Roxie grew up in a large family and spent half of her childhood with her nose buried in the pages of a book; the other half writing her own stories, escaping off into other worlds.

Roxie lives in the UK with her husband and two children. She loves to spend time by the seaside, especially if there is an opportunity to sit down and read while enjoying some sunshine.

For my husband, who graciously lets me spend some evenings with imaginary men.

For VT and AH, for your constant encouragement and for the laughter.

Roxie Holland

PROTECTING HER HEART

AUSTIN MACAULEY PUBLISHERS

LONDON * CAMBRIDGE * NEW YORK * SHARJAH

A CIP catalogue record for this title is available from the British Library.

ISBN 9781035883059 (Paperback)
ISBN 9781035883066 (ePub e-book)

www.austinmacauley.com

First Published 2025
Austin Macauley Publishers Ltd®
1 Canada Square
Canary Wharf
London
E14 5AA

Also by Roxie Holland

The Love She Forgot

1

Zoey

"Good morning, Ms Taylor." The security guard smiles as they open the building door for me. I smile back at her as I walk past, putting down the holder that contains the four coffees I've just picked up on my way into the office. I pull one out and hand it to her.

"Here you go, Olivia, one steaming hot black coffee for you. One latte for Jake, too." I put the second coffee on the counter.

"You're the best." Olivia grins at me.

"I'm running late, unfortunately. I'll see you later," I say, picking the holder with the two remaining coffees in it and crossing the lobby, the heels of my boots clicking on the marble flooring as I walk. I swipe my pass at the turnstile and head in the direction of the lift, ignoring my mobile phone that is ringing from within my handbag. It's my personal mobile making the noise so I'm confident it will either be somebody I don't want to talk to, or somebody I just don't have the time for right now.

The lift doesn't take long to travel up the five flights to where my office is situated. I put a cup of coffee on the desk for Abigail, my personal assistant, before stepping into my office and shutting the door behind me. I open the blinds in the office and look out at the landscape ahead of me. It's a built-up area but if I focus, I can see the sea. Or at least that's what I like to convince myself on stressful days, days where I'd love to be sitting on one of the sandy beaches of the south coast of England with nothing to do but watch the sea race up the sand.

Today is going to be one of those days. I can feel it in my bones.

I sip my coffee as I look out of the window. My phone rings again. This time, I rummage in my handbag to find it. Glancing at the screen, I see it is my friend Lizzie. I let the call divert to answerphone, planning on sending a text later to tell her we'll talk at dinner tonight. Lizzie is used to my radio silence, and graciously patient with me.

"Zoey?" A voice calls, followed by a knock on the office door.

"Come in, Abigail," I call back to her, and then she steps into the office.

"Thank you for the drink, though I keep telling you, you don't have to buy me coffee. We have a perfectly good coffee maker here," she teases.

"I know, but I like the ritual of stopping for coffee, and I don't like turning up empty handed for others." I smile. There hasn't been a day in the years I've run this business that I haven't stopped at the independent coffee shop down the street. I'm sure they set their watch by me.

"Here's your post. I'll be outside, shout up if you need me." Abigail puts down a stack of envelopes at my desk. She thinks it's weird that I don't have her open my post. She opens the bulk of the post, but anything that is handwritten to me, I open it. Sometimes it sits in my drawer for days on end until I get a gap in the diary. Mostly, it's usually shitty circulars or stuff that doesn't merit my attention, landing straight in the recycling bin, but it's another ritual I've done since the business started, another thing I can't seem to let drop.

"Thanks. I'll be out shortly. We can run through the diary."

"Sure thing, Zoey." Abigail shuts the door behind her.

I sit down at my desk, sipping a little more coffee. I glance at the calendar on my desk, shaking my head at the date. I grab the stack of post, looking for a distraction.

The first piece I open is an invitation to join a conference being run in London, for women business leaders. A quick run through the proposed itinerary makes me move it to one side of my desk, mentally labelling it as a possibility. It's hit and miss at these conferences. Sometimes it seems more geared on how to make your mark as a woman, rather than women celebrating their successes. I used to go to the first type of conferences, with Caterina, my business partner, where she'd smirk behind her hand at the presenters and scoff afterwards at their advice. Face to face, though, Caterina was a master at working the room, probably why we were always welcomed back, despite any bad behaviour we would display.

I open the second. It's a request from the university I attended, asking if I would come and talk to their economics and finance students. This lands in the recycling pile. Not because I have any bad feelings towards my former university, just the last time I attempted this, somebody had asked me how'd I'd continued with the business after my personal tragedy. At the time I'd laughed it off and commented about the audacity of kids these days, but it had left me unsettled for weeks afterwards and I've avoided going back.

I alternate between sipping my coffee and landing the post between the possibility pile, and the recycling pile. As usual, the recycling pile is considerably higher.

One of the envelopes contains a suggestive picture of a man, suggesting we meet up for a date. He's half dressed in the photograph and has the eyes that remind me of mug shots presented on the news to warn of an escaped convict. Post like this isn't unusual. My business model is based on security for women, and it makes us a natural target for men who feel threatened, or men who take it as a challenge. This guy looks like he fits the group who feel threatened and want to exert their manliness.

I've never understood why men feel threatened, I'm not challenging their existence, just making it possible for women to go about their lives without strange men posing a risk in certain situations. I'm not a threat to men, the way men can be to a woman, but it still makes us a target for hate mail or lewd messages.

At least I can handle the post that comes to me, rather than upsetting somebody like Abigail if she had to deal with it. Our incoming social media is monitored by a man, because I'd never subject another woman to the disgusting bullshit that gets sent that way. Some men like to attack our business in a way which illustrates exactly why the business exists and thrives.

I shake my head and reach for the last piece of post, a yellow padded envelope, planning to get the day of meetings started. I try to shake the last envelope contents out of my mind, but this envelope is worse, much worse, and I drop the envelope in shock when I see the contents, knocking over my coffee cup in my surprise.

∞∞∞∞∞∞∞∞

I grew up knowing to be wary of men. My father was a difficult man to live with, with mood swings that were impossible to predict and protect myself from. He'd have weeks of being loving, a doting father and a good husband to my mother, but then out of the blue, there would be months of ducking and making myself scarce when he was in a bad mood. At some point, around when I was seven, the weeks of doting became less frequent, the bad mood more permanent, and any good memory I had of him became hazy, like I'd imagined it all.

The first time I realised it wasn't just my father I had to be careful with, I was fifteen years old. An older brother of a friend touched me inappropriately when I was at their house for a sleepover. When I froze like a rabbit in the headlights, he apologised and told me he had misunderstood my signals.

He convinced me I had misunderstood him, too.

The second time, I was eighteen. I was drunk and a man in the club wouldn't take no for an answer. Somehow, I ended up in a cubicle in the bathrooms with him, my top pulled away from my body, breasts exposed as I struggled to get away from him. By the time I found somebody to help me, the guy was long gone.

I was told it was my fault for having a drink.

The third time, I was nineteen, at university. I met a guy online. I did my due diligence. We talked for ages before we met and when we did meet, it was in a neutral, public location. We had a few dates before I revealed where I lived. The first time I went to his house, he pinned me on the sofa and tried to force himself on me. He called me a prick tease as I left. For good measure, he spent several nights outside my house, standing in the street, staring at me whenever I came home.

The police told me they couldn't do anything, as he hadn't made any real threat.

When I started talking to my friends, I realised I wasn't the only one. Every woman had a story. Every woman knows it's not *all* guys, not even *some* guys, but they have had a bad experience with at least *one* guy.

The leery guy at the bus stop.

The guy who followed in the dark.

The over friendly family friend who hugged a little too long, with hands that roamed.

The good guy friend who showed his true colours once in devastating fashion.

The guy who thought every woman wanted to be choked during sex, never asking for permission.

The taxi driver who drove routes down deserted streets and joked it would be a perfect place to hide a body.

The guy who thought they were owed sex and objected their length of time in the mythical friend-zone.

By twenty, studying economics and finance at university, a course where men outnumbered women two to one, I'd toughened up. I was sick of hearing the stories, sick of being told how I should behave around men to keep me safe, like I was accountable for their bad behaviour and actions.

I was determined to make a difference in the world. I had a business plan. A plan to make things better, to take the niche markets of women providing safe services for women and building it into an empire. It wasn't enough to have a local taxi company where the drivers were women, or a couple of companies where women provided trade services. I had a vision of all these services sitting under one umbrella. Sitting under *my* umbrella. Services provided by women, exclusively for women. Women learning their craft from other women. Providing safety as well as excellent, skilled services.

It took years to get off the ground, years to get the company to the level it is at now. Years for me to be able to sit back and breathe. Except, in the minute it's taken for me to open the padded envelope, it appears my peace is going to be shattered.

I look at the paper again, just in case I'm hallucinating, but it is still the same. The words appear to be cut from a magazine and stuck together on the paper to make a statement. Again, I feel surprised that this kind of thing happens. It seems so cliché, so low budget horror film.

I'm going to make you pay. I'll make you bleed and beg for mercy, you cunt.

Attached to the paper, paperclipped neatly in a stack, are six photographs of me. One of me outside the office. One of me at the train station. One of me outside my doctor's medical practice. One of me walking out of my favourite coffee shop. One of me getting into my car in a multi-story carpark in town. One of me walking into my house.

I put the paper and the photographs onto my desk, onto the padded envelope they'd arrived in, and sink into the highbacked leather chair. Before I've even engaged my brain, my hand is on the telephone receiver. Dialling the number is like muscle memory. Ten minutes ago, I'd have sworn I'd forgotten this number. But ten minutes ago, my heart wasn't pounding in my chest.

Apparently, adrenaline works wonders for my memory.

Or, maybe, I've never really forgotten.

"Aiden Slater," the voice barks down the line.

It's been almost two years since I heard this voice.

I take three steadying breaths. "I need your help," I say.

"Zoey?"

That he recognises my voice makes me take another steadying breath.

"Yes."

Now I hear his steadying breath. There's a beat of silence between us. One. Two. Infinity.

"I haven't changed my mind." The sentence is firm, strong. No wavering in his position.

"Wait. Don't hang up." The words rush out. He'd have every reason to hang up.

"I'm busy," he says flatly.

"I had a threatening letter, at the office," I throw back.

One. Two. Infinity.

"I'll be at your office in an hour," he says, and then the line goes dead.

I pop out of the office and clear my throat to get Abigail's attention.

"Are you okay, Zoey?" she asks, surprise on her face.

"Yes. I'm fine. Can you please rearrange my schedule for this morning?"

"Including your eleven o'clock with Mr Hammond?" Abigail prompts as she checks my calendar on her laptop.

I shouldn't miss that meeting. I can't believe I forgot about it. My brain feels to be working at half speed.

Aiden should be gone before my scheduled meeting with Robert Hammond. I'm expecting Aiden to breeze in, tell me I have nothing to worry about, mock me for contacting him, then leave again. Perhaps throwing the same sentences he'd said last time, over his shoulder as he storms out.

"I'll keep that one. What do I have this afternoon?"

Abigail looks back at her laptop.

"Lunch at twelve until twelve thirty. At twelve thirty, you have the finance heads for the month end review. At two, you have the software team for the latest reporting capabilities. Two-thirty, it's the external communications team so they can show you the latest advert. Three fifteen, you are meeting the new interns. You've got a fifteen-minute gap at four fifteen, then you're with HR until five.

You've got a private call scheduled at five. At six, you're meeting Lizzie for dinner."

She reels off my appointments with a frightening speed. It's not actually a busy day for appointments. It's rare for me to leave the office for six, although I rarely let my meetings go past five because I don't want to impede into their personal lives.

"Rearrange them all, please. Keep the coffee and food for the interns and book it again as soon as you can. Send my apologies to everybody."

"Zoey, what's the matter?"

"Nothing. Can you call security, tell them I'm expecting Aiden Slater. Please make sure there is a pass ready for him and bring him straight to my office when he arrives. He should be here in an hour. Thank you."

"Yes, Zoey, of course." Abigail's voice follows me as I step into my office, and I shut the door firmly behind me.

I look at my watch. Ten minutes since I called him. Fifty minutes until he said he'd be here. Fifty minutes for me to calm myself down.

I rummage around in my desk drawers and find some napkins. They bear the logo of the coffee shop down the street; I assume I swept them in there one day after ordering a pastry for breakfast. I use them to mop up the coffee spilt on my desk. The desk remains slightly sticky given the squirt of syrup I always add to my order, but at least the desktop looks clean.

I check my watch again. Forty-eight minutes. I pace around the office.

It shouldn't make a difference given there are more important things to worry about, but I still look down at my outfit to check how I look. Charcoal grey blazer, matching skirt. Cream silk blouse. Black ankle boots. I'm glad it's Monday, not a Friday. We have dress-down Friday and I try to join in, leading from the top. Somehow, I feel more comfortable seeing Aiden when dressed like this than I would have been wearing jeans and a quirky top.

Glancing at the letter and photographs again, I shake my head. I'm not comfortable, I'm far from comfortable. This feels unsettling.

I'm used to abuse. I'm sure most women in power experience it. Most successful women will have had at least one encounter where a man questions their success. My bonus payment and salary are published in the company accounts. The first time it was published was not long after a local paper published their 'top thirty women to watch'. Some man, some random stranger who didn't know me from the next person on the street, took the time to screenshot my profile and my payment information, asking me how long I'd spent on my knees earning my bonus, blowing my boss. Clearly misunderstanding that I am the boss, and that my bonus was down to my blood, sweat and tears.

I'd been through three women in the position of monitoring the social media inbox before I'd relented and hired a man, moving the women to other positions because they were sick of the abuse, the dick pics, the innuendo about what we would be better doing. The abuse has always been directed at the business, rather than a threat to an individual person.

This, though, this is extreme. Maybe Aiden will tell me it's a joke, some kids trying to get a reaction from me. Except the pictures feel intrusive, designed to scare me.

They're doing a damn good job.

I stand and pace the office, anticipating his arrival. Maybe he won't come, maybe he'll delegate and send somebody else from his company. Except, he had said he would be here, and I called his personal number. I'd be surprised if he turned up as he'd had every right not to, but Aiden has always been a better person than me.

I check my watch after I feel like I've paced for an eternity. Thirty minutes since I called. Thirty minutes until he'll tell me to rip the photographs up and put them in the bin, forget all about them, and forget about him while I'm at it.

I glance at the pictures again. The one taken outside my home is recent because in it, I'm wearing a dress that I only got a couple of weeks ago. I've only worn it twice. The one outside the doctors must be recent too, other than my visit last week, I haven't been to see the doctor in years.

The phone buzzes, making me jump and audibly yelp.

"Yes?" I ask as I answer the phone.

"Aiden Slater is here." It's Abigail, sounding slightly stressed which is unusual for her. She's been my personal assistant for the last year, and she is amazing under pressure, usually. Except she usually knows what the pressure is. All she knows right now is that there is something going on and I'm not telling her a thing about it.

"Can you—" I start but she carries on talking.

"I'll bring him up now, Zoey, I just thought you might want the warning that he's early."

"Thank you, Abigail. Come up."

I hang up the phone and take my blazer off, tug the front of my shirt to pull it a couple of times, creating a little swill of air around me because I'm suddenly sweating.

I'm not sure if it is the note and photographs, or that he is in the building.

I still feel far too hot. My long hair, hanging to the middle of my back, suddenly feels like a hot carpet of lava against me. I root around in my desk drawer for a hair tie. I spot one, tucked into the top corner of my second drawer. I grab it and pull my hair into a ponytail. I know it won't look as sleek as I'd usually do, but the cool air around my neck feels like relief. It was either a hair tie or hacking it off with scissors.

There is a knock on the door.

"Aiden Slater for you," Abigail says politely when she opens the door. He steps around her and into my office, and she shuts the door behind him, her the other side of the door, leaving me and him in the office.

The sight of him renders me momentarily speechless. He looks exactly the same as the last time I saw him, except this time he's fully dressed. He stands in front of me, wearing a dark suit and white shirt, slim black tie completing his look. His black hair is still in that stylish crewcut fashion he has always favoured. It looks a little longer than usual. It looks the perfect length for a woman to twist her fingers through as he kisses her.

His deep grey-blue eyes stare at me.

"You're earlier than you said," I comment.

"Traffic was light," he replies, short and brisk-toned.

"How fortunate for me," I murmur as I sink down into my chair.

Aiden takes a step closer to my desk. His jaw is set in a firm line, like he's clenching his teeth together. His discomfort seems to come off him in waves.

"You said you'd had a threatening letter."

"Yes, here, look," I say, and I slide the offending article to the edge of the desk. He takes a couple of steps closer so he can see what I am trying to show him. A second later, he snatches the item off the table. He pulls the photographs out of the paperclip and flicks through them.

"Do you know when these were taken?" he asks. Business mode switched on. Whatever discomfort he had at being in my office appears to have gone. This is Aiden, focused.

"That second photograph, I've only had that dress for three weeks. I wore it the first week I got it, and I wore it last week. That third photograph, it's taken

17

at my doctor's. I was there last week. So, I'd guess, sometime between three weeks ago and now."

He looks at the photographs again, turns them all over in his hands.

"Do you have security here, other than the guards downstairs?"

"It's a small crew, we never really needed much more."

"What about at home?"

"Why would somebody like me need security at home?" I huff out a little laugh.

"I meant what security measures do you have at home. Cameras? CCTV? Panic button?"

"Next you'll be asking me if I've a panic room," I tut.

"Wouldn't do any harm." Aiden shrugs.

"It's just a hoax, right? Some guy who hates my business?" As I speak the words, I realise how much I'm hoping he's going to tell me that's all it is. I also know I'd never have called him if I thought this was a hoax.

"What makes you think it's a man?" he asks.

"I don't know any woman who uses the word cunt," I reply.

"Whoever it is, they appear to have an issue with you," Aiden comments. He puts one of the photographs onto the table, picture face down on the desk so the back is visible.

"I didn't see that," I whisper. On the back of this photograph is a written note.

There's nowhere you can go.

Aiden puts a second photograph down.

Nowhere you can hide.

He puts a third down.

I will find you.

He puts the fourth down.

You'll never be safe.

Down goes the fifth on the desk.

I'll make you suffer.

He puts down the sixth.

You'll pay with your life.

"Have you contacted the police?" he asks.

"The only person I have contacted is you."

"You should contact the police."

"You want to pass me off to the police? I thought this is what you did for your business," I scoff. The handwriting on the back of the photographs has made me feel a little sick and a lot on edge.

"No, not pass you off. There's not much point in me providing security if you're not going to report this. The police need to investigate otherwise the threat won't ever go away," Aiden points out.

"Your company will provide security for me?" I ask, to clarify because I'm still a little concerned he's about to tell me he's done. It's his core business to provide personal security but I'm sure he'd usually care if his clients were harmed. Me, I'm not sure if he would.

"I'll do it."

"You, your company, or you, as in you?" I stare at him. His grey-blue eyes hold my gaze.

"Me, maybe a co-worker. We can talk about that later," he replies. He rests his palms against my desk, leaning forward, still maintaining eye contact. It makes me uncomfortable, so I look slightly higher up, focussing on the scar that runs through his left eyebrow, causing a gap in the brow and the only flaw on his face.

"Okay." I nod.

"I'll need to know everything, Zoey. Somebody appears to have an issue with you. This is directed at you, not your business. I'm going to need to know every threat you've had, go over every person in your life to assess them. You're going to need to be with security, twenty-four seven."

"Until this is resolved?"

"Until this is resolved," he confirms. He points towards the padded envelope. "Is this what it came in?" he asks. I nod.

"It was in the stack of post I opened this morning."

"Why the hell are you even opening your post? You're the boss, not some girl Friday," he snaps.

"I don't open all the post. It's just a habit. Caterina and I," I start but then I falter over the rest of the sentence.

Aiden doesn't acknowledge what I've said. Instead, he reaches to grab one of the clean, discarded napkins from where I'd left it on the desk. He seems to use it as a protective barrier as he picks up the envelope, glancing inside. He frowns. "Right, we're going to get out of here and go to the police. Right now, Zoey."

"What…" I start.

"This didn't come through the post. This was hand delivered."

"That doesn't mean anybody has been in the office. The post comes into reception and then is distributed from there. Abigail passes me anything directly addressed to me," I argue. With that, Aiden twists the envelope in such a way that I see what is inside, the item I haven't seen before.

The silver surgical scalpel seems to glisten at me.

"Now, Zoey," Aiden commands, and the tone of his voice, like so many times before, has me doing exactly what he says.

I pick up my handbag, the laptop that I haven't even switched on yet, and follow him as he walks out my office.

"Is everything okay?" Abigail gives me a concerned look.

"Fine, I'm going to be out for the rest of the day. Can you please rearrange Mr Hammond as well, for his earliest availability?" I ask.

"Sure. I'll sort everything here," she promises me. Of course she will. Abigail is worth her weight in gold. I linger at her desk.

"Zoey," Aiden's tone is half coaxing, half a warning. I follow him in the direction of the lifts.

"Do you think I should tell her what is going on? What if something happens today, here?" I start to fret as we reach the lifts. I never fret. I'm disappointed in myself. One threatening letter and I'm a mess, fretting about things, spilling coffee, calling Aiden.

"The threat is for you, Zoey, not the office. I'll speak to security though before we go to the police," he offers. He presses the call button for the lift and the doors open.

We both step into the lift. I press for the ground floor and as the doors shut, I feel a little claustrophobic. Somehow, the air between us in the lift feels oppressive, thick and stuffy. I remind myself that it's five floors, we will be out the confines of the lift soon.

Aiden sighs, and I know he feels the same discomfort I do. I glance over at him.

"Thank you for coming," I whisper.

"It's my job." He shrugs as the lift reaches the bottom floor.

The doors open and it's unclear which of us is most relieved that we're out in a wider space. As I follow him towards the reception area, I question my decision to call Aiden. It seems logical, he's a bodyguard. There isn't anybody more qualified to protect me if there is a threat in my life, even if the last time we spoke, he told me to stay out of his.

∞∞∞∞∞∞∞

"Why are you here with Mr Slater?" the police officer asks. "Why was he your first call, instead of the police?"

"I've known Aiden for twelve years. This is exactly what his family business is about, he seemed a logical person to call." I shrug.

The room we are sat in is small and reminds me of the types that appear on TV shows, more akin to interviewing and intimidating a bad guy than making a woman who essentially received a death threat feel comfortable.

It is not a death threat. I chide myself, but it doesn't do anything to make me feel better, especially when I remember the words on the last photograph. I can try to tell myself it's not a death threat, but the words are still there. Pay with my life, that's clearly a threat, whether I want to admit that, accept that.

The police officer has the photographs and the letter on the table in front of him. They're right there, on the table, splayed out for me to see. How did I not know somebody was following me? How had I not seen that somebody was taking photographs of me?

"Both your names come up in our records. Quite the complicated past you have had with him, and he was still your first call," the officer muses. I bristle. Knowing this officer has read past cases and made assumptions about me, it makes me feel vulnerable, but I'll be damned if he knows that. I force myself to stare at him.

"I'm here to discuss a present threat going on in my life, I'm sure this is not connected to anything in my past. That was years ago." I keep my tone even.

"Have you noticed anything else unusual? Any other letters?"

"No." I shake my head.

"You haven't noticed anybody outside your house?"

"No." I frown.

"We can come to your residence and assess it for security," he offers.

"It's okay. I'm sure Aiden will have that in hand."

The policeman frowns slightly, but it isn't like they'd be offering twenty-four-hour police protection outside my house. Whatever I end up paying Aiden's company, it'll be more security than what the police would have provided anyway.

"We will investigate this and be in touch. We may come to your office building as well, increase the police presence around the area."

"Can I go now?" I ask. I feel like we have been here for days, but it has only been an hour since Aiden had guided me into the police station.

When the policeman nods, I get up and follow him out of the room. Aiden sits in the reception area. He looks uncomfortable on the chair, his long legs stretched out in front of him. He is suddenly alert when I clear my throat. He's out of the chair in an instant, standing tall in front of me.

"Ready to go?" he asks.

"I should get my car," I blurt out. He'd driven me to the police station, I hadn't thought to mention that my car was parked in the office carpark.

"Is it secure, for tonight?"

"Yeah, I guess," I reply, thinking of the barriers to the carpark, the security cameras covering the entrance and exit.

"Okay, let's get ahead of this, we should go to yours and assess your security requirements."

I nod and follow him out of the police station. He doesn't say another word to me, just leads me towards where his car is parked. He opens the car door and I get into the passenger seat.

"Aiden," I start, but then I fall silent because I'm not sure what I should say to him.

"You still living on Grove Street?" he asks as he starts the engine.

"Yes."

"When will Caleb be home?" Aiden doesn't look my way as he talks. He pulls away from the kerb, eyes focused on the road.

"Caleb is in the States at the moment," I explain.

"When will he be back?"

"You said earlier that it might be you and a co-worker who takes on the job. how is this going to work, Aiden?" I ask, changing the subject. I don't want to talk to Aiden about Caleb, not yet. Caleb and I are complicated. Caleb, Aiden, and I are a goddamn minefield.

"One of my colleagues will come to your house later today. We can talk about it in more detail then," he replies, his tone brisk.

"Okay." I shift around in my seat again, keep my focus out of the window, watching the scenery change as we head in the direction of my house. All there is between us is the silence, and the same thick atmosphere we'd had in the lift, caused by two years of silence and the words left unsaid.

2
Aiden

Zoey sits in the passenger seat of my car, a frown on her face. She doesn't say anything to me as we drive across the town, out on the quieter roads towards the little village where she lives. I've only been to her house a couple of times, never in the past two years, but I feel like I would know the route to her place blindfolded.

I pull my car onto her driveway and look around. The house itself looks secure enough but the grounds could do with a bit of tightening up. At the right of the property, there is a wrought iron gate which leads onto the back. It doesn't look like it's locked. I want to scold her for being so lax with her security, but I know it's not the right time. It might be enough to push her over the edge after an already unsettling day. The last thing I'd want to do is hurt Zoey. Not more than I've already done. Our history is long, and complex.

The first time Zoey and I met, I felt like we were kindred spirits. I'd heard stories about her from Caterina, my girlfriend and Zoey's housemate. Mostly I'd heard from Caterina about how Zoey was tough and strong. Except, as I laid eyes on Zoey for the first time, I had seen through the bravado.

Zoey was tall, lean and angular, with sharp cheekbones and dark blue eyes. Long blond hair and an air of haughtiness around her. An air that I knew was fake, something she projected to protect herself. I recognised it as a front she put on because I had the same front myself. Wounded people can always recognise when they're with somebody else who has been wounded.

Caterina was the opposite of Zoey in every way. Caterina was from an affluent family whereas Zoey had cut ties with hers. Everything about Caterina was short and sweet, from her little button nose to her sugary smile and her bubbly personality. Caterina was the type of woman who was destined to wear designer outfits and carry her miniature dog in an expensive handbag as she dashed off for another lunch with the ladies. Zoey was the type of woman who was destined to make waves. Somehow, they fit together perfectly.

Over the years, Zoey and I had been through so much together. A decade of us going through everything together, feeling like we were battle weary soldiers. The last two years, however, had been nothing between us but silence.

A sensible man would have arranged for somebody else to go to Zoey, assess her needs and provide security until the threat is resolved. I have enough people working with me to arrange that, but when it comes to Zoey, I've never been able to be a sensible man.

"Stay in the car, pass me your keys and I'll check the house out," I cut the engine to my car.

"Do you really think that is necessary?"

"I'd rather err on the side of caution," I reply. I don't want her to be more frightened than she already is, but I need to take this seriously. Somebody has been following her. Somebody has been taking covert photographs. Somebody has threatened her. I'm going to do everything I would usually do for a client, and then do it better and harder, because it's Zoey.

"Here," she murmurs, handing me a set of keys. Her fingers brush against mine as she passes them to me. I notice that her hand is trembling and now I'm not sure she should be left alone. What I should have done is arrange for Isabelle, one of my employees, to be here by the time we'd arrived. She could have looked after Zoey as I secured the property.

"Why don't you come with me?" I suggest. She straightens up in the seat.

"I don't think I'm a damsel in distress who can't be left alone. I'm not that bad."

"It's up to you." I shrug. She gets out of the car, so I follow her lead, and together we walk towards her front door.

She doesn't take her keys back from me, so I take the lead and unlock the porch door and then the front door. I'm impressed that she locks both doors. The amount of people I know who only ever locks one door when they leave the property empty is shocking.

We step into the hallway together and she puts the alarm code into the box as it starts to beep. Another plus.

"I always put the alarm on," she says. So far, so good.

"I'm going to look around, and then we can sit and talk. It's up to you if you want to walk around with me or stay downstairs." I turn to lock the front door behind me.

"I'll put the kettle on," she replies.

Her front door and hallway are in the centre of her house, and she turns to the left in the direction of where I know her kitchen, dining room, utility room and a cloakroom is located. I follow her and check out those rooms first. The windows are all shut. The window for the utility room looks like it should be replaced. I make a note of it on my phone.

I join Zoey in the kitchen. She's by the kettle.

"Are there any areas you'd prefer to look at with me?" I ask but she shakes her head.

"Do what you need to do, Aiden," she shoots back, her focus on the boiling kettle and the mugs she's placed on the side.

I leave her in the kitchen and head towards the right side of her property. I check the living room first. Her patio doors that lead onto the back garden are locked and secure, as are the windows in the room. I open the patio door so I can step into the garden. In the garden there is a high fence running around the boarder of the property, a decked area at the end of the grounds, and the rest of the garden appears to be split into zones, an area for outdoor cooking and entertainment, an area where she has clearly taken up gardening. In the garden, there are no external lights, and the wrought iron gate to the front of the property is not properly locked, as I'd suspected.

I go back inside, locking the patio door again before walking through the rest of the downstairs rooms. Her study is secure, the window is a porthole style that does not open. I get to the staircase leading to the second floor of the house. The second floor has two guest bedrooms, a family bathroom, then her bedroom, dressing room and connected ensuite. All rooms are exceptionally neat, the only area of concern I note is a damaged window panel in one of the guest bedrooms, and that the little window in her shower room is open.

I pause at her bedroom door. There's something not quite right about the room, but I can't put my finger on what it is that seems different. She's decorated since I last visited. The room is now a jade green. It's not the colour of the room that feels odd, I just can't decide what it is that seems troubling.

I shut the bedroom door and head back downstairs.

"You've left the window open upstairs, in the ensuite," I say as I reach her in the kitchen.

"The cat uses the window to come in and out when I'm at work," she comments.

"When did you get a cat?" I laugh because Zoey is not the type of person to have a pet.

"Cats are low maintenance." She sounds defensive.

"What did Caleb say when you suggested a cat?" I ask.

She shrugs. "Well, he's away."

Her tone sounds odd, and I think of the bedroom upstairs and I suddenly realise why the room seemed odd to me.

"When did you break up?" I ask, as I think about the distinct lack of male items in the bedroom. She and Caleb got together five years ago and now I think about it, I haven't seen much in the house to suggest he has lived here in a while.

"Does it matter?" She glances at me.

I bristle. "Of course it matters, Zoey. You received a threat today. I told you; I need to know everything."

"You cannot possibly think that Caleb is a threat," she scoffs.

"Well, that depends. It depends on things like why you broke up, and who instigated it."

She picks up the mugs of coffee she appears to have made when I was upstairs. She walks towards me, and for a second, I'm convinced I'm going to end up wearing one of the contents. Instead, she puts one of the mugs on the countertop in front of me.

"Perhaps," she says, her dark blue eyes boring into me, "Caleb realised I was a terrible person, and decided he wanted nothing more to do with me. He wouldn't be the first, would he?" she asks, and then she stalks out of the kitchen, heading towards the living room.

I hear the door slam shut behind her.

I stay in the kitchen. I pick up the coffee she'd abandoned in front of me. I take a sip. She's made it exactly how I like it, but it still seems bitter in my mouth, mostly because I'm biting back the shame of what she's just said to me, and the fact that I had no comeback.

∞∞∞∞∞∞∞∞

I let Zoey have some peace in the living room as I finish my coffee in the kitchen. Once I've finished my drink, I put the mug into the dishwasher and then head in the direction of the living room. I knock on the door.

She doesn't acknowledge my knock, but she doesn't shout at me to go away, although Zoey's forthright, if she didn't want me in the room, she'd have shouted something much stronger than 'go away'. I know her silence means she's thinking so I push the door open.

Zoey is sat in the armchair, her knees curled underneath her, her arms wrapped across her chest. She's always sat like this when she's upset, like she is trying to pull herself into the smallest shape she can make with her body.

She glances over at me.

"I'm sorry," she murmurs.

I step further into the living room and take a seat on the two-seater sofa which is positioned the closest to the armchair she's sat in.

"What are you sorry for?"

"Everything. For snapping at you in the kitchen. For calling you this morning," she explains.

"Do you want me to get somebody else to take over your case?" I ask. I'm not sure I trust anybody else to take care of her until whoever sent the letter is caught or is no longer a threat, but I hate the idea she is uncomfortable by my presence.

"No, but I don't know how this is going to work. You said I need somebody with me all the time, and that might not be for a long time, if the police can find the person who sent the package, but…you can't watch the house all day and night," she points out.

"That's why Isabelle is on her way. I'll introduce you to her, you can get to know her, and then it is up to you to decide how you want this to work. You can have either Isabelle or me with you in the day, and we'd switch for keeping an eye on things at night. You can choose. You're supposed to feel comfortable with the people providing your security. If you really don't feel comfortable with me, I can arrange somebody else, as well as Isabelle."

"What do you usually do, the days or the nights? When you're guarding the rich, the famous, and the important, I mean."

For the first time today, her smile seems halfway to being genuine. She used to tease me about my job, telling me I was getting an unfair deal whenever a high-profile client was travelling overseas and needed security. I've been to more countries than I can count, but it isn't like I got to enjoy the places where I went, too busy minding the rich, famous and important, as she likes to call them.

"I don't particularly mind. We usually split to two twelve-hour shifts, seven until seven, but we'll base it around your schedule," I explain instead of acknowledging her comment.

"Okay," she replies. We're quiet for a moment.

"So, Caleb. Come on, what happened?"

"I doubt this is anything to do with Caleb," she mutters.

"You don't know that."

"Weren't you the one who told me he was spineless?" she tuts. I give her a small smile.

"I don't remember calling him spineless. I think I told you he reminded me of wet lettuce."

"Warm, wet lettuce was your exact assessment, I think," she replies, and then there's a little giggle that I didn't expect from her today. Not with the shock of what she's had. She rights herself. "Look, I don't think Caleb is a threat. He's a nice guy, you know that."

"Why did you split?" I try again, gently.

"You can count him off your list, okay? He doesn't have hurt feelings. He was the one who ended it. He moved to the States a couple of months ago, to be with the woman he met on a business trip a while ago." Zoey shrugs as she finishes talking.

I'm surprised that he is the one who ended it. I'm surprised he met somebody he thought was better. Caleb never struck me as the type who would have the balls to cheat. He followed Zoey around like a lapdog, always at her feet, desperate for her attention. He always acted like she walked on water, and he indulged her for every whim, because he was devoted to her.

I wonder if he ever knew that his devotion to her wasn't reciprocated with the same loyal enthusiasm. I make a mental note to check into his location, make sure he is where he says he is, investigate if he could be involved. Even if he is in the States, like she seems to believe, it doesn't mean that he isn't the one behind this, having somebody else do his dirty work for him.

"Was it amicable?" I wonder.

"Is it ever?" She looks at me again, holding my gaze. "Nobody ever really gets out of a relationship fully intact, do they?"

"Zoey," I start but she waves away my comment.

"Sorry, that was uncalled for. I think it's just the stress of this morning."

My phone beeps so I take it out of my pocket, unlock it to see a message from Isabelle.

"Isabelle is here. Let me answer the door for her and show her around, then I'll introduce you. You can get to know her once I've got her up to speed," I suggest, and I stand up, making my way to the living room door.

"Hey," Zoey calls.

I turn to look at her. "Yeah?"

"Why a woman? Are all your men on assignments?" She almost sounds like she's teasing.

"No, I just thought you might be more comfortable with a woman. I mean, your whole brand is about women taking care of women." I shrug.

Neither of us comment that, if I'm providing security, it goes against her brand. We both know that over the years, I've been her exception, like she's been mine, and regardless the way we spoke to each other last, nothing has managed to sever that connection. It might have been radio silence between us for almost two years, but the minute she opened that envelope, us reconnecting was inevitable.

I just hope we'll both survive it.

∞∞∞∞∞∞∞∞

"So, how do you know her?" Isabelle asks after I've given her the tour of the house. We're in the kitchen together, talking before I introduce her to Zoey.

"I met her when we were at university," I reply. I think back to that start of my final year at university, she and Caterina in their second year.

"She called you directly?"

"Like I said, we go back, so yeah, she phoned me directly."

"Okay, so where are we so far? Other than the assessment of the property, what are you thinking? What's going to be the big issues?" Isabelle fires questions at me.

We always comment that every client has a weakness, something that becomes a big issue. I've worked security for famous people, minding their teenage children who seem to find it a personal challenge to see if they can evade me. Isabelle once had a high-profile client who had a penance for hookers, and liked to try to sneak them into the hotel rooms she was standing guard at. I've had multiple clients who were obsessed with uploading their every move to social media, tagging themselves, almost giving a map for the people who wanted to harm them.

Everybody has a weakness, and I wonder for Zoey whether it will be her stubbornness.

Isabelle hadn't noted anything that I didn't see when I did my initial assessment. We both agree the house is secure enough, just a few minor changes. Zoey, on the other hand, I suspect will be resistant to the changes we'll propose to her daily schedule.

"She's the owner of her company, she has a busy schedule, and I suspect she'll be resistant to us being there all the time at work. She's stubborn as hell," I reply.

Isabelle looks thoughtful. "How well, exactly, do you know this woman?"

"I'm professional, Isabelle."

"You betcha, boss man. Though, I'm assuming there is more history that you want to tell me about."

"How about you follow boss man, and I'll introduce you to Zoey?" I laugh.

"Does your dad know you've taken this case?"

"I put the details in the system." I shrug.

"You're going to get so much shit from Richard." Isabelle laughs.

"Maybe."

We walk out of the kitchen together and down the hallway.

I know why Isabelle is concerned. This security company is the one my dad, Richard, set up. He's run the company for years. When I left the armed forces, he was keen for me to join him. I started working at the company, from the bottom rung of the ladder. I've done my fair share of crappy assignments, also more than my share of high-profile or overseas trips as my experience and reputation grew. The past couple of years, Dad has been pushing me to switch roles, to stop being one of the team who provide the security, to somebody who is running the business instead. He wants to retire. He wants to hand over the business to his family.

I don't think I'm cut out to be that son for him. A few months ago, we'd argued when I realised that he'd stopped assigning me on some jobs, taken on additional staff to cover the workload, trying to force my hand into moving into management instead. Taking this job, adding it to the books, assigning myself and Isabelle without discussing it with him, it'll be seen as defiance, and a

31

disappointment. If I'd just assigned it to other people, that would have been fine, but my involvement is not going to go down well with him.

Especially when he realises that Zoey is the client.

Maybe Zoey isn't the only one where stubbornness is their worst trait.

I'd left the living room door ajar when I'd gone to let Isabelle into the house, so I can see Zoey is still in there, sitting in the armchair, her laptop on her knee. She's hunched over, typing furiously. The keys in her laptop sound like they're about to give up against the frantic tapping.

I clear my throat and she jolts in her seat, startled.

"Shit," she mutters.

"Sorry, I should have knocked," I apologise. I feel like a dick. She received an envelope with covert photographs and a fucking surgical scalpel inside, and I can't think to knock on the door to avoid scaring the life out of her? I'd never have done that with another client. My history with Zoey is going to be something I'll have to get a grip on.

We can get through this, and then we can get back to where we were, radio silence and vowing never to talk again.

"Hi, I'm Isabelle," Isabelle says brightly. She crosses the room to Zoey who stands, putting her laptop on the cabinet behind the armchair.

"Zoey Taylor." Zoey offers her hand for a handshake.

"It's nice to meet you, I'm so sorry it is under these circumstances. How are you feeling?"

"I'm okay, now. I think the adrenaline has washed out of my system. Some work crisis took my mind off it for a minute," she says, gesturing at her laptop.

"I'll leave you two to get acquainted. I'll be in your study, if that's okay, Zoey?" I ask. Zoey nods.

"I'll come find you when we're done," Isabelle suggests. I leave the two of them in the living room, shutting the door behind me so they can talk privately.

I make it to Zoey's study before my phone rings. I know it will be my dad, so I'm not surprised to see his name on my display.

"You took a job?" he asks as soon as I answer.

"Yes, I'm just assessing everything now."

"Why are you doing it, Aiden?" he asks and even though it's just a phone call, I can sense his disappointment.

"I didn't think you'd mind."

"I thought you were going to start moving into a management role." Dad sighs.

"I know."

"You haven't put a lot of details into the system," he starts, but I cut him off.

"I'm still getting the details together. I just wanted the job logged, but I'll update the client account later," I reply. I'd input only basic information about Zoey's case into the system, something I'd quickly done on my work phone when in the lift with her assistant. She's listed currently as Jane Smith.

"It's an unconventional way of processing things."

"Dad, let me handle this. I know the rates to charge, I know how to do this. Isabelle and I can take care of this account."

"Make sure you update everything on the system as soon as you have the details. How long do you anticipate the job lasting?"

"I don't know yet. It will depend on how quickly the police find the person who has made the threat," I explain, and I sink into the chair at Zoey's desk. Her desk, like everywhere else in the house, is neat and tidy. Aside from her personal laptop, the only thing on the desk is an envelope, bearing the name of an expensive solicitors. I wonder what the letter is about, whether it could be linked to whatever has triggered somebody to make a threat against Zoey. For now, I push it to the back of my mind, whatever the contents of the letter, it'll come up later when we go through all Zoey's acquaintances and connections with her to establish anything we need to be aware about.

"I can have either Nolan or Pratt free to take over from you," Dad offers. I knew they were free, both recently back from an assignment overseas. It would have been easy enough to assign them to Zoey's case, but this is something I don't want to pass onto somebody else, no matter how uncomfortable it will be working with Zoey.

"It's fine. Look, I'm supposed to be going over everything with the client. I'll call you at some point in the week, okay?"

"Okay," he relents. I know he's still pissed off. "Are you still okay to take us to the airport on Wednesday? We'll be away for Jonah's birthday. I assume this job won't get in the way of your home duties?" He asks it like a question, but I know it's a command.

"Yes. Give my love to Mum, okay?"

"I'll speak to you soon, Aiden," Dad says, and then he disconnects the call.

I stay sat in the chair until Isabelle comes into the study. She looks at me and smirks.

"Richard got a hold of you, I guess?" she says. I smile wryly at her. She knows me so well.

"Yeah, I'm surprised he hasn't called you and asked you for details."

"He did, but I didn't answer. I can talk to him later. I didn't want to put my foot in it, something like how our client isn't really Jane Smith but a Zoey Taylor."

"Whatever he asks, that should be the information you don't correct him on."

"Fair enough. You know when this job is done and dusted, I'm going to want all the details from you, about your history. I asked her a question in there about you and she was evasive as fuck." Isabelle stares at me. I know she's trying to gauge my reaction.

"Are you two done?" I ask.

"Yeah, time for us to do the deep dive into all her acquaintances."

I follow Isabelle and we head across the house. Instead of going into the living room, Isabelle takes me in the direction of the dining room where Zoey is sat at one end of the dining table. There are three glasses of cranberry juice on the table. Isabelle and I take a seat opposite Zoey, next to where two of the glasses have been placed.

"Okay, let's do this." Zoey sighs. I take out my phone and launch the app where I'm tracking information for Zoey's case. We'll work through all the people she knows, all the incidents that could have escalated into something like this, and I'll update the work system with any relevant information.

"Is there anybody that jumps to your mind if you think about who could have sent the letter?" I ask.

"You mean, do I know somebody who might want to hurt me? No." Zoey frowns as she talks. Her right hand is on the table, index finger tapping slightly against the tabletop.

"Is this the first threat you have received like this?" I can't stop looking at her finger as she increases her frequency.

"We get the usual shit on social media, the usual comments. Earlier in the year, we had to get the police involved when some incels were getting a bit too carried away with their comments, but they have been quiet for ages," Zoey explains.

Her use of the term incel won't be hyperbole. I've never known her use words like incel, misogynist or abuser without there being significant cause and evidence.

"Do you have issues on your personal social media, or just work?" Isabelle cuts in.

"I don't have my own social media accounts. I closed them a few years ago," she explains. She glances over at me but then quickly looks back at Isabelle.

I had wondered if she had deleted them all and started a new profile under a different name, blocking me from view. The absence of social media helps, there is nothing like having to explain to a prolific social media user that they should change their posting habits when something like this is unfolding.

"Who do you interact with, day to day?" Isabelle asks.

Zoey frowns. "Mostly, it is people from work. We only interact at work though, and our employee satisfaction scores are very high."

"What about unsuccessful applicants, have there been any recently? Anybody who might feel disgruntled at being rejected?" Isabelle prompts.

"Nobody that I'd have been involved in hiring, firing, or rejecting. The last interview I did was for Abigail and that was over a year ago, when my previous assistant relocated after she chose to be a stay at home mum. Before that it was about four years ago, when I had to replace my chief accountant."

At this, I see Isabelle sit straighter in her seat.

"Why did you have to replace them? Some people can hold a grudge for a long time, are you sure the previous accountant couldn't be involved?" Isabelle wonders.

"To put it bluntly, no, they're not involved. I know they aren't involved because they died. That's why I needed to interview." Zoey's tapping ceases and her eyes meet mine. I wonder if she's thinking the same as me, about how she had reacted to Dominic's death, all the circumstances surrounding it.

"Okay, well, we'll still look into your employee records, if that is okay." Isabelle smooths over the uncomfortable air that seems to have descended in the room.

"What about friends?" I ask.

"I spend a lot of time with Lizzie. Elizabeth Chapman," Zoey elaborates. I haven't heard her name before. I search for her on social media and Zoey confirms the correct profile. Lizzie's profile is wide open for the public. It never fails to surprise me how trusting people are, what they'll put out for the whole world to see.

Lizzie's photographs contain mostly pictures of her with her pets, or with Zoey. There are multiple pictures of Lizzie and Zoey, arms around one another, huge smiles on their faces. It looks like they must have been on holiday together as there are pictures of them in bikinis sitting at the poolside, cocktails in their hands, wide sunglasses on their faces.

I haven't seen Zoey looking this relaxed with a female friend since Caterina.

I turn my phone towards Zoey.

"I'd advise her to keep her profile page private, or at least stop tagging herself in locations and noting that she is with you. You might not be tagged as you don't have a profile, but her status today reads that she's looking forward to dinner with you tonight, six o'clock at Bailey's Bistro." I show her what I'm looking at and she flushes.

"Well, given I don't have a profile, it isn't like I knew she did that. Of course, I'll have a word with her."

Isabelle looks over at me, then back at Zoey. "I think Bailey's Bistro is too exposed. We don't really know what we're dealing with right now. Could you perhaps suggest dinner here instead," she suggests.

Zoey snorts. "What, a nice dinner for me and my best friend and two bodyguards? She'll think I'm paranoid and crazy."

"Better crazy than sorry." Isabelle shrugs. "Besides, once you've decided which shift pattern you prefer, it would be you, your best friend, and one discrete bodyguard."

"Fine, I'll ask Lizzie to meet me here and we can order something in." Zoey looks frustrated. I knew it wouldn't be long before she was.

"Why are you using Hammond solicitors? I saw the envelope in your office." I know I'm risking her being angry, given she's already frustrated, but it is important for the background checks that Isabelle and I will need to run, for us to work out where all the possible threats might be coming from.

I watch as she sits upright in her seat, like her spine has just become a metal rod. She shifts so she is more angled to focus on Isabelle.

"Aiden seems to think I'm being naïve when I say my ex, Caleb, is not a threat. Hammond is the solicitors I'm using to finalise our separation. Caleb believes he is entitled to some of the house. Legally, he isn't. The house is in my name. I pay the mortgage. He lived here with me, but he never contributed financially. The solicitor is doing the final work to settle that," she explains.

"That could be an important factor, Zoey," Isabelle replies, tone gentle.

"He just wants money," Zoey snaps back, looking frustrated.

"It's never just money." Isabelle shakes her head. We both know how powerful a motivator money can be, but it's often coupled with something else. We've seen enough of it in our line of work, from abduction plots to blackmail. We both know that an angry person with hurt feelings can be ruthless. Combining hurt and greed, it can be deadly.

"I have his details," I say to Isabelle.

"Anybody else worthy of noting?" Isabelle looks back at Zoey.

"Just the people I pay for running the house. The gardener, the cleaner, the window cleaner, that kind of stuff. I keep my circle pretty small. Now, if you excuse me, I need to make a call." Zoey pushes her seat back and then stalks out of the dining room, leaving her glass of juice untouched.

"A small circle? One person is not a small circle. It's a full stop," Isabelle mutters.

"She doesn't trust many people," I reply.

"Well, good for us, she seems to trust you, even if only a little," she muses.

"We both know what it's like when somebody betrays you." I shrug.

"How about you look into this ex of hers, and I'll wait for her to calm down so I can get the details of the people that help around the house?" Isabelle suggests.

"Sounds good." I nod and focus on my phone, starting the request for a background check on Caleb Lowe. He might have always struck me as being limp and pathetic, but if he is anything to do with this threat, I'll make him suffer for it.

"When are you going to tell me the history you have with her?" she adds.

"Later. It's a long story," I reply with a sigh. I'm thankful that she falls into silence, busying herself with her task as I scroll through Caleb's social media pages, desperate for a clue.

The history I have with Zoey, it's long and complex, something we both have figurative and literal scars from. I'm sure if I tell Isabelle, she'll advise me to walk away and that's the one thing I can't do. Protecting Zoey is something that has felt like an instinct from the day I met her, and I don't think I'm capable of stopping that now.

3
Zoey

Twelve Years Ago

The sound of the front door slamming as Caterina arrives home makes me jolt and drop my textbook.

"Zoey?" she shouts from the hallway.

"Just recovering from that mini heart attack," I call out to her.

She laughs as she comes into the living room. "Sorry."

"I'll forgive you." I pick my book back up.

"How was your day? Are you all relaxed and chill?" she asks. I glance over at her because I know she's after something.

"What do you want?" I laugh.

"Nothing but your time. Were you planning anything tonight?"

"Why?" I ask, non-committal because I want the option of an out.

"I really want you to meet Aiden." Caterina stares back at me with her usual pleading expression on her face. It's the one I expect she would use in front of her father when asking for a new car.

"I was actually," I start, but I should've known better than to give her an opportunity. I should have told her no immediately, made up some plans.

"Please, please, please?" she wheedles.

"Do you ever let anybody say no?" I grumble.

She laughs at me and shakes her head, her long dark hair swishing around her shoulders as she does so.

"Not really, it's just easier this way. You could say no, I would try to convince you, you'd eventually give in, and then you'd be moaning that you wish you had time to get changed."

She says this as she looks me up and down.

"You're kidding right? You want me to get changed?" I laugh.

"Yes, I do. Come on, chop, chop."

"You're intolerable, you know that?" I tease.

"No, I'm adorable, and you love me." Caterina smiles back at me. She's an animated smiler, she shows off every tooth when she does. She told me her family had paid a small fortune for her perfectly straight and pearly white teeth, maybe that's why she shows them off. I'm more of a closed mouth smiler when I do smile.

I get up from my horizontal position on the sofa, the position I would have been quite happy to keep all night. I put down my textbook and stretch slightly.

"I do find you adorable, but this guy better be worth it," I warn.

"Oh, he is, I promise." She follows me as I walk through the house, intent on going upstairs to get changed.

"I'll take your word for it. You have a bad habit of picking up duff ones. I'm sure you only do it to piss off your dad," I joke.

"The university years are for getting it all out of your system, right? Before we find somebody to settle down with." She shrugs and I laugh.

"For you, maybe. For me, these years are all about getting myself sorted for my career."

She follows me into my bedroom. She's a little intrusive sometimes but I know once she critiques my outfit, she'll at least leave me alone so I can get changed in private.

"Do you want me to pick you something to wear?"

"I'm perfectly capable, thank you." I roll my eyes at her and then open my wardrobe. It isn't bursting with options so it's easy for me to shift through my clothes. "I'm just meeting him here, right? Then you're going out?"

"No, come for drinks with us. I really want you to like him and get to know him properly."

I push the hangers with jeans and jumpers to one side. Caterina's version of drinks is not a dive bar with sticky floors, where jeans and a pair of boots is almost a requirement to get in. She means a fancy wine bar. She also means she'll be paying for the drinks, so the least I can do is oblige her by putting on a dress or a skirt.

"You sound like you really like him," I comment as I pull out a dress and a skirt and top combination to show her. She points at the skirt and top, shaking her head and wrinkling her nose, so I put it back into the wardrobe.

"He's lovely. I think he could be *The One*," she says dramatically, putting air quotes around the last words.

"Is this somebody Daddy will approve of?" I tease. The men she has dated through our first year and a half at university have not been the type that her father would approve of. She tended to pick up men who she hoped to change, but they'd still be people her father would refuse to let her be with. She'd typically pick people that came from my own social circle, with my background.

I get a pass from her father as I'm not a threat to her inheritance. I'm not jumping into bed with his daughter in the hopes I'll be bagging an easy future. I genuinely care for Caterina, and every day I count myself lucky that we'd been matched up together for our accommodation.

"Aiden is actually from good standing," Caterina says with a small smile on her face. Good standing probably means his family is worth a million or so, not quite the big leagues of her own family.

Caterina's dad, Ronan, started some tech company early in his life and before the big tech boom. He made an absolute fortune when he sold it. Caterina's life has always been parties on yachts and winters in the Caribbean as a default. She's the youngest of his three children. Her two older brothers both have their own businesses, apparently funded by their trust funds when they finished their degrees. It's apparently a stipulation of their inheritance, finish university, turn twenty-one, have a viable business plan, collect your money.

I can see Caterina staring at me as she waits for my response. She's probably expecting me to be sarcastic.

"I'll remember my manners tonight, shall I?" I grin at her, and she relaxes.

"Please. You're important to me, Zo, but he is too," she says. Quite how she has been with Aiden for three months and not introduced us yet is beyond me. Most of her other boyfriends, I've seen them within a few weeks. Usually, I'm telling her they're not worth her time, and they end up on the scrap heap shortly after.

"Will this dress do?" I shake the dress on the hanger in front of her.

"It'll do. It isn't like I can loan you anything of mine, is it?"

"Absolutely not, not unless you're expecting me to be flashing my underwear," I joke. Caterina is only five foot two. I'm five eight. Caterina and I might have shared a home for the last couple of years, we might have shared our deepest secrets over copious bottles of wine, but sharing clothes has never been practical.

"Not the kind of impression I want you to make, Zoey," she smirks.

"Is he meeting us here?"

"No, the wine bar in town. In an hour. Hurry up and get changed."

"You're lucky I find you adorable given this is such late notice." I roll my eyes at her as she starts to retreat out of my bedroom. At this rate, by the time I have got myself ready, we'll have to leave to get the bus into town.

"I'll get us a taxi, don't worry," she calls over her shoulder. Then she's gone, leaving me in peace and quiet for me to get ready.

∞∞∞∞∞∞∞∞

We make it to the wine bar before Aiden. We would have been earlier if Caterina hadn't vetoed my first choice of shoes.

I order us both a glass of wine at the bar as Caterina finds an empty table. The bar might be busy, but I know she will find one, it is like a special power she has. Sometimes, I imagine the oceans themselves would part, should she need to cross them. She seems to live a completely charmed life which should be irritating but she's always so endearing that it's hard to feel anything but affection for her.

I stand at the bar as I wait for our drinks. The barman, a guy I know to be a complete womaniser, gives me a leary smile as he slides the drinks across the bar to me.

"Enjoy these, sweetheart. You let me know when you want another, or something stronger," he suggests.

There's a little wink thrown in my direction. I know he does this to all the women he serves. I also know he doesn't ever recognise me as the girl who sits behind him in our economics lectures. Mostly this is because Caterina makes me dress up and put on some makeup when we are going out, and I don't feel the need to do the same for a university lecture.

I don't acknowledge the barman beyond my curt nod. I pick up the glasses and head to find Caterina. She's found a table, of course she has. She smiles widely as I sit across from her. I pass her the glass of wine and then take a sip of my own.

"So, tell me what I need to know about Aiden," I say once I've put my glass down.

She shifts in her seat, leaning forwards, an excited smile on her face.

"Okay, so first, he's a total dish. Honestly, I think he's the best I have ever been with, looks wise. Tall, dark, handsome and all that."

"You said that about Shawn." I grin at her. I did have to hand it to her, Caterina has the habit of attracting exceptional looking men. Mostly because she is also exceptional looking. I guess people gravitate to their equal.

"Shawn was all muscle, no brains. Aiden is smart."

"Looks, brains, from a good standing family, where is the flaw?" I joke.

"He doesn't have a flaw," she protests.

"Everybody has a flaw." I laugh.

"Oh, what's mine?" she asks, a grin on her face.

"You're a hopeless romantic with terrible taste in wine," I tease. She leans over and swats me on the arm.

"Alright smartarse, what's your flaw?"

"When I said everybody, I meant aside from me. I'm perfect, obviously." I giggle.

"Your shockingly bad confidence, that's your flaw," Caterina teases.

"You know I buy into the whole 'fake it until you make it' school of thinking." I shrug. She opens her mouth to speak and I'm sure it'll be another of her lectures to not critique myself, and I'm not in the mood for it tonight so I cut her off instead. "So, come on, Aiden. Three heads? Small dick? Too fast in bed? Mummy issues, or worse, Daddy issues?" I prod and she shakes her head, giggling.

"One head. Lovely dick. Strong bedroom game. Seems fine about his family."

"Stingy? Doesn't tip? Rude to servers? Shit at mental maths? Chews with his mouth open?"

"You're the worst, Zoey," she protests but she's still giggling. "He pays for dinner. He always tips. Nice but not over the top with servers. Knows how to do math. Could eat in front of the royal family."

"Does he kick kittens and puppies for fun?" I ask.

"Not for fun, maybe for competitive sport." The voice that comes from behind me makes me jump. I whirl around in my seat and Caterina is on her feet, stepping around the table to stand in front of the man, throwing her arms around him.

"Aiden," she exclaims.

"Fuck," I mutter to myself. Of course it's Aiden. This is mortifying. I'd much rather it had been the flirty guy from behind the bar who was stood behind us.

"Hi, sweetheart, sorry I'm late," Aiden says to her, but he's glancing in my direction as Caterina still has her arms around him.

"Do you want a drink?" I ask, standing up, hoping he'll say yes so that I can have a moment to compose myself. I hate that he's caught me talking about him to Caterina.

"I'll go, why don't you sit and get to know each other?" Caterina suggests as she pulls away from him. She gives him a kiss on the cheek and then skips off to the bar without waiting for a response.

"I'm sorry, I didn't mean anything by it. I was only teasing her," I apologise as I sit back down. Aiden shrugs and sits down next to where Caterina had been sitting.

"So, any questions you want to ask me? A bit of probing about my family life, to see if I really do have any Mummy or Daddy issues?" he asks.

I feel my cheeks flush, and I know they'll be bright red. I'm grateful for the slightly dim aesthetic in the bar. I'd rather the ground open me up before I apologise for a second time so instead, I force myself to grin at him.

"At least you now know she thinks you have a lovely dick and a strong bedroom game," I joke.

Aiden, thankfully, laughs. "Zoey, right? You're studying economics?"

"Economics and Finance," I confirm.

"That's a hard course to get into. Smart girl," he comments. I'm assuming he means the grade requirements to get in, but it rubs me up the wrong way. I worked hard to get the grades for my course.

"What are you studying? Or are you working?"

"Psychology," he replies, tone even.

"Smart boy," I shoot back at him.

He smirks. "Caterina told me you two have lived together since your first year."

"Correct. I feel lucky to have her as my housemate. She's awesome." I smile. He looks over towards the bar.

"Yeah, she's one of a kind," he muses.

"Well, don't hurt her. If you did, I'd have to chop your arms off and beat you to death with them," I say, grin on my face, but I'm serious. Caterina might be demanding, she might be a little spoilt, but she has a heart of gold and I love her to pieces. There isn't anybody in my life I love like Caterina.

"What makes you think I'd hurt her?" Aiden scoffs. He leans closer towards me and even under the dim lights, I can see the depths of his grey-blue eyes. They remind me of the skies on a stormy day, right before the rain comes.

"I'm just letting you know that you'd have me to answer to if you did." I shrug.

"How, exactly, would you chop my arms off?" His mouth twitches and I'm sure he's trying to hide a smile.

"Possibly with a rusty chainsaw." I take a sip of my wine, stare at him over the glass, and then we're both laughing.

"Relax, Rambo. I'm sure Caterina and I will get out of this relationship fully intact."

I frown because I'm sure Caterina isn't expecting that either of them is going to get out of the relationship. She's imagining *The One*, but I don't say anything as I'm sure any guy who has only been dating for three months, they're not thinking of marriage and happily ever after. They're thinking about how long they need to remain on their best behaviour to still get some action for their dick, how long until they're sure the relationship is secure enough to let down some of the standards they'd been upholding.

"Sorry, the bar was so busy, but I got us some menus, I thought we could order some food and really make a night of it." Caterina sounds breathless as she gets back to the table. She has a pint in one hand, three menus in the other. She puts Aiden's beer down, takes her seat and then puts the menus in the centre of the table. The expression on her face makes me smile to myself because I know we're going to order food now, whether we are hungry or not.

"Zoey was just telling me I need to treat you right, otherwise she's going to make sure I suffer." Aiden reaches for her hand, and she giggles.

"Oh well, Zoey is my biggest champion."

"I was wondering who is going to protect me from you?" he teases. I grab one of the menus from the table and make myself appear busy reading it as I feel like their conversation should be private.

"I won't hurt you, baby," Caterina tells him, and she sounds like she's never been surer of anything in her life.

Aiden's phone beeps and he pulls it out of his coat pocket, glancing at the screen. He grimaces slightly.

"That looks ominous," I comment.

"Somebody is having a crisis and wants to talk." Aiden is now frowning.

"Who is it?" Caterina asks.

"Jonah, my brother."

"Tell him to come. I'd love to meet your brother," Caterina gushes.

Aiden fires off a text, the frown still on his face. His phone beeps in return and then he looks at us in turn.

"Jonah is on his way. He's not far, he says he'll be five minutes or so. Do you two mind if we wait for him before we order? I'm not sure if he will eat with us or if it will be a flying visit," he says.

"I'm sure he'll want to stay for food. He's your brother." Caterina is all smiles, but she comes from a family where family is everything. She can count on her dad and her mum, both of her brothers, if she needed them, they'd be there like a shot.

I glance over at Aiden, and I can tell from his expression that he knows personally that family dynamics are sometimes difficult and hard.

"Older or younger?" I ask him.

"Same age, actually."

"You never said you had a twin," Caterina says. He shakes his head.

"We were both adopted," Aiden clarifies. He puts his phone back in his pocket and he looks thoroughly annoyed.

Interesting dynamics.

"How old were you when you were adopted?" I ask.

"I was seven when I was adopted. Jonah was older when he was adopted, he was ten." Aiden doesn't seem bothered by the intrusive questions.

"Is Jonah at university, too?" I continue my questions.

"Yes, studying Theology."

"Are you close?" I risk a third question but before Aiden can answer, Caterina pushes a menu towards him.

"I think I'm going to have the grilled salmon, what do you think Aiden?"

I grin at her. "Is that your subtle way of telling me to shut up?"

"I was about to ask why you didn't study psychology, too." Aiden smirks. His head jerks up slightly when we hear somebody shouting his name. "I'll be back in a moment, excuse me, ladies."

Aiden stands and heads across the bar. I watch as he stops in front of the man who I assume to be Jonah, the two of them immediately looking like they're in an intense conversation. Aiden looks like he might be shouting though I can't be sure from the distance.

Caterina taps my arm to get my attention. I turn to look at her and she smiles at me.

"Come on, what do you think?" she asks.

"I was only talking to him for what, five minutes." I laugh.

"I know, but you always say you trust your first instincts."

"He seems nice." I shrug.

"Nice? He's amazing," she gushes.

I think of his comment about them both getting out of the relationship fully intact. I think about the fact that he seems to be shouting at his brother in the bar. Before I can answer, Aiden arrives back at the table with Jonah at his heels.

If he hadn't told me they were both adopted, I would never have picked them for brothers. Aiden is taller and leaner than Jonah's shorter and stocky frame. Where Jonah has blonde hair which looks like it is long overdue a cut, Aiden's black hair is in a short, stylish crew cut.

Jonah fixes his blue eyes on me.

"You must be the third wheel," he grins.

"Hey, at least I was invited." I shrug.

Aiden laughs. "Caterina, Zoey, this is Jonah."

"Are you going to join us for some food, Jonah? We were just about to order." Caterina smiles brightly at him.

"Sure, I'd love to," he replies. When he takes a seat next to Caterina, I see the flash of annoyance over Aiden's face. I slide over to the next seat so he can sit down between me and Caterina.

"I'm still thinking of the grilled salmon, how about you guys?" Caterina asks after we have all studied the menu for a minute. She pulls her mobile phone out, opening her notes app so she can make a note of the others.

"The salmon sounds good, I'll join you." I smile at her, and she adds my order onto her notes.

"Put me down for the fillet steak," Jonah drops his menu onto the table.

"Are you paying for it?" Aiden stares at him.

"Don't be silly, it's my treat," Caterina scolds. She's generous to a fault. Or rather, her dad allows her to be generous.

"Why don't we add a couple bottles of wine, seen as we're making a night of it." Jonah looks like his night has just turned for the better.

"I'm sure you can afford your own food and drink," Aiden shoots at him.

"It's fine, it was my idea. I'll just put it on my card." Caterina shrugs and she fishes out her credit card. The credit card her father settles on her behalf every month, no questions asked, as far as I can gather.

I'm fairly sure that of the four of us gathered around the table, I'm going to be the only one leaving university with a mountain of debt.

"I'll come with you to order," Jonah offers, and he stands with Caterina.

"What are you having, Aiden?" she asks.

"The cheeseburger," he replies, naming the least expensive thing on the menu, like it will go some way to offset Jonah ordering the most expensive meal. Caterina leans to kiss him before heading to the bar with Jonah. Aiden and I sit in silence for a couple of minutes.

"Not a lot of love between you and your brother, is there?" I comment, breaking the silence. I don't look at Aiden as I talk as I'm busy putting the cost of my meal into the notes on my phone, into the document I keep titled 'to pay back to Caterina'.

I might not mind her paying for drinks every now and again, but I track everything else so I can pay my way whenever my cash flow allows.

"What's that?" Aiden asks.

"What I owe Caterina." I shrug and put my phone away. He raises his eyebrows momentarily, but he doesn't comment.

"Jonah and I are just opposites in every way. He can sometimes be an entitled asshole who thinks the world owes him a favour. But he's my brother, and I love him, regardless of how we act with each other."

"Is he single?"

"Why, are you attracted to arrogant dicks who think respect in a relationship means trying to remember to wear a condom when he fucks somebody else?"

I snort. "Well, safe sex is safe sex, so maybe he gets some points there. However, I was asking because if he is attached, it means I won't have to listen to Caterina trying to cajole me into dating him."

"Zoey, please, dating brothers would be so much fun," Aiden mimics Caterina with such precision that it has me giggling.

"Yes, exactly that." I grin.

"Your life is none of my business, but if she pushes, don't do it. Seriously, he needs to do a lot of growing up."

"It might not be any of your business, but it is not going to happen. I'm sworn off boys. Too much to focus my attention on, not to mention there are a lot of assholes out there, and I have no time for that shit," I explain.

"Oh Zoey, don't tell me you're boring Aiden with your anti-men stance?" Caterina teases as she and Jonah arrive back to the table.

"Lesbian?" Jonah raises an eyebrow.

"No, you asshole." I roll my eyes at him. "I'm waiting until they're worth my time."

"Ah, a virgin." Jonah looks at me like I'm suddenly a conquest for him to make. I flip my middle finger at him.

"I unfortunately discovered that most people my age with dicks are, in fact, dicks. No offence to you two, I'm sure you're both fine gentlemen," I joke. "Anyway, I vowed to put all that dating shit on one side, until I'm older, and they're older. Maybe then I can easily spot the bad apples."

"I keep telling her to find an older man to date. Some nice thirty-year-old who has his life sorted." Caterina laughs.

"I keep telling you, a thirty-year-old man who has his life sorted should want no business with a nineteen-year-old university student," I remind her.

"It's not as unusual as you think," Caterina protests, as she always does.

Caterina has dated a couple of older guys before. Last year, in our first year at university, she'd spent two months convinced she was in love with a twenty-eight-year-old she'd met in a bar. He was a walking red flag, may as well carried a sign that flashed in neon lights that he was a toxic asshole. Fortunately, she'd seen sense and ended things, but I know it wasn't her first relationship with an older person, she dated one of her eldest brother's friends when she was only seventeen. As far as I know, nobody in her family batted an eyelid about it.

"Enough of my love life, thanks. So, Jonah, tell me about Theology." I lean closer towards him. He gives me a big smile and shuffles his seat closer towards me. Aiden and Caterina turn their attention to one another, and the four of us sit having crossed conversations until the food arrives.

∞∞∞∞∞∞∞∞

"Another glass, ladies?" Jonah holds the bottle of wine up to both me and Caterina. It's the fourth bottle that appears to have made its way to the table as we'd had dinner.

"Not for me, thanks," I reply, holding my hand above my glass because the last time I'd said no, he'd poured me one anyway.

"I think I've had enough for tonight." Caterina giggles and then she leans against Aiden. He kisses her temple.

"Oh sweetheart, looks like you need to get home to bed," he says, affection in his tone.

"No, I think we should go dancing. It's way too early to go to bed. We're too young to be going to bed this early," she protests. "Right, Zo?" she asks, looking at me.

"Excuse me for a minute," Jonah says as he stands. A second later, he's disappeared from the table.

"Come on, Zoey, dancing!"

"Don't pull me into this, I think I'm going to head home. Some of us have work in the morning," I remind her. Saturday and Sunday mornings are when I do my regular shifts in the local supermarket. It helps pay the bills, and I like the discount I get on food. I pick up any extra shift I can in the week, trying to balance my need for cash with my need for hours to study, especially when some of those precious hours are so often stolen by Caterina.

"You are such a spoil sport." She sticks her tongue out at me, but I know she won't be dancing anywhere tonight. She looks exactly as Aiden suggested, ready for bed.

"I think once the fresh air hits you, all that wine is going to go straight to your head, and then you'll be complaining that the world is already dancing," I tease.

"No way, I'm fine. I can handle my alcohol. Besides, dancing seems like such a good idea. I haven't been dancing in ages. Come on you two, don't be spoilsports." She pouts as she finishes talking.

"Fine, but I can't stay long. Some of us don't have the luxury of Daddy's credit card," I remind her.

"I'm sure it wouldn't matter if you missed one shift." Caterina rolls her eyes at me.

"Did I hear we're settled on clubbing?" Jonah arrives back at the table.

"Come on, let's get going before these two stick-in-the-muds change their minds." Caterina grins at him.

We all stand to join Jonah and walk out of the wine bar. As the fresh air hits us, I feel a rush, like the alcohol has finally found its way to my head. By the giggles I can hear from Caterina, I'm convinced she is experiencing the same as me. Aiden has his arm around her, supporting her.

"Come on, Zoey, let's get that body of yours on the dancefloor." Jonah puts his arm around me. I carry on walking but step slightly away from him. "Come on, I'm just being friendly."

"Aw, look at them," Caterina croons behind us.

Again, I step away from Jonah's embrace. He reaches out for me again, his arm snaking around my shoulder, his hand on the top of my chest. Aiden's hand lands on Jonah's, grabbing his hand and pulling it off my body.

"Leave her alone," Aiden warns.

"I'm just being friendly, don't overreact. It's not like I'm groping her." Jonah rolls his eyes. There is a second of quiet between us all, then Aiden's expression changes.

"What have you taken?" he snaps.

"You've got such a stick up your ass, Aiden," Jonah groans.

"You promised me you weren't taking anything," Aiden shouts.

Caterina grabs my hand and pulls me towards her. We stand and watch Aiden and Jonah, both looking furious.

"It's just a bit of coke, stop being such a fucking baby." Jonah jabs him in the shoulder. Aiden turns to look at Caterina and me.

"I'm sorry, I'll get you two a taxi and then sort him out." His expression is a mix of frustration and remorse. I wonder how many times he has had this exact argument with Jonah.

"Sorry ladies, Aiden's a bit sensitive when it comes to drugs, given that's how his dear mummy and daddy died," Jonah mocks, and the next second, he and Aiden are on the floor, fists cracking, curses and insults being exchanged.

"Stop it," Caterina screeches. It only seems to take a minute for Aiden to have subdued Jonah on the floor, then Aiden is back on his feet, Jonah still on the floor. He sits up straight and wipes the blood from his mouth.

"Fuck, Aiden, you could've knocked a tooth out," he complains.

"You'd deserve it," Aiden shoots back. He looks around, seemingly for a taxi, but then he groans when Caterina leans over and vomits in the road. I rush towards her.

"Oh Zo, I don't feel well," she moans. I know the chances of us getting her home in a taxi are non-existent. Taxi drivers take a firm stance on picking up passengers who might lose their stomachs in the car.

50

Aiden looks at me. "Can you walk?"

"Yeah." I nod my head. Watching him fight with Jonah, watching Caterina throw up in the street, it's made me feel suddenly sober.

"Come on sweetheart, piggyback time," Aiden coaxes Caterina. She looks like she's too drunk to argue. She half clambers onto Aiden's back and he shifts her position. She moans slightly when he moves her but then rests against him.

"What about Jonah?" I ask.

"He's had plenty of experience in taking care of himself when he gets into this state, right, bro?" Aiden glares at Jonah who nods as he gets up from the floor. For somebody who just got put in his place, he seems remarkably chipper.

"Are you sure you don't want to come dancing, third wheel?" he asks, grinning at me.

I shake my head. "I'll pass, thanks."

"Suit yourself," he mutters, and he walks off in the opposite direction of the one we will be walking in to go back to my place.

Aiden starts to walk, there is no second glance in Jonah's direction to make sure he is okay. I follow him. Caterina appears to have dozed off on his back, so I walk a step behind him, my arm ready to catch her if she looked like she was going to tip backwards.

"Sorry about that," Aiden says.

I laugh. "I'm not sure what you have got to apologise for."

"Nothing like a complicated family, right?" he asks. I think of my own family, the one I haven't spoken to since I left for university, the one where if you looked up the word dysfunctional, you'd probably see our picture.

"Was Jonah telling the truth, what he said about your parents?"

"My biological parents, yes. Within a year of one another. Mum first, then my dad. I was in foster care when my dad died. He kept saying he'd get it under control so he could get me back, but the drugs were more important, apparently."

There's a beat of silence between us.

"I'm sorry, Aiden."

"I'm not looking for sympathy, Zoey." His response is quick, his tone sharp.

"I didn't think you was, but you have it anyway," I reply. I watch as he shifts slightly, moving Caterina into a better position. "Did she know?" I wonder.

"No, but based on how much's she's drank tonight, she'll probably have forgotten by morning. Though maybe she'll remember enough and won't ever suggest you date Jonah."

"No offence, but I'd rather sew my vagina shut with a rusty needle than let Jonah anywhere near it," I tell him, and he stops walking, laughing loudly.

"Don't make me laugh, I don't want to drop her," he complains, composing himself.

"Given dropping her would hurt her, causing me to cut your arms off with the rusty chainsaw, I guess I'd better behave," I tease.

He looks my way, grins, and then he starts walking. We walk the distance to our place, chatting together, him still carrying Caterina, me still a step behind, just in case.

By the time we reach the house, I've sobered up. If Aiden had been feeling any effects of the alcohol, it doesn't show.

"Where do you want her?" he asks when I let us into the house.

"Can you manage the stairs with her?" I ask, but at that moment, Caterina stirs.

"Why do I smell sick?" she asks, and she hops down from Aiden's hold. He stretches once free of carrying her weight.

"The fresh air got to you," I tease.

"Oh, embarrassing," she moans. She looks at Aiden. "Did you just carry me from the taxi?"

He laughs, "Try all the way from the wine bar, you lightweight."

"Do you want to stay?" she asks him. He's not stopped over at ours before.

"I'm going to get home. I'll call you tomorrow, okay?" he asks, and he kisses her temple.

"Goodnight, Aiden," she murmurs.

"Sleep well. Goodnight, Zo," he calls. He gives us both a quick wave and then he shuts the door. I lock it behind him.

"So, what do you think of him? I think he really is the one, you know," Caterina says, taking my hand and pulling me up to the stairs.

"He seems like a really nice guy," I agree. We both go into the bathroom, and I reach for my toothbrush and the toothpaste. I want to get to bed so I can get some sleep. Caterina grabs her own toothbrush, grimacing, no doubt tasting the effects of being sick earlier.

"You should date Jonah. It would be amazing if we dated brothers," she exclaims once she has brushed her teeth, like the idea hasn't been on her mind all night. I knew this was coming and it makes me laugh.

"You know I'm not even looking at men right now. Now, get to bed. I've work tomorrow."

"Thanks for going out tonight."

"Anything for you, Cat, you know that." I smile.

"Love you too, Zo." She beams at me, and for the millionth time, I feel grateful for my best friend, wondering what I would do without her.

4

Zoey

"Zoey? Can I come in?"

I pull a face. Even though it's still early, I'm tired, a weary tiredness that I can feel in my bones.

"Yes, Aiden," I call back and then he steps into my study. He looks at me with an expression which seems a little like it is judging. Given it's not yet three and I'm sitting with my feet up on my desk, a decanter of expensive brandy in front of me, my half finished second glass in my hand, I can't say I blame him. "Do you want one? It's good." I gesture at my glass.

"No, thank you. I don't drink when I'm working."

"Usually, neither would I, but it's been a hell of a day," I mutter. I've only just finished with Isabelle, updating her with names and numbers of everybody I can think of as being involved in my life. I'd spent the whole time wondering if I could have done anything to upset anybody enough to have sent me the package.

"Isabelle and I need to know what your preferences are when it comes to the shift pattern you prefer from us. Whoever is going to do the night shift will need to get some sleep," Aiden explains.

I put my glass down onto the desk and then pinch the bridge of my nose. It should be such a simple decision. I make what feels like hundreds of decisions every day, but this one feels tricky. Do I want Aiden around me at night? Do I want him with me in the day?

"Whoever does the night shift, I assume they stay in the house?"

"Yes, we secure the property and then we stay alert, usually downstairs, with periodic checks upstairs. We're not going to be sat outside your bedroom door all night," he says, and I feel myself flinch. I drop my hands back into my lap.

"In the day, when I'm at the office, where will people be placed then?"

"Outside your office, and then with you when you leave it. We'll make sure we secure the house before we leave and check it when we get back."

I rub my eyes and sigh.

"What's your preference, Aiden?" I ask, but he doesn't answer. He looks like he either wants to pinch the bridge of his own nose or try my alcohol. "Fine, maybe it will be better for Isabelle to be with me in the day," I suggest. The idea of either of them being in my house at nighttime makes me feel on edge, but it would mean less time with Aiden. He'd suggested seven until seven. I can have early nights; it would limit the amount of time we need to interact.

"I'll let Isabelle know. I'll get going, to get some sleep. I'll be back for seven. I'll bring some items for the house, to give you increased security."

He turns as if to leave and I clear my throat.

"Aiden?"

"Yeah?" He doesn't turn to look at me.

"Thank you," I add.

He gives a curt nod and then steps out, shutting the study door again behind him. My hand reaches for the glass of brandy but my mobile phone beeps so instead of drinking, I answer the phone.

"Hey, Lizzie," I say, brightly.

"Zoey, I wasn't sure if you would answer, I tried the office, but Abigail said you weren't there." Lizzie sounds bright, like she always does. She's one of those types of women who thinks a smile and a positive attitude can remove every barrier. It's something I've seen in action, when we went on holiday to Miami and there was a mix-up with the rooms, Lizzie's bright smile and sweet nature when complaining had secured us a discounted room and a generous amount on a free tab behind the bar.

"It's been a weird day. I meant to phone you, anyway. I know we were supposed to be going out tonight but," I start but she cuts me off before I can finish.

"Do not even try to cancel on me. You deserve a night out. Especially given you're calling Caleb today. I promised you some consolation cocktails after you deal with him."

"I'm not speaking to him today. I rearranged. Well, Abigail did. I rearranged everything from today."

"Why, what happened? I got the message that you were rearranging with me, that's why I was calling, to check what is going on."

"I was hoping you would come for dinner at mine. Tonight, instead of going out. Perhaps I can pay for your taxi so we can have cocktails here instead of going out?"

"Why, exactly, can't you go out?"

"I'll explain it when you're here. If that's okay. If you can't make it, we can rearrange." I tilt my head to hold the phone between my ear and shoulder, and then I scratch at a sore spot on my arm.

"I can come to you. What time do you want me over?" Lizzie asks.

"Shall we say six, same time we should have met?"

"Sure, I'll finish work and come straight to you. Are you okay, though, Zoey? You sound a little off."

"I'm okay. I'll tell you all about it when you get here. Do you have anywhere in mind for where you want me to order from?" I keep scratching my arm. The skin starts to look red, but I can't stop myself.

"We can order from Bailey's. Why don't you text me with what you want, and I can pick it up on my way over to yours. We can get right onto the food and cocktails, and you can tell me whatever is bothering you, okay?"

"Sounds good. I'll see you later."

"Bye, Zoey," she sing-songs and then she ends the call.

I know she'll find it incredulous when I tell her what has happened today. I can still barely believe it. Lizzie lives a charmed life, the idea of a threat on her life would be something she'd only expect from a thriller film. I don't even have a copy of what was sent to me, the police kept it, so I'm sure she'll joke that I'm making it all up, hired personal protection as some practical joke I'm playing on her.

I put my phone back into my pocket, finish my drink and then head towards the kitchen. My phone beeps, a reminder from Lizzie for me to send my food order before five. The thought of food makes me realise I haven't eaten anything today, and I feel rude because I never thought to ask Isabelle or Aiden if they wanted something to eat. The only thing I've done is give them cups of coffee and glasses of juice.

I find Isabelle in the kitchen when I get there. She gives me a smile.

"I thought you might want a coffee," she says, gesturing at the kettle that she's put on the boil.

"Did Aiden tell you that I'm on the verge of getting drunk?" I wonder and I step around her to put the brandy glass in the dishwasher.

"No, he didn't say that, not really," she says with a small smile, so I'm sure he said something to her, perhaps just not insinuating that I'm a day-drinking alcoholic.

"I think knowing somebody hates me enough to want to hurt me should be enough of a validation to have a couple of stiff drinks," I bristle.

"I'm not judging you, Zoey. I imagine you're still quite shocked and reeling from what has happened. I'm sure it will get a little easier, with time, but try not to worry. You're completely safe with us."

"How did you get into personal security?" I ask. I take two mugs out of the cupboard so I can take over making the coffee.

"I was in the armed forces. Did twelve years. When I left, I wasn't sure what I wanted to do with my life, but I met Aiden through a friend. We talked a bit, got friendly, then a job became vacant, and he asked if I wanted to apply," she explains.

The term 'got friendly' hangs in the air, an intriguing piece of information. It makes me wonder how intimately she knows Aiden.

"Have you worked together a lot?" I ask.

"We've paired up a few times."

"Have you worked there long?" I busy myself putting the coffee granules into the mugs.

"Eighteen months, give or take," she informs me. Eighteen months ago, Aiden and I were not talking. We'd had six months of no contact by then, and I wonder how well he'd been doing in his life then.

"How do you like your coffee?" I ask.

"Black is fine."

I pour the water into the cups. "How long was the longest job you worked with Aiden?" I ask as I add milk to my own cup.

"We did three months with a family who were travelling and wanted security. There was four of us in the team, so we got a bit of time off to enjoy the sights and the location."

"It must be a bit odd, having to uproot everything to work in different locations. Your family doesn't mind when you're not around?" I hand her the coffee.

"It's nothing different to being in the army, I guess, but I don't have a family at home waiting for me. Footloose and fancy free. I get to travel a lot, when the jobs are there, and I like seeing different places, when we get some time off." Isabelle smiles.

"I'm guessing working this job is a bit of a come down." I smile back at her.

"Honestly, Zoey, I think this will be a quick job. We'll be out of your hair in no time, I'm sure."

"Then it's back to overseas and glamorous jobs for you and Aiden?"

"For me, yes. I expect this will be the last job I work with him."

"Why so?" I ask, and I hope the curiosity isn't written all over my face.

"Aiden's dad is pushing for him to move into the offices rather than working in the field," Isabelle explains.

"Richard always wanted him to be in the office." I shrug. It's a step too far, naming Aiden's father, because Isabelle's eyebrow lifts slightly.

"You and Aiden must go back a long time," she says. She'd asked me a similar question earlier and I'd avoided answering.

"We met at university," I state. It feels like the simplest explanation, an innocuous sentence that will stop her asking any further questions.

"Did you lose touch? I've worked with Aiden a few times and he never mentioned you. I hope that doesn't sound insensitive. It's just an observation."

"We lost touch about two years ago." I nod. I curl my fingers around my coffee mug and take a sip. She seems to think that it's a sensitive topic. She gives me a warm smile.

"So, why don't you tell me what a typical workday looks like for you, seeing as I'll be with you tomorrow," she suggests.

"It varies day to day. I don't know what my diary looks like for tomorrow. My assistant, Abigail, she rearranged several meetings from today, they may have ended up in any free slots I had. You'll probably be bored tomorrow if I'm in meetings most of the day."

She laughs, "I'm sure I'll survive it; I've had worse assignments."

"Abigail will look after you."

"Is there any dress code you want me to follow?"

"It tends to be business casual. Except on a Friday, we still do dress down on that day, so feel free to wear jeans, trainers, whatever you like." I smile.

"I'll do my best to blend in. Aiden said you probably want as little attention drawing as possible."

She gives me another curious expression, but I don't want to be drawn into anything about Aiden. Instead, I smile at her.

"It sounds like a weird question, but when Lizzie comes over, she's going to stop at the bistro to pick up some food. Would you like something? It would be for around six," I explain.

Isabelle laughs, "It's okay, Zoey. I'll get something to eat on my way home. You don't have to feed me."

"Oh, okay." I put the coffee cup down and take my phone out, planning on texting Lizzie to tell her what I want to order from the bistro, but I can't help thinking about Aiden. He'd left here around three and he's supposed to be back at seven. His flat is at least a forty-five-minute drive from mine. It doesn't give him long to get some sleep, pick up the equipment he has apparently told Isabelle he is getting, as well as eating.

"Aiden can take care of himself, too." Isabelle's tone makes me feel like she can read my mind. *I feel the flush of a blush on my cheeks.*

"I'm going to be in the living room. I'm going to email Abigail and let her know to expect you tomorrow. I'm sure she'll pull out all the stops, I bet she'll organise you a desk." I smile.

"Oh, I've never worked in an office before. This might be fun, a new experience to make up for the lack of pristine beaches," she jokes.

"Please come through if you need me for anything." I pick up my coffee cup again and then I walk through to the living room. She doesn't follow me, and I'm partly relieved. Isabelle is nice, she strikes me as somebody professional, but she's still a stranger in my home, at a time when I feel vulnerable.

I pick up my work laptop from where I'd abandoned it earlier, put my coffee cup down on the side. I text Lizzie with the food for tonight, and then I email Abigail, giving her a long update about what is happening, and what she can expect tomorrow.

I check through my emails after finishing my update to Abigail. I've a message from the security team, confirming they plan to double up the security guards for the time being. I read through the emails from the HR team who have sent through the latest employee satisfaction scores and summaries. I read the emails from the external communications team, watching the draft video they have attached. I busy myself with all the emails until I see the latest one that arrives in my inbox.

From: Caleb Lowe
To: Zoey Taylor
Subject: Are you kidding me?

Why are you still messing me about, Zoey? You were supposed to be updating me today with the settlement fee, now you've finally agreed to be an adult and speak to the solicitors. I expect an update from you at your soonest with reference to my compensation.

Caleb.

I roll my eyes and supress a laugh. Caleb has never used phrases like 'at your soonest', nor would he have previously suggested he needed compensation. He's also never been pushy before. When we were together, he was always sweet and gentle.

I could email a reply, or I could delete the message and ignore it. Instead, I pick up my mobile and scroll for the number of his place in the States. It's stored in my phone as 'his mistress', not that I'm Caleb's wife, but we had been together for five years. Finding out he was screwing a woman from the New York office was a shock, especially when it was due to him being lax about deleting the photographs she'd sent him 'to keep him entertained until he returned'.

I might not have been saintly, but I never blindsided him like that.

Michelle is the vice president of her department and technically would have been one of Caleb's superiors, but Caleb has always had a type of woman he prefers. Strong. Independent. Resilient. All the things I'd presented when we met, until I'd had a situation that made me question myself. When I'd needed a moment of somebody taking the strain from me, Caleb couldn't deal with that, and instead of waiting for my wavering to be over, he found himself another strong independent woman. Michelle is a little older than I am, seemingly highly ambitious. If we'd met in another lifetime, I'm sure she and I would have been friends, kindred spirits. Instead, she's now the one pushing Caleb to get everything she thinks he's due after five years with me. Five years of him taking my money, five years of him basking in my success, and six months of him cheating on me with her every time he flew to the States for business trips.

It's not the cheating that bothers me. It's what he thinks he's entitled to.

I connect the call and listen as it rings.

"Zoey?" Caleb sounds surprised to hear from me, "I thought you couldn't call today?"

"What's with the email, Caleb?"

"What email?"

"The one you just sent, telling me to update you about your compensation." The tone of my voice leans heavily on the word compensation. I'm sure he can hear the mystic air quotes around that word.

"I didn't send any..." he starts, but then he falls silent, "Michelle," he mutters.

"Perhaps you can tell your lovely girlfriend to stop emailing me, pretending to be you. If she has something she wishes to say to me, she should have the guts to do it in her own name," I snap.

"She's just trying to make sure I get everything organised and resolved. She doesn't want any lingering ties to you."

"There are no lingering ties. You'll have to tell her to wait patiently. I'll see the solicitor as soon as I can, hopefully tomorrow, but I'll remind you, this house and mortgage is in my name. I don't owe you anything. I hope she won't be too disappointed when the solicitor confirms what I've been saying."

"Zoey," he sighs. "I just want to wrap this up. I don't want you being hurt, but my life is here, with Michelle. Like I said, she just wants me to get things with you resolved."

"I'm sure it can wait a couple of days. Tell her to back off."

"We're getting married," Caleb replies. If I was the type of woman who wanted to marry Caleb, the idea of him putting an engagement ring on another woman's finger, it might hurt, but I never expected to marry him. I'd made that clear to Caleb from the very start of our relationship.

"Congratulations." I force myself to sound bright. I'm not hurt that he's starting a new life with the woman he cheated on me with, I don't have feelings for him now, and I wasn't the best girlfriend for him anyway, but it is still hard to muster enthusiasm for what he is telling me.

"Update me after the meeting with the solicitors," he adds. I don't bother responding, I end the call and drop my phone back onto the sofa.

I get back to my emails and try to ignore the frustration about Caleb. I open the email from the accounts team. I read through every attachment, look at every reconciliation summary, check every action point that has been highlighted in the report. The accounts are neat and tidy, but scrutinising every transaction for the last month gives me something to focus on and pass my time.

∞∞∞∞∞∞∞∞

Lizzie arrives exactly at six. She's always punctual, I can set my watch by her. I get up to answer the door but as I reach out for the handle, Isabelle appears from behind me and stops me.

"It's Lizzie," I protest.

"Until Aiden comes back later with the CCTV, you shouldn't just blindly open the door," she reprimands.

"Well, forgive me for not knowing the proper way to deal with a threat."

"The only thing you need to do is let us do our job properly," she soothes, and she opens the front door. I want to ask why it's okay for her to open the door without knowing who is on the other side, surely anybody posing as a threat wouldn't pause to ascertain it is me answering the door, but then I realise the front porch is locked. Lizzie is visible on the doorstep, looking confused why the door is locked. Usually, when I'm expecting her, the porch is open, and the front door is unlocked. We've been friends for eighteen months and for at least a year, she has let herself into the house when I know she is visiting, just like I let myself into her house.

"Oh, am I early? I didn't realise you had company," Lizzie says once Isabelle has unlocked the front porch. Lizzie checks her watch.

"It's fine, Lizzie. This is Isabelle."

"Nice to meet you," Isabelle says as she shakes Lizzie's hand.

"You too. Zoey didn't say you were joining us, I only got two meals, but I'm sure there is enough to go around," Lizzie frowns slightly.

Again, I feel bad that I'm socialising, and Isabelle is going to, what, stand on guard at the dining room door?

"Just act like you would do if I wasn't here," Isabelle suggests, as if she can sense my uncertainty.

"Come on, Lizzie." I gesture in the direction of the dining room. We walk together, leaving Isabelle in the hallway.

"Who is she?" Lizzie asks as I shut the dining room door behind us. She takes a seat, putting the bag that contains our food order onto the table.

"She's personal security," I explain, and I feel an involuntary shudder because it makes me feel like a weak, entitled asshole.

"What on earth do you need security for?" Lizzie takes the food containers out of the bag. She puts two smaller containers to the side of the plates I've laid out, then passes me one of the larger containers.

I dish my food order onto my plate. The smell of the chicken and chorizo is usually heavenly but tonight it makes me feel like my stomach is turning.

"I had a threatening letter today," I admit as I stir the noodles on my plate, mixing with the oils from the chorizo and the sauce for the dish.

"A threatening letter?" Lizzie repeats. She stops what she was doing, leaving half her spaghetti and meatballs still in the takeaway dish, looking distracted by what I've said.

I sink into my chair.

"Somebody sent a letter to the office. It said I would pay. There were photographs of me, taken when I have been out in different locations. They all had a threatening sentence on the back. One said I'd pay with my life." My voice hitches as I talk.

"Oh Zoey, that sounds more than a threatening letter. That is like a death threat," she exclaims.

"I keep trying to tell myself it isn't a death threat, that it's just some sick joke, but it's had me on edge all day. I called a security company as soon as I opened it, and now I have security who are going to watch everything until the person who sent it has been found."

"Did you go to the police? I hope you have. You can't trust a security company to fix everything for you, I don't think they can investigate and arrest somebody, or can they?"

"I went to the police. I was there this morning. They have the letter and the photographs, and they will investigate. It's the police who would need to arrest somebody. The security company will just keep me safe until then," I explain.

"This sounds awfully scary. How are you feeling?" she asks. She gives me a sympathetic look and then finishes dishing up her dinner. "Eat, Zoey, you look like you might pass out." She gestures at my dish.

I pick up my fork and twist some of the noodles around the prongs and stab a small piece of chicken. It's my favourite dish from the bistro and my stomach feels empty, but as I chew, it tastes a little like cardboard.

"I don't know if I can eat this," I say once I have finished the forkful.

"You must try, otherwise you are going to be lightheaded," she reprimands but her tone is soft.

I take another bite, this time adding some of the chorizo. It still feels like cardboard, but I force myself to eat it as I know she'll only worry if I don't.

"How has your day been?" I ask and she laughs.

"Zoey, why do you even think we're changing the subject yet?"

"Maybe because there is nothing else to say." I manage a grin.

"I have questions," she interjects.

"Go on then."

"Who is your security team? Is it a team?" She stabs a meatball with her fork as she talks.

"It is a team of two. Isabelle is going to be going to the office with me," I explain.

"Totally on brand for you." Lizzie grins.

"The second person will be here at night. You'll probably meet him when you go, I guess."

"It must be weird, the idea of somebody in your home when you're asleep," she muses.

"The only other option is to not have the security and then worry all the time that somebody is going to try to get to me. I'm sure it'll get easier. I'm sure it's just somebody playing a horrible joke."

"I could stay with you. I could cancel my study course. Surely that will make you feel more comfortable than a stranger." Lizzie stares at me. She's the closest thing I have to family, the person who has been my go-to for the last eighteen months. She lives alone, but I couldn't ask her to uproot everything for me. I also couldn't ask her to cancel her planned training course for work, she's been talking about it for months and would undoubtedly get in trouble with work if she didn't go.

"I can't ask that."

"You're not asking. I'm offering. It could be like an extended sleepover."

"What, doing each other's nails and singing into our hairbrushes every night?" I grin.

Lizzie giggles. "You and I had completely different styles of sleepovers. Mine was usually sneaking in bottles of alcohol and trying to see how much pizza I could eat before I was sick."

"As fun as it sounds, I'm sure I'll be fine. They've said to keep everything as normal, so after today, I'm just going to go about my day as usual."

"I'm sure it will all be okay. Like you say, it'll probably be some joke of a man with a little dick who's having a tantrum." Lizzie shrugs.

I find her words reassuring. I can handle somebody who is just lashing out, that it is not personal. The idea that it's somebody who knows me personally and hates me enough to threaten me, that's another matter entirely.

"I hope so." I sigh.

"Okay, I feel like a change in topic is required, not because this isn't important, but because you're looking stressed out."

"Well, in other news, I spoke to Caleb today." I move some of my food across my plate, looking for a distraction.

"How did that go? What has the rat bastard got to say for himself today?" Lizzie grimaces and it makes me laugh. She hadn't been Caleb's biggest fan.

"He and Michelle are getting married," I say.

"Probably only marrying her for his ticket into the country." She shrugs and her assessment makes me laugh.

"Hopefully the two of them are so focused on the wedding that they forget all about me, and what he thinks he's entitled to."

"Right, eat up. I'm going to go grab a bottle of booze as you look like you need something to help take your mind off the day."

"I'll go get the drink, you're the guest." I laugh as I stand up. She gives me a smile as I leave her in the dining room. I keep my alcohol in my study. I don't often drink in the house, but when I do, it's after I've been working late.

I'm not sure where Isabelle is, she is obviously discrete in her job. I'm hoping the same will be true in the office tomorrow. The more discrete they manage to be and integrate into my daily routine, the more likely it is I'll keep them and not end their oversight before the police have resolved the issue.

I step into the study, focused on the little cupboard in the corner which holds my alcohol, a couple of bottles as well as a couple of my favourites in decanters. I've always found decanters fascinating. I used to buy them from charity shops and car boots when I was at university. My favourite is the one Caterina gave me as a gift when we landed our first contract.

I kneel so I can pick out a bottle of vodka so I can take it back to Lizzie. As I turn to walk out of the office, the movement of another person in the room makes me yelp.

"I'm sorry, I didn't mean to scare you," Aiden says. He's stood on a little step ladder, half hidden behind the back of the study door.

"What the fuck are you doing," I gasp out and I clutch the bottle of vodka to my chest. My heart is racing.

"Putting up the security cameras," he points out. At the top of the shelving, I can see a small camera. Aiden gets down from the step ladder.

"You're early." My tone is much sharper than I intended, but it's the shock of him being here, hidden away in the study. I'm also concerned that he's here before seven, given he'd barely had enough time to go home and be rested before starting the overnight watch.

"It's fine. I wanted to get all the cameras set up when Issy was still here. She's just putting some upstairs," Aiden explains.

It's the first time he's called her Issy. I shouldn't be surprised because he's always shortened names, especially when he's close to the person. He'd been the only person I knew beside me who called Caterina Cat. He was also the only person beside Caterina who would call me Zo.

"Issy," I murmur.

"Isabelle," he corrects himself.

"You two seem like you have a lot of history together," I comment.

"Yeah, we've worked a few jobs together. She's a good friend." He shrugs as he talks.

It's on the tip of my tongue to ask him whether she is a good a friend as I was. It feels like I'm suddenly thrown into a showreel of my friendship with Aiden. It's a reminder of every conversation, every laugh, every time he'd joked that he was my truest bestie, every promise we'd made to one another, counterbalanced by all the hurt and pain we'd been through together, inflicted upon each other.

I can't say any of this to him. I can't ask him anything about his relationship with Issy. We've left that part of our relationship in the past. Instead, I clear my throat.

"Where are the cameras being placed upstairs?" I focus on the topic. Whatever history he has with Isabelle is none of my business. I've no right to ask him anything.

"There are a couple on the landing, in different directions to give a full view. Nothing in the bedrooms or the bathrooms, if that is what you're worried about."

"Thank you," I reply. I should have known they wouldn't put a camera in my bedroom, but still, it is reassuring to know.

"I'm going to finish setting everything up. You get back to your dinner," he suggests.

"I should say goodnight to Isabelle before she goes." I frown as I check my watch.

"She'll let you know when she's going. Get back to your friend, Zo," he says. I nod and leave him in the study, heading back to Lizzie, feeling as uneasy as I had as soon as I'd opened the letter, and not entirely sure why.

∞∞∞∞∞∞∞

At ten, Lizzie gets up from the sofa. We'd moved into the living room after we'd finished dinner and the dessert she'd picked up from the bistro. Isabelle had left at seven thirty and told me she'd see me tomorrow. She's due to drive me to the office, given my car is still in the carpark.

"I should get going, I need to finish packing before I set off tomorrow afternoon," Lizzie says. She fishes her car keys out of her handbag. In the end, we'd only had one drink together. Earlier in the evening she'd told me we were going to go out for cocktails as soon as the situation was resolved.

"Thank you for coming over." I get up so I can walk her to the front door. Aiden is in the hallway.

"My, oh my," Lizzie murmurs to me when she sees him.

"Lizzie is going to go home now," I say to Aiden, ignoring Lizzie's reaction to him. Aiden is a good-looking man. I've seen many women fawn over him. I've seen a fair share of men fawn over him, too.

"I'll walk you to your car," Aiden offers.

"Well, isn't that nice of you?" She smiles at him.

I stand next to him as he starts to unlock the front door. Just as he reaches for the key, there is a large thud above us. The next thing I know, Aiden's arm has thrust in front of me, his arm against the top of my chest, sweeping me out of the position I was in next to him so that I'm stood behind him. The stance he has in front of me screams protection and alertness.

"It's the cat," I explain.

"What?"

"That's the sound of the cat coming in through the bathroom window," I elaborate. I know it's unexpected as the first time I'd heard it, I'd jumped what felt like a mile.

As if to illustrate my point, Simba comes running down the stairs and past us in the hallway. Aiden relaxes his position.

"I'll check outside." Aiden clears his throat and then opens the front door, stepping outside. Lizzie doesn't follow him immediately, instead she turns to look at me, a grin on her face.

"Wow, Zoey. That…" she starts, and she mimics the gesture Aiden had made when we'd heard the noise. "Hot as fuck," she concludes, still grinning.

"Go home, Lizzie. Text me when you get in, okay?"

"Will do. Goodnight, Zoey." She blows me a kiss and then leaves me in the hallway.

Simba circles at my feet. I kneel so I can stroke his head.

"Come on, Simba, kitchen." I coax and he totters after me. Behind me, I can hear Lizzie's car engine starting, and I prepare myself for the first night of trying to sleep while Aiden roams my house.

5

Aiden

I watch Zoey's friend drive away and take a couple of deep breaths before I go back into the house. A cat. A goddamn cat has got me acting like a grenade has been thrown. I tell myself I need to get a fucking grip.

I lock the porch and then the front door. I can hear Zoey in the kitchen, so I walk in that direction, planning on checking whether she's heading to bed. If she's heading to bed, I can stay downstairs without feeling like I'm intruding.

It feels weird being at Zoey's house. I've worked personal security for years. I've been an invisible presence in the homes and lives of people and never felt awkward before. Now, I just feel self-conscious.

Zoey's putting food down for the cat. She coos over the cat as she puts down the dishes before straightening up.

"That has to be the biggest house cat I have ever seen," I say when she glances at me.

She gives me a wry smile. "Simba's on a diet, but I think somebody else is feeding him as he isn't losing a lot of weight. He's better than when I took him in, though. He was like a beer barrel."

"How long have you had him?"

"Only two months. I got him after Caleb left."

"How long ago did Caleb move out?"

"Four months ago. Though it was over a long time before that, really. He had been seeing Michelle for six months before I found out, planning the best way to tell me, apparently. As soon as I knew about her, that was it, he hightailed it to the States and moved in with her," Zoey explains. She sounds factual rather than emotional.

"I'm surprised," I admit. Caleb used to look at Zoey with an expression on his face that he was the luckiest guy in the world. Cheating on her seems so out of his character.

"I was going through something, and he got tired waiting for me to snap out of it," Zoey admits. She leans against the kitchen cabinets and stares at me. I take it as an invitation to keep the conversation going.

"What were you going through?"

"My dad died."

The words are like a kick to the guts. I didn't know her father, but I know she had a complicated relationship with him when she was younger, and that she stopped speaking to him when she left home for university and hadn't spoken to her parents since. I also know that there was a time this would have been something she'd have talked to me about, that the moment she knew, she'd have turned up at my doorstep. She'd have told me everything. She might have cried as she talked, and I'd have wiped away her tears, told her that everything was okay, told her that I was always there for her, told her she could lean on me.

I'm the one who closed that door, and I feel like an asshole.

"Oh Zoey, I'm sorry," I murmur. She looks awkward.

"I didn't expect to feel sad. I guess I thought I wouldn't feel anything given it had been so long since I'd seen him, spoke to him."

The hitch in her voice makes me want to cross the kitchen and hug her, but I'm sure she wouldn't want it, and there is no way I should cross a line given I'm here to do a job. Except, I'm always crossing lines for Zoey.

I clear my throat. "It's completely normal for you to grieve for him. He was still your father. It's natural to have complicated feelings for the people we have complicated relationships with."

"I'm better now. It just threw me through a loop, and I needed a bit of time to get myself through it. Caleb didn't want to wait, but that's fine." She juts her shoulders back.

"He's wet lettuce, Zoey," I reply.

"Warm, wet lettuce," she corrects.

"On top of an otherwise perfectly fine burger," I add, remembering the conversation now so vividly. She'd laughed then. Now she just gives me a small smile. "What about your mother?" I ask.

"It's complicated. She's still in the house I grew up in. I think she wants to make amends, and I know I should, but it's still something for me to work through. I know he treated her as badly as he treated me, if not worse, but…" Her voice trails off.

"But she was your mother, and she should have put you first and protected you," I say, gently and she bites her lip, nodding slightly but not answering.

I know her feelings towards her mother are complicated. When she'd first told me about her parents, about the reason for their absence in her life, she'd told me she couldn't understand why her mother wouldn't leave her father. Zoey had told me she'd spent most of her childhood praying for the day her mother would pack a bag for them both, disappear across the country, fading into the rearview of her father's oppressive nature.

Zoey is quiet for a moment. She glances down at Simba who is making fast work of his food.

"He's a rescue. He lived with an older lady who died, and the cat was taken to the shelter. She'd looked after him but clearly indulged him. He's massively over-weight, old as the hills, blind in one eye, deaf in one ear too."

I know she's drawn a line under the conversation of her parents, of anything to do with grieving. That's all too much to fit into one night.

"He's lucky to have you," I comment. Not many people take on animals with issues, especially at the age Simba appears to be. A lot of people would walk past this cat, looking for the younger, cuter ones, the ones with no health problems and a long life ahead of them. It's Zoey all over really. She projects this armour that she's tough as nails, but she has a soft spot underneath that sometimes you're lucky enough to witness. When she lets you see it, it's like watching the light return after a total eclipse, basking in the warmth. Once you're in the inner circle, she'd walk to the end of the world for you.

"He tends to stay downstairs at night, though if he needs to go out, he goes out the window. I thought I'd let you know just in case he startles you in the night," she explains. There is a small tug at the side of her mouth, and I know she's suppressing a smile after my reaction in the hallway earlier.

"Simba's going to get his own background check," I mutter and Zoey laughs.

"I don't think he's quite mastered the ability to cut out words from newspaper headlines."

"He could have an accomplice," I tease.

"Oh come on, it's bad enough me thinking somebody I know hates me enough to do this, don't make me think of two people," she grumbles.

"I've not seen anything so far that makes me think it is somebody you know, but we're still waiting for information to come through. Speaking of which, did you know your gardener has a criminal record?" I wonder. I'd meant to let Isabelle ask her tomorrow, Zoey seems a little more relaxed with her.

"Yeah, I knew. Jamie did his time and is trying to get his life back on track. He isn't some violent criminal who went around hurting people on purpose. He wasn't terrorising or attacking people. He went to prison for," she starts, looking annoyed with me.

"I know what he went to prison for, Zoey. I was checking if you knew, that's all," I cut in.

"Okay. Well, I knew, so that's the end of that." Zoey shrugs.

"I'll let you know if there is anything else I find, I still have some files to go through," I tell her.

"I'm going to go to bed. I'll see you in the morning, I guess."

"Goodnight, Zoey."

"Goodnight, Aiden."

She leaves me in the kitchen with Simba. Simba struts over to me, rubbing against my ankles, purring.

"Well, you can act as cute as you like, I'm still putting you on the list of potentials," I say as I stroke his head.

I hear Zoey's footsteps on the floor above me and I stand, listening until there is no more noise. I assume she's now in bed. I walk around the downstairs rooms, checking the positioning of the cameras and that the windows are still secured. I finish what I'd started earlier, attaching alarms to the windows that will trigger when they're opened. I still have the CCTV to set up but it's easier to do in the daylight, so I plan to leave that until the morning, after Zoey has gone to work with Isabelle, and before I go home for some sleep.

Instead, I unlock the front doors and install the doorbell camera before locking everything up again. Once everything is set up, I sit in the living room. It's the closest of the rooms to the staircase and somehow, I feel like Zoey will be more comfortable with me in here than her study. I'd left my bag in here earlier when I'd arrived, Zoey busy with her friend, and now I pull my laptop out. I log into the system I've just set up, checking over the cameras and making sure all the views are clear, that everything looks secure.

I make a note that she needs a security light installing in the driveway. Another job for me to do tomorrow. I can pick a light up on my way home and install it when I get back. I'll need some sleep tomorrow, given I didn't get chance to sleep today.

I log onto the work system and pull up the job I'd created for Zoey's case. I'd input only brief details but promised my dad I would update properly and if I don't, it'll only raise questions I don't want to answer.

I keep Zoey's name as Jane. Something tells me updating to her real name would land me in waters I'm not ready to be in. Under the section for codename, something any other team member and I would use to communicate to one another about Zoey, I input Rambo, a small smile on my face when I think of it. I update the details about the threat Zoey had received, the content of the envelope. I input the police contact name, the officer who had taken the paperwork and promised to update us. Under the type of threat, I select direct. She might want to skirt around the words 'death threat' but this is clear to me, it's a direct threat to her safety. I update with the kit I've added to her home for additional security measures. I update the names of close contacts, a lot shorter list than I'm used to but on reflection, it wouldn't be dissimilar to how mine might look, just a list of casual acquaintances.

There is a section to update as a contact in case of an emergency. I leave it blank because I'm not sure what Zoey would want me to put in there. I'll have to ask her tomorrow when she's awake.

I save the details and then open the files that have been collected already on the people that Zoey had noted as close acquaintances, the names I'd requested from the admin team earlier today. I'd only skim-read them earlier, looking for anything glaringly worrying, but the only thing I'd seen was that the gardener had been in prison. I want to read them all thoroughly just in case I missed something in the first review.

I read through the information on Jamie the gardener first. By all accounts, Jamie had been an upstanding citizen until his life took a turn. He's thirty-seven, a single father of a teenage child. His profile reads like a saintly member of the community, he'd volunteered at various charities, worked as a social worker, taken care of his wife when she'd been sick, juggling that with his job. He'd taken on a second job after his wife was unable to work due to her condition. In the early hours of one morning, after a long night shift, he'd offered to drive three of his colleagues given they lived in his direction. He'd fallen asleep at the wheel, the passenger in the front was not wearing a seatbelt and had been ejected from the car, dying at the scene. One of the passengers in the back was also unbuckled and only lived long enough to be transported to the hospital. Jamie himself had been uninjured.

Jamie had been convicted of causing death by dangerous driving. The judge had been lenient, but he still received a custodial sentence. His wife had died when he was in prison. When he had been released, he'd fought to get his child back. Due to his conviction, he was unable to return to his main job. Instead, he'd set up a gardening business and appears to be doing well, enough to support him and his child. He hasn't had a moment of stepping out of line since he got out of prison. Everything about him suggests he's a man who made a mistake, paid the ultimate price, and has fought to get his life back on track.

There is nothing in Jamie's file that would suggest he would have an issue with Zoey. She'd been one of his first clients when he started the business, looking at the dates she said she'd employed him and when he'd started the business. Based on the pristine garden I'd seen earlier he clearly does a good job here. I know Zoey, she'll pay him well and she's given him an opportunity to start over again.

I close his file. Nothing about him seems suspicious, a threat. I also don't see anything of suspicion in the files for the other people Zoey pays for jobs around her house. I wasn't expecting to, but I don't want to leave any stone unturned.

Since I'd last logged on, there is a new file that has been pulled together. It's a file about Caleb. I open it to read through. There is confirmation that he is living in New York, with a woman called Michelle Bell. There isn't anything surprising in Caleb's profile, nothing new that I don't already know about him, other than his new woman's name.

I open social media and log into the profile that I haven't used in a long time. I find Caleb's profile. Weirdly, in the time we weren't talking, I'd looked for Zoey's profile many times, but I'd never allowed myself to look at his. I wonder now if I'd just been concerned about what I might see if I had opened it. Zoey's social media used to be updated infrequently, usually little comments about something she'd been proud about related to work. Caleb used to post long, gushing messages about her. I think I've avoided looking at his posts because I knew they'd hit a nerve to read them.

I scroll through the history of his posts. It looks like he's carefully edited the past because all the posts about Zoey are gone. Every gushing message, every outpouring of love, every photograph he'd uploaded of her, they're gone. I wonder if Zoey knows. I wonder if she cares either way.

His latest posts are about his new girlfriend. Similar, sickeningly gushing posts about her and how he feels. Uploaded today is a photograph of the two of them, his arm wrapped around her, one of her arms outstretched to show the sparkling engagement ring on her finger. By the size of it, I'm surprised she can hold her hand up.

Again, I wonder if Zoey knows. Again, I wonder if she cares.

I click onto Michelle's profile. She hasn't been so diligent at removing historical posts. When I scroll back, I can see the posts that she'd written in the time-frame Zoey said Caleb had been with her. There are cryptic posts about a new love, about missing somebody, about counting down the days until they can be together again. Her newest posts are openly hostile about how somebody needs to 'get a grip', and 'give people what they're due'. I wonder if it's aimed at Zoey, or whether Michelle is just focused on what she wants from life. Her profile doesn't have anything openly threatening and it's clear she thinks she's an important woman, holding a high position in her company. Given her job title, and Caleb's, I wonder why they need to petition for money from Zoey. I suspect it's more than the money. Some people can forgive cheating. People don't always forgive people trying to take something they're not entitled to. I wonder if that's Michelle's strategy, to make Caleb somebody undesirable to Zoey, making him more than a cheater, making him seem like a money grabbing entitled asshole.

I flip back to my own social media page. I barely post, I never have been a big fan of sharing my life online, but there are photographs I'd uploaded, years of my history. Me, Caterina, Zoey, Jonah. Things I couldn't quite bring to delete entirely. In the folder called 'Uni Days', there are so many pictures of us. In the last couple of months at university, Jonah had buckled down. He'd stopped doing the occasional line of coke, seemingly getting his life together that year. He was more tolerable, and we'd spent lots of long nights with Caterina and Zoey. Zoey referred to us as 'Cat and Aiden, the third wheel and the uninvited', but she was always smiling when she said it.

Zoey took Jonah's blatant flirting with her in good humour. Whenever Caterina suggested she date Jonah, Zoey would shake her head and find a nice sentence to say no. To me, though, she'd mimic the movements of somebody sewing and it would always make me laugh, thinking of her comment that first night. The first birthday she'd had after I met her, I'd given her a sewing kit as a joke, labelling it 'just in case'.

Jonah and I graduated university first, a year ahead of the girls, both of us leaving with excellent degrees. Dad and Mum had been so proud when we'd graduated, joining Caterina and Zoey who had clapped and cheered us on.

Caterina and Zoey had graduated the year after. Zoey had smashed it, not that there had ever been any doubt. She's one of the smartest people I know and at university she was hyper focused. It hadn't taken me long to work out she'd decided getting a first-class degree would be her best option to open job opportunities, a way to support herself given she'd already decided she would never go back home, not that she would have been able to rely on her parents for support anyway.

Caterina didn't have the same concerns for her future, the doors would be opened for her based on her background and connections, but she had also done well. Four graduates, feeling proud of what we had achieved.

I stare for a moment at one of the photographs I'd uploaded years ago. It's one of the four of us standing in a line, Jonah's arm over my shoulders, a picture of brotherly solidarity. Caterina and Zoey are stood in an embrace beside us, both with wide smiles. We all look so innocent, like the world was at our feet, ours for the taking.

I close the social media page down in frustration. Taking trips down memory lane is not something I should be doing. Not when I'm working for Zoey. I need to keep my focus. I'm already going against most of the guidelines my father dictates in the contracts and employee guidelines. We shouldn't let our clients know much about our private lives, but Zoey knows everything about me. We shouldn't talk much, let the client lead the conversation, but I've spoken enough today, strayed into topics I shouldn't. My focus should be on the task and present threat, not thinking about the past and the things we both wish we could take back.

∞∞∞∞∞∞∞∞

The house is quiet until five-thirty in the morning when there is a thud upstairs and Simba comes running downstairs, announcing his arrival. I don't know what time he'd snuck out, he seems to exit the house gracefully, but his arrival back is another story. I've never heard a cat make so much noise before, and I'm surprised Zoey seems able to sleep through it.

The next noise comes at six. It sounds like Zoey is up. Forty-five-minutes later, she's downstairs. She's dressed for work, wearing a smart trouser suit and shirt. Over the years I've worked personal security, I've noted the decline in the business workwear, people aiming to project a more casual, friendly work environment, but Zoey looks sharp. Her hair is up in a ponytail again but today it looks much neater than yesterday.

"All quiet in the night, I take it?" she asks with a tentative smile. She looks more relaxed than she did yesterday, almost like some of the jarring shock has worn its way out of her system.

"Aside from Simba coming back in, yes." I smile back because I prefer seeing Zoey relaxed. I feel like we have both put the awkwardness of meeting again behind us. She needs a job doing and trusts me to do it. I can do that job and want to do it for her. We can both retreat to our own corners when this is resolved, like boxing opponents taking a break between the rounds of the match.

"Yesterday, when you moved me behind you, your free hand went to your hip," she comments. I'm surprised she noticed.

"Force of habit, sometimes." I shrug.

"From carrying a gun?" she asks. When I've worked overseas on long assignments, if the country is more relaxed about carrying weapons, it isn't unusual for us to be issued with a gun.

"Yes, but don't worry, I'm perfectly able to protect you, even if I'm not carrying a gun here."

She frowns, "I wasn't suggesting you couldn't, I was just thinking about it. So, if it came to it, and you really needed to protect me, how do you defend me?"

The phrase 'with my life' hangs in the air.

I clear my throat. "If your life is in danger, I can use reasonable force. You remember I'm a black belt in both kickboxing and jiu-jitsu?"

"Yes," she murmurs and from the look on her face, it's like she's thinking of the time I tried to teach her some basic jiu-jitsu moves.

"Do you still practice?" I ask, trying not to fall down that rabbit hole.

"No. Maybe I should consider it though."

"I could…" I start but stop myself. Teaching a client self-defence is not my job, it isn't where my attention should be focused.

"Do you want breakfast?" She changes the subject and I'm grateful for her evasiveness, for a change.

"It's fine, I'll grab something on my way home."

"Aiden," she says with a sigh. "It's already awkward as hell. Please eat breakfast with me."

"Me eating breakfast is going to make it less awkward for you?" I laugh.

"Both you and Isabelle. It'll make me feel less weird, okay?"

"Sure." I shrug. Having breakfast here gives me the ability to pick up the security light and then go home to crash straight into bed.

"Does Issy like eggs?" she asks. I note the use of the term Issy.

"Isabelle likes eggs," I confirm, non-committal, but I know exactly what she is hinting at.

"How does she like her eggs?" Zoey's face is a mask of innocence.

"Why don't you just come out and ask me what you want to ask, Zoey?" I ask.

"What on earth do you think I want to know?" Her hands are now on her hips, looking indignant.

"You want to know if I've ever slept with her."

"I want to know nothing of the sort." She rolls her eyes at me.

"Why, Zo, you almost sound like you're jealous," I tease.

"Oh my God, get over yourself. How big is your ego?"

"Only as big as my dick, plenty big enough," I shoot back, because she's asked me this before, and I've said the same response to her. From her facial expression, I can tell she's thinking of previous conversations, the jokes and laughter in our history.

She shakes her head. "I was just curious," she protests. She sighs when I don't answer. "Shall I do poached eggs?"

The doorbell rings before I can answer her. I start to walk towards the front door.

"No," I call over my shoulder.

"No to poached eggs?" she asks. I pause at the doorway and turn to look at her.

"No, I haven't slept with her, or want to. Nor does she want to sleep with me. I'm not her type."

"Too much penis?" she guesses.

"Too much emotional baggage," I clarify.

She looks pained. "Aiden," she starts, but the doorbell rings again and she falls silent.

"Poached eggs would be great. Isabelle won't eat. She gets up at five for breakfast so she can work out before work," I tell her, and then I leave her so I can answer the door for Isabelle.

"Morning, boss man, I assume everything was all nice and quiet for Rambo?" she asks with a grin when I let her into the house. At some point, she's clearly read through the updates I'd put on the system.

"All quiet. Word of warning though, for when I'm not here, the fecking cat sounds like a tank. Come on through, Zoey is making breakfast. I said you'd probably eaten but she's only just started."

"I ate. Go get breakfast, Aiden, you look whacked." Isabelle looks sympathetic. We both know it's probably not the lack of sleep that has me looking whacked. We're both used to stints of no sleep, both from time in the army and on the job.

"I need to install the CCTV camera before I go, then swing by the office to get a security light for the front. I'll go home and crash after that," I explain as we walk towards the kitchen.

"Do you want me to do the CCTV when I get back?"

"No, it's okay, I want it setting up and recording for when she isn't here. I have it ready to go, I just thought better to do it in the light."

We get to the kitchen where Zoey stands next to the hob, a saucepan of water on the boil. There are four slices of bread in the toaster, waiting to be toasted. The kettle is boiling.

"Coffee, Isabelle?" she asks, voice bright, big smile on her face, like she's welcoming home a family member rather than somebody being paid to provide personal security.

"I'm okay thanks, I'll get one at the office later, if that's okay," Isabelle replies.

"Actually, me too. I always stop at the coffee shop just down the road from the office. That's okay, isn't it?" She looks at Isabelle with a hopeful expression.

"The coffee shop you were photographed at?" I bark. I suddenly feel like a dog with all its hackles up.

"Yeah, but," she starts.

"You should go straight to the office, Zoey. You shouldn't stop at places where you were covertly photographed." Isabelle manages to sound much nicer than I did.

"There was a photograph of me at the office, but I'm going there," Zoey points out.

"Until I've scoped out the coffee shop," I start but Zoey sighs and cuts me off.

"Aiden, what is going to happen to me in a little coffee shop? I know the people that work there. I stop every day. I'm nice to everybody there. I always tip. I spend a lot of money there. They're not going to hurt me."

"You don't know who is going to hurt you, Zoey, and you don't know how! Those pictures, those notes, they were a direct threat. *'You'll pay with your life'*, remember?" I snap.

She almost looks like she's going to burst into tears.

"Is there a drive through at the coffee shop?" Isabelle cuts in.

"No."

"What about another coffee shop, with a drive through option?" Isabelle offers.

Zoey shakes her head. "It's fine, forget it."

She cracks four eggs into the saucepan and puts the lever on the toaster down. She keeps her attention on the things she is doing, ignoring the kettle when it finishes boiling.

Isabelle looks at me, her eyebrows raised. She mouths something that looks like 'sort this out, you idiot'.

I sigh. "I'll drive behind you. I'll assess the place. Then you can go in, okay? If we're satisfied with the place, you two can go tomorrow and I won't bat an eyelid. Okay?"

"Okay," she mutters, still refusing to look at me.

"We're trying to keep you safe, Zoey. We need to assess the places you go, to make sure there isn't a threat. I don't want you to be frightened, but you don't know yet what somebody wants to do. It might be a hoax, it might not be, but we wouldn't be doing our job if we let you walk into some place without us knowing the lay of the land. You understand that, right?" I add.

"Okay," she repeats. She busies herself buttering the toast when it pops up, putting two on each of the two plates she's laid out. She dishes up the eggs. She grabs both plates and two sets of cutlery. She walks towards me, still not making eye contact. She dumps my plate and cutlery onto the breakfast bar and then stalks out of the room with hers. The slam of the dining room door echoes around the house.

"Eat, Aiden," Isabelle prompts.

"I told you she was stubborn," I mutter. I stab at one of the eggs. It's perfectly poached and looks delicious but I'm not in the mood now.

"Eat," Isabelle commands, and then she heads in the direction of Zoey, clearly braver than me if she's willing to risk her ire.

∞∞∞∞∞∞∞∞

After breakfast, once the house is locked and secure, Zoey gets in Isabelle's car with her. I get in mine and follow Isabelle on the drive to the coffee shop that appears to be important to Zoey.

I assess the location. It's quiet inside, just a couple of employees and a couple of people who are too engrossed in their coffee to notice me. One looks like a businessman who is trying to gear himself up to go into the office for another day of the usual nine-to-five, or eight-to-six given he looks knackered. One is a woman, typing enthusiastically on her laptop, a dreamy look on her face.

On the wall adjacent to the coffee counter there are hundreds of photographs. I stare at them for a moment until I work out it's photographs of regular customers and people who have spent time here but then gone on to have successes. I recognise some photographs of a local science fiction writer, there is one of him typing on his laptop, a drink and pastry next to him, then another of him with the first book he'd published, smashing to the top of the book charts. As I look at the other photographs, I suddenly understand why this place is so important to Zoey. There are pictures of her and Caterina, young and full of smiles, one of them at a table in the coffee shop, a massive pile of paperwork in front of them, and another, the day they'd signed for the building where their offices are located.

Zoey doesn't say a word to me when I go back to Isabelle's car to say it's okay to go in, and I don't comment about what I have seen on the walls. Isabelle gives me a sympathetic smile as I get in my car. I need to go back to Zoey's, then to pick up the security light, then home for bed. My lack of sleep is making me short tempered, clearly.

I'm halfway to Zoey's when my phone beeps and the automated reading app I use kicks in.

'Just an update; Rambo's car was damaged last night.'

Isabelle's text reads out over my speaker system. I swear. I glance behind me, the road is clear of traffic, so I pull over and pick up my mobile. Isabelle's message is followed by several photographs of Zoey's car. The tyres are slashed, and the paintwork is scratched.

'I'm on my way,' I fire back.

'I can deal with this myself. I'll wait for the police. Go to bed.' Isabelle's text commands.

Except I can't do that, because despite what I said to her two years ago, it's clear that when Zoey needs me, I'm going to turn up. Like I promised her years ago, regardless of what we mean to one another, I'm there for her. Always.

6

Zoey

Eleven Years Ago

"Zoey, come on!" Caterina exclaims.

"Give me a minute," I grumble. I give myself one last look in the mirror. I'm sure most graduates look far more excited than I do right now, but most graduates will have a bunch of friends and family there, ready to cheer them on, celebrating their moment of glory, the recognition of the hard work. The only person who cares about me graduating is Caterina.

I smooth down the dress that Caterina had insisted on buying me, to wear underneath the graduation gowns we'll put on later. She'd called it a graduation present. I have to hand it to her; she knows how to pick an elegant outfit. The dress I'm wearing screams that I'm a woman in charge, a force to be reckoned with. The black shoes she's made me wear pinch my feet slightly, but I'm sure I'll be able to suffer through it.

I walk out of my bedroom, joining Caterina on the hallway.

"Happy graduation day, we did it," she exclaims, and she throws her arms around me, pulling me close for an excited hug. As usual, it's hard for me not to be swept up in her enthusiasm.

"I'm so proud of you, Cat," I say, kissing her cheek. She pulls away and beams at me.

"I'm super proud of you, Zo."

"I'm glad somebody is." I force a smile. She looks at me, sympathetically.

"Fuck your parents," she declares.

It was my decision to cut ties with my parents, my decision to leave the house I'd grown up in and not look back. I'd spent my childhood wishing my mother would come to her senses, move us far away from my father, but it had never happened. As far as I know, they're still together, no doubt living unhappily in

83

the little house, my mother knowing when to keep quiet to avoid his wrath. I don't know if they're still together because I don't keep in touch with anybody from my hometown. I haven't been back there since the day I left.

I wonder if they know I'm graduating today, and if they did know, I wonder if they care either way. I wonder if they even know where I'm based. I never told them what university I was going to study at. In my final year of A levels, when applying for university, I'd pleaded with my mother to move with me, suggesting I could study somewhere and we could live together, away from my father, but she had shaken her head and told me she loved him. After that, I never told her anything about university. I declared myself legally free from my parents, I applied for the required loans to get me through the years, and I moved halfway across the country to study.

When I left, I had no idea how I was going to cope. I was lucky to get a job straight away, working enough hours to support me between loan payments. I know I was lucky enough to end up in the same house as Caterina. She'd immediately taken me under her wing. I don't know if she knew how hard those first weeks were for me, wondering how I would survive being an adult when I was barely legally one. I had no fallback, no backup, no option. The only thing I had was Caterina.

My first year, the questions about my family would seep in during the night. I'd toss and turn and wonder how they were. Was my dad in a perpetual dark mood, making the house feel oppressive and leaving my mother living like a timid mouse? Or were they happy, that somehow the removal of my presence in the house had lifted the gloom and misery that seemed to saturate through their marriage. Without me, were they happy? Do they walk hand in hand, full of love for one another, like the photographs that I'd seen of their early relationship, pictures of my parents looking so in love that I'd have sworn they were doctored images given it was a million miles away from what I knew about them. Over the years, though, those thoughts have gone, and the only thing I'm left with is the disappointment that they treated me the way they did.

It's all been my decision to leave my family and forget about them, but that doesn't mean there aren't days when it doesn't sting, doesn't hurt to know the people who brought me into the world don't give a shit.

Today is one of those days where it hurts a little more. I'm sure tomorrow, I'll be okay. The days might occasionally sting, but it is never enough for me to try to reach out to them, to see if I can reconnect the ties I'd severed. Sometimes, things are irreparable.

"Did you say Jonah was coming today?" I ask, stepping away from Caterina so I can gather the things I need for today.

"He said maybe. He said he had something else he might have to do, but who knows with Jonah." Caterina laughs.

Jonah and Aiden had graduated last year. Aiden had applied for the army, despite Caterina's initial upset about it. He gets home as much as he can and when he does, he and Caterina seem to disappear from the world, catching up on lost time. Jonah decided he wanted to see the world and spent a couple of months travelling, but when he is back in the UK, he joins Caterina and me for drinks and a catch up. When it's the four of us, all in the same place at the same time, that's when I feel the happiest. Jonah, despite his raging flirting and occasional inappropriate behaviour, is a good friend. Aiden, when I manage to spend time with him when Caterina isn't around, is one of my best friends.

I know Caterina and Aiden have talked about living together when he gets discharged from the army in a couple of years, and I'm happy for them, but I can't help feeling a little sad that I'll move out and not live with Caterina. For now, though, we're due to leave our student accommodation and move into a house that Caterina's parents have paid for.

"Your family are coming today, right?" I ask, though there is no reason to. Of course, Caterina's parents are coming to see her graduate. I'm sure her brothers will be there, too. I know Caterina has lived the type of life I could have only dreamt about. A family who would turn up, to both the big things and the little things. Sometimes, I wonder if it's why Aiden, Jonah and I gravitate to Caterina, the three of us having had loneliness etched in our bones from a young age. Even though Aiden and Jonah love their adoptive parents, I know they both remember the uncertainty that existed in their formative years, Aiden with his parents who struggled with drug addiction, Jonah with parents who had neglected and physically abused him, leading to his eventual placement in social care before being adopted.

"Yep, and we're all going out for dinner tonight. So, the plan for today is graduation first, then you and I are going to go for a few drinks, then dinner with my family, okay?" Caterina confirms, cutting into my thinking.

I frown. "You should just be with your family."

She laughs at my expression. "You are my family, silly."

I feel a rush of affection for her. She might sometimes not listen to me, but she's the best person in my life. Her family are amazing, too. Whenever I see them, they welcome me with open arms. I know they love Aiden too, him getting the seal of approval from Ronan, Caterina's father.

"I have told you I love you, yes?" I clarify and she snorts.

"Every bloody day, to the point I'm going to ask whether your man-ban is because you are batting for the other team."

"No, I don't think so." I grin. I enjoy sex with a man. I'm just very careful on how I select people now. Not many men make it through my stringent assessment of character and usually they end up disappointing me, but at least I've occasionally scratched the itch, hooking up with a guy for some no-strings attached fun. Usually, it is with male friends who I know will be safe, who won't push for anything further.

"So, now university is over, are you lifting the no-boyfriend ban?" she teases. She picks up her own things and grabs her car keys.

"Maybe. I guess it depends on who is out there."

"Well, there is always Jonah. I'm sure he'd be more than happy to give you a roll in the sack." Caterina opens the door and we both step outside. The sun hits my face and I have a big smile on my face.

"That man would likely give me an STI," I joke.

As friendly as I am with Jonah, I know he's not faithful. The only person he is faithful to is himself. Based on what he brags about, I'm surprised he doesn't have a string of knocked-up women knocking on his door, or a line of disgruntled boyfriends who are furious their girlfriend decided one night with him was worth their relationship. Once, we'd played truth or dare in a big group and when he'd been asked his favourite sexual position, he'd joked 'bareback, preferably via the backdoor'. More than one woman in the group had looked like they'd had firsthand experience.

"I'm sure if you were the one asking, he'd wear a condom. He looks like he's a man dying of thirst when he looks at you," Caterina teases as we get into the car.

"No, thank you. Besides, when you're in a committed relationship, when you're faithful, I like skipping the condom. Jonah's the type of man who you'd never fully trust. Every time a condom would come out, it would be a reminder that he can't be trusted."

"I prefer a condom. And the pill. Aiden and I are taking no chances." Caterina laughs.

"You trust Aiden though, don't you? Trust him not to cheat, I mean?" I'm surprised. She's never said anything that would indicate she doubts Aiden. Aiden and I talk a lot and we confide in each other; he's never said anything that would make me doubt him, either.

She laughs, "Of course I do. It's just neater."

"Why am I not surprised. You just don't want your silk sheets stained by a wet patch," I joke.

"You know, for somebody who rarely dates, you sure have strong opinions about spunk."

I can't stop myself; I snort. "Caterina Miller. Spunk. Seriously? You should wash your mouth out with soap and water."

She laughs. "Oh, I know all the slang."

"I'm going to drop as many slang names in during dinner with your family." I giggle.

"If you can manage to say jizz in front of my mother, I'll transfer you a grand," she offers.

"You're terrible." There is absolutely no way I'd say jizz in front of Jessica. I'd consider sex with Jonah before upsetting her. Jessica Miller is exactly the type of woman I can see Caterina being when she's older. Classy and generous, loving, and welcoming.

"All I'm saying is you should give Jonah a chance. He's a nice guy. He's looked after me since Aiden joined the army. Whenever he's away, Jonah makes sure to check in on me."

"Why don't you stop the matchmaking for today? I think we have bigger things to focus on." I smile.

She smiles back, flicking the radio on and skipping to find a station she wants. With upbeat music blaring out of the speakers, she carries on the drive, and we both sing loudly to the music, feeling like the world is at our feet.

∞∞∞∞∞∞∞∞∞

The graduation ceremony is exactly as I expected it would be. There seems to be hundreds of family members milling around, waiting for their loved one to take the stage, collect their diploma and bask in the recognition of the hard work.

When it's my turn to cross the stage, above the polite clapping that everybody in the audience seems to do for any student, I hear my name being chanted out. I squint in the direction of the voice, unable to see clearly who it is that is shouting my name, cheering like I'm a celebrity rather than just another girl leaving university with a first-class degree.

When the ceremony is over, Caterina tells me she is going to find her family. I tell her I'll see her later, and I mingle my way through the crowds, smiling at classmates, ducking my way through other families who are catching up. As I reach the edge of the crowd, I hear my name being called.

I turn and before I can register what I'm seeing, Aiden's arms engulf me in a hug.

"Oh my God, what are you doing here?" I exclaim.

"You really think I was going to let my best friend cross that stage feeling like there wasn't somebody there to cheer her on?" he scoffs. We text a lot and I'd told him how I felt; graduating and severed from my family.

"You didn't have to come."

"I wanted to."

"Was it you who was cheering my name like an idiot?"

He grins. "Of course."

"Does Caterina know you're here?"

"I told her I was coming. We all thought it would be a nice surprise. We're joining you two for lunch," he explains. I don't need him to elaborate to know he means Jonah.

"Please tell me you're not joining Caterina in the championing me and Jonah getting into the sack?"

"No, besides, you've just graduated top of your class, you've far too many brain cells for him." Aiden laughs, "Come on, let's go find Cat," he suggests. We walk together to join Caterina and her family.

"Aiden?"

"Yeah?" He stops walking to look at me.

"Thanks for thinking to turn up today."

"Anytime." He gives me a warm smile.

"I mean it, thank you for being here."

"Always, Zo," he promises, and I count my blessings that I have two people who care about me as much as I care about them.

∞∞∞∞∞∞∞

"So, what's next, third wheel?" Jonah asks as we sit in the summer sun in the beer garden.

"I'm not sure yet, uninvited," I shoot back, and he laughs, good naturedly.

"Come on, Zoey, I know you, you'll have a plan."

I sigh. I do have a plan for my future, but I don't know how I'm going to make it happen, yet.

"Zoey wants to start her own company. She's going to change the world, aren't you, chick?" Caterina says and I feel the flush on my cheek.

"One day."

"What if one day could be sooner than you thought?" she asks.

"I don't see how." I shrug.

"Well, I have been thinking. Your business plan is sound, Zo. I even spoke to my father about it, showed him everything you've shown me."

"Please tell me you haven't asked your father to be my business partner." I laugh.

"I'm offended. I was thinking me, not my father," she suggests, and I feel my heart skip a beat.

"What?"

"I get my inheritance. Dad's completely on board with me using the money to start our business."

"I don't have the capital to match you, Cat," I say, and I know I never will.

"I know you don't, but it doesn't matter. Look, you're clearly the brains between us. You've got the plan and you've got the know-how. I've got the cash to get us going. We can do this, I know we can, the only question is whether you want to do it with me or not." Caterina looks at me, patiently waiting for me to digest what she's saying.

"You'd do that with me?" I feel like I'm holding my breath.

"Of course. What do you think?"

I don't answer her. Aiden and Jonah are both quiet as I almost leap onto Caterina. My arms are around her in a big hug, and I kiss her on the cheek.

"I would love to," I exclaim.

"Have I just witnessed a business being born?" Aiden teases.

"I reckon we need more champagne." Jonah gets up from the table and heads towards the bar.

"Are you sure, Cat?" I ask.

"Of course, I'm sure. Do you want me to take a blood oath right now because I will. I'm not changing my mind. You know me, once I've decided something, that's it. You'll never get away from me," she jokes.

"I can't think of a better thing, ever." I beam at her.

"When are you going to get started?" Aiden asks.

"Tomorrow. Nothing like striking when the iron is hot. Zoey's business plan is tight, Aiden, I've never seen anything more detailed. It's all there, exactly what we need to do," Caterina explains. I get the sense that she hadn't told him what she was planning on doing.

"I'd expect nothing less from Zoey." Aiden grins.

"We are going to be so rich." Caterina claps her hands together in glee. Her faith in my plan has me feeling like I'm on cloud nine. Jonah arrives at the table just as Caterina is painting a picture of her plans when we make our first million. He has two bottles of champagne in his hands.

"I always knew you'd marry an independently wealthy woman," Jonah jokes as he sits between Aiden and me.

"Hey, he'd have to ask first," Caterina says with a grin.

"Seriously, Jonah?" Aiden glares at Jonah, and he looks furious.

"Wait…were you…" Caterina starts.

"I knew you'd be a pussy about it, thought I'd give you a little push," Jonah jokes. From the look on Aiden's face, I can tell he was likely planning on proposing to Caterina at some point today and he thoroughly regrets his decision to let Jonah know any of his plans.

"Aiden; were you going to ask?" she asks. He groans.

"I'm only back for today and I already thought I was going to be stealing your thunder from graduation, but I'd assume my asshole brother would have realised I would postpone it, rather than stealing the limelight after your business decision," Aiden explains. He shoots Jonah a dirty look.

"I personally can't think of anything better to steal the limelight." I grin at Aiden.

"Aiden," Caterina whispers.

"Okay, fine, if this is the place, this is the place," Aiden starts, and he slips off his chair, kneeling on one knee in front of her, pulling a ring box from his pocket.

"You're seriously asking?" Caterina stutters, and for the first time since I've known her, she suddenly looks speechless.

"I'm asking if you, Caterina Miller, would like to marry me." His voice betrays that he feels nervous, despite the encouragement and joking. He clicks open the ring box and nestled inside is a gold band with a solitaire diamond.

"Yes, Aiden!" She gets out of her chair and flings her arm around him.

"I'm so happy for them right now," I say to Jonah.

"I'm really looking forward to banging you, bridesmaid. Perks of the best man," Jonah jokes, winking at me. Caterina and Aiden pull away from one another. Aiden sits down on the chair, pulling her to sit on his lap.

"Who said you were going to be best man?" Aiden raises his eyebrows.

"Who said I'd ever consider banging you?" I add.

"I like how the third wheel never questions if she is going to be bridesmaid." Jonah tuts.

"Because some things in life are absolutely certain. There's not a chance in the world that I'd be getting married without Zoey as my bridesmaid," Caterina vows.

"I'm trusting both of you not to put me in some hideous dress." I grin.

"Go for something easy access, with a fuller skirt. I don't like to work too hard getting a woman out of her clothes," Jonah jokes, and for once, none of us reprimand him, we all start laughing, and I wish I could freeze this moment in time, as I can't imagine anything better than this.

7

Zoey

Aiden's car screeches to a stop just outside the gated entrance to the carpark where my office is. Given I'd parked my car yesterday in a space at the top of the carpark, closest to the back road, I can see him get out of his car. He looks furious as he walks towards me and Isabelle.

"What are you doing outside?" he asks.

"What harm do you think I'm going to come to in the carpark, Aiden?" I shoot back. I'm still upset with him for trying to block my visit to the coffee shop.

I know if I'd explained to him what the coffee shop means to me, he'd have been nicer about it. When Caterina and I were setting up the business, we'd found the coffee shop and made it our home, both of us agreeing that we'd get more done if we were planning and working in the coffee shop rather than at home. Once we were ready to find an office location, Caterina had taken it as a cosmic sign when the building down the road had become vacant. We'd celebrated in the coffee shop with a chocolate chip muffin, begging the owners to let us light a candle that she'd stuck in it, too impatient for us to wait to go somewhere fancier to celebrate our success. After we'd moved to the offices to work, we still stopped by the coffee shop every morning on our way in.

"Are the police on the way?" Aiden turns his attention to Isabelle. She doesn't seem fazed by his mood.

"Yes, I called them after I sent you the messages. It would have been low on their priority list if it wasn't for the threat being reported yesterday. They're sending the same officer over," Isabelle explains.

He nods curtly and then walks around the car to inspect the damage. The state of my car makes me grateful that it is still early, that the carpark hasn't yet started being filled up by employees, because I don't want people to see this. The slashed tyres on my car are more of an annoyance and inconvenience. It's not cheap to replace four tyres for alloy wheels, but it's something I can easily arrange. If it was just the tyres, I could sort that out today and be back on the road. The paintwork is another matter. On the passenger side of the car there are a couple of deep gouges, long scratch marks. The driver side is another level. Words have been etched into the paintwork.

Bitch. Whore. Cunt. Sinner. You'll pay.

Aiden's expression changes when he sees the words. I don't think Isabelle had sent photographs of that side of the car, just the passenger side. I suspect she was hoping Aiden would have decided he didn't need to come down.

"Where are your cameras in the carpark?" Aiden barks.

"I've already checked it, Aiden. There's no footage. The cameras are here, look, and there," Isabelle explains, and she points to each of the cameras that are positioned in the carpark. They cover the entrance and exit and some of the surrounding area. Isabelle has already told me, in a gentle tone, that I park my car in an alleged blind spot. She'd admonished me for parking too far from the building, even if it is where I always park. We've already taken a quick look through the security footage with the security guards who are working this morning. Based on the first view, there is no image captured of whomever has come into the carpark and vandalised my car.

"The police are here," I say, staring at the police car that has parked up behind Aiden's car. The same police officer I'd met yesterday gets out of the car. He walks around Aiden's car, scowling at it, before crossing and coming into the carpark.

He looks at Aiden. "Your car is parked illegally."

Aiden stares at him. "So is yours."

"I'm on official police business." The police officer shrugs.

"I'm sorry, what issue do you two have, and what does it have to do with the fact we have a vandalised car here?" Isabelle puts her hands on her hips, and everybody falls silent.

"Mr Slater took offence to some line of questioning yesterday, something he clearly still has an issue with, based on his current attitude."

Aiden doesn't respond and I wonder what was said between them. All I can remember is that Aiden had spoken to the police officer when another officer had taken my fingerprints, for elimination purposes, and he'd looked pissed off the entire time we were at the station. I wonder what Aiden had said to the officer, as both look equally pissed at the other.

"Aiden, why don't you move your car in here, get it off the double yellow lines?" I suggest. I pull off my work pass, the one that operates the doors and the car parking barrier. I hold it out for him, and he takes it off me before stalking off towards his car. I don't think the police can issue Aiden with a parking ticket, but this officer seems like he wants to make a point, and getting Aiden to move his car seems like the easiest way to dilute whatever aggravation exists between them.

The police officer looks slightly less disgruntled now Aiden has stepped away.

"Why don't you tell me what has happened?" he suggests.

"All four tyres of the car have been slashed, and the paintwork has been damaged." Isabelle points towards my car and he looks at me.

"What makes you think this is related to the letter you received?"

"Are you kidding me? How many people do you think I've pissed off in my life, to the point one sends me a surgical scalpel and somebody else decides to vandalise my car the same night?" I snap at him. I pinch the bridge of my nose, frustrated. I'm grateful that Aiden is still moving his car into the carpark because I think he'd probably punch this guy, and the last thing I need is for Aiden to be arrested.

"Ms Taylor, I'm just trying to get the information for the report." He sounds so unbothered by what is happening that now I wish Aiden was already back in the carpark, not to punch him but to hold me back before I can lash out.

"I'd say it is highly probable that the events are linked, and that this is an escalation of the situation. Based on what I have been told, some of the words from the note and the photographs are the same as the ones scratched into the paint." Somehow Isabelle sounds calm and collected. Maybe she'll hold me back if I lose control with this police officer. Officer West. His name comes to me in a flash. I focus on Aiden who is now through the barriers, pulling his car into a space near to my own damaged car. Despite all the tension between us, I'm oddly relieved when he gets out of the car and walks towards me.

I turn my attention to the officer. "Officer West, I assure you, I have never had any type of threat like this before."

"There are reports that people have targeted your business," he says.

"Nothing like this. We had some guys who thought it was their job to be vocal about the existence of the business, but it was all words on emails, albeit filthy, derogatory ones. We've never had a physical threat," I explain. I'm frustrated because we went over this yesterday.

"I'll take the details down. I'll call for the scenes of crime officers. The SOCO unit can check the security cameras and we'll probably take the car away for analysis. Do you have anything in the car you need to remove?"

"No." I scratch the side of my arm, frustrated by everything that is happening. Aiden arrives and stands next to me.

"Well, that's all I really need from you. Can you direct me towards the place where I can review the footage from the cameras?" Officer West asks.

"We already checked them, and there is nothing to note," Isabelle replies.

"Perhaps this is something best left to the police, to people who know what they're doing, not some amateur crime detective wannabes."

I keep scratching at my arm. Aiden reaches over to me. He takes my hand away from where I'm scratching.

"Don't," he says. I look at the skin, the redness I've caused around the old scar. He lets go of my hand and then looks at Officer West. "Are we amateurs or wannabes?" he asks.

"There is no need to be rude, Mr Slater."

Aiden scowls. "Except you're being rude, and unprofessional."

"Why don't we all just take a breath? How about I take you to the security office?" Isabelle smiles brightly at Officer West. He nods curtly and they walk off together.

"Don't you need to let them into the building?" Aiden asks when I don't make an immediate start after them.

"Isabelle has an all-access pass to everywhere in the building. Security issued her one this morning. She can get in without me," I explain.

"Well, you're still supposed to stick with her," Aiden points out.

"Maybe you could be a gentleman and walk me to the door?" I tease. "Besides, if you come with me, I'll get you a pass, too. Just in case you have to come by again. I wouldn't want you to get a parking ticket for abandoning your car on the double yellow lines." I grin at him. The earlier anger I'd felt about his reluctance for me to go to the coffee shop now seems insignificant.

"Hey, if you read the contract that you signed yesterday, you'll find there is a clause about you paying any fines I incur during official duties." He shrugs but then I see the little tug of a smile on his face.

I laugh. "I'll get that contract novated once I've issued you a parking pass."

"Come on, I'll walk you to the office," he offers. I could catch up with Isabelle and Officer West, but instead, I let him walk me.

"So, what did Officer West say to you that has you so pissed off?" I ask.

"Nothing. Forget it," he mutters.

"Well, it would be nice to forget it, but this is the police officer who is investigating what is happening, so maybe if you acted a little nicer it would mean he doesn't put my paperwork to the bottom of the pile."

"Fine, but I feel like you drew the short straw in getting him as the one assigned to your case." Aiden sounds frustrated and suddenly exhausted.

"Why don't you get going?"

"I want to talk to your security team," he says.

"Isabelle can do that," I remind him. So far today, she's demonstrated grace under pressure.

"Are the guards from last night still here?"

"No, because the guards are only here until seven. There isn't a reason for them to be here later. All the staff are gone by six. Usually, I'm the last one out," I explain.

"You should consider twenty-four-hour patrols." His tone is almost like a reprimand.

"I'll think about it, okay?"

"It wouldn't cost much more than what you already pay, certainly less than what you would lose if you had to suspend work because the building was damaged."

"I said I'll think about it, okay? I'll also organise getting some extra cameras in the carpark."

"Good," he says.

We reach the main door to the office building. Isabelle and Officer West are in the lobby together, looking completely at ease, all tension gone. Aiden stifles a yawn.

"I think you should go home. I appreciate that you came over, but you are supposed to be getting some sleep," I remind him.

"I need to go do the CCTV at your place," he says.

"You can do that later. There are cameras in the house, right? Plus, the doorbell camera will activate if somebody comes to the door." I stare at him as I talk, hoping he'll relent because he looks shattered.

"What time are you finishing today?" he asks.

"Six. I have a packed day, what with rearranging meetings from yesterday," I explain. I'm sure Isabelle is going to get bored as the day goes on.

"There isn't much point in Isabelle driving you home. By the time she gets there, it'll be time for me to take over."

"I can't finish any earlier, I still have a business to run, no matter what else is going on in my life." I start to scratch my arm but the stare he gives me stops me in my tracks.

"Does that still bother you?" he asks.

"When I'm stressed, yes," I admit. There is a flash of something across his face, almost like pity or remorse, but then he rights himself.

"Look, it'll make more sense if I come here and meet you at six. I can take you home," he suggests.

"Okay. Come on, pop in and I'll sort your pass, then you can park in the carpark when you get here. You know, just in case some police officer wants to make an example of you by getting a parking warden to slap a ticket on your car next time you abandon it," I joke.

"Fine," he grumbles, glancing at Officer West through the glass door.

I push the door open and walk up to the security desk. The security officers on today are two that have worked here for several years. They're efficient and friendly.

"What do you need, Zoey?" Nicole asks.

"Can you do a pass for Aiden Slater? A permanent one, I'll tell you when to end-date it, okay?"

"Sure thing." Nicole taps away on the system to organise a pass for Aiden. I look over at Isabelle and Officer West who are still deep in conversation. I watch as Jackson, the other security officer on duty today, passes Officer West a disc. I assume it's a copy of the security footage for last night.

"I'll see you later, Zoey," Aiden says once Nicole has given him his pass. He nods in the direction of Isabelle and then heads back outside.

Officer West finishes with Isabelle and starts to cross the lobby to leave, but he stops as he reaches me.

"I think you need to keep in mind that most people who receive threats like this, it is from somebody they know," he says, and his gaze seems to follow Aiden as he walks through the carpark.

"Aiden was at my house from about six-thirty yesterday until this morning, so if you are suggesting he is the one who damaged my car, you are way off base. I was with him all night." I sound far snappier than I'd intended but he does seem to irritate me easily.

"That sounds cosy," Officer West muses.

"Do you need anything else?" I glare at him.

"Goodbye, Ms Taylor. I'll arrange for your car to be towed," he says and then he's gone. I wonder if he can feel the weight of the scowl that I give him as he leaves.

"He's a charmer, isn't he?" Isabelle comments.

"Asshole," I mutter. "Come on, I'll give you a quick tour now the car drama is over." It was what I had intended when Isabelle and I had arrived, but the sight of my car had thrown me off track.

"Okay, lead the way."

Isabelle follows me as I walk through the building. I point out various offices as I walk past them, telling her who is based in each area we pass. The second floor is my favourite space, it's mostly open space with collaborative areas, comfortable sofas, and then an area for pool and table hockey. There are a couple of darts boards which always have a queue to use during lunchtime and breaks. I know a lot of the people who work for me end up forming friendships with other team members and it always makes me smile whenever I see people laughing and catching up on this floor. It's brightly decorated with noticeboards in several areas which are always filled with little jokes and cartoons people have written up. There's usually a couple of games of hangman and noughts-and-crosses on the go on the board too.

As I walk Isabelle through the fifth floor, I point out the departments based up here. I share the floor with the finance teams. I reach the section where my office is. It's an unusual set up, it's a large area that has been split into three sections, one larger office with two offices inside it. Abigail's desk is in the first section of the office. She is already at her desk. She'd passed through reception earlier when I was with security looking at the camera footage, and the coffee I'd got for her from the coffee shop is on her desk. I have no idea where mine is,

I vaguely remember that I put it down in the security office and forgot to pick it up again.

Across this section of office, there is a new desk for Isabelle to sit at when she is here. I have to hand it to Abigail; she is very efficient.

"Hi, Abigail. Let me introduce you to Isabelle. Isabelle will be with us for a while, she'll just shadow me around the building," I explain, though I have already emailed Abigail with a brief summary of Isabelle.

"Nice to meet you." Abigail smiles.

"What's on the diary today?" I ask. Abigail glances at her computer, taking a breath and then reeling my meetings off with a frightening speed. The only gap I have is at two-thirty, for forty minutes. I'm hoping I'll be able to convince Isabelle to walk with me to the coffee shop, or at least drive me if she won't concede to a walk. The idea of not getting out for a moment of fresh air in the busy diary seems like torture. I find myself longing for the beach again.

"Are there any issues with the diary?" Abigail asks. I shake my head.

"I'm going to get started, can you send the marketing team in when they get here?"

"Sure, Zoey." Abigail gets up, presumably to show Isabelle her desk.

"Whose office is that?" Isabelle asks and she nods in the direction of the office door next to mine.

"It's Caterina's," I reply, feeling short with her. I smile brightly. "I'll see you in a bit, Isabelle."

I leave her with Abigail and step into my office, shutting the door behind me. I put my laptop on my desk, take my jacket off and sit in the chair, waiting for the marketing team to arrive to start my day off with a bang.

∞∞∞∞∞∞∞∞

When my break in the diary arrives, Isabelle looks like she'll be agreeable to a walk. I step out of my office, taking my handbag with me, and clear my throat.

"Are you bored to your back teeth?" I tease.

She laughs. "It's not been too bad. Abigail has been showing me the ropes of everything she does."

"I think a couple more days, she'll be ready to take over my job." Abigail grins.

"Don't you dare think about leaving me, Abigail," I admonish.

"I wouldn't dream of it. Who else has a boss who buys them coffee every morning."

"Speaking of coffee, Isabelle, do you think we can get out of here for a bit? I need some food. I'm sure you're hungry too."

"I can drive you to the coffee shop," she offers.

"It's a nice day for a walk, don't you think?" I ask and she laughs.

"Don't push it. Come on."

"Do you want anything, Abigail?" I ask. She shakes her head.

"No thanks. I'll see you in a bit."

I follow Isabelle towards the lifts.

"Abigail is nice," she comments and when we step in the lift, she grins at me. "She's not just nice, she's very professional. She guards your door like it's to a secret lair."

"I know, she's ruthless. It is usually busy. She stops a lot of crap coming my way, but she knows to rearrange the diary if there is a genuine need. She hustles people out of the room if there is a chance they're going to make the meeting run over." I laugh. Abigail might be slight in stature, but I wouldn't want to try to slip something past her.

"I think if you introduced her to Aiden and he saw how efficient she is, he might reconsider if you need security in the office."

"I half expected him to tell me yesterday that I was over-reacting. I still think this might be a bit much. It's a threatening letter and some damage to my car, not…"

"Zoey," she cuts me off as we exit the lift. "I don't want to scare you, but you need to see the pattern. This isn't a letter and some damage. This started with somebody following you, for at least a few days. It was then the letter, and then the vandalism. This is escalation. I really want you to keep your wits about you. I don't want you to be frightened, but I do want you to be prepared that this could get worse before it gets better."

"How exactly do you think it could get worse?" I ask.

"In my experience, if there is somebody going to this much trouble to try to affect you, they'll keep doing things, and then they might take it a step further."

"By step further, you mean you think somebody is going to try to hurt me, physically," I comment, trying to keep my voice neutral.

"Like I said, I don't want you being frightened, I just want you to remember how serious this could be."

"I am taking this seriously. I wouldn't have called Aiden if I wasn't," I shoot back.

We exit the building and walk towards her car. She looks at me a couple of times, I am sure she wants to ask more questions about my history with Aiden. There is curiosity on her face. I wonder if I'd had a similar curiosity on mine this morning when asking Aiden about Isabelle. I feel a little cringe in my body when I think about my questions, trying to sound innocent. There was a time I'd have just asked him directly if he was having sex with her.

"So, tell me more about the company. I got the glossy run through from Abigail earlier, but what makes this place your passion?" she asks. From the expression on her face, I'm sure she was going to ask something different, but changed her mind like she knew I wouldn't answer her.

Isabelle unlocks her car and I get into the passenger seat.

"I know it will sound cheesy, but I'm passionate about what we provide as a business. It's changed over the years, because the world has changed since everything started, albeit the change is slow, and sometimes it feels like society takes a step forward but two back. I love knowing we provide a little bit of security. Originally it was mostly young women who were our client base, but we get a lot of elderly people too. I like knowing we've helped one vulnerable person feel a little less vulnerable."

Isabelle swipes at the barrier and turns onto the main road, heading towards the coffee shop.

"Abigail said you started initially working as a facilitator company, but now have some of your own services?"

"Yeah, originally we went out to smaller businesses and convinced them to work with us, to let us book jobs for them and take over a lot of their admin burdens, their advertising and things like that. It was a bit like food ordering companies convincing lots of restaurants to let customers order through them, that's the best way to describe it. Then we noticed there was gaps in businesses and so we went down the route of setting them up as departments underneath us."

"The staff I have seen coming in to have meetings with you today all seem very happy," she comments as she nears the coffee shop. It's a little frustrating that she's insisted on driving, given how close the coffee shop is, but at least we are out of the office.

"I meant it when I said we have high employee satisfaction scores. People spend a lot of their time at work, and I want people to be happy there, as well as doing a good job. I've had some employees who have been there from the start. I'm a big believer of promoting from within the company when we have an open job, and we have a graduate programme. We employ apprentices and train them in various skills, too. Omar and Heather, for example, they started on a rotation scheme, worked most departments to develop their skills, and now they both run their department."

"You seem to be doing well," Isabelle says as she pulls her car into the carpark at the side of the coffee shop.

"Well, it's one of the reasons I'm sure whatever is going on, it isn't being caused by any of my employees." I get out of the car. I spot the small frown she has on her face that I haven't waited for her to get out of the car first.

She stands close next to me as I walk towards the door to the coffee shop.

"Hey, Zoey, do you want your usual?" Jon asks from behind the counter. He's the son of the owner and is working here in his gap year before planning on going to university.

"Yes please, Jon, to take away." I smile at him. "Do you want anything?" I ask Isabelle.

"Just a black coffee for me, please."

"Coming right up. You're lucky, Zoey, we had a run on these today, but I saved you one," Jon says as he reaches for a wrapped bag which I know will contain my raspberry jam filled croissant. I love these, the jam being baked into the croissant is somehow much nicer than dipping a plain one into some raspberry jam. Also, far less sticky for when I'm at my desk later.

"You are an angel, Jon. I'm going to miss you when you go to university, are you sure you don't want to defer another year? I told you working for a year and saving money is going to make it easier for more time for studying, but think of two years wages and tips," I tease. He busies himself with making my vanilla latte and Isabelle's coffee, but he turns to give me a grin.

"I'm pretty sure my dad would have something to say about that. He keeps joking about how he is going to turn my room into a man-cave once I get out of the house."

"Your dad has loved having you work for him this year, but you're right, he would have something to say if I convinced you not to go. He'll be proud as punch when he gets to see you graduate."

I smile at him. He returns to the drinks, looking pleased at the praise. Jon is a timid guy. His dad, Mike, had told me Jon struggled to fit in at school, but I've seen him grow over the last nine months. His confidence has grown so much, dealing with the customers every day. I've tried my best to encourage him, help him see his potential. I hope he finds somebody who'll carry on supporting him when he gets to university.

When he puts my order through the till, I pay with my card, drop some cash into the tip jar, and give him a little wave.

"Have a great afternoon, Zoey," he says.

"You too. Tell your dad I said hi," I call as I walk towards the front door. This time, I'm sensible enough to wait for Isabelle to take the lead.

"Let me guess, that's why you're convinced the coffee shop is safe?" Isabelle asks.

"Yes. I know these people. I've known Mike for years, his wife Sally too, plus all the other staff they have," I explain as we head towards her car.

"You're forgetting that people can hide their true nature," she admonishes. I get into the car, put my pastry down so I can strap myself in. I stick my coffee cup into one of the cup holders as she gets into the car. I look at her as she puts her seatbelt on.

"I'm not underestimating or forgetting anything. I know the statistics," I say. She raises her eyebrows.

"Go on then, tell me some statistics," she challenges as she starts the car.

"I know that in one year in this country, female victims make up around thirty percent of murder victims, and in around ninety percent of the cases, their murderer was male. I know that when a woman is murdered, around sixty percent of them knew their killer. I know that in one year for women in this country, there are over sixty-five thousand cases of rape, and over a million cases of domestic abuse. I also know that these statistics are under reported."

"Yet you seem so reluctant to think the person doing this could be somebody you know."

"I only said I don't think it is anybody from work or the coffee shop." I sigh as I talk. Isabelle is sometimes as frustrating as Aiden. I look at her as she drives towards the office carpark. "I don't really know any other people, and those I do, they're on your list to look into, okay?"

"Has Aiden said anything to you about the checks?" she asks, seemingly switching tactics from making me feel naïve for not wanting to believe somebody like Jon could want to hurt me. It isn't that I don't think people can hide their nature, it's that I can't see what I would have done to warrant such vitriol.

"Not much, he just asked me if I knew my gardener had been to prison. I told him I did, which is true. Oh, and he joked about giving the cat a background check, at least, I assume it was a joke." I can't stop the little smile on my face as I think about how jumpy Aiden had been when Simba had come into the house.

"Well, I expect Aiden is making sure all the I's are dotted and the T's crossed."

"He's very thorough," I muse.

"He is indeed," she comments, and as she pulls up into a car parking space, she gives me a knowing look. I don't answer her comment. Instead, I focus on getting my coffee and croissant, and the plan for the rest of my day.

8

Aiden

I wake in the afternoon feeling like I've had enough sleep, though I know I probably haven't had enough. It had taken me a while to stop tossing and turning and fall asleep. An escalation of a previous threat is never a good sign. It just reaffirms that whoever is behind the threat to Zoey, they're serious.

I get myself ready and even though I know I'm too early to go to Zoey's office, I pack my things and get in my car, driving towards the police station we'd been at to report the initial threat. Officer West pisses me off but I want him removed from Zoey's case because he seems incompetent. If he appeared competent and pissed me off, I'd put up with it, bite my tongue, but he strikes me as somebody who isn't going to put the effort into looking at what is going on.

In the past, I've listened to many of Zoey's points, times where she's reeled off statistics about police failures when it comes to protecting women, or where the police themselves missed opportunities to take down one of their own before they hurt a woman. I've listened to the police press conferences where they insist that they're getting better, that they're cutting out officers who are misogynistic, abusive, racist, homophobic, those that do not have the correct values. I just know it's not fast enough.

When I get to the police station, I ask for a senior officer. My experiences with the police are usually positive but I've never had much need to complain before. I sit in the chair of the little room I'm ushered into to wait. It's the same room where Officer West had insinuated that I was a threat to Zoey, asking if we'd had a lover's tiff and I had constructed this situation to swoop in as Zoey's saviour. Clearly, there is enough in the police records to make him think that, but he's way off track.

"Mr Slater, I'm Officer Kim. What can I do for you?"

He's an older officer and he moves in a way that makes me think of other people I know from the army, people who have seen a lot and still have it weighing on them.

I clear my throat. There's no point being coy about what I want.

"I wanted to discuss whether there was an option of changing the officer who is assigned to Zoey Taylor's case."

"Is there a problem?" Officer Kim asks, one eyebrow slightly raised.

"West doesn't seem to take it seriously. He was rude and dismissive this morning when her car was vandalised."

He frowns at me. "You say her car was vandalised? There is nothing in the report I just read about that."

"This is exactly my point. It was reported this morning. There shouldn't be a reason the information isn't updated on her case yet. She got sent the package yesterday and that night, her car was vandalised. It's clearly an escalation."

"We are a very busy force, Mr Slater. Surprisingly, Ms Taylor's case isn't the only one we have on our plate."

"I get that, I do, and I know I have the luxury of only working for one client at a time, I'm just worried that something is going to get missed and she'll be hurt." I sigh and lean back in my chair.

"Officer West put a note on her file that we should look at your background. Is that why you seem to have a problem with him?"

"No, but he's wrong. He's basing his assumption on something that happened six years ago but if he'd bothered to read the files properly, he'll see that we were both innocent in what happened. Even if we weren't, I can promise, there is no way I'd hurt Zoey. If you need to investigate me, that's fine. Put me on your list of suspects, just…don't waste too much time and forget to look for the real culprit."

Officer Kim is quiet for a moment. I can't help but think about what he is referring to, something that changed my life, Zoey's life, fractured us to where we are now. I've spent years trying to be impassive when somebody brings this topic up, but I know it's probably written all over my face, the pain and the hurt, something else I wish I could take back and change in my past.

"I'll look at the case, I'll keep an eye on things. Here, take my card. If you need anything, call me. I'll keep Zoey updated, and I'll find out what has happened to the case notes from this morning." He smiles and slides me a business card. I pocket it, give a curt nod and stand.

106

"Thank you," I say, ready to turn and leave.

Behind me, Officer Kim clears his throat. I stop to look at him and the look of sympathy he has on his face takes me off guard.

"For what it's worth, Mr Slater, I believe you, and we are taking things seriously. I read through all the cases Officer West highlighted where your name, or Zoey's, comes up. I'm sorry for the things you have gone through."

"Yeah, me too," I reply, shrugging as if it doesn't bother me.

I leave the police station, checking my watch. Waiting for somebody to talk to me at the police station has taken far more time than I'd wanted, and I know I don't have enough time to do anything but drive to Zoey's office.

I arrive at Zoey's office at five-fifty, pissed off because people don't seem to know how to drive through rush-hour traffic. When I walk in the entrance of the building the guard who was on this morning is still there.

"Good afternoon, Mr Slater. Zoey left a message that you could go straight up. She's still in a meeting. Do you know where her office is, or would you like me to take you up?" She smiles brightly as she talks. I wonder how many people Zoey lets traipse unaccompanied through the office building, and I wonder why the guards never seem to question her decisions.

"I know where her office is," I reply.

I walk through the building, the pass I've been issued only needed to get through the main door after the lobby. After that, it's like free rein. It might be fine for Zoey's staff, but she ought to be more careful with visitors.

I knock on the door to the main office where Zoey's office is nestled inside. Isabelle opens the door.

"Hi Aiden, you're looking better than this morning," she comments.

"How has it been today?" I ask. There isn't anybody else in the main section of the office and the door to Zoey's office is closed.

"It's been okay. She's been in meetings most of the day. Don't worry, I checked she was alive after each meeting," Isabelle jokes. She sits at the desk that has been placed opposite to the one I'd seen Zoey's assistant sitting at yesterday.

"She'd better be alive, Issy," I mutter. I perch at the edge of her desk.

"She's fine. She seems okay, better than she was this morning. Probably because you've not been here to piss her off." Isabelle grins at me.

"Maybe," I agree.

"I took her out at lunch, but only to the coffee shop. Other than that, there isn't anything to report."

"I went to the police station on my way here. I asked them if it was possible to change the person investigating."

"Oh good, because that guy is a dick. He doesn't like you, but I don't think he likes me much, either." Isabelle rolls her eyes.

"Why don't you get going? I'll see you tomorrow, at Zoey's. Or maybe it's easier if we just meet here, swap over at the office?"

"Yeah, okay, that sounds like a good idea. It saves me doing a bit of running around. Text me later and tell me the time Zoey plans to get here tomorrow and we'll use that as our handover time, okay?" Isabelle asks as she gets her things together.

"I'll message you."

"Right, well, I am going to cram some fun into my evening before another thrilling day in the office. Tell Zoey goodnight for me." Isabelle laughs and then she waves goodbye before she walks off.

I move to sit at Isabelle's desk rather than on it. A couple of minutes later, the door to Zoey's office opens. Abigail and a man step outside.

"Oh, hello there," Abigail says to me. "Zoey is in there. I'm going to walk Mr Hammond back to the main reception and get going myself."

"Sure," I reply. I glance at Mr Hammond, the lawyer that Zoey had mentioned yesterday. I wonder if she's resolved her issues with Caleb. Abigail gathers her things from her desk and then smiles at him, leading him out of the office.

Zoey steps out of her office. She doesn't look surprised to see me instead of Isabelle.

"I won't be long. I'm just going to get my laptop and stuff and then I'll be ready," she explains. "Come through, if you like. You know, just in case there is a monster hidden in the office."

There's a small hint of a smile on her face and I shake my head.

"It's not funny, Zo."

"It's easier to joke than it is to keep thinking how terrible it is." She shrugs.

I follow her into her office. She packs away her laptop into her bag, shifts through a pile of notebooks, throwing some into her desk drawer and locking it, the others going into the bag with her laptop.

"So, how did the meeting go with Mr Hammond?"

"Really well. Not that I was expecting it to go any other way, I know Caleb was out of order with what he was demanding, I just needed to get somebody official to say it. Hopefully that will keep him quiet."

"You let Abigail sit in on personal meetings?" I ask, curious.

"Well, Abigail knows everything about me, but she was only in for the last five minutes. I don't like keeping her late, but she offered, just in case I needed support. I think Isabelle being here is making her feel a little unsettled." Zoey shrugs.

"Why is she unsettled?"

"Abigail is used to being in control of everything, but she isn't, currently. She doesn't know the variables and it's uncomfortable for her."

"She should try working for my company."

"I don't know how you do it," she muses.

"I just try to plan for every eventuality. We should start thinking about past this week. I don't think the police will have made much headway on your case by then, so you'll need to let Isabelle and me know what you had planned for the weekend so we can plan for that," I explain.

Zoey slings her bag onto her shoulder and gestures towards the main door of the office. I walk with her.

"I am not seeing anybody this weekend. Lizzie is away on a training course so the things I'd usually do with her at the weekend aren't happening. I had planned a personal appointment on Thursday night, but I will rearrange it. I had hoped to go to the beach because I haven't been in ages, but I'm guessing that's out of the question?"

We reach the lifts. She looks at me with a hopeful expression on her face. I know how much she loves the beach.

"I'll talk to Isabelle about the beach," I concede. It'll be a logistical nightmare given the weather is warm and the place will be packed, but if she hasn't been in a while, it might not be anywhere somebody expects her to go. The photographs that had been taken of her suggested they were recent followings, so maybe the beach will be unexpected.

"Thank you," she says, stepping into the lift as it arrives. I get in with her and she presses the button for the ground floor.

"Keep your other appointment, just let us know the schedule so we can plan it."

"No, thank you."

"Zoey, you can go about your usual business if we have planned for it. Whatever appointment you had planned, you can keep it. We'll just check the area out first."

"No, thank you," she repeats, and I can't work out why she won't look at me.

"Zoey, if it is important then…"

"It was a bikini wax, okay?" she cuts in. She turns to stare at me. "I don't particularly want to have you sitting in the reception area when I'm having it done, okay?"

The lift comes to a stop on the ground floor with a little bump. I count to ten in my head as the doors open, trying not to think of Zoey lying back on the beautician's table.

"I could ask Isabelle to take you, but I've taken people to all sorts of appointments, Zoey," I shoot back, once I've got a hold of myself.

"I'm sure you have, but it's not important. I'll last a little longer," she replies, and then she blushes furiously. She stalks out of the lift. I walk with her, scanning around the ground floor which looks empty except for the security guard who is sat near the entrance.

Zoey calls her goodbyes to the guard, and then we leave the building, walking to where I have parked my car, just in front of the reception. There is nobody around in the carpark. I zap to unlock the car and she gets into the passenger seat. I get into the car and start the engine.

"You know, there used to be a time when you were very comfortable making jokes with me about your waxing schedules," I say, trying to lighten the atmosphere between us.

"I know that. I remember. I'm not trying to make this weird, or any weirder than it already is. Maybe I just don't want to think the woman who waxes the hair off me might want to kill me. You and Isabelle have me looking suspiciously at everybody," she grumbles as I swipe the pass that I'd been issued at the barriers to get out of the carpark.

"Zoey, what could you possibly have done to the waxer to make them send you threats and vandalise your car?" I ask, a small smile on my face.

"I don't know, but what could I have done to the gardener, or to the guy who owns the coffee shop, or his son who serves me every day, because they're the people you two already seem so suspicious of." She gives a little shrug as she talks. I turn the car onto the side street and start heading towards the main road.

"I saw why the coffee shop is so important to you. I'm sorry for being a dick," I say as I reach the turning to the main road.

"You weren't being a dick. I know you were trying to keep me safe, given that's what I am paying you for. Oh, speaking of what I'm paying for, I read the fine print in the contract when I got back from lunch. It states about payment for food. Why were you so arsy about having breakfast?" She glances over at me with a curious expression on her face.

"I don't think I was being arsy, I'm sorry if I was."

"Was it because I was trying to wheedle information out of you," she guesses as I look in the rearview mirror to see if there are any cars behind us. The traffic has died down in the short time since I'd arrived at her office, there are only a couple of cars behind us. The two immediately behind us both contain families, harassed looking parents in the driver's seat, sullen looking teenagers beside them. The third car behind us seems to only contain the driver.

"No, but in future, just ask outright," I suggest.

"Okay, outright question, have you eaten today?" she asks. One of the cars behind us indicates off the road and takes the side street, followed by the other car containing the family. The road is quiet now apart from our car and the car with what appears to be a male driver. I make a mental note of the model of the car and commit the number plate to my memory.

"Not since the poached eggs," I reply. "I do have some dried noodles for later though."

"Aiden, that sounds grim."

I glance at her and laugh when I see her facial expression.

"Don't knock them until you try them."

"Absolutely not. There is no way dried noodles will ever compare to something fresh," she argues. She shifts in her seat, angling her body in my direction. "Do you remember those noodles at that restaurant we went to?"

"The char kway teow?"

"Yes, those!"

"I remember the food poisoning we got when you tried to cook it." I laugh.

"That was your dodgy prawns," she protests. "I know you're probably not looking for anything big to eat, given technically this is your breakfast time, but I bet I could find us a place that would deliver us a dish, if you fancy it later?"

Suddenly, I feel ravenously hungry.

"Sounds good. Why don't you order for whenever you think you'll want to eat? I'll eat whenever you're ready."

I glance in the rearview mirror again and the car is still there. It hasn't closed the gap between us since the other two cars have left. In theory, given I'm driving a little under the speed limit, the car should have closed the gap between us. They're either driving below the speed limit because they've had lots of speeding tickets, or there's a reason they want to keep a little distance between us.

"Oh, I found one," Zoey says. She's back to facing forwards, tapping away on her mobile at a food ordering app. "Do you want anything else? Or just the char kway teow?"

"I'm easy," I reply as I speed up the car, hitting the speed limit.

"What's up?" she puts her phone down for a second and looks around. "You think we're being followed?"

"I don't know," I admit.

"Aren't you supposed to make four right turns or something like that?" she asks. She twists in her seat. "Oh, that's Omar's car."

"Who is Omar?"

"One of my employees. He heads up the procurement team. He lives in this direction. He'll take the next right," she says. I pass the right turning she'd mentioned and when the car behind draws closer, they indicate off.

"He drives under the speed limit," I grumble.

"Yeah, he had a bump in his car a few months ago. Somebody was speeding and drove into the back of him. He's been a bit nervous of driving since," she explains.

"He didn't come out of the carpark behind us," I point out.

"No, because he was at a conference run by one of our suppliers. They're based on the other side of town."

"You seem to know a lot about this employee, accidents he's been in, where he lives, where he's been." I can't help but wonder if I sound as curious about Omar as Zoey had sounded this morning when asking me questions about Isabelle.

"I know where he was today because I signed off on him attending the conference, dummy. I know about the accident because he was off work. I know where he lives because I dropped him home when he returned to work, before he got the courage to drive again." She rolls her eyes at me.

"I'm only teasing."

"Well, I'm just glad it was him in the car behind us, rather than somebody crazy."

"I'm sorry if I worried you."

"I'm not worried, Aiden. I'm in the car with you. I trust you to get me home safely." She gives me a small smile and then falls silent for the rest of the drive. I fall silent too, because I have no idea how to respond.

∞∞∞∞∞∞∞∞

As soon as we get to Zoey's house, I check everything is secure and then she disappears upstairs, telling me she's going to change before doing some work in her study. I know she'll probably be catching up on work emails until dinner arrives. She's always worked hard. I wonder if Caleb ever used to lecture her, if he'd put his hands on her shoulders to massage them, whisper in her ear that she's too tense, suggest they go to bed for a bit. There's something about Caleb that makes me think the answer is no. I think he'd probably have enjoyed her working hard, thinking of the financial benefits.

I don't see Zoey come downstairs and go into her study as I'm busy with the jobs I needed to do in the house. I set up the CCTV and install the security lights I'd picked up. Once I've finished with them, I feel more at ease. I know we'll be able to keep an eye on the property when she's not here.

I get to test the setup of the CCTV when the alert goes off as the food delivery guy arrives. I take the order from him, lock all the doors again and then go knock on Zoey's door.

"Zoey, the food is here," I call to her. She steps out her study a minute later. She's changed out of her suit, now wearing a pair of soft looking blue jeans and a black vest top. Dressed like this, she looks much younger than she did earlier, less pressured by everything she has on her shoulders.

"Good, I'm starving," she announces.

We walk through to the kitchen so I can dish up the food she's ordered. There are two portions of char kway teow as well as a starter platter for two.

"What did you have at lunch?" I ask, wondering why she's so hungry.

"A pastry and a coffee. I didn't get chance for lunch at the usual times. By the time I had a break in the diary, the restaurant was closed. Isabelle took me to the coffee shop though."

"I'm sure you could have had something more substantial than a pastry for lunch," I point out. Zoey passes me two plates and two bowls for me to put the food in while she pours two glasses of juice.

"I could have, yes, but if I've got loads of meetings in the afternoon and I don't have a full hour lunch, I just get something light. Otherwise, I feel uncomfortable. It's middle age, Aiden, it creeps up on us," she jokes.

"You're thirty-one." I laugh.

"Okay, third-aged then, providing I get to live to ninety-three."

"It's a lot more than some people get," I reply, and I immediately regret my words. We both know what it's like to be touched by loss. It still shocks me that I'm older than either of my parents were when they died. They were twenty-five when they died.

"Shall we eat in here, instead of the dining room?" she suggests, ignoring my comment. I nod and move the plates over to the breakfast bar she has in the kitchen. Zoey's kitchen is the type you'd expect to see in a magazine for a show home, all the mod cons, exposed beams in the ceiling, but somehow it feels comfortable and homely. She puts two sets of chopsticks onto the table and we both sit up at the breakfast bar.

"I haven't had this dish in years," I admit. I ignore the appetisers she's added to the order for a moment, taking a bite of my dish. The flavours that hit me when I take a bite are amazing. I'd forgotten how good this was. The pack of noodles I have in my bag would have tasted like cardboard if I'd tried to eat them now.

"Good, right?" Zoey grins.

"Jesus, I'd forgotten just how good this is," I reply once I've swallowed my first bite. She picks up one of the spring rolls and bites into it.

"Oh, so good," she murmurs once she's swallowed.

"I'm starting to think I'm getting too good a deal, providing security for you." I pick up one of the spring rolls to try it myself. Like she'd said, it's delicious. I'm going to have to find out where she's ordered this from so that I can order it for myself once things go back to normal.

"Don't tell me the rich, famous and important don't feed you or treat you to amazing food," she says, picking up her chopsticks.

"I've never eaten with a client before, Zo," I reply.

It's another reminder that Zoey is always my exception. Usually, if a client wants to go out for dinner, I get to stand guard somewhere. When they eat at home, I tend to check the grounds and make sure the property is secure. Mostly, clients I work with just want the comfort of security, rather than having an active threat.

"When was the last time you had a job that took you overseas?" she wonders.

"A year ago. Dad's keen to move me into management rather than active duties."

"How do you feel about that?" she asks.

"I don't know. I get it, being based in one location instead of being up and running around to different locations seems like a good idea. It's not exactly conducive to a stable home life when you're hardly at home. Even without being overseas, most clients we get are either based in London or travel a lot to London. Putting roots down seems like a nice idea. I just don't know how I feel about management, about being primed to take over from my dad. Maybe I'll think of something different to do. Put my degree to good use." I shrug.

"You already put your degree to good use. You get into the minds of people, understand what makes people tick," she explains.

I laugh. "That makes me sound really devious."

"Not devious. Perceptive," she counters.

"There's plenty of people I don't think I'll ever figure out," I reply. I pick my chopsticks back up.

"Like who?"

"You," I admit.

"Really? Sometimes, I'm sure you're the only person who ever really knew me," she says, her voice soft.

There was a time I'd agree with her. That there was a time I knew her inside and out. I knew the things that made her tick, knew the things that kept her up at night, keeping her awake when they were on her mind. I knew how she reacted to pressure, knew how best to help her kick off a little of that pressure she feels on her shoulders. I'd have agreed that right from the start, she was the one who knew me best, even better than Caterina who had my heart, even better than Jonah who knew me from when we were kids.

"Zoey, about what I said, the last time we spoke, before all this, I mean, I…" I start but the flash of pain in her eyes stops me talking.

"Not tonight, Aiden. I just want to enjoy the food, okay?"

"Okay," I agree. There's a small silence between us and I worry I've upset her. "So, tell me about Lizzie," I suggest, breaking the silence.

"What do you want to know?"

"Where did you meet? How long have you been friends?"

"We met about eighteen months ago. We kinda just kept bumping into one another. She goes to the same gym as me, we'd kind of seen one another around but then we were both sat in the reception room for…oh, gosh, why is it that this whole evening seems to end up being about waxing?" she finishes with a mutter, and I smirk.

"Don't tell me she's the person who waxes you, as that is the weirdest foundation for a friendship."

She laughs. "No, you idiot. She was waiting for an appointment at the same time as I was. So, we struck up a conversation, you know, the whole 'don't you go to the same gym as me' thing, and it went from there really. We started meeting up to go to the gym together, and we'd get a coffee afterwards, and she's become a good friend."

"I'm glad you have somebody you can rely on." I focus on my food, ignoring the stab at the thought that she used to be able to rely on me.

"She got me through some stuff, I guess. She's been very supportive since Caleb left."

"I wish you'd reached out," I say with a sigh. "I wish you'd got in touch when your dad died, or when Caleb left, or…"

"Don't, Aiden," she warns.

"Okay."

We fall into a silence as we finish our food. Once dinner is finished, I help her stack the plates into the dishwasher. Once we're done, she disappears into the living room for a bit, telling me she's going to watch some television before she goes to bed. I don't see her again until ten thirty.

"I'm going to go to bed. I'll see you in the morning," she says.

"I'll be driving you to the office tomorrow. Isabelle and I decided it'll be better to swap over there. I'll take you for coffee in the morning, okay?" I offer and she gives me a little smile.

"Sounds good. Can you listen out for Simba? I have put food down for him, but he isn't in. I'm sure he'll turn up in the night, but just make sure the kitchen door is open so he can get to his food and water, please."

"Sure, no worries. I'll see you in the morning."

She gives me a nod and heads up the stairs. I go back into the dining room, looking over the documents I'd been looking at before I'd heard Zoey walking out of the living room. I finish the request for chasing up the check on Zoey's friend Lizzie. I know Zoey doesn't appreciate it, but all close contacts should be checked, just in case.

I think back over our dinner together and regret pushing her to talk about the past, making it awkward and stilted between us.

I know our past has been complicated; I know we both have lots of things we regret. There isn't a day that I don't wish that certain things had unfolded differently, that I still had Zoey in my life. Our friendship used to be so easy. Back in the days when it was Caterina and me, Jonah and Zoey, it had felt so effortless, there wasn't a single thing we couldn't talk about, not a single time we'd been awkward or stilted. I couldn't see that it would ever change, but there had been a lot of things I'd assumed would have always remained as they had been when we first met.

All I know is that, although I wasn't the one who set everything in motion, I was the one who made the first decision that changed all our trajectories, changed the future we'd all had planned out.

Our dreams for our lives were so different to how it is now, and I can't decide how much of it was my fault, or how much Zoey holds me responsible.

9

Zoey

"Here's to a successful second year of trading, we are awesome," Caterina exclaims. She has a big smile on her face as she sidles into the seat next to me at the conference hall we'd booked to hold our celebrations.

Gathered around us are all our employees and everybody looks so proud of themselves. I'm ridiculously proud. Every person has worked so hard but we're doing so well. The celebration evening has involved food, presentations and awards, and lots of laughter.

"I'm so happy right now," I tell Caterina. She reaches over for the half empty bottle of champagne on the table and pours me a second glass.

"You are my favourite person. This is all your doing. Do you know how awesome you are? Look at what you have created." Caterina gestures out to the hall. Despite it being a Thursday night and there being work tomorrow, everybody is still celebrating, a few people have started to dance, others are sat in groups, talking and laughing. The night is showing no signs of slowing down.

"Caterina, I could not have done any of this without you." I reach out for her hand, giving it a squeeze. "You and me, we are unstoppable, and I am so grateful for you."

"We are going to do this every year. Except next time, on a Saturday night, on a huge yacht."

I laugh at her exuberance. "You are very confident about the future."

"I'm sure about what we have planned. We should dance, come on," she urges, trying to pull me from the chair.

I laugh. "I am not going to subject our lovely employees to my dancing."

"We should kick back and let them know how human we are." Caterina grins.

"Maybe we should go dancing next weekend."

"Aiden is back next weekend, he gets in on Friday," she says, getting a dreamy look on her face.

"Ah, yes, I forgot. He'll arrive on Friday, leave on Sunday, and I won't see a peep of you." I grin at her.

"We are not that bad. I'm sure we can surface for an hour or two, for us all to go out for lunch. Aiden likes to see you and Jonah when he's home, too."

"I'll speak for both me and Jonah when I say it's fine. If he's only home for a weekend, we won't take a minute from you."

"I've missed him, so much," she muses. Aiden's been stationed overseas for six months. I know she has missed him desperately, especially when she's seen information on the news about the situation where his unit is deployed.

"I might actually go away next weekend, to give you two some alone time."

"There is no need for that. It's your home, you idiot. Unless, of course, you tell me that you have some hot guy you're secretly seeing and you're going away for a dirty weekend, in which case, I'm all for it. I'll even help you buy some slutty underwear," she teases.

"Caterina," I scold, looking around at whether anybody can hear us talking.

She laughs. "Chill out. Seriously, though, do you? Is there some sexy side piece? I haven't heard you talking about a guy since Seth and that was four months ago."

"I've been busy. I do have a date, though, Saturday morning, a breakfast date."

"Saturday morning is a weird time for a date. That's usually what people do after a successful Friday night date."

"He's a paramedic, we're going out before he has to go on a shift," I reply with a smile. I met Logan on a dating site, one I'd signed up to when Caterina's teasing had made me consider what I want from life. I don't know how to balance my working life with a romance, but it's been a while since I've had sex and maybe it's time for me to find the balance that she's suggested.

"Oh wow, that's kinda hot, a man who knows his way around the body."

"Well, I'll let you know how the date goes."

"I expect all the dirty details. Now, if you're not going to dance with me, I'm going to go have some fun," Caterina announces. She gives me a quick kiss on the cheek. I wince. Caterina frowns. "You seriously need to get that tooth sorted."

"We've been busy," I remind her.

"Not busy enough to ignore your health," she admonishes.

"I'll get it sorted; I promise. I have an appointment after work tomorrow. Go enjoy the celebration, Cat," I urge her.

Caterina stands and goes to join the throng of people now gathered on the dancefloor. I sit back and watch her, smiling to myself as she disappears into the crowd, accepting hugs from team members and shouting to the DJ to turn the music up. I am sure half the company will be at work tomorrow with hangovers, Caterina included.

I try to focus on the team and ignore the niggle of pain in my tooth.

∞∞∞∞∞∞∞∞∞

I wake in the morning with more pain in my tooth. My dentist appointment is at six, so I console myself it'll be sorted soon. I dress and head downstairs for breakfast, finding Caterina already in the kitchen.

"I'm going to go to my parents' house straight from work. I forgot it's my grandma's birthday dinner. Well, I didn't forget, Grandma decided one celebration wasn't enough and has dropped a surprise dinner in," she says as I put some bread into the toaster.

"I love how you're describing yourself. I don't think one celebration is ever enough for you," I tease.

"You're so funny, but yes, I believe in celebrating life, even if it is last-minute. I won't be back until Sunday afternoon," Caterina says.

"I'd rather a last-minute celebration than the dentist, but I am looking forward to getting this sorted out." I rub my cheek.

"Do you want me to stay and look after you?"

"And deprive your grandma of your presence? I don't think so." I grin at her.

"If you change your mind, just let me know. I'm sure the family would understand, they love you," Caterina says, and I shake my head.

"It's fine, I'm sure it just needs some antibiotics. Anyway, I'm going to have my toast and then head into the office. I'll drive myself today if that's okay, so I can go straight to the dentist."

"Yeah, I'm heading to Mum and Dad's straight from work anyway. I'm going to get going now, I'll see you in the office," she replies. She gathers her things and gives me a wave and heads out of the house.

∞∞∞∞∞∞∞∞∞

I let myself into the house, my face feeling half numb and half on fire. I'm pretty sure the right side of my face is swollen, making me look like a hamster with a cheek full of food. It's going to be such a good look for my breakfast date tomorrow. I'm partly grateful that Caterina is away as I am sure she would laugh at me before the sympathy arrived. The downside of her being away is that I will have to go back to the chemist myself to pick up the painkillers and antibiotics given I'd been too late for the usual chemist and now need to wait for the emergency one to open.

I shrug out of my jacket, drop my bags by the front door and my jacket on top. I walk through to the living room, my mind thinking the sofa will be a better place to rest because if I go to bed, I will fall asleep and I'm pretty sure I'll wake in agony if I don't get the tablets.

I yelp when I see somebody is sitting on the sofa, a bouquet of red roses in their hands. It takes a second for my brain to engage at what I am seeing; that it is Aiden on the sofa.

"You scared me," I exclaim, but the words are muffled given one side of my face is still numb.

"What the hell is wrong with your face? Why can't you talk? You're not having a stroke, are you? Oh Zoey, come on, hospital." Aiden gets up from the sofa, dropping the flowers on the coffee table, stepping towards me. It's times like this that always reminds me that Aiden is a man of action and how calm he is under pressure, even if he is wrong.

"I had a tooth removed, dumbass," I explain.

Again, the words are slurred, and even though my face is partly numb, I'm pretty sure I'm drooling. Gingerly, I raise my hand and touch my mouth. I grimace and groan when I find my fingers are damp.

"I think I heard tooth, but I'm pretty sure I misheard you calling me a dumbass." Aiden grins at me. He picks up the box of tissues from the coffee table and I take one, dabbing softly at my mouth, wincing.

"Why here?" I ask, hoping fewer words is going to be easier until the numbness wears off. I don't think it will be long, given my cheek has started to tingle, just below my eye. I'm sure the numbness will wear off quickly, sweeping down the rest of my cheek until it'll be jaw level and then the pain and tenderness will hit me.

"Why am I here? I was trying to surprise Caterina. I told her I had next weekend here, but I'm back until next Sunday. I thought it would be a good surprise, but I also thought she'd be home by now. I've been here for about two hours."

"Parents," I say.

"Sit down, Zo, you look pale."

I take his advice and flop onto the sofa, groaning. He sits down next to me. I can feel more tingling in my cheek now and I move my jaw, trying to see if it'll make it easier to get the feeling back in my face. I wipe my mouth again.

"Grim," I grumble.

"Not planning on giving any blowjobs this weekend, are you?" he teases, and I push him on the arm.

"Fuck off," I mutter.

He laughs. "Oh, now that one I understood."

"Good."

"Do you want a drink of water?" he asks. I shake my head and fish around in my trouser pocket for the information sheet the dentist had given me. I hand it to Aiden, and he looks at it, studying it.

"Okay, so no food or hot drink for three hours. Soft food only for the next day. No sucking. Blow jobs are definitely out," he reads. I grab the sheet of paper from him and read it myself.

"No sucking the wound, dumbass." I snort.

"Your insults would be far more insulting if you weren't drooling." He takes the sheets of paper back from me with a smirk on his face.

"I don't need words," I shoot back, flipping my middle finger at him.

"This says you should be taking antibiotics and painkillers, where are they?"

I check the time on the clock on the wall. I'm pretty sure there is still another half-hour before the chemist opens.

"I'll get them later," I reply, grimacing as the tingling in my cheek comes a bit further down.

"I'll go. I'll be back in a min. You stay here and try not to drool all over the cushions." Aiden gives me a grin and he stands up, holding my prescription. My face hurts too much to think of an insult so I just settle back on the sofa and try not to move, listening to the sound of Aiden's footsteps as they go down the hallway and out of the house.

∞∞∞∞∞∞∞∞

"Hey, Rambo, come on, wake up. Time for your tablets." Aiden shakes me awake.

I open my eyes and he's stood in front of me holding a glass of water and my tablets. The numbness in my cheek has gone and now everything is just tender. I take the glass from him and take a tentative sip of water then swallow the tablets he has in his hands.

"Thank you for getting these for me," I tell him once I've put the glass down.

He smiles. "Sounds like your anaesthetic has worn off. Proper words, no drooling."

"That is good news because I do have a date tomorrow."

"Somebody new or somebody you have been seeing a while and not told me about?" he asks.

"Somebody new, we're going for breakfast."

"Please tell me you're not so busy that a breakfast date is all you can fit in."

"Actually, this time it is because he is busy." I roll my eyes at him.

"Where did you meet him?"

"On a dating app," I explain. I get up from the sofa and head towards the kitchen, Aiden at my heels.

"What's his name?" he asks.

"Logan Boothe. He's a paramedic."

"I thought you might be telling me you've finally given in to Jonah," Aiden comments and I laugh.

"I had a wisdom tooth out; I didn't lose my wisdom."

"Come on, show me Logan's profile. I'll see if he's worthy of my best friend," he offers.

"Funny that my other best friend was so thrilled at the idea of me getting laid that she didn't make me show her the profile, just offered to buy me slutty underwear," I joke. I take my mobile phone out of my trouser pocket and pull up the dating site I've been using. I find Logan's profile and hand the phone over to Aiden, watching as he skims through the pictures and the profile information.

"He's good-looking. Looks like he's nearly the whole package," Aiden comments.

"Nearly?" I frown, taking my phone back from Aiden and skimming over Logan's profile again, wondering what it is that I've missed.

"Well, clearly I'm the only perfect guy in the world, but he looks like he could be a close second."

I laugh. "Oh my God, get over yourself. How big is your ego?"

"Only as big as my dick, plenty big enough," he shoots back.

I'm sure that if we were any other people, this would be the moment any perceived sexual tension broke, where they'd be up against the counter worktop, a tangle of mouths and limbs, both wondering where the condoms were, fumbling with clothes, hoping they were wearing decent underwear.

Except it's me and Aiden. So instead, we're grinning and laughing.

"You are so full of shit," I admonish.

"Well, when you and Logan marry, I'll be cheering you on."

"Not even had one date yet, you idiot." I roll my eyes at him.

"Speaking of dates, you said Caterina was at her mum and dad's. Why is she there? When is she back?"

"She said her grandma wanted a birthday dinner or something. She's supposed to be back on Sunday morning," I explain.

"Don't tell her I'm here. I really want to surprise her. I'll just wait until Sunday morning."

"Okay," I reply and then I wince when I close my mouth too forcefully and it irritates where the tooth has been extracted.

"Yeah, definitely no blowjobs tomorrow," he jokes.

"First, it's a breakfast date. Second, blowjobs are more a second date activity." I smirk at him, but the expression makes my face ache and I wince again.

Aiden snorts. "Rest your mouth, Zo. I'm going to go see my family and hide out there until Sunday. I'll see you later, okay?"

"See you later, Aiden."

He gives me a hug before he leaves, leaving the flowers he'd had earlier on the coffee table. I pick them up and put them into a vase. If Caterina is back before Aiden gets back home on Sunday morning, I can lie and say they're flowers from my date. Knowing Aiden, he'll bring another bunch home for her for Sunday, just to show her how much he loves her.

∞∞∞∞∞∞∞∞

"I had a really nice time, Logan," I say as he walks me back towards my front door. My mouth feels so much better than yesterday but still a little tender, especially after eating breakfast. Chewing breakfast on one side of my mouth while trying to look elegant has felt like a struggle.

"Thank you for being so accommodating with my rubbish schedule," Logan replies. I smile at him. He strikes me as the type of man who is used to women accommodating him. He's tall and blond, deep brown eyes and a friendly smile. He's a gorgeous man but also seems modest about it. At breakfast, he'd ticked all the right boxes, said all the right things. He's either a genuinely nice guy, or he's used to playing one.

"I know what it's like to be busy, but I am looking forward to dinner next Sunday evening." I smile at him. He'd asked me to dinner when he'd driven me home, and I am excited by the idea we can have a longer date, more time to talk and see where the night might lead us.

"I look forward to seeing you again, Zoey," he replies. He reaches for my hand, giving me a kiss just above my knuckles. "It was very nice meeting you."

Logan saunters down the path, heading towards his car. I know he's going straight to a long shift at work. I watch as he takes his phone out of his pocket as he walks towards his car. A second later, my phone beeps. I take it out to read the message, smiling when I see it is from Logan.

I remember you'd had a tooth out, but I wish I'd been able to kiss you goodbye properly today.

I type a message back.

Looking forward to next Sunday, if that is what is on offer for dessert.

I unlock the front door and step inside, still smiling to myself. I drop my keys on the countertop and kick off my shoes. I pause for a second, listening. The noise I thought I'd heard when I'd put my keys down happens again, the slam of a door, coming from upstairs.

I head upstairs, trying to keep my footsteps light, skipping the step that always creaks. I'm not expecting anybody to be home. Caterina isn't due home until tomorrow morning. Aiden said he wouldn't be back until Sunday, either.

I stop at the top of the stairs, listening for the direction of the noise. There's another drawer shut, and it sounds like somebody is sniffling. The noise is coming from Caterina's bedroom.

I take a tentative step, peering through the door which is slightly ajar. Aiden is kneeling on the bedroom floor, pulling clothes out of the drawer.

"Aiden? What's going on?" I ask. He turns to look at me, and the expression on his face catches me off guard, making me drop my things to the floor and rush to kneel in front of him. I put my arms around him and hold him close. "What's happened? Is Caterina okay?"

For a moment he doesn't answer, he just lets me hold him and then he pulls away, wiping his eyes.

"She's fine," he replies eventually, clearing his throat.

"What are you doing?" I ask, looking around the room. He has two holdall bags at his knees, piles of clothes in front of him.

"It's over. I'm clearing my stuff out," he explains.

"Caterina broke up with you?" I ask, surprised. Aiden refuses to look at me, his eyes seem suddenly fascinated by the pile of clothes next to him. I grab his face with both hands, moving his face so I force him to look at me. His grey-blue eyes look dark and stormy.

"I broke up with her."

"Why?" I exclaim. The idea that Caterina would break up with Aiden felt shocking, that he may have broken up with her seems scandalous.

"Zo, you're my best friend, I wouldn't ever lie to you, but do not ask me questions about Caterina."

"What happened?" I try again.

"I mean it, Zoey."

His tone is sharp, and he looks serious. I watch as he shoves some of his clothes into one of the bags.

"Let me help," I offer.

I take the shirts out of the bag given they're all scrunched up. I refold them and put them into the bag neatly. Aiden leans against the base of the double bed, resting his chin on his knees. When I've finished packing one of the bags, I zip it up and reach for the second bag. I open the bag up and start putting the other items he's already pulled out of the wardrobe he'd shared with Caterina. I pack away his jeans and trousers, underwear and socks.

"Thank you," he says once I've finished packing the bags. I sit down next to him.

"Can you please tell me what happened?" I ask.

"It's over."

"But why? I don't understand."

"I need to get the rest of my things from the rest of the house," he says, dodging my question.

"Where are you going to put them all?"

"I've rented a storage unit."

"You have thought this all through," I comment. He stares at me.

"This is not a rash decision. I've thought this through. I have some flatpack boxes downstairs, then I'm getting out of here."

"I'll help you."

I stand up and my legs feel shaky, my stomach feels like it's swimming. Four years. Four years they've been together, engaged, planning a life and a future. I can't understand how it is all gone.

Aiden gets up from the floor, carrying the two bags with him. He walks down the stairs and I follow him, still desperate to know what has happened.

Aiden dumps his bags on the floor near the front door and then walks into the living room. I follow him, seeing the flatpack boxes he's picked up from somewhere. He builds one of the boxes, not making eye contact with me, dumping the box onto the coffee table. He walks through the living room, picking up various items and putting them in the box. Aiden's things have always slotted nicely into the house, things I've barely noticed but now seem to leave gaps in the room.

I help him pack his things into the boxes. When the last item is boxed up and all the boxes are stacked in the hallway, I go to the kitchen to make us a cup of tea, pulling Aiden with me. I make us both a dink and hand one to him. He looks shellshocked as he sits in the seat.

"Thanks," he murmurs.

"Where are you going to go?" I wonder.

"I'm going to put my stuff in storage until I get out of the army. I can go there whenever I want today. I'll stay with my mum and dad until I'm due back on base," he replies.

"Let me help you with the storage unit."

He shakes his head. "I'll get a taxi."

"Aiden, please. You're my friend. I'm not going to let you do all this by yourself." I sigh. Before I can say another word, Aiden has his arms around me, holding me in a bear hug.

"I don't want to lose you too," he whispers.

"You won't lose me, you're one of my favourite people in the world. I don't know what happened between you and Caterina, but I'm going to do my best not to take sides. I'm here for both of you. I don't want anything to change between us," I tell him.

"I don't know what I'd do without you," he murmurs. He pulls away and takes a deep breath.

"I'm going to nip to the bathroom, then I'll come back and finish my tea, and then we can do whatever you need," I say. He nods back at me.

I go upstairs and as soon as I'm in the bathroom, I sit on the side of the bath and take my mobile out of my pocket. I text Caterina, firing off questions.

Me: *Caterina, I don't know what is going on. Aiden is here, he says you have split up. Are you okay? What happened? When are you coming home? Why didn't you call me?*

My phone buzzes only a minute later, and I'm grateful that I didn't have to wait because I feel like my nerves are all on edge.

Caterina: *I'm devastated, but I am okay. I am with my mum and dad. They'll take care of me. I'm going to stay here for the week, can you cover me at work? I'm sorry, Zoey. I love you. I'll phone you tonight.*

Me: *I love you too, but I don't know what is going on. What happened?*

Caterina: *He just broke it off with me. I can't deal with this conversation right now. I'll call you later.*

I stick my phone back in my pocket, still confused because this makes no sense. They've been so solid for years, I've listened to them talk about the wedding plans and Caterina has told me all about the dress style she wants to wear, what song she wants to play as their first dance, asked me if I'll join forces with her in getting Aiden to learn to do some ballroom dancing as she wanted their first dance to be 'epic'.

I go back downstairs to Aiden. He looks wretched, like his whole life has just exploded. It's completely different to how he was yesterday when he had arrived. I know there is no way he came home for a week to surprise Caterina and break up with her. I know there is no way Caterina had planned to break up with Aiden. I don't understand why neither of them want to tell me what has happened, but I know one of them will tell me once they're over the shock of what happened.

"Do you think there is any chance you'll get back together? Is this just a blip?" I ask.

"No, this is it," he replies. He gets up from his seat. "Finish your tea. I'm going to get some fresh air."

"I don't want it." I shake my head. The idea of drinking the rest of my tea makes me feel queasy. I follow him through the house, I grab my car keys.

We load Aiden's things into the back of my car, filling the backseat and the boot. I drive in the direction of where he tells me the storage unit is, and I help him unload his stuff into the storage unit, leaving just his two bags of clothes in the car. I drive towards where his mum and dad live.

"Thank you for this, today," he says once I pull up outside the house.

"Give me your key to the storage unit." I hold my hand out.

"Why?"

"So that you have a reason to call me," I say.

"You know I don't need a key as a reason to call you." His facial expression is soft.

"I know, just…" I start, but he drops the key into my open palm. He leans over and kisses me on the cheek.

"I'll see you soon, Zo," he says. He gets out of the car, grabs his bags from the back seat, and then disappears down the path to the house.

∞∞∞∞∞∞∞∞

"Cat, are you going to tell me what happened?" I ask as soon as she calls me. The sigh she gives down the phoneline doesn't convince me that she's going to tell me anything of substance.

"He just said he doesn't see a future for us," she sniffles.

"That's ludicrous," I scoff. Turning up with the flowers on Friday night, to surprise her, that doesn't suggest Aiden doesn't see a future with Caterina.

"I don't know what else to tell you, Zo. He's a bad guy."

"I know you're hurting right now, but you know he's not a bad guy," I say, gently. I sit down on my bed.

"Did he say anything to you when he was at the house?"

"He just said that it was over. I helped him clear his stuff from the house," I tell her, and I bite my lip because I'm not sure how she's going to be when she gets home and all of Aiden's stuff is gone.

The sound of her crying pierces my heart. It's worse than seeing Aiden so distraught because I hate knowing she's upset, and she isn't with me for me to comfort her.

"Will you be okay at work next week without me?" She hiccups as she speaks.

"Forget about work," I reply.

"See, I know it's bad if you're saying not to worry about work," she cries.

"Work isn't important right now. I've got you covered. I wish I could be there to give you a hug. Are you sure you don't want to come home early?"

"I'll be back next weekend, and I'll have a big hug from you then, okay?"

"You bet, Cat."

"I'm going to go. My mum is shouting me. She thinks a bit of shopping is going to help. Daddy's credit card is going to take a hammering, apparently."

"Call me later, please? I'm worried about you."

"You're a good friend, Zoey," she says, and she disconnects the call before I have chance to reply.

I flop down on the bed and as I shift to get into a comfortable position, the key to Aiden's storage locker digs into my hip. I get back up off the bed and I put the key into my trinket box. It's still early in the day but I feel exhausted so I climb back into bed, pinch the bridge of my nose, and wish it would all go away.

10
Zoey

It's strangely unsettling getting ready for bed and knowing Aiden is downstairs, even being the second night. Last night when I'd gone upstairs, I'd paced around for a bit until I got into bed, wondering if Aiden could hear my footsteps from where he was. I'd sat on the bed, unable to sleep for an hour.

Tonight, my emotions feel like they've been put through a spin cycle, everything too much to deal with. Threats aside, seeing Aiden again was always going to be uncomfortable given how we left things, and any time I attempt to smooth things over, I feel like I'm being dragged back into the past.

I have always hated how we left things, how we were so hurt and wounded, retreating from everything and leaving only silence between us. I even hate the way we left things tonight. I've tried to be friendly this evening but all I feel now is sadness, sadness about how awkward this is now compared to how we used to be.

I get into bed, pulling the covers around me, lying on my side. I reach for my phone and text Lizzie to ask if she's free. Instead of a message back, my phone rings, Lizzie's name on my screen.

"Hey, how's tricks?" she asks.

"Surviving. How's the training course?"

"I'm not going to lie, it's as boring as fuck," she grumbles, and I can't help but giggle.

"Didn't you once tell me not to use that sentence as it implied that I had a terrible sex life?" I remind her.

"Well, I'm going through a dry spell, so my sentiment is correct."

"I thought you'd got some hot date lined up when you get back from your course?"

"I do, but honestly Zoey, it's been so long since I got laid, I think I've forgotten how to do it," she complains.

"I'm pretty sure it's like riding a bike, once you know, you never forget." I laugh.

"I don't usually go for sex on a first date but if Ben looks anything like he does in his profile picture, and is half as entertaining in real life as he has been in print, I'm going to be breaking that rule because he is hot as hell. Speaking of hot as hell, who the hell is that security guy of yours? He's freaking amazing, he looks like the type of guy you find shirtless on erotic romance stories."

"Lizzie, he's a bodyguard, he isn't there to be drooled over," I scold.

"What's his name?" she asks.

I hesitate. I've told Lizzie briefly about my history with Aiden, but she doesn't know him in person, she doesn't know what he does as a job. For some reason, I can't bring myself to tell her who he really is, the same way I haven't felt comfortable in giving Isabelle too many details about how I know Aiden.

"James," I tell her.

"Well, you can tell that James of yours that I would quite happily let him frisk me," she jokes.

"You better get laid soon, I feel like you're one inappropriate comment away from a police warning for harassment," I tease.

"How have things been today? No more threats, I take it?"

"My car was vandalised," I admit with a sigh. I hear the shuffling she makes as she shoots up from whatever position she was in, clearly shocked by my news.

"Please tell me you're kidding me."

"No. I'd left it at the office on Monday because I went straight to the police with the security team, and then came straight home. I thought it would be safe in the carpark at work, but nope. It's all scratched down one side, and then horrible words cut into the paint on the driver's side."

"Oh Zoey, I'm so sorry. I wish I was there. I could give you a big hug."

"I'll accept your verbal one." I smile to myself.

"Well, in that case, super big hugs. What did James say?" she asks, and it takes me a second to realise she means Aiden.

"I was with the other team member when I saw it, Isabelle. She's with me in the day. Isabelle was nice about it, she took care of it and looked after me as I'll admit, it freaked me out."

I think back to the morning, seeing the devastation of my car, wondering again what I've done to make somebody hate me so much, who could possibly despise me to the point they'd risk getting caught damaging my car. I still feel so stupid that I'd overlooked the way the security cameras were set up in the carpark. Not just for my car but for knowing something like that could have happened to one of my employee's cars. It's my responsibility, and I overlooked it. I'm the one who dropped the ball, even after I vowed that I'd never drop the ball again.

"What did the police say?"

"The guy looking after my case wasn't helpful, but at least the car got taken away to be looked at."

"Have you got enough security at home, and at work? I'm worried about you. This seems scary, Zoey," Lizzie frets.

"I think work is okay. There are enough cameras in the building. I promised that I would get some additional cameras sorted for the carpark, and I said I'd think about extra security patrols," I explain.

"What about home, though. How safe are you right now?"

I think about Aiden, patrolling the house. I know how easily he can be ready for action, engrained in him from being in the armed forces and for years working security.

"I'm perfectly safe, Lizzie."

"You should get a really big dog," she suggests.

I laugh. "I think Simba would have a lot to say about that."

"At least tell me you have a baseball bat by your bed."

"I'm pretty sure it's not legal to defend yourself with a baseball bat." I grin to myself.

"I'd get you out of prison, I promise."

"I don't need a baseball bat. I'd probably only end up injuring myself anyway."

"Did you say you were getting more security at the house?" she asks.

"Yeah. I've got new security lights, front and back garden. I've got CCTV on the front. There are cameras in the house, too. I'll keep everything up until this thing goes away."

"I'll admit, CCTV seems a bit extreme, but I'm glad you have it up, for now."

"I'm perfectly safe," I promise her.

"If you are feeling safe, why are you sounding weird?" Lizzie prods.

"I'm just…off kilter, I guess is the right way to describe it."

"I'm not surprised. Who do you think is behind it?"

"I don't know. I'm feeling suspicious of everybody. I was supposed to be getting waxed on Thursday and even that has got me stressed out."

Lizzie laughs. "You think Cheryl would harm you?"

"How about you get a threatening letter and see if you find yourself getting suspicious," I joke.

"I don't think I'd ever leave the house. You're so much stronger than me, and braver."

"I doubt that. I'm feeling like I'm putting on a brave front, but I'm an anxious mess underneath it all," I admit.

"Maybe you should get an early night. Some sleep always makes me feel better," Lizzie suggests.

"I'm in bed now. I'm going to sleep right after we're done talking."

"In that case, I'm going to wish you goodnight. I'll speak to you in the week, okay?"

"Goodnight, Lizzie," I reply. She wishes me goodnight again and disconnects the call.

I reach over to put my phone on the charger before lying back on the bed. I pull the covers tighter around me, hoping that if I'm wrapped up like a burrito, I'll quickly fall asleep.

∞∞∞∞∞∞∞∞∞

I wake, disoriented. I reach over for my phone, checking the time. It's one in the morning. I hate waking up like this, far too alert, far too early in the morning. I sit up in bed, propping myself up on the pillows because I know getting back to sleep straight away is not going to happen.

The house is silent but it's not unusual. The house has been silent since Caleb left, but even before he left me for Michelle there were long periods where he worked away so I was by myself, but it never bothered me.

I know I'm not going to get back to sleep anytime soon so I get out of the bed, picking my cardigan up from the dressing table chair, pulling it on. I potter down the hallway and down the stairs, planning on getting a glass of water. When I reach the bottom of the stairs, I see Aiden.

He's standing alert at the bottom of the stairs. I assume he's just come out of the living room or my study.

"Are you okay?" he asks.

"I can't get back to sleep. I was just going to get a glass of water," I explain. I walk past him down the hallway, heading towards the kitchen. Aiden falls into step beside me.

"Do you want some warm milk instead?" he asks and I start laughing.

"I'm not some pensioner."

"No, but warm milk can help you fall asleep," he reminds me.

"Fine," I reply, but only because it's been a long time since anybody has made me a drink before bed.

I walk through the kitchen, flicking the light switch for some of the spotlights to come on. I love my kitchen, after my study it is my favourite room in the house.

Aiden looks through my cupboards. I assume he's made himself familiar with the cupboards in the nights he's been here as he doesn't have a problem locating the milk pan, a silicone spoon, a mug. He gets the milk out of the fridge.

"One warm milk coming right up," he says.

"You're not having one?" I ask.

"You forget I'm supposed to be standing watch." Aiden looks at me with a small smile on his face.

"I feel really bad," I admit.

"Why? If I wasn't working here, I would be working somewhere else," he reasons. He measures out some milk and puts it into the milk pan, lighting the hob and putting the pan on it.

I sit up at the breakfast bar, watching him as he stirs the milk around the pan. I clear my throat.

"You don't have anybody at home, getting frustrated that you're not there?" I ask, my voice quiet and soft. It's been a long time since we have talked like this.

"No, I'm not with anybody."

"How long have you been single?" I ask.

"I haven't had anything serious for years." He shrugs. "Have you seen anybody since Caleb?"

"No, I've been single since he left, but it's fine. I like the peace and quiet, plus I've had a lot to deal with."

"I can imagine you have," he muses.

"I kinda miss sex though. Not particularly with Caleb, just in general." I laugh, and he snorts.

"Does that explain the waxing appointment?"

"My cancelled appointment, you mean?"

"If you wanted to go, I can ask Isabelle to take you. Honestly, it wouldn't be weird, for either of us. We've been to worse things with clients."

"It might not be weird for you, but it would feel weird for me."

"Okay, well, if you change your mind, let either of us know. I think we can agree to the beach, too, if there are no more incidents this week," he offers.

"So, what's the worst place you have had to take a client?" I ask.

"Don't try to get information out of me, I sign confidentiality agreements before every assignment," he reminds me, but when he turns away from the hob, I can see he has a small smile on his face.

"I'm betting it involved strippers."

"What can I say, not every client is as innocent as you," he teases.

Aiden pours the heated milk into the mug he'd taken out of the cupboard, turns and crosses the kitchen to put it in front of me.

"Hardly innocent," I scoff.

"Trust me, you're practically an angel," he says, and he has a soft, affectionate look on his face. I open my mouth to protest, to remind him of the things I blame myself for, but he shakes his head. "Don't argue with me. I know you. You're the kindest person I know, under that tough exterior of yours."

"Aiden," I start, but he carries on as if I haven't spoken.

"You're the reason I got through my last year in the army. After Caterina and I split, I struggled, but your emails and updates kept me going. Knowing that if I had a bad day, I could call you and talk about everything and nothing all at once, it got me through."

There are so many responses I could give to this admission, so many responses that could lead us down various paths of thorny subjects, but I don't feel strong enough to take any of those paths tonight. Instead, I look at him and give him a small smile.

"Is that why you'll consider the option of going to the beach?"

"One of the reasons. Besides, I like the beach."

"I'm not going to the beach at night, Aiden," I complain.

"If we go, it'll be me and Isabelle with you."

"You wouldn't have had any sleep," I point out.

"I'm used to it. Besides, I can always grab a few hours' sleep before we go. I'll talk it through with Isabelle," he replies.

"Thank you, for the drink and for thinking about the beach idea," I say, feeling optimistic about the idea of going to the beach at the weekend. I know it would have taken a lot for Aiden to consider it as an option.

He nods and starts to clean away the milk pan. I drink the warm milk he made me. I put the mug back onto the breakfast bar when I'm finished, keeping my hand around the mug, feeling the heat on my palm and fingers.

Aiden reaches for the mug so he can put it in the dishwasher.

"You should get back to bed, Zoey. I'm sure you have a busy day tomorrow," he says.

"Thank you, Aiden. I'll see you in the morning," I reply. He doesn't say anything else as I leave him in the kitchen and head to my bedroom.

I get back into bed and settle under the covers. I still don't feel sleepy. I don't know whether the warm milk is going to make me feel sleepy either, I feel far too hyped up to sleep.

I reach over for my mobile phone and launch the internet, logging into a personal email account that I haven't used in a long time. As soon as I'm logged in, I can see the folder of all the emails between me and Aiden over the years. I haven't read through these in ages, but I used to read through them regularly, remembering how we used to be.

The emails are in date order. I scroll through the hundreds of email threads until I get to the year he and Caterina had broken up. The first week after they'd separated, everything had felt weird. Aiden had been off the radar, only answering my text messages infrequently. Caterina had refused to entertain the conversation with me when I'd pressed her for details about what had happened between them. I'd even reached out to Jonah, and he'd replied with a message that he was travelling and would get in touch when he got back. I felt like I'd been the one left behind in a fractured family.

I open the email chain based on the first email I'd sent Aiden after he'd gone back for his final year, the weekend after he'd broken up with Caterina. I scroll to the start of the email chain, to that first email.

From: ZoTaylor
To: ASlater
Subject: The Power of a Key

So, I was thinking last night about this storage locker key you gave me. You're very trusting, you know that? I could use this key and sell all your possessions. You could get out of the army and find you don't own a single pair of boxer shorts.

How are you? Are you going to tell me what happened between you and Caterina?

From: ASlater
To: ZoTaylor
Subject: RE: The Power of a Key

You realise I wear underwear in the army, right? I have enough to keep me going, should I find that you're a boxer selling fiend and not the honourable person I think you are. Unless you're hard up for cash, in which case, I can transfer you some. It'll be easier than having to replace all my underwear.

I'm fine. How are you? How's the paramedic? Did your mouth survive the blowjob?

From: ZoTaylor
To: ASlater
Subject: RE: The Power of a Key

You can't swing from honourable person to giving blowjobs after the first official date. I told you, it's second date activity. He's nice. We're going out on Thursday night, an official second date, or third if we count Saturday breakfast.

I don't need your money, thanks. I'm pretty sure I earn more than you. Though, worn underwear is apparently a profitable market. Maybe I should look at it as a side business.

Are you going to tell me what happened between you and Caterina?

From: ASlater
To: ZoTaylor
Subject: RE: The Power of a Key

Sorry it's been a while. Been unable to access my emails for a while, busy on a job.

I'm sure that yes, you earn more than me and yes, worn underwear is profitable, but I'm also sure it's more women's underwear that makes the money.

How was the second/third date with the paramedic? If it went well, I assume you have had more, or is he too busy saving lives and you're too busy changing the world to have scheduled something?

From: ZoTaylor
To: ASlater
Subject: RE: The Power of a Key

The paramedic and I have had five dates. He's very nice, ticks all the right boxes.

Everything seems okay, but I feel like there is something missing. I can't put my finger on it, maybe it's just me overthinking things. He seems to have had such a charmed life. His parents have been together since they were teenagers. He's got a brother and sister, they're all successful in their fields, shacked up with the loves of their lives. His family get together every other weekend, shifts depending, and they have dinner together. They have a group family chat. They play board games together. He's totally designed for the whole 2.4 children, house with a picket fence, dutiful wife and golden retriever kinda life.

We're going out tonight. I'll let you know how it goes.

Have you heard from Jonah? He seems to have disappeared from the face of the earth. He doesn't answer my messages.

I'll ask again…Are you going to tell me what happened between you and Caterina?

From: ASlater
To: ZoTaylor
Subject: RE: The Power of a Key

Jonah is fine.

No, I told you, I'm not going to talk about what happened with Caterina. It's over, and that's all there is to say. However—I'm curious—does she know we talk?

From: ZoTaylor
To: ASlater
Subject: RE: The Power of a Key

Of course she does. I don't tell her anything we talk about though, but I won't hide my friendship with you from her, even if neither of you want to admit to me what happened. You're both very frustrating, but I'll take the hint and shut up about it. I'm sure one of you will tell me one day.

From: ASlater
To: ZoTaylor
Subject: RE: The Power of a Key

How was the date with the paramedic? It sounds like you're being put off by this idyllic childhood and family life. Why does that frighten you?

From: ZoTaylor
To: ASlater
Subject: RE: The Power of a Key

You're the one with a psychology degree, and you're asking me why that idyllic family lifestyle frightens me? I thought you graduated top of your class.

From: ASlater
To: ZoTaylor
Subject: RE: The Power of a Key

Oh, I know why it frightens you. I just wondered if you knew.

From: ZoTaylor
To: ASlater
Subject: RE: The Power of a Key

Yeah, I know. Some scars run deep. I know you know what I mean.

From: ASlater
To: ZoTaylor
Subject: RE: The Power of a Key

I do know what you mean. Just don't let a shitty mum and dad be the reason you miss out on everything you deserve. The paramedic might be the right guy for you, he might be your happy ending, but you'll never know if you don't give him a chance.

Sometimes, it's far too easy for us to still be that little kid, with all that hurt around us. When you feel like that, you tell me, and I'll remind you how strong you are.

From: ZoTaylor
To: ASlater
Subject: RE: The Power of a Key

I'll always be the one to remind you how strong you are, too.

I took your advice and gave the paramedic another chance, but I think it'll fizzle out. He's too soft in bed, and yes, before you ask, I gave him more than one opportunity to prove it to me.

From: ASlater
To: ZoTaylor
Subject: RE: The Power of a Key

Okay, I'm laughing, but please tell me you didn't tell him he's too soft in bed? That'll do nothing for his ego.

From: ZoTaylor
To: ASlater
Subject: RE: The Power of a Key

Ha, not like that! That would have done nothing for my ego. I don't have a big ego like yours.

I mean he's too gentle and emotional.

From: ASlater
To: ZoTaylor
Subject: RE: The Power of a Key

My big ego is on a break. We had a weekend off base. I met a woman in a bar. First time I've been with somebody since I got with Caterina. It went fine but took me a while to deal with it in my head. But…life moves on.

From: ZoTaylor
To: ASlater
Subject: RE: The Power of a Key

Life moves on, but I'm always here for you, Aiden.

I close the email thread. That thread took place over the course of three months. He'd started another thread a week later with a different subject title. We talked about everything that whole year. He tells me about women he'd met, one-night stands that left him feeling empty. I tell him about giving Logan another chance and how he'd introduced me to his family, how I'd wished I'd said no because I bailed on our fledgling relationship immediately after, too overwhelmed by what he seemed to want. We console one another and cheer each other on, and I knew through the emails he was feeling better after being blindsided by whatever happened with Caterina.

In my inbox, there are loads of different threads, different subject titles. The last one is titled *got my discharge papers and I'm coming home. Do you want to…*

I know without opening it, the body of his message was 'help me move and eat a shit tonne of pizza?', and I'd replied only with the word 'abso-fucking-lutely'.

As I put my phone away, I feel an ache through my body, an ache for who we were, for how we used to be. I ache for who we became, before everything blew up on us.

It's on my mind as I fall asleep, and I know it'll all haunt my dreams.

11

Aiden

I'm reviewing one of the background checks on one of Zoey's acquaintances when I hear her footsteps coming towards the living room.

"Morning," she says, a smile on her face. She's dressed for work, a black dress on, her hair down instead of the ponytail I've become used to seeing her in.

"Did you sleep well?" I ask.

"Eventually. Warm milk clearly does nothing for me. I wondered if you wanted some breakfast?"

"Breakfast would be nice," I reply, and I put my laptop down. I follow her towards the kitchen.

"Didn't Simba come in last night?" she asks, a frown on her face when she sees the bowl of water and food which looks untouched.

"I'm sure if he had come in, you'd have heard him. I'm still not convinced he's a housecat," I joke.

"He usually comes home at night. I'm sure somebody else is feeding him, so maybe he's shacked up with another family. Typical man, abandoning a steady home in favour of a quick treat." She smiles wryly.

"I'm sure he'll turn up, when he realises that he's much better off here."

"Do you want a cup of tea? I assume a coffee this late in your day would be a disaster," Zoey says, filling the kettle with fresh water.

"Actually, a coffee would be good. I'm taking my parents to the airport today. They're going away for a week. Dad hates the idea of leaving his car in the airport parking, and Mum hates flying without saying goodbye," I explain.

"Where are they off to?" she wonders, flicking the kettle on. "Poached eggs okay, or do you want scrambled?"

"Either is fine. Whatever you prefer. Do you need a hand?"

"No, take a seat. You must be tired," she comments.

"A bit, but I'll last until I get back from the airport. They have an afternoon flight, so I'll drop them off around midday before catching some sleep at home."

I take a seat at the breakfast bar and watch as she gets things ready.

"So, where are they going?" she prompts.

"Oh, France. They've a place in Marseille. They always get away this time of year."

There is the smallest change in the way Zoey holds herself. I notice her spine straighten slightly and her movement slows. She doesn't acknowledge the significance we both know is there. Instead, she busies herself with making coffee and breakfast, eventually pushing a plate with scrambled eggs on toast and a steaming cup of coffee towards me. Unlike yesterday, when she'd stalked off to the dining room with her breakfast, she sits next to me with her own plate of scrambled egg and toast. She has no cup of coffee, and I know she's anticipating that I will take her to the coffee shop, like I'd promised yesterday.

"How are Grace and Richard?" she asks, referring to my parents, genuine interest etched into her facial expression.

"Mum keeps nagging Dad to give up work. She wants to travel the world, apparently."

"Smart woman."

"At some point, I'm going to have to step up to the plate, be the dutiful son and take over from him," I admit with a sigh. I take a forkful of my scrambled eggs and wonder how she's made them so light and fluffy. "This is really nice, Zoey," I comment.

"The eggs?"

"Catching up."

"Well, there's nothing like the threat against your life to bring you closer to people," she snorts.

"You're much calmer than you were on Monday when you phoned," I say, cutting a piece of toast to have with the eggs.

"I think I've levelled off to a new normal." She shrugs and eats some of her scrambled eggs, but I spot that her arm looks like she's been scratching it, irritating the skin near her scar. I put my knife and fork down and reach over to her arm, tracing my finger down the red area.

"Is this your way of accepting a new normal?" I ask, frowning.

"I was just a bit anxious trying to get back to sleep last night. I'm fine today," she reassures me, but her voice is hitched slightly so I take my hand away from her. I focus back on my breakfast. Zoey does the same and we don't talk again until the plates are cleared.

"That was great, thanks Zoey. Much better than the sad sandwich from the petrol station I thought would end up being my breakfast," I joke.

"I'm starting to think your security job is just an elaborate way to get people to feed you proper food." She tuts as she clears the plates from the side, putting them into the dishwasher along with the pan she'd used to make the eggs. I finish my coffee and then get up to put my mug into the dishwasher.

"Let me know when you're ready to go into the office," I say, planning on heading to the living room to get my things.

"Oh, I'll be ready in a second. I just need to get my jacket from upstairs," she replies, and then she heads towards the stairs. I leave the kitchen door open for the cat as I'm sure he'll come home for food when we're gone, and I wouldn't trust that cat not to eat through the door to get to his food.

Zoey's back downstairs quickly, joining me in the hallway near the front door. I unlock the front door, stepping into the porch, Zoey behind me. She locks the front door as I scan the driveway before unlocking the porch door. She locks up behind me and then I walk her to my car, letting her into the passenger seat. There's nobody around on her street, the road is quiet. As soon as she's settled into the car, I open the app on my phone, setting the motion sensors to active, then I start to drive towards her office.

The roads are deserted given it is early, but I still scan around, looking for potential threats as I drive her towards the office. Zoey sits in the passenger seat, tapping away on her phone, a small smile on her face.

"Are you looking at dating profiles? You know I'd need to background check them all, right? I bet if I search hard enough, I can find out all their kinky habits, save you a bit of legwork," I tease. I remember her words from last night, telling me she missed sex.

"Fuck off, you deviant. I'm texting Lizzie." She rolls her eyes, but she has a smile on her face. We're about halfway to her office. We're going to be early meeting Isabelle, even factoring in stopping at the coffee shop. It doesn't bother me though. I don't mind chatting with Zoey, especially since she seems much more relaxed than our terse exchange on Monday.

"Is Lizzie married?" I ask. The team at work that investigate the close acquaintances haven't yet returned anything about Lizzie, and although her social media is wide open, there isn't much on there, other than posts about her pets and her time with Zoey. If she's changed her name recently, that might be why we haven't found anything. That, or she's saintly. It's unusual for people not to have something about their life online these days.

"No, she's not married," Zoey replies.

The beep of my mobile phone stops me replying. It's the alert tone I'd set up for the motion detectors I've set up in Zoey's front garden.

"Are you expecting anybody at your house today?" I ask.

"Why?"

"Motion detector," I explain. "Maybe it's the post."

"No, I get my post held at the post office and collect it once a week." Zoey is quiet for a minute, a frown on her face. "Maybe a delivery that I've forgotten about. I usually get a subscription delivery around this time in the month. I might have just missed the reminder email on the date they're sending it. They'll just leave it behind the planters in the garden, that's what they usually do."

"I can check the cameras when we get to the coffee shop. I assume you want to go there this morning?" I glance over at her.

"Yes, please," she replies. She's quiet for a second. "Oh shit. I need to go back to the house. I've forgotten my laptop. I'm sorry."

"No problem. We have time before we're supposed to meet Isabelle. I'll message her to update when we get back to yours."

"I feel like an idiot, I'm sorry."

"You're acting like you've committed a crime." I laugh as I turn the car off the side street so I can turn around and go back to Zoey's.

"I can't believe I forgot it. I don't know where my mind is at." She sighs and puts her phone away in her bag.

"Zoey, it's been a stressful week. You can't expect yourself to be perfect all the time," I chide.

She doesn't reply, she just sits and looks out of the window as I drive us back towards her house. The roads are still quiet.

I pull my car onto her driveway. She unclips her seatbelt and we both walk down her driveway.

I spot it before Zoey does, and I step in front of her.

"What's the matter?" she asks with a little huff of laughter.

"Go wait in the car," I bark, much harder than I intended.

"Aiden, what's going on?" she asks, trying to look around me.

"Zoey," I warn, but she steps around me, gasping when she sees the same thing I've seen, the body of Simba the cat, hung by his neck on her porch door. Smeared onto the window in what appears to be blood are the words *you're next.*

"Oh my God," Zoey gasps and she kneels over, vomiting into a large ceramic planter which resides next to the porch. I'm quick enough to grab her hair and hold it back. She heaves for a second time but nothing else comes out of her. She sinks to the floor, resting against the side of the porch, her head in her hands, shaking.

"I'm calling the police, and I'm asking Isabelle to come here," I tell her, already pulling my phone out of my pocket. "We'll have captured them on camera, Zoey," I add, though I know it'll be of little comfort to her.

She looks up at me, her eyes brimming with tears.

"Who would do something like that to an innocent cat?" she sobs. I sit on the floor next to her, pulling her close to me in a hug. She weeps against me.

"I'm so sorry, Zoey," I murmur.

I should be calling the police right now to explain what has happened, to report this as a crime, to demand they turn up right now and find the culprit. Instead, I keep my arm around her, texting Isabelle with my free hand, telling her to come to Zoey's and asking her to call the police, adding the words that her cat was killed. I click send, then wrap my other arm around Zoey, pulling her closer.

∞∞∞∞∞∞∞∞∞

The police arrive at the same time as Isabelle's car screeches to a stop outside of Zoey's house. I'd managed to convince Zoey to sit in the car, more comfortable than on the floor and at least Simba is out of sight. In the time we have been waiting, I've reviewed the security camera recording, keeping it from Zoey as she doesn't need to see again how they'd treated her cat.

I get out of the car, ready to give an update to everybody. I groan slightly when I see it is Officer West, but at least he's flanked by Officer Kim.

"I'll stay with Zoey," Isabelle offers, a sympathetic look on her face.

"Do you want to tell me what has happened?" Officer Kim asks.

I gesture towards the house. "It's over here. We haven't been inside the property. We got home and this was waiting for us. We haven't been away long. There is a video of the person coming to the door, but they're wearing a balaclava, but maybe the video will help with your investigation."

"I'm assuming you can account for your whereabouts?" Officer West asks. I want to deck this guy, he's a real piece of work.

"You have got to be fucking kidding me," a voice mutters from the car, then Zoey is on her feet, standing in front of Officer West, her hands on her hips. "Aiden was with me. He was driving me to work. How the hell do you think he managed to orchestrate this when he was with me?" Zoey continues to snap.

"It would be easy enough to have an accomplice," Officer West mutters.

"Zoey, calm down," Isabelle warns, but Zoey is on a roll.

"Before you start with the snide innuendo, Aiden was watching over the house all night. The security system will show he never left the house until we went to work," she continues, a look of fury on her face. This is Zoey when she's pushed to the edge and defending where she sees injustice. If it wasn't for everybody standing around us, I'd hug her.

"I am sure Mr Slater can take us through all of this today." Officer West sounds snippy, glaring over at me. Still Zoey isn't done. She steps in front of him.

"I'm not finished talking. No, Aiden will not take you through anything. He has something he needs to do this morning. Isabelle is perfectly capable of showing you what you need, and if you have any questions for Aiden, you can come here and ask them later, when he is doing his job, as you ought to be." Zoey finishes her rant. I look at Officer Kim, ignoring Officer West who frankly looks like he's never been put in his place before.

"I have to take my parents to the airport. You have my number, if you have any other questions," I remind him. He nods.

"Zoey, why don't you tell me what happened this morning?" he suggests to Zoey.

"Aiden, I'll see you later, at the office." She directs this to me. I'm torn, wanting to stay here and support her, knowing I need to get my parents to the airport.

"I can…" I start, but she shakes her head.

"Go. I'll be okay with Isabelle."

Zoey turns her attention to the police officers. Isabelle gives me a small smile.

"I'll look after her," Isabelle promises.

I get into my car, checking my watch. I'll have just enough time to get to my parent's house and take them to the airport. I linger on the driveway for a moment. I take my phone out of my pocket, firing a text to Isabelle.

Do not let her out of your sight, not for a single second. And make sure she eats lunch.

∞∞∞∞∞∞∞∞

"Here you go, safe and sound, delivered to the airport in one piece," I joke. It sounds forced to me, but my parents don't seem to notice. Mum's been complaining about my driving the whole way to the airport, apparently the stress of this morning has given me a heavy foot on the accelerator.

"Are you okay, Aiden?" Mum asks as I park up. It's too long a conversation to have in the carpark of the airport, given how much they charge per minute for parking here. I'm sure there are probably strippers who are cheaper than parking at the airport.

"All good, Mum. Just a bit of stress at the job I'm on," I say as I get out of the car. I walk to the back of the car so I can get their cases out of the boot.

"What's going on?" Dad asks. I should have kept everything to myself because he might not like me having taken the job on, but he likes to keep on top of all the business.

"Somebody killed her cat this morning," I explain, feeling sick as I think about the cat.

"That's awful," Mum exclaims.

"The police are on it. I captured some images on the security camera, hopefully the police will be able to do something with it." I hand Mum her case and reach into the car for Dad's. He's busy checking through his carry-on bag, presumably for their passports because this is a routine I know well. I don't think we have ever travelled without him doing this same old double check before he's willing to enter the airport.

"You look exhausted," Mum comments.

"This one means a lot," I admit.

"Why so?" she asks. Dad's still busy with his bag.

"It's Zoey," I whisper to Mum. Mum's hand flies to her mouth to stifle her gasp.

"Oh my goodness," she exclaims.

"What's the matter, Grace?" Dad asks, finally locating the passports.

"His client, it's Zoey," Mum murmurs.

Dad grabs his suitcase from me. The expression on his face is exactly the one I'd imagined he would have.

"Get this case wrapped up now," he snaps.

"I'm not rushing it, Dad, and I'm not going to leave her defenceless. Some sick bastard just killed her cat and hung it on her door," I snap at him. Dad looks frustrated, like he knows he's not going to win this argument with me. I wasn't going to walk away the moment Zoey got the envelope, somebody will have to drag my dead body away from her now.

"Come on, Grace, we'll be late for our flight." Dad hustles Mum across the carpark and towards the departures entrance at the airport. He doesn't look back, but Mum does. The expression on her face is still shocked and a little worried. Then she turns back and follows Dad.

I close the boot of the car, get into the driver's seat ready to drive out of the carpark. I knew it was a bad idea for them to know I've been in touch with Zoey. It's been years since I mentioned Zoey in front of them. I should've known they would react like this, but the morning has thrown me off kilter.

Before I can drive away, my phone beeps. I'd switched off the functions in the car to read my messages aloud, not wanting Mum and Dad to hear my messages, so I open my phone to look at what has arrived. It's a message from Isabelle, reassuring me that Zoey is okay, promising again that she won't leave her side and, of course, she'll make sure she gets lunch.

I send a message back, telling her thanks. Then I drive out of the carpark, heading home, desperate for my bed.

∞∞∞∞∞∞∞

Zoey and Isabelle are waiting for me in the carpark of Zoey's office when I get there in the evening. I park up next to Isabelle's car and get out of my own.

"What's gone off?" I ask, surprised to see them both outside.

"Zoey's tired and keen to get home," Isabelle explains. Zoey gets into the passenger seat of my car. She looks exhausted.

"She should have gone home hours ago." I sigh, watching as she settles into the seat, clipping her seatbelt on, resting her head against the window.

"I don't think she knew what to do with herself today," Isabelle says, glancing into the car, sympathy on her face.

"How was it with the police this morning?" I ask.

"That second officer is going to take over everything, apparently. They took a copy of all the CCTV. They took the cat away too. Zoey wants him back, when they're done. She says she wants to bury him properly. I cleaned up the door when they'd done, before I drove her to work. It wasn't blood. It looked like cornstarch and food dye. I suggested she stay somewhere else, but she was adamant about going home."

"I did tell you she was stubborn," I remind her.

"Well, I tried, she shot me down in flames."

"Just so you know, my dad knows this is Zoey's case. If he tries to pull you off the case, can you let me know?" I ask. Isabelle frowns.

"I don't know what happened between you, Zoey and your dad but Richard's not going to put somebody in harm's way."

"I'm just being over-cautious. We'll swap over here tomorrow, okay?"

"Sure. Take care, Aiden." Isabelle looks troubled but then she gets into her car, driving towards the exit barrier of the car park. I get into my car and look at Zoey.

"Don't," she says. Her eyes are closed.

"Don't what?" I smile to myself.

"Whatever lecture you want to give, about how I underestimated the situation, or that I shouldn't have gone to work today, or that I should go stay somewhere else, or whatever else might cross your mind…I'm too tired for it," she complains, eyes still closed.

"Actually, I was going to thank you for having my back with the police this morning."

Her eyes fly open, and she turns to look at me.

"Of course I'd have your back, Aiden. Plus, that guy is a dickhead."

"I think you made him feel about five inches tall this morning," I joke.

"Which would be about four inches taller than he should have felt," she scowls.

"Well, thanks, anyway." I shrug and start the car.

We drive home in silence, Zoey alternating her time either staring out the window or sitting with her eyes closed. When we pull up to the house, she doesn't immediately get out of the car, instead she waits for me to get out and look around first. There doesn't seem to be anything untoward now, so she gets out of the car and follows me to the house.

Once inside, she heads to the kitchen. I follow her and watch as she picks up the bowls of cat food and water from the floor, dumping the biscuits in the bin, the dishes into the dishwasher.

"I have been thinking about those bowls all day, every meeting I had, I was thinking *'his food is still in the kitchen'*, knowing he'll never come home for it," she says with a shaky voice. She takes a deep breath. "Do you want something to eat? I have some chilli I defrosted, I was going to reheat that and make some rice."

"I can eat with you," I reply, and then I can see she looks exhausted. "Why don't you go relax in the living room, and I'll make the chilli?" I suggest.

I half expect her to protest, but instead she nods. "That would be great. I'm going to get changed and I'll be in the living room."

I watch as she walks out the kitchen. I can hear her on the stairs and then the sounds above me as she moves around in her bedroom. I take a quick look in Zoey's freezer, finding it neatly organised, food she appears to have batch cooked and frozen in single portions. I open the fridge to find the chilli she had talked about. I know from experience, it'll be spicy as hell, just the way I like it.

I work in the kitchen, getting the food ready. I don't rush, trying to give Zoey enough time to relax before I disturb her. I finish the rice and chilli, putting everything into two large bowls from her cupboard, grabbing two spoons. I take everything through to the living room. I know she has the dining room and the breakfast bar to eat at, but sometimes there is nothing better than sitting on the sofa with something hot and nourishing.

Zoey's asleep on the sofa. For a moment, I wonder if I should leave her asleep, but I know she should eat before it gets too late. I put both bowls onto the floor so I can shake her arm gently.

"Zo, come on, you need to eat," I coax. She takes a deep breath as she wakes and then sits up on the sofa. She's changed into a pair of pyjamas.

"Sorry, I didn't mean to doze off," she apologises.

"I wasn't sure if I should wake you, but the chilli looks really good." I smile at her, picking up the two bowls and handing one to her. She breathes in the scent of the chilli and gives a small smile.

"I think it's always twice as spicy after it's been frozen and reheated," she says.

"I'm sure I'll manage," I reply. We both settle on the sofa, bowls in our laps. I take my first spoonful and the flavours hit me like a bomb. "I swear, nobody has ever made me a hotter chilli." I smile at her once I've swallowed the first spoonful.

"Caleb hated it. He hated anything spicy or hot."

"That's because he's a wet lettuce," I remind her.

We eat for a while in silence. Halfway through her bowl, Zoey looks at me.

"He told me that I was not capable of loving somebody apart from myself," she tells me.

"What a wanker."

She snorts. "So, you're aiming for a wanking wet lettuce as an assessment of his character?"

"Yes, I am. There's not much else I can say about him, but you know I never liked him." I shrug. I eat some more of my chilli, and she finishes hers. When we're both finished, we walk through to the kitchen together. I put everything in the dishwasher.

"I think I'm going to go upstairs to read, maybe call Lizzie and tell her everything that happened today. Do you mind?" she asks.

"Of course not, you're supposed to go about your normal life," I remind her.

"Goodnight, Aiden," she says. She starts to walk out of the kitchen.

"Zoey?"

She stops to look at me. "Yeah?"

"You know what Caleb said was complete bullshit, right?"

"Yeah, but he was partly right. I didn't love him the way I should have." She gives me a little shrug.

"Do you think he ever knew?" I ask.

"What, that I cheated on him? No, I don't think he knew. I don't know why he didn't realise, but maybe that's why he said what he did. People who love, they don't cheat, and I feel like that behaviour has defined my whole life. So, maybe he's not that far off the mark, after all," she says.

"Zoey," I start.

"Goodnight, Aiden," she repeats her earlier sentiment, and then she walks out of the kitchen, refusing to carry on the conversation with me.

She judges herself harshly, but we both know all too well that the first time she cheated, it wasn't on a man, it was on her best friend, and I helped her do it.

12
Zoey

Seven Years Ago

"Zoey!" Aiden calls out to me. He waves as I cross the road to join him.

"Hey, how are you doing?" I ask, throwing my arms around him.

"Better for seeing you." He flashes me a grin.

"You always act like you haven't seen me in ages," I say, punching him softly on the arm.

"Zo, if that's your version of self-defence, you have to join me the next time I go to jiu-jitsu," he jokes.

"Fortunately, I wasn't trying to hurt you." I roll my eyes at him.

"Good, because that was shit. Come on, before the film starts without us." He gestures towards the cinema behind us. We walk in together.

"My turn to get the treats," I remind him as he puts his card into the machine to print off the pre-booked tickets he's already paid for, despite it being my turn.

"Have you told her yet that we're meeting up?" he asks as we walk towards the counter where the popcorn, hotdogs and nachos are giving off a heavenly smell.

"No." I sigh, and I feel guilty. "She knows we've talked, but not that we meet up."

Aiden has been home after finishing the army for seven months. I've seen him once a week since. The first time was when he picked up the boxes that he'd stored at the storage unit, and he needed me to turn up with the key. That day, I ended up helping him move his things into his new place. It's a flat on the opposite side of town to where Caterina and I live. I'd helped him clean it, unpack his boxes, taken in his deliveries of a bed, sofa, dining table, bookcase. I'd helped him build the flatpack and put everything away with him. To thank me, he'd asked me for dinner the following week.

The following week, we'd met in a sports bar near his where we'd caught up over plates of overly cheesy lasagna and slices of garlic bread. We'd talked about his final year in the army, where he'd been, the skills he'd learnt. He'd told me he was going to work for his father, getting his licence to be a personal bodyguard and providing personal security. His training would take some time but once he had some experience, it offered him the opportunity of working abroad with clients. He told me he was excited about the future. I'd talked about where the business was and how proud I was for what we were building, how everything was unfolding. We avoided the topic of Caterina, like two friends from formerly warring countries who couldn't bring up the topic of the war fought.

The next week, I invited him to a football match that I'd been given tickets for. We'd eaten pie and chips, cheered along the team and drank slightly warm beer from plastic cups. The following week, he invited me to join a bunch of his friends from the army when they went paintballing. I'd ended up bruised in several places, hiding them from Caterina by wearing too long sleeves required in the weather because I didn't know how to explain them. The week after, I had tickets to a festival and Caterina was supposed to go with me, but her parents had invited her to join them on holiday, skiing in Italy. Instead of letting the tickets go to waste, I'd invited Aiden and we'd stood in the field, singing our hearts out to the bands on stage.

Since then, Aiden and I have fallen into the habit of watching the previous weeks cinema release together. The film is released on the Friday, and we wait until the Wednesday to watch the film and get a drink afterwards. Caterina never asks where I have been.

"I think you should tell her," Aiden says when we reach the front of the queue. He orders our usual, he always has nachos, which I invariably steal half from his tray. I always have a hotdog and we split a bag of popcorn.

"She still cares for you," I tell him. Any time I've mentioned speaking to Aiden, Caterina gets a longing on her face.

"She needs to move on. It's been a lifetime," he mutters. I pay for our items, and I pick up the popcorn and my hotdog.

"But you'd planned a lifetime together. She's struggling that all of that was taken away from her. She had the dress picked, Aiden. She had plans for what you'd call your children," I remind him, keeping my tone gentle.

"That future is gone, Zoey," he says, firmly. He picks up his nacho tray and we walk towards the guy manning the barrier for the admission to the screenings.

"Perhaps if you talked to her, told her why, she might…" I start, but the huff he gives stops me talking.

"She knows. All that bullshit she gives you about how I broke up with her and never told her why, it's a lie. She knows why. Don't let her keep playing the victim."

"What happened between you?" I ask. I've asked before, but whenever I ask Caterina, she tells me Aiden's decision was out of the blue and whenever I ask Aiden, he's evasive.

"That's between me and Caterina." Aiden passes the tickets to the guy, and he beams at us.

"Nice to see you again. I could set my watch by you two," he says, handing our tickets back to Aiden.

"We're becoming predictable, Zo," Aiden says with a laugh. I smile at the guy and then follow Aiden so we can find our theatre.

"Maybe next week we should do something different," I comment. Aiden stops at the door to our theatre.

"Only if you tell Caterina that we meet up."

"Fine," I grumble. He opens the door wide for me and I step past him, leading the way to find our seats.

∞∞∞∞∞∞∞∞∞

After the film finishes, Aiden and I go to a bar for a drink. We've both caught the bus into town for the film, like we usually do. I order us both a cider as Aiden grabs a table for us.

"Here with a friend?" The man standing at the bar next to me asks.

"Yes, you?" I ask. I'm hoping the bartender will hurry up with my drinks because I don't want to be drawn into conversation and the guy next to me looks like he's a chatty type.

"Let me pay for your drinks," he offers. "My name is Jasper."

"Thanks for the offer, but I'm okay." I pull my cashcard out of my jeans pocket.

"Don't I at least get a name?" He laughs.

I tap my foot, feeling impatient at the barman. I look around behind me to see if I can see Aiden.

"Here you go," the barman says, handing the drinks over and he brings the machine to me but before I can pay, Jasper has swiped his card on the machine, the beep indicating he's been charged. He grins at me.

"What are you doing? I said no thanks," I snap.

"I'm just paying for your drinks, where is the harm in that?" Jasper is still grinning at me.

"The point is I said no."

"Not now I've paid for them, but you can get your next drinks in, unless I'm too quick for you again." He leers at me.

"Typical man, being too quick," I mutter. I grab both glasses from the bar and step away from him, looking for where Aiden is seated. Before I can take a step, Jasper grabs my arm, pulling me backwards. The drink sloshes over the top of the glasses.

"You don't get to talk to me like that, I just paid for your drinks, you should say thank you," Jasper snaps.

"What the hell are you playing at?" I exclaim. He doesn't let go of my arm.

"Take your fucking hands off her." Aiden seems to appear out of nowhere. The expression on his face is dark and dangerous.

"Yeah, mate, this is between me and her," Jasper spits. Aiden grabs Jasper's hand, twisting it up and behind his back. The sudden move makes Jasper yelp.

"She's my friend, but even if she wasn't, I'd make it my business to interfere if you're going to treat somebody like that. Now why don't you skulk back to the dark corner you came from, and try to be a better man," Aiden hisses. He lets go of Jasper's arm.

I half expect Jasper to react, but whatever Aiden has done to his arm appears to render Jasper immobile for a minute. Aiden nods in the direction of the table he'd managed to secure. I walk with him, glaring at Jasper over my shoulder. I put the drinks down on the table and try to shake the spilt cider from my hands.

"Asshole," I mutter.

"Wanker," Aiden clarifies.

"He's the exact reason why the business is going so well. Imagine if he's a tradesperson. If he's willing to be leery and grab hold of me in a crowded bar, what is he willing to do in a private home with a female client?" I sit down.

"He's the exact reason why my dad's business does well. The number of clients we have who are female and need protection because they're being stalked or threatened, it is mind blowing." Aiden sighs.

"It's like we're on opposite ends of the see-saw. I try to prevent people being put in that situation, and you deal with it when everything has failed," I muse.

"That's depressing."

"Maybe, but at least we're doing something about it rather than just living the status quo and turning a blind eye."

"I have my first overseas assignment coming up," Aiden comments.

"Oh Aiden, that's amazing. When?"

"Week after next. I'll be gone for three weeks," he says.

"Well, here's to you." I lift my glass to toast him. I know how hard he's been working and I know he wouldn't have an overseas assignment if he'd been doing poorly. I expected nothing less from Aiden though, he's dedicated to everything he puts his mind to, and I expect he's worked extra hard to impress his father.

Despite my excitement and pride for what he is doing, I get a funny feeling in my stomach. I wonder how dangerous the job he'll be doing. It can't be any more dangerous than when he'd been in the army, where he'd been stationed overseas and had seen things he doesn't like to talk about, but I still feel anxious about the job he'll be doing.

∞∞∞∞∞∞∞∞∞

'Wednesday. My place. Bring workout gear.' Aiden's text arrives on Monday. Usually, he'd text the name and time of the film we're seeing. A second text arrives. *'Did you tell Caterina?'*

I can hear Caterina in the kitchen, looking through the cupboards and fridge, sounding disgruntled at what she finds in there.

"I think we should go out for food," she calls.

"We went out for food yesterday," I remind her.

"Zoey, you can be such a spoilsport," she mutters as she comes into the living room.

I laugh. "I'll cook us something."

"I guess I'll help," she says, her tone dramatic.

"Come on. Kitchen." I grin.

I tuck my phone into my pocket and walk with her. I open the fridge and pull out the chicken breasts I'd got when I did the shopping, planning on making a pie. It won't be the five-star meal she's used to, but it'll be nice to eat something homecooked, just the two of us at the table.

"What do you want me to do?" she asks.

"Take a seat and listen to me for a moment," I say in a rush, suddenly feeling brave.

She grins at me as she takes a seat. "Oh, this sounds ominous."

"It's about Aiden," I blurt out. Once I say his name, I know she won't let me chicken out of telling her what I need to say.

"What about him? Oh my God, is he seeing somebody else?" she exclaims.

"First, I'll remind you that you have dated a lot since you two broke up," I point out, but her dating has never been serious. She always compares them to Aiden, back in the days she spoke positively about him.

She pouts. "That doesn't mean I want the bastard dating somebody else."

"This isn't about him dating. I told you I spoke to him, that we message."

"Yeah."

"It's just a bit more than that. I see him occasionally. By occasionally, I mean I see him weekly. I'm sorry Caterina, I knew it would upset you, but he's my friend too." Every word is a rush.

She doesn't talk for a full minute, but it feels like much longer than that.

"Does he talk about me?"

"Not really," I reply as gently as I can.

"I can't stop you, Zo. You're right, he was your friend." She shrugs as she talks and then she pulls her mobile phone from her back pocket. She taps away on the screen.

"Who are you texting?"

"Jonah. I'm asking him if he knew that you see Aiden."

"Why would that bother Jonah?" I laugh. Jonah moved further away for his job a couple of months ago, he barely gets opportunity to see us.

"Aiden is rude to Jonah; did you know that?"

"It's none of my business." I sigh. Jonah and Aiden's relationship has always been complicated, something Caterina never really understood. I don't think she's ever had a cross word with her family or had one of her brothers be as hurtful to her as Jonah sometimes is to Aiden.

"Okay, well, don't come crying to us when Aiden ghosts you, the way he did us."

"I won't. I just want to make sure you're okay with me being friends with him."

"Yeah, it's fine. Just, if you know he starts dating again, find out who it is, so I can kill the bitch."

"Caterina," I admonish, and she laughs.

"Get cooking Zoey, otherwise I'm going to make you take me out for food."

I look at the chicken breasts. The date is good for another couple of days. Caterina seems relaxed at what I've just told her about Aiden. I smile at her.

"Screw it, let's go to the pub."

"We deserve it." Caterina grins back at me.

"We do, but hurry up, before I change my mind." I joke, putting the chicken back into the fridge.

"I'm just going to change," Caterina says, and she heads out of the kitchen. I pull my phone out and text Aiden.

'Told her. Still breathing. See you on Wed.'

His response is almost immediate. *'Good. Looking forward to it, Zo.'*

I put my phone away and wait for Caterina, ready to give her my full attention for the rest of the night.

∞∞∞∞∞∞∞∞

"Okay, why exactly did I need to bring workout gear?" I ask as Aiden opens the door for me on Wednesday. He's wearing grey sweatpants and a top, the white tee-shirt stretched across his chest. He's also wearing a wide grin, so I know he's got something ridiculous planned.

"Come in, go get changed," he suggests. I've come straight from the office and my smart trouser suit is on the opposite end of what he is wearing.

"There had better be something more exciting than exercise, Aiden. I'm giving up our treats, blockbuster films and cider for this." I pout.

He laughs. "Stop stalling. I'll feed you afterwards."

I kick off my high heels, drop my work bag and handbag in the hallway with the shoes and then take my tote bag with me to the bathroom. His bathroom is neat and tidy, much cleaner than most men's bathrooms I've been in. I strip off out of my clothes, standing naked for a moment in his bathroom before I pull on the clothes I'd exercise in. Sports bra. Boy short underwear instead of my usual Brazilian style. Light weight top and yoga pants. I pull my hair up into a ponytail, fold up my other clothes and then go to find Aiden.

He is in the living space. The dining table he has in there, he's pushed it to the far wall, and the rest of his furniture has been rearranged, clearing a space in the centre of the room where he has placed some soft looking mats.

"What on earth are we doing?" I laugh.

"I'm going to teach you some basic jiu-jitsu, to see if I can entice you to come training with me." He grins at me.

"Jiu-jitsu? Not kickboxing?" I grin back at him.

"I want you to know how to defend yourself. Everybody should learn some self-defence. You need to know how to fight back if your life was ever on the line. I thought I could show you a few moves and then you can decide if you want to train."

"Fine, what are you going to show me? Let's get this over with so you can feed me, before this turns nasty," I joke.

"I'm going to teach you how to get out of a situation if a guy has you on the ground. The position I'll do is the mount, and I'll show you how to get away."

"The mount? You make me sound like a barn animal." I laugh.

"Lie down, Rambo." Aiden grins. I lie on the floor, my knees bent. "Okay?" he asks.

I nod. "Mount me, Aiden," I joke.

He snorts but then gets into position. He straddles across my hips, his ass just above my pelvis, the back of his thighs resting on mine.

"This is a dangerous position if somebody has you on the ground. From here, they could hurt you, cause a lot of damage. What's your instinct?" he asks.

"To punch you," I reply, and I extend my arm from the floor like a mock punch. His hands are free, and he blocks me effortlessly, then holds my arm. My elbow locks into place, and my arm is rod straight. I get the sense it would be easy for him to hurt my arm, to pin me down.

"No, your best option is to get out from under me," Aiden explains.

"You're so much bigger than me," I complain. He's only about five inches taller than me, but he's so much stronger, and the idea I can get from underneath him feels like a joke.

"It's about using my strength against me. If you're down on the ground like this, somebody could try to choke you. It only takes a couple of seconds and a couple pounds of force to become unconscious."

"There goes my plans to try choking during sex," I joke.

"Zoey," he warns.

162

"Fine, o mighty master, teach me your wise ways."

"Grab my arm," he says, a grin back on his face. I grab his wrist.

"Like this?"

"No. It's much stronger if you grip like this," Aiden says, and he holds my wrist with thumbs and fingers together to show me what he means. "Grab the wrist like this, and then use your other hand to grip like you would usually do, around their forearm."

"Like this?" I follow his instructions.

"Yep, now, your foot should do this," he starts, reaching behind him with his free hand, grabbing my foot and moving it into the position he wants. "Then this leg, push up with it." He taps the opposite leg to the one he's moved to hook around his leg. "Then move your hips, use all your strength here to flip me over." He puts a hand on my stomach.

"Ready?" I ask.

He puts his free arm back against me, like he is using it to attack.

"Ready, but for future reference, try to take an attacker by…"

I follow through the instructions he's just told me and amazingly I manage to flip him over me so that he lands onto the floor, me on top.

"By surprise?" I finish his sentence. For a second, I feel smug that I've managed to do it on my first attempt, but before I can tell him I'm a master, he's flipped us back around again and I'm on the ground.

"Time to be smug when you've got away from an attacker," Aiden teases.

"Fine, come on, teach me more, but I bet by the end of the session, I can beat your ass."

He laughs. "Bring it, Rambo."

∞∞∞∞∞∞∞∞

Aiden teaches me various moves for the next forty-five minutes. I've worked up a sweat and my muscles are aching, but I feel like I have learnt a lot.

"One more move, then we can get something to eat," he suggests.

"You're a pain in the ass, Aiden," I grumble because I'm getting hungry.

"You want to stop? Make me." His tone is light and teasing. I'm still on the ground and he stands above me.

"I think it's time for me to show you my own moves," I joke, and I lift my leg, extending it out. I'm aiming to push against his stomach, but my foot lands lower than I'd anticipated, connecting instead to his groin. For a second, neither of us move.

"Zoey, that's my dick," Aiden says gruffly.

"Is it? I can barely feel it, the ladies must be so disappointed," I tease.

"You can't belittle somebody into submission if they attack you," he groans at my apparently poor student attitude.

"No, but I'm pointing out the area I'd go for, should the need arise." I move my foot as I talk. His eyes darken slightly.

"Rookie mistake, I told you to keep your leg straight, to stop somebody doing this," he says, and he pushes against the leg I've been pointing at him. My unbent knee offers little resistance to him, my leg falling and hitting the floor as he lands on top of me. He shifts his position, straddled over my waist, his hands on my shoulders. "So, how are you getting out of this one?" he teases. I don't feel unsafe under him because these are all moves that he showed me earlier, but there's still a flutter of butterflies in me, a strange anxious feeling rather than fear, like the air in the room has suddenly changed density.

"You forget I can do this," I say, and I do the move he taught me earlier, grabbing his wrist with one hand, his forearm with my other, hooking my foot around his ankle, pushing my pelvis up and using all my core strength to flip us over. He lands on the floor with a thud and with me now sitting on his pelvis.

I try to focus. I know the next move that he taught me is how to retreat from this position safely, to get away from an attacker, but I cannot for the life of me summon the will to move from this position. I know I should, I just...can't. I'm suddenly hyper aware of how firm his body feels below me, especially the place I'd previously been telling him was too small for my foot to notice, because, joking aside, it's now not anything I can ignore.

Aiden is perfectly able to move, I know this because he demonstrated it earlier. Except, he doesn't move either. Instead, I move above him. It's only the smallest fraction of an inch but he moans underneath me, and I feel an explosion in me, like every nerve has been switched on. His moan is the singular, sexiest sound I've ever heard.

"Zo," he murmurs. I stare at him, his pupils are large, his eyes dark, his expression fierce. I know this is when I should get up. He shifts slightly and now it's my turn to moan, a little whimper of need and red-hot desire.

He holds my gaze. The air seems charged around us and there is utter silence in the room.

One. Two. Infinity.

He reaches and strokes my cheek, his fingers gentle on my skin.

"How the hell would I ever be able to tell her," I whisper, thinking of Caterina, thinking of what a betrayal it would be if I was brave enough to lean forward, into what we both seem to be feeling.

"How the hell can I live the rest of my life without regret, if I don't tell you how I feel?" His voice is soft and gentle.

"How," I start.

"I love you, Zoey. I've been falling in love with you every day. I know it's complicated, but how I feel about you, how I think you feel about me too, it's too much to ignore. I love you," he murmurs.

His hand is still on my cheek and my heart is thudding in my chest. I think of everything that has been going on between us since he came home. How the days I see him are the highlight of my week. How the feeling I'd felt when he said he was doing a job overseas was because, deep down, I knew I would miss him. How I've denied what I have been feeling, because of Caterina.

"I love you too," I whisper. "But…" I start, because although this man on the ground beneath me is everything I want to have, and although he's captured my heart, he still belonged to the person who means the world to me. I didn't realise until right now just how deeply I feel about Aiden. I want so badly to be selfish, to take what I want, but I know it will break Caterina's heart.

"Don't overthink this, Zoey. What we feel, it's pure, it's real," he urges.

"I…" I start again.

His hand slides down, his fingers caressing down my chest, skimming along my side. The touch of him makes me shiver, the movement of my hips again making it painfully clear how much both of us seem to want to give in.

"Kiss me, Zoey. One kiss, and then tell me you can walk away," he murmurs.

I lean forward, my lips meeting his. As soon as our lips touch, any thoughts of what I should be doing disappear. His tongue moves against mine and his fingers slip underneath my top. I move above him. I can feel his erection and every fibre of my being protests about the few layers of fabric that exists between us. I need more of him, right now.

Aiden appears to have the same thought as me as the next second, he's rolled us over and I'm back in the position on the floor, his body above me. The position he has me in is delicious. He carries on kissing me, his tongue exploring, his teeth occasionally nipping my bottom lip, making me gasp and pant and writhe underneath him.

Aiden pulls my thighs, hooking my legs around his waist. With a swiftness and movement that seems to defy the laws of physics, he manages to get up from the floor, pulling me with him, until he's stood, holding me, my arms and legs wrapped around him. He covers my face with a flutter of kisses and then strides towards the bedroom, carrying me with him.

"I'm all sweaty," I pant, half apologetic.

"I'm sure we're about to get much sweatier," he growls, pushing his bedroom door open and then kicking it shut behind us once we're inside. I glance over at his bed, the same bed I'd built with him.

"Aiden, you better be planning on throwing me on that bed and fucking me," I groan. I want him now, more than I've ever wanted anything.

"I've thought of nothing else for a while," he whispers against my neck.

Aiden puts me down onto the bed. He stands at the edge of the bed, looking at me like he wants to devour me. He reaches a hand over his shoulder, grabbing his tee-shirt and pulling it over his head. He drops the top to the floor, still staring at me, watching as I drink in his body, and lick my lips in anticipation.

I sit up on the bed, pulling my own top over my head, then my sports bra.

"Don't judge my underwear. Nobody wears their fancy underwear when working out," I grin as I fall back on the bed, but the way he stands looking at my breasts makes all my joking vanish.

"Some of us don't bother with it," he replies, inching down his sweatpants. Underneath, his skin is bare, and I groan again. I pull down my yoga pants and underwear. I lie still on the bed, naked and ready for him.

"Now, Aiden," I bite my lip, looking at the length and width of his erection.

"Now?" he teases, leaning forward, resting one hand on the bed. He strokes a finger across my sweet spot, circling my clitoris. "Oh Zo," he murmurs when he feels how slick I feel. Each stroke he makes is slow and calculated, touching me in a way that makes me whimper. I'm hyper aware of how wet I must feel on his fingers, but it drives me crazy how much he seems to enjoy it.

"Oh God, do you want me to beg you?" I groan when I cannot take it anymore.

"Fuck, Zoey, do you want this to be over before it's even begun?" he growls, and he withdraws his hand, getting onto the bed with me, his whole weight above my body. His hips are above mine and it takes all my self-control not to wrap my legs around him and pull him harder onto my body.

"I'm covered, and tested negative when I checked after my last relationship." I tell him, thinking of my last trip to the doctors for a comprehensive checkup and an IUD fitted. I haven't been with anybody in ages.

"Me too. Full checkup after the army, and no sex since then," he explains.

"Good, because I don't think I could wait another minute, if you needed to find a condom. I might explode."

He flashes me a grin and then shifts to kiss me again. As he kisses me, he snakes a hand between our bodies, gripping himself for a better position against me, and then with a flex of his hips, he enters me. It's barely an inch to start but it has me gasping against him. He kisses against my neck and pushes all the way into me. Both his hands reach for mine, fingers circling around mine. I groan underneath him and grip his fingers, feeling like I need to hold on.

"Is this okay?" he murmurs.

"This is more than okay, Aiden, this is amazing. Don't stop," I plead.

"Only you saying 'no' could stop this. A fucking tornado could sweep through this room right now and I wouldn't notice." He moves his hips, just once and it's exquisite.

"I'm going to get such a jaw ache when I blow you later," I gasp, and then he really starts to move, making me fall silent as all I can do is form an oh with my mouth.

His fingers are still clasped around mine, my hands slightly pinned to the bed. I hook my legs around him, shift my hips, moving with him. He looks at me with such devotion on his face, it's so intense. I'm not used to making eye contact during sex and the intimacy takes my breath away and I look away from him.

"Zoey," he murmurs, slowing his movements. "Look at me," he coaxes.

I look back at him and he starts moving again. Every movement is exquisite, and when I climax, I'm still staring into his eyes, feeling like we're the only two people in the universe. When he climaxes and collapses against me, he pulls me close to his body, and it feels like everything in the world has changed. When he whispers again that he loves me, I feel like I'm seeing everything clearly for the first time in my life.

∞∞∞∞∞∞∞∞

"I wish you would stay," Aiden says as I stand by the door to go home. We both know the only reason I'm going home is because of Caterina. If things were different, I wouldn't be leaving him right now. I'd be still wrapped in his arms, in his bed, feeling cocooned from the world.

"You just want to go for round three," I tease. "I'm not sure my jaw will survive it, but I'm sure I'll have recovered by the time you get back from the States," I add, and I lean up on my tiptoes to kiss him. He scoops me into his arms, his lips crushing against mine. It's like an onslaught on my senses, the firmness of his body, the desperation in his kiss, the scent of him. I've showered so I can go home but he hasn't yet, and he smells manly and like sex.

"Drive safely," he murmurs once he lets me go. I squeeze his hand and then pick up my things to go home.

When I arrive home, fortunately Caterina is out. She hasn't left a note to tell me where she is. I get changed into my pyjamas and crawl into bed. As soon as I'm in bed, the guilt and shame washes over me.

There is no way I can balance my love for Caterina with my love for Aiden. There is no way she'll see me sleeping with Aiden as anything but a betrayal, but the only way forward would be to tell Aiden it meant nothing, and that my confessions of love were just me being swept up in the moment.

As I fall asleep, I can't decide which will hurt me more.

∞∞∞∞∞∞∞∞

Aiden and I exchange messages in the few days he has before he's due to fly to the States. Whenever he brings up the topic of us, I'm non-committal, gearing up to lie to him, to break off our connection for the sake of my friendship with Caterina.

Like a wimp, I don't text him until I know he's in the air, flying for his three-week job. I tell him it was a mistake, that we were wrong, and it meant nothing. He doesn't reply, though I know he's read my message.

For three weeks, I throw myself into work and being with Caterina. I'm the best friend that I could ever possibly be, though the shame of what I've done aches in my bones. Every night, I cry in my bed, trying to convince myself I've made the right choice.

The day he's due to fly back from the States, Aiden texts. *Please meet me at mine this evening, I'll be home about eight. We need to talk.'*.

I don't reply, but at seven thirty, I wait outside his flat. The weather is warm and sunny, I'm wearing a sundress to keep me cool, but I feel sick and hot, dreading seeing him again, dreading the idea of lying to his face.

It's just before eight when I see him, walking down the path to his flat. The second I see him, it's like I'm a greyhound, released from the gates for the race. I rush over to him, throwing myself into his arms. He catches me, his hands under my ass as I wrap my legs around him.

My mouth is on his before he has chance to talk. This kiss feels like a release I've been desperate for, something I never want to end. Every idea I'd had about lying to him seems ludicrous.

I nip his bottom lip and he growls.

"Are you done pretending it didn't mean anything?" he asks.

"Yes," I whisper. I can't pretend and it feels ridiculous that I ever thought I could.

My fingers curl into his hair. Aiden keeps hold of me with one arm, walking me to his front door, dragging his small suitcase with the other hand. I could get down, to make this easier for him, but something about the way he holds me against his body makes me think he wouldn't let go.

He unlocks the front door and carries me inside.

"Good, because it meant everything," he murmurs between kisses. He leaves the suitcase by the front door, locking the door behind him and then he carries me to the bedroom.

"You're everything," I gasp as he tips me and lands me on the bed.

"I missed you, so much. Don't do that to me again," he tells me. His eyes are dark. They remind me of the colour of the skies before a storm; before the roar of thunder comes. I know what we're doing now is something that will cause the biggest storm in my life, but I can't walk away. I want to hold his hand and dance in the thunderstorm with him.

"I missed you. I want you. I love you," I pant. He inches himself down the bed, pushing the bottom of my dress up so it's around my waist.

"Say it again," he commands.

"I missed you," I start.

He rubs a finger over the underwear I have on.

"Definitely not the type of panties one wears to exercise," he murmurs.

"Three weeks in the States and you've picked up all the lingo," I tease.

He laughs. "What's your preference?"

"I don't care what you call them, just get them off." I writhe slightly on the bed. He inches them down.

"Still waiting for a repeat of those words, Zo," he says once he's got them halfway down.

"I want you," I repeat, my whole body seemingly screaming in confirmation.

"Try again," he says. Now my underwear is off, and he's slipped my little ballet slippers off my feet.

"I love you."

"There's the magic words," he groans, and I'm rewarded by him inching two fingers inside me. He looks at me, a slow, lazy smile on his face. "I love you too," he says, and then he lowers his head to where his fingers are already working their magic and making me feel like I'm about to combust. It doesn't take long until I'm bucking underneath him, panting and desperate to feel him inside me.

"Do you want me to beg? It's been a long three weeks, Aiden," I pant. I watch as he strips his clothes off until he's naked and glorious in front of me.

"There isn't much point begging when the opponent is going to fold like a stack of cards," he says. He climbs onto the bed with me, straddled above me, and he pins my wrists to the bed.

"Oh my God, yes," I hiss and despite him saying he'd fold like a stack of cards, I can't help but whisper, "Please fuck me, right now."

Aiden doesn't hesitate, he's in me in seconds, and like the two times we've made love so far, I know the pleasure is going to overwhelm me. This time, I have no problem keeping my gaze on him, watching how he looks at me like I'm the most precious thing in the world as he pushes to further heights of bliss, ecstasy, and love.

After, I lie in his arms. He wraps his body around me.

"I can't tell her. Not yet. I love you, Aiden, but I love her too. Can you live with that for a bit?" I whisper.

"I can, but we'll need to tell her at some point. I love you. I belong to you," he vows.

"I couldn't possibly belong to anybody else," I vow back and the beat of my heart in my chest makes me sure I won't walk away from him, even though it risks my friendship with Caterina. Not now.

Once, you can claim you made a mistake. Twice, it's a choice made to throw caution to the wind. Three times, it's a habit, an addiction, a precious secret you'll protect with your life.

I'll protect us, with my life.

13

Zoey

Somebody killed Simba.

Somebody killed my cat.

Somebody hung my cat by his neck.

It doesn't matter how long it's been since finding him this morning, what happened to Simba has been running around my head all day. I faked cheeriness at work today and when people asked how I was, I told them I was fine, but my mind was screaming I wasn't, that nothing about this situation is fine.

Poor Simba.

Isabelle had insisted that it wasn't Simba's blood that had been smeared into the glass in the porch, but she'd added she knew it would be of little comfort.

What kind of sick person does something like that? Who have I pissed off so badly that this is the way they want to punish me?

I'm exhausted when I get to my bed, and so grateful I've already changed into my pyjamas. I know going to sleep just after eating chilli is a bad idea, as is the idea of going to bed this early because I'll either get indigestion or I'll be awake in the middle of the night again. I resist the urge to climb in the bed and sleep. Instead, I pick up my phone from where I'd left it on charge. I sit in the bed, propped up against the pillows.

My fingers hover over the option of logging into the email account I'd looked at last night. I know taking another trip down memory lane and reading emails between me and Aiden would sting, but part of me wants to, to let me fall into it all for a bit before I rip the plaster off again.

Since he got here, we keep falling easily into the people we used to be, throwing ourselves down the path we've travelled together. It's too easy for me to remember how I'd felt in the first few weeks after Aiden and I first slept together. How giddy I felt, like a teenager with their first crush. My heart would skip a beat every time I had a new message. We'd email a lot, back and forth, hundreds of messages a day, partly because I thought it was easier to hide from Caterina. If his name wasn't popping up on my screen, but hidden away in an email folder, it felt less obvious. Outwardly, I probably looked the same as I always did. Inwardly, I was a ball of emotions, blissfully in love, pretending I wasn't betraying my best friend.

Sometimes, the guilt about betraying Caterina would drive me crazy, especially when I thought about all the things she'd told me over the years about her plans with Aiden. She'd imagined their wedding, showed me the dress she wanted, the carriage she wanted to arrive in, the private villa she wanted him to take her to for her honeymoon. I knew Caterina had planned a life with Aiden, but it didn't stop me from being with him, from talking about our own future. After that first time I'd tried to tell him it was a mistake, I'd never considered it again. I was in love with him, and I knew he loved me, too. We were destiny, and I lived in hope that, in time, Caterina would accept us.

Now, the memories of what happened between us start to overwhelm me, as they often do. The ache in my heart hurts, and my stomach twists. I squeeze my eyes shut for a moment, hoping it'll block everything out. When that fails, I look back at my phone, scrolling my contacts and connecting to call Lizzie.

"Everything okay, Zoey?" she asks as soon as she answers the call.

"I just wanted to hear a friendly voice," I admit.

"Well, consider me flattered. What's wrong? You sound weird," she says.

The tears that I've been holding back since the police left and Isabelle drove me to work finally break through.

"Somebody killed Simba," I cry.

"Zoey, I don't know what you're saying, I can't hear you through the tears. Take a deep breath," she instructs. I take one, then another, and another.

"Somebody killed Simba," I say for the second time. It still feels unbelievable.

"Oh my God, that's horrible! What on earth happened? Please tell me the police have some leads." Lizzie seems to gasp as she talks. I can imagine her in her hotel room, her hand raised to cover her mouth.

"They left his body at my door."

"Did your cameras capture anything?"

"Just somebody coming up the path, with Simba. The person was wearing a balaclava, and they didn't seem to be in a car. I'm not sure how much the police will be able to work out from that." I wipe my eyes as I talk.

"I hope they find something. This is scary, Zoey. I'm really worried for you," Lizzie frets.

"I'm sorry to dump this on you. I just wanted to talk. I'm okay. I shouldn't have said anything, now I've given you a terrible image before bed."

"It's okay, I'm about to watch some crappy television, that'll take my mind off it. How about you, how are you going to take your mind off it?" she asks.

"I think I'm going to try to get some sleep," I tell her, though I'm sure it's going to take me ages to fall asleep, despite how tired I feel.

"We can talk longer, if you like," she offers.

"I shouldn't have called. You're back on Tuesday, right?"

"Yes, maybe we can go for dinner, or I can come to yours if you're still on some sort of lockdown."

"I'm hoping it's all sorted by then, I'm not sure how much more of this I can take."

"Get some sleep," she suggests.

"Goodnight, Lizzie," I say. She wishes me goodnight, so I hang up. The icon for the emails appears to be screaming at me and this time, I give in and open it, reading through some of the emails. I only want to allow myself to read one, but I can't resist opening thread after thread, immersing myself in the past, my heart aching until I fall asleep, phone in hand, memories dancing in my head.

∞∞∞∞∞∞∞∞

Aiden is in the hallway as I walk down the stairs in the morning. I'm dressed and ready for work, and I know that I don't look like I've been awake half of the night, scrolling through our history, mostly because I have a lot more makeup on than I'd usually wear.

He looks utterly exhausted, like the tiredness is etched into his bones. I wonder how much he slept yesterday before he'd come to meet me at the office. He was supposed to be dropping his parents at the airport then going home to sleep, but maybe he was as freaked out by the morning as I had been.

I glance at my watch. I'm downstairs early, there is ages before we're supposed to meet Isabelle.

"Why don't you ask Isabelle to meet us here?" I blurt out.

He looks at me, a bemused expression suddenly on his face. "What's up, can't face another car ride with me?"

Despite his amusement, he can't disguise the tiredness in his eyes.

"I was thinking you could go to sleep. Here, I mean," I explain.

"I can go home to sleep, Zoey," he replies.

"Yes, I know, but you could get at least three extra hours sleep if you just stay here, until I get back from the office. You could sleep in one of the spare bedrooms."

"I don't have a change of clothes with me."

"I'm sure I have an old tee-shirt of Caleb's somewhere."

The grin on his face gets wider. "What do you expect me to do for underwear when I wake up, Zo?" he teases.

"I expect you're used to going commando," I smirk.

"This is a mad idea, I am capable of driving home," he protests, but he doesn't sound like he's got much argument left in him. "Are you sure?" he adds, but he already has his mobile phone in his hand.

"Yes, I'm sure. Besides, what kind of job are you going to do if you fall asleep at the wheel driving me to work?" I ask, and I know it's enough to make him agree with me.

"I've gone longer without sleep," he comments. All it does to me is reaffirm my thought that he got very little sleep yesterday.

"Well, you're old now," I tease.

He busies himself with his phone and then looks up at me.

"Okay, Isabelle is going to come here," he says. "And fuck off with the old, you're only a year younger than me."

"Breakfast?" I suggest. "Then you can get to sleep."

"Breakfast sounds good, but I'm not going to sleep until Isabelle gets here," he replies, and then he follows me into the kitchen.

∞∞∞∞∞∞∞∞

Isabelle doesn't look fazed by the change in the planned routine. She also doesn't look fazed at the fact that Aiden walks me to her car and then heads back into my house.

She drives towards the office and automatically stops at the coffee shop.

"Let's get this day started. A shot of caffeine might do you the world of good," she says as she gets out of the car. I follow her towards the coffee shop.

"Coffee is my favourite way to start the day."

"Are you having breakfast, I wouldn't want to get in trouble with Aiden for not making sure you're fed." Her voice has a teasing tone to it.

"I already had breakfast," I reply.

"With Aiden?" she prods, opening the door for me.

"Yes, with Aiden," I clarify, a small smile on my face. Evidentially, Isabelle is still curious about me and Aiden and is as coy as both Aiden and I have been about trying to find information out of each other.

"How is he?" she asks as we reach the counter.

I smile at Mike. "Morning, Mike. Black coffee, vanilla latte, two flat whites and a cappuccino to take away please."

"Freshly baked raspberry croissant too?" he offers. I nod my head and look at Isabelle.

"Do you want anything?"

"Nothing to eat, thanks. Who are the other coffees for?" she asks.

"The two security guards on today and Abigail," I explain.

"Zoey's generous nature keeps my business afloat." Mike chuckles as he hands me my wrapped pastry. Mike busies himself with making the drinks. I glance at Isabelle as he works.

"Aiden seems exhausted. I'm a bit worried about him," I admit.

"He's always professional, but he's taking this case very personally," Isabelle replies. She looks like she's trying to sound uninterested, but her expression gives her away.

"Do you think I should ask him to find somebody else to take over from him?" I ask.

"Honestly, Zoey, even if it was the best thing for him to do, I don't think he'd listen. He's sticking this out to the end."

I'm not surprised by her answer. Aiden's dedicated to his job, and we have a twisted, complex history which makes this situation more complicated. I think I've known since the moment he saw the contents of the envelope that he would stick this case out, despite the initial awkwardness and hurt between us.

Mike puts my order onto the countertop so I can pay. Isabelle helps me carry the items to the car, but she doesn't prompt me to carry on our conversation, and I'm grateful because I wouldn't know what to say. The idea of Aiden pushing himself too hard or too far when working my case makes me feel anxious, but the idea of him saying goodbye feels worse. Even with all the hurt and history between us, I feel safe with Aiden. A part of me doesn't want to let him go, but the larger part of me knows how much it'll hurt when I inevitably do.

∞∞∞∞∞∞∞∞

Aiden is waiting on the driveway when Isabelle pulls her car up to my house.

"Are you sure you don't want to come in for some tea?" I ask as I reach for the door handle on the car.

"Thanks for asking, but I'm actually going out on a date tonight." Isabelle smiles and for the first time since I met her, I see her as something other than the always-in-control, level-headed person she usually appears to be. There's a hopeful tone to her voice, and a little blush on her cheeks. She looks like any other woman who is going on a date with somebody they really like, full of excitement and hope.

"I hope it goes well for you. I'm going to be asking you all sorts of inappropriate questions tomorrow," I joke, and she chuckles.

"I look forward to it. Go on, before Aiden busts a gut waiting for you."

Isabelle waves at Aiden as I get out of her car, laughing and calling my goodbyes. She's driven away by the time I reach Aiden.

"You look much more alive and alert," I comment.

"Well, your spare bed is very comfortable. I slept like a baby."

"Glad to hear it." I smile at him and can't help but think of Aiden curled up in my spare bed.

We walk into the house, and I put my laptop bag down in the hallway, dumping the post I've just picked up at the post office onto the coffee table as Aiden locks both the porch and the front door.

"Why don't you have your post delivered like a normal person?" he asks with a wry tone when he sees the stack of envelopes.

"Habit, I guess. I put a hold on the post a couple of years ago, after Caleb changed jobs and was travelling overseas a lot, while I was trying to expand the business and spent ages up and down the country. We were coming home to find days' worth of post, making it obvious that we weren't here. I just never updated them to send the post properly when our jobs became more routine. Besides, it gives me something to do with all my spare time," I joke.

"You need a hobby." Aiden laughs as we walk through to the kitchen.

"Hey, I have hobbies," I protest.

"Yeah, what are they, given you haven't told me about a single activity you do other than work, and occasionally going out for dinner with a friend," he challenges. He has a knowing smirk on his face.

"I like walking on the beach, I asked about that," I remind him as I look through the fridge for some inspiration on what to cook for dinner. My eyes fall onto the packet of bacon and I'm pretty sure nothing is going to satisfy me more than a bacon sandwich now.

"What an inspirational hobbies section you'd have if you were writing a dating profile," he teases.

"God, a proper day of sleep and you're on top irritating form." I roll my eyes at him. "Besides, if I was going to write a dating profile, you know I'd be direct about what I wanted. I wouldn't list a load of fake hobbies."

"My name is Zoey and men who are immature and selfish need not apply," he quips.

"My hobbies include walking on the beach, being horny, and extensive masturbation," I joke.

He snorts. "You'd have all the right types of guys lined up for your attention with that."

"Then it's a good job I'm not writing a dating profile. Bacon sandwich?" I ask.

For a second he looks confused by my change in the conversation, but then he nods.

"I'll help," he offers.

"So, what would be on your dating profile?" I ask. I pull the packet of bacon and the butter from the fridge.

"Oh God, I think I'm ready for the scrap heap." He takes the pack of bread out of the breadbin, not looking at me as he talks.

"No, you're not." I laugh. "I'd bet you have plenty of women climbing over one another to get in the front of the queue for your attention."

"Doesn't matter if it's not the person I want to be there." Aiden shrugs.

For this, I can't answer. Instead, I focus on getting out the frying pan, lighting the hob, adding the bacon when the pan is heated. Aiden doesn't say anything either, buttering the bread, finding the sauces in the cupboard.

Once the bacon is cooked, I assemble the sandwiches and we sit up at the breakfast bar together. We eat in silence.

"When did you last date?" I ask, breaking the silence once I've finished my sandwich.

"I had a couple of dates with a woman called Emma a few months ago."

"What happened?" I wonder.

"She just wasn't what I wanted, and I didn't want to string her along. Have you dated since Caleb?"

"Nope," I reply. He's finished his sandwich, so I pick up both plates and put everything into the dishwasher. "I'm going to changed and then I'll probably watch some television in the living room. Something for me to add to my hobbies," I joke. "If you've nothing better to do than monitor the CCTV, you could watch some mindless crap with me."

"Sure," he replies.

I head upstairs to my bedroom. I strip out of the clothes I'd worn to work and have a quick shower, washing the day from my skin, scrubbing the makeup off my face. I dry off and dress in a pair of jeans and a casual shirt, socks on my feet and my hair back in a ponytail. I go back downstairs, grabbing the post from the side table as I walk through to the living room.

Aiden is already in the living room. He's set up his laptop so he can monitor the CCTV, his mobile phone with the sensor alarms next to the laptop.

"Do you want to watch anything in particular?" I ask, picking up the remote controls and switching the television on.

"Whatever you want, Zoey."

"Here," I warn, and I throw the remote towards him. He smiles and starts browsing the television menu as I stand near the sideboard, opening my post, discarding the rubbish and circulars into a pile. There's some post I hadn't noticed when I'd collected from the post office, addressed to Caleb. I hate it when this happens, it always means I have to redirect and send it to him.

I open a stack of bills, getting frustrated when I realise it's more paperwork from companies I've already asked to change to online billing. I'm frustrated by the time I get to the third example. I'm still frustrated when I pick up a brown envelope, too distracted by my minor irritation to notice it's a handwritten envelope, too distracted to do anything but gasp when I unfold the content of the envelope.

"What's the matter?" Aiden asks, fully alert. He crosses the distance between us in two short strides. He glances at the item I have in my hand. It's the same style letter to what had appeared at the office. It's a printout of a photograph, something I vaguely recall being on the company social media page from years ago. We'd been at a celebration night, Caterina and I are flanked by Dominic, the former chief accountant, and Laurel who headed up the procurement team before she'd been diagnosed with cervical cancer and given up work due to her aggressive treatment. All four of us have our faces crossed out with a red marker, and the words 'you're next' are stuck to the top of the page.

"Oh my," I whisper, and my fingers curl together, scrunching the paper in my hand.

"Zo," Aiden says gently, "I'll need to keep that to pass it to the police."

"Oh my," I repeat. Aiden takes the paper from me, putting it onto the sideboard.

"Come here," he murmurs. He pulls me into his arms. He holds me close with one arm around me, the other he raises and puts his hand against my cheek, stroking my cheek. "It's okay," he adds, and he kisses me on the forehead, before the second arm drops from my face, wrapping around me and pulling me close.

Aiden's touch takes me by surprise. For the first few years I knew him, there was nothing but affection between us, but then our relationship had changed, and every touch had felt charged, electric, usually culminating with me jumping into his arms, my legs wrapped around his waist, desperate for him. This touch is different. This is Aiden at his most affectionate, his most caring, his most tender.

For all the times we have been together in the past, for everything we have done together, this feels like the most intimate we have been in years.

His arms around me are strong and firm, holding me close like his only intention is to protect me, like he'd lay his life down for me if it came to it. Despite the security he offers, I feel terrified. My legs feel weak, and it has nothing to do with the threatening letter that is now lying on the sideboard.

"I'm afraid," I whisper.

"I'm not going to let anybody hurt you," he vows.

"I know," I murmur.

"What do you want to do? I can call the police now and get them over, or," he starts, but I shake my head. I'm still in his arms so the action makes my head rub against his chest.

"I just want to forget about it for a while. Can we please just sit and watch television and pretend it didn't happen? Just for now," I plead.

"Okay, come on, sofa," he suggests, pulling away from me and taking me by the hand so he can lead me to the sofa.

We sit together and he switches to a movie channel that plays old movies. There's an old scary movie just starting, a black and white one which I think is more suspense than gore.

We settle back to watch the film. It feels completely natural for us to sit closely on the sofa. It seems completely normal for me to reach for his hand when there is a scary scene in the film. It feels completely reasonable for him to stroke his thumb across my hand. It feels perfectly acceptable for me to rest my head against him as the film progresses. It feels logical for him to put his arm around me and pull me close.

Except, there is nothing natural about the way my heart pounds in my chest.

There is nothing normal about the fluttering feeling in my stomach.

There is nothing reasonable about how the rest of my body is responding, skin tingling, blood pooling in places that make me ache.

There is nothing acceptable about what I want, what both my body and brain are telling me to ask for.

There is nothing logical about wanting to climb on top of the man I'm paying to protect me.

It's been months since I've had sex. It's not the longest I've been without it, but I'm suddenly hyper aware of how long it's been, and how good it always is with Aiden. Remembering how good we were doesn't mean anything, because I remember how much we have hurt one another in the past.

As the film finishes, he seems to shift uncomfortably in his seat. Neither of us move for a moment but then I stand.

"I should probably get to bed," I say. It's not what I want to do, but it would be the most sensible thing to do. Aiden stands next to me. I take one single step and he reaches out, catching me by the elbow. His thumb caresses down the curve of my elbow, and even though he's touching my shirt rather than my skin, I feel like I'm ice and he's fire. The warmth of his touch seems to radiate through my whole body.

I stare at him, and he looks like he's holding his breath, unsure of what he should say, what he should do.

My heart thuds in my chest. All the questions that have buzzed around my head for the last hour and a half seem so stupid. Of course I'm still attracted to Aiden. Of course I still have feelings. He was the love of my life. Right now, he's stood in front of me, there for me if I can only be brave enough to lean into what I'm thinking, what I'm feeling, what I want.

We've been here before, the indecision hanging between us, the fear we both had at the idea of leaning towards what seems to be inevitable. It was like this the first night we'd been together. Even now, years later, I can recall how my heart had pounded as I'd bent to kiss him, to give him that one kiss he wanted before I tried to walk away. I remember how I'd felt his heartbeat too, how the moment our lips touched, I knew I was in trouble.

"Goodnight, Zoey," Aiden murmurs. "I'll see you in the morning," he adds. It could be a dismissal, but I see it as a junction, a fork in the road for me to take, if I want to be brave enough to take it.

"Or you could come upstairs with me," I suggest.

"To make sure you get to bed safely?" he replies, although we both know that was not what I was suggesting.

"I'm not tired, Aiden. I don't want to go to bed to go to sleep. I'd really like it if you wanted to join me. What do you think?" I ask. I search his grey-blue eyes for clues about how he is feeling, holding my breath as I wait for his answer.

14

Aiden

The air between us feels like it's far too heavy. Zoey holds my gaze and I feel like I'm about to be set on fire.

"We shouldn't," I tell her, although I want nothing more than to be with her.

"Don't make me beg, Aiden, because I will," she warns.

Her warning is what tips me over the edge, that and the desire on her face. I've spent most of the film feeling like my body was about to combust, and seeing this replicated on Zoey's expression as she talks is a validation that I'm not crazy, I'm not imagining this, that the passion that has always existed between us is still there.

I stop thinking about what I should do, about what would be right for me to do, and think only about what I want. I pull her towards me. She lands against me, looking up at me, her blue eyes icy. I've always loved her eyes; she has always had a way of looking at me like she's seeing my soul.

She inhales deeply as I put my hand against her face, caressing her cheek with my thumb. She groans and the second I hear it; I know I'm screwed.

"Upstairs," I growl. There is no way I want to have sex with Zoey as some quickie in her living room. I want to spend forever exploring her body, getting reacquainted, taste every inch of her skin. I want to watch her come undone, time and time again. I want to hold her tight and never let her go again. I want to promise her the world. I want to promise her my heart. I want her to promise me hers.

Zoey turns and walks out of the living room, pulling me with her. I let her lead me up the stairs and towards her bedroom. She stops at the bedroom door.

"I want you, Aiden," she says, and then she's in my arms, her legs wrapped around my waist, my hands under her ass to keep her steady. This is a position I've held her in many times, one I love. Her fingers are in my hair.

Another thing I've always loved about Zoey is what she does to my hair. Whenever she twists her fingers through it, it's like a direct line to my dick.

"You have no idea how much I want you," I murmur between kisses.

I open the door and carry her towards the bed. I place her on the bed, as gentle as I can, trying to balance my need to get everything started with my desire to make this last.

She stares at me as I stand at the foot of the bed. I lift her right foot, pulling off the lightweight sock she has on. Her toenails are painted a pale pink. I trace my fingers down the sole of her foot, feeling the curve of the arch. I press on a few pressure points on the soles of her foot, and she flexes in response. I'm not usually a fan of feet but Zoey has beautiful, slender feet. I kiss the top of her foot, kissing down towards her toes, and then I suck her big toe. She shudders on the bed.

I nip my teeth against the inner curve of her foot, and she lets out a hiss. I pull up her other foot and take off the sock from that foot, repeating the same process, watching her eyelids flutter.

I reach up towards the waist of her trousers, undoing the button and the zip, inching them down her body. When they're off properly I get on the bed with her. I kiss my way up one leg, starting with the ankle, up the curve of her calf, over the knee, up her inner thigh. I cross to her hip, kiss along her stomach and hook my fingers into the sides of her violet coloured underwear.

"Oh, fuck, Aiden, you're making me so wet," she groans.

Another thing I've always loved about Zoey is how she talks when we're in bed together. All decorum leaves her, and it drives me wild.

"Nice panties," I tease.

"Call them what you want, just get them off." She gives a little huff of laughter.

"Who am I to argue?" I grin at her as I inch them down her body, throwing them onto the floor. "Hmm, and there was me thinking you wanted a wax," I tease, my fingers tracing over the small section of hair.

"I told you I could last," she replies, her cheeks a little flush.

I slip one finger across her, seeking out her clitoris, watching as her mouth parts slightly.

"Can you last?" I murmur, no longer talking about waxing, but marvelling about how slick she feels against my finger.

"No, I can't last," she whimpers.

"What do you want, Zo?" I ask, stroking her. "What do you need?"

"You know what I want," she gasps. "You always know what I need."

"Use your words, honey. Tell me," I coax, stroking her again. She fixes her gaze on me and licks her lips.

"I want you to put your fingers inside me and make me come against your hand. Right now." Her tone is a cross between desperation and a demand.

Another thing I've always loved about Zoey, she's not shy about telling me what she wants. She has no idea how much it turns me on. She used to say she liked me being in control in bed, but she's never realised that she's the one in charge, she's the one who can command my every move.

"Like this?" I tease, slipping two fingers inside her. She's wet and slick to my touch. I push my fingers up, searching for the sweet spot inside her, my thumb brushing over her clitoris. She mewls and grinds against my hand. I lift my other hand and when she raises her hips to grind against me again, I slip my hand under her backside. Her mouth falls slack because we've done this before, she knows what I'm thinking. She keeps her hips raised.

"Fuck, yes, Aiden, do it," she groans. I push my thumb on that hand against her backside, pushing against her anus, slipping slightly inside. She gasps and bucks, tight around me. I keep up the same movements with two fingers and two thumbs until she climaxes, her body twitching and spasming against my digits. I love watching Zoey when she climaxes. She always looks like she's doing it for the first time, surprised by what her body is capable of.

I withdraw my fingers and she breathes heavily as she lies on the bed. I look over at her bedside table, spotting a packet of wipes. I reach over for one, cleaning my hands.

"Are these your wipes for when you've finished your horny masturbating?" I tease, throwing back the words she'd told me earlier.

"They're for removing makeup, you deviant," she laughs. She shifts a little on the bed and I look at her.

"You know we're nowhere near done, right?" I ask.

"I was hoping you'd say that," she replies, and she lies back on the bed.

"What do you want, honey?"

"I want you to go down on me as I go down on you," she says, no hesitation in her voice. Always in charge on what we do.

"You have far too many clothes on," I growl, pulling her back up from the mattress so I can undress her.

I unbutton her shirt, slipping it off her body. Her bra is violet and lacy, a bright contrast against her pale skin. I unclip her bra and then kiss across her chest, my hands reaching for her breasts, skimming my thumbs across her nipples. She pushes her chest firmer into my hands and then her own hands are on my clothes, pulling off the tee-shirt she'd loaned me this morning, followed by undoing my belt buckle, the button and zip on my trousers. I shrug out of all my clothes, yanking off my socks and then we're both naked on the bed.

She runs her gaze down my body, looking hungry.

"I'm going to get such a jaw ache," she murmurs, and she lies back onto the bed. It's hard not to feel ten feet tall when she says stuff like this to me, but it has always paled into insignificance to how it feels when she tells me she loves me.

I'd do anything to hear that again.

"You ready, honey?" I ask. She flashes me a cheeky smile. I snake my arm under the back of her thighs, pulling her down the bed so she's more centralised.

"I love it when you do that," she groans.

"Yeah, how about this?" I ask, and I get into a position we've been in many times, my knees either side of her head, me facing away from her. I lower my head and she shifts her legs, parting her thighs to give me access. My tongue brushes against her clitoris and she moans.

"Yes, Aiden, you're so good at this," she calls, but then she takes my dick in her hands, guiding it into her mouth. I push my tongue against her, groaning slightly because this is so good, the taste of her on my tongue, the smell of her, the feel of her mouth, hot around me. Our actions are like reflections, her tongue swirls across the head of my dick, my tongue swirls around her clitoris, she sucks at me, I suck her, she cups my balls, I slip my thumb inside her.

I try to keep my focus on what I'm doing but there are moments where the feel of her mouth on me makes me want to lose my control. When she gives a little tug on my balls, the sensation is amazing, and I bury myself further into her. She feels so good, she's everything.

She groans as she climaxes, spasming against my tongue, sucking me tighter with her mouth as she rides the wave of her orgasm. I keep my tongue against her until she stills. Her mouth is still hot and tight around my dick. I pull away from her because that's not how I want to come, and I don't want to wait to feel her all around me.

"Oh God, Aiden," she pants. "Please don't make me wait."

I reposition myself on the bed, facing her.

"What do you want, Zoey?" I ask. My whole body feels taut with need and desire for her.

"I want you to flip me over and fuck me. I want you to pin me down, I want you in me, right now," she gasps as she talks. She might be breathless, but she speaks with direction and clarity, no hesitation in telling me what she wants.

"Condom?" I ask. Zoey's the only person I've ever had sex with without a condom on.

She shakes her head. "I'm covered. I want to feel all of you. I want you to come inside me."

I snake my hand under her waist and hold her firmly, flipping her over on the bed so she's lying on her front. She positions her face to the side, and I watch as her mouth forms a small oh. Her hair has fallen across her face, so I smooth it back, tucking it behind her ear, my fingers running down her neck. I reach and grab her right wrist with my right hand, holding it tightly, pinning her arm onto the bed. A ripple of desire runs across her face.

Oh God, don't let this end. I think.

"Is that okay?" I murmur into her ear. She nods against the mattress and mumbles something incoherent. "Say the words, Zoey," I tease.

"Yes, yes, yes," she cries out.

My left hand circles around her left wrist, and I pin it to the mattress.

"Okay, Zoey?" I ask, checking she's still okay with this, with me doing what she's told me to do, with what I feel desperate for. I nip at the skin below her shoulder blade, a ticklish sweet spot I know she has which makes her buck slightly underneath me. I groan and nip again, just to see her reaction.

"Don't stop," she pleads. Her fingers are splayed out on the mattress.

"Do you want me, Zoey?"

"I do," she pants. "Always."

Her wrists are pinned, the weight of my body against her. She moves her bottom half up, pushing against me. I move and grind against her. She groans, it's a sexy, throaty sound. I won't survive more of this. I let go of one of her wrists so I can grip my dick, lining myself up against her, then I push inside her and pin her wrist back onto the mattress.

"Oh God, Zoey," I groan. She's warm and tight around me, there's nothing better than this feeling. She keeps arching her hips as I move inside her, matching me stroke for stroke. I let go of her right wrist, snake it under our bodies, my fingers finding her clitoris, resting my finger there so that every time we move, my finger brushes lightly against her clitoris. We keep moving together, bodies tightly together, every move feeling like the pressure is going up another level. There's a sheen of sweat on both of our bodies, like we've both run a marathon, the finishing line in sight.

"I'm already so close," she whimpers. It doesn't take much more, just a few more thrusts, a few more movements of my finger, she loses her control, climaxing underneath me, crying out my name. When she twists her head to look at me, telling me she wants to feel me come inside her, any hope I had of lasting even a second longer is gone and I climax, collapsing on top of her as my orgasm rips through my body.

"You're a vixen," I finally manage. I kiss along her shoulder before pulling out of her, lying on the bed next to her, pulling her closer towards me.

"It's always so good with you. I never come like that with anybody else."

I laugh. "You're so full of shit."

Zoey twists on the bed so she is facing me. She looks up at me.

"I swear it's true, Aiden. You're the only one who can make me come that hard, and more than once."

"I'm flattered." I grin at her. Despite the grin, I'm being truthful, but she under-estimates how she makes me feel. I've just come harder than I have in years and yet she still manages to make me feel like I could do it all again, right now.

"Well, you should be flattered. I have very high standards," she teases. She traces her fingers across my chest. "I should go get myself cleaned up, but I don't think my legs are ready to function."

"Wait there." I lean and give her a kiss on her forehead and then get up from the bed. I walk through to the little ensuite connected to her bedroom. There is a sink in here, so I clean myself up and then wet the flannel under the hot tap, taking it and the little hand towel back into the bedroom. I sit down on the bed next to her, gesturing for her to lift her hips.

"Such a gentleman," she teases as I put the little hand towel under her backside. I use the flannel to gently wash and clean between her legs. I dry her with the towel and then put both items on the windowsill, getting back into bed with her, pulling her close to my body again.

"There you go, all clean." I kiss her temple again. She murmurs something I don't catch, and she snuggles against my chest, one hand resting on me. We're quiet for a few minutes and I feel completely content.

"I'm going to assume I get some sort of discount for tonight, given you're taking far too long of a break," Zoey says teasingly, breaking the silence.

Her joke makes a pin prick of reality seep back in and I sigh.

"I should really get dressed and get back to my duties."

"Can't you stay here for a bit? I'm sure nobody is going to try to kill me right now. I think they're done for today."

"What makes you so confident about that?" I stroke my fingers down her arm.

"Well, it's been one thing a day, as the pattern. Monday, the package. Tuesday, the car, Wednesday," she starts but then she stumbles on her words. I feel her shudder and I feel it echoed in me, thinking about poor Simba. She takes a big breath. "Tonight, letter," she concludes.

"That letter could have been sent any time since you last picked up the post," I point out.

"Regardless, I'm sure there's nothing happening tonight."

"Maybe, but I'm not going to be doing any good for you if something does happen, and I'm still naked with my dick hanging out," I point out. I wish, desperately, that things were different. That so much was different, different enough that this could have been our life, minus the threats. Zoey and I, laughing and joking, naked in bed with one another.

"Please don't go," she whispers.

"What do you want me to do?" I ask.

"Can you just stay here, until I fall asleep, please?"

"I can do that," I murmur back.

"I feel very satisfied right now. For future reference, if I tell you I can't sleep, this is a much better way at settling me down than warm milk."

"Next time I offer warm milk, please feel free to suggest this instead, as I don't think there is anything better." I smile to myself.

"We were always good at this, Aiden. This was never our problem."

"Zoey, are you sure you want me to stay? Here tonight, and working your security, I mean. The last thing I want to do is hurt you. I can get somebody else to come here, if you think we've crossed the line," I murmur. Even though I

189

know I've crossed the line, I still let my fingers trace down her arm, across her smooth skin, and I watch as she snuggles up further against me.

"I'm sure. I don't want anybody else. I feel so safe with you. Please stay," she whispers back. I get the feeling she's exhausted, that everything is finally catching up with her.

"Okay, I'll keep working. I want to protect you, Zoey."

"I meant for you to stay here with me tonight, too," she clarifies, her voice still quiet.

"How about I hold you until you fall asleep, and then I get back downstairs to work?" I suggest. Leaving her bed is one of the last things I want to do, but it trails behind seeing her getting hurt. Her safety is always going to come above my desires.

"That sounds nice."

"Then I'll stay," I promise. There's a moment of silence between us before she speaks again.

"You're the only one who ever makes me feel like this," she murmurs. I'm sure she's halfway to sleep.

"Like what?" I half expect her to laugh and tell me something like 'thoroughly fucked'.

"Cherished," she replies, softly.

Her voice is barely audible now, and almost immediately, before I can reply, she's slack in my arms, fast asleep, her hand still resting on my chest. I lean and kiss across her eyelids, holding her tightly until I'm sure she's in a deep sleep. I roll her gently out of my arms, tuck the covers around her, then I get up and dress. I sit on the edge of the bed for a minute, watching her peaceful sleep. She murmurs my name and I wonder if she's woken up, but then she's quiet again, a small smile on her face. I hope she's dreaming something pleasant. I know my most favourite dreams all feature Zoey, as do my favourite memories.

"I love you, Zoey," I whisper, then I get up from the bed and head downstairs.

I should be smart enough to relinquish my presence on Zoey's case, regardless of her preference for me to stay. I should have Isabelle run this, find somebody else to replace me. Sleeping with a client is unethical and strictly prohibited in the code of conduct, but Zoey was never going to be just a client. She's always been much more to me, my best friend, my lover, the love of my life, the other piece of my soul. If you put stock in the ancient Greek theory about soulmates, Zoey is the one I'd have been designed to wander the world to find.

Zoey is everything to me, the person I love beyond reason and logic. I'd loved Caterina when we were together, but I had felt differently with Zoey, a deeper love, a fiercer need and desire, a deeper connection. I used to wonder what would have happened if I hadn't separated from Caterina, if we'd married and followed the path expected of us, I'm sure I'd have fallen in love with Zoey at some point. It would have been wrong, but inevitable. Perhaps I wouldn't have acted upon it, I'd have pined for the woman I hadn't married, but that love would have been there. It's not hard for me to know that Zoey was the one I was made for.

I know in my heart that when Zoey and I fell for one another, we did nothing wrong. The only barrier was Caterina, the betrayal of a best friend for Zoey. I'd never wanted to hurt Caterina, even after everything that had happened between us, but it had happened, and it had caused irrevocable damage, hurt Zoey especially. Damage that I know still exists, still causes her pain, still keeps us apart, despite what just happened between us.

It doesn't matter how much fire and passion there was between us tonight. I know nothing has changed. Whenever this situation about her security is resolved, I'll be banished again because I'm the reason Zoey's heart broke, and she's never been able to forgive me.

I don't blame her.

I've never been able to forgive myself, either.

15
Zoey

"Happy birthday, honey," Aiden murmurs down the line. It's barely my birthday, only just clocking past midnight.

"You could have waited until the morning," I say, quietly, but I am smiling to myself.

"I wanted to be the first to say it."

"What time is it there?" I yawn. I'd gone to bed at ten, but the phone had woken me.

"Four in the morning."

He's been away for the last two weeks, providing security for a family he's worked for before, charged with watching their teenage kids on the family holiday in the Maldives. I've missed him desperately, just like I do every time he's worked away. Most of the time, he's worked in the UK, mostly spending time in London but often in our town. He's had a couple of quicker stints abroad. This is the longest time we have been apart.

"What's it like watching the rich, the famous, and the important?" I ask.

"Not as interesting as when I get to watch you," he jokes, voice husky.

"Remind me, when are you back."

"Very early Friday morning, honey. I can't wait."

I sigh, because as much as I've missed him, Friday is going to be awkward.

"Are you sure you're okay with this party idea?" I ask. I sit up in bed.

"It's bad enough I can't be with you right now, I don't want to miss seeing you because of this party Caterina has organised. So, I'll attend to see you, even if it means I have to keep my hands off you." He sighs. It's still a point of contention between us, the question of when and how I'm going to tell Caterina, something I've dodged for the last five months. It always comes up as a problem when we can't meet up, when there isn't a way to explain my absence to Caterina.

For the most part, hiding my relationship with Aiden is easy. Caterina and I are so busy with work, everything has really taken off for the business, and we're often running around in different locations, meeting clients and securing jobs. Days like that, it's easy for me to go to Aiden's flat on the way home, to sneak an hour or so with him before I go back to Caterina's house, claiming the traffic has been terrible. I still meet him every week, nights when Caterina thinks we're catching up. Those are the nights I love, where we're locked away in his flat, eating dinner, watching TV wrapped in each other's arms, and invariably having several orgasms before I go home.

At Christmas, when Caterina had joined her parents on holiday, I'd deliberately neglected to update my passport so I couldn't join her when she invited me. I'd insisted she went away, telling her I was going to enjoy the downtime, something she hadn't questioned as she knew I'd never been a big fan of the festive period. When she'd left, I'd spent a couple of days with Aiden and it had been blissful, both of us agreeing that it was how we wanted the rest of our lives to be.

When Aiden works away, I spend my time with Caterina, but regardless how much I bend to her every whim, be the best friend I can be, the guilt is still there. When she talks about Aiden, there's still an edge, and I'm painfully aware she considers they have unfinished business. She'd decided a party at our house was required for my birthday, and reluctantly suggested that I could invite Aiden, telling me Jonah was also invited.

"You're not worried about seeing Jonah or Caterina?" I clarify. His relationship with Jonah seems to be in one of their downturns, something he doesn't want to talk about.

"I'm more worried about spending the night with a raging erection," he jokes.

"I'm sure I can sneak away with you for a bit to take care of that for you."

"Zoey," he growls.

"You're not on duty, are you?"

"Yes, but I'm on a break, it's fine," he says.

"Oh, and there was me thinking you could video call me and show me what I'm missing. I'd show you what you're missing too, to keep you thinking about me until you get home," I tease, feeling the usual stirrings of arousal I get whenever I'm in any sort of proximity to Aiden.

"What are you wearing?" His voice is a little tighter.

"Something obscene," I joke, looking down at my pyjama shorts and top.

"Can you get away a week on Saturday, for the night?" he asks.

"Maybe. I think Caterina is travelling to see her mum and dad, for their anniversary. I don't think she's back until Sunday."

"Then pack that obscene outfit, Zo, I want to take you away for the night. A big bed in a secluded hotel, with nothing to do but explore each other."

"I'd go anywhere with you, so long as it's me and you," I murmur.

"I've got to get back to work, honey, but happy birthday. I love you."

"I love you too," I whisper back. He lets out a soft sigh and then he's gone, and I lie back in bed, feeling like I'll be counting the hours until he's back.

∞∞∞∞∞∞∞

"Happy birthday, Zoey!" Another reveller shouts on Friday night as they walk past me to the back garden. The house and the garden are packed, mostly friends from university, people I know from work. Caterina is in her element, air kissing people as they arrive, opening bottle after bottle of wine. As part of her gift to me, she'd paid for catering and through the downstairs of the house, there are discrete staff handing out food and drink. Music is pounding on the stereo system.

Outside in the garden, Caterina has erected a small gazebo, some outdoor heating lit to take away the winter chill. Caterina is outside. Jonah has just gone outside, studiously ignoring Aiden when he had arrived.

Across the room, Aiden is with some people he knew from university. Every time I look at him, I feel a thud in my heart and a longing, wishing everybody else could disappear so it's just me and him. Every time his eyes meets mine, there's a flicker of acknowledgement on his face and I know he is feeling the same as me.

Aiden's eyes meet mine again, and I mouth the word 'upstairs' before I excuse myself from the group of friends that I'm with, heading upstairs. Upstairs is quiet, Caterina had already instructed people that they were to use the downstairs bathroom if needed and it appears everybody is listening to her, as people often do when she speaks.

Thirty seconds later, Aiden's hands are on my waist. I pull him in the direction of my bedroom and shut the door behind us.

He stands still in front of me for a second but then he lifts me up and I take the position I'm so used to with him, my legs around his waist, my arms around him, my fingers curling through his hair, and my lips on his.

"Fuck, Zo, I missed you," he says when I pull away.

"Please tell me you're not going away again for a while."

"I promise."

"Good, because when you're away, I get very needy," I joke, and I hop back down, my feet on the floor.

"Needy?" he teases. I pull up the floaty skirt I'm wearing and rest his hand on top of my underwear.

"Needy," I repeat. His fingers find their way underneath the fabric, stroking against me. There's no surprise on his face when he finds I'm ready for him. I'm always ready for him, the minute I see him. His fingers keep teasing until I'm clutching onto his arms, wanting to surrender.

"Do you want me, Zoey?" he asks as he strokes against me.

"Yes, Aiden, I want you. I love you."

"I love you too," he whispers. He strokes against me again and I groan with want. "Kneel down," he commands, his voice thick with lust. "Lean forward," he adds. I follow his instructions. He hikes up my skirt and pulls down my underwear.

"Aiden," I gasp, and I hear him unzipping his jeans.

"Tell me how you want it, honey," he growls.

"Desperately. Right now. Fast," I beg.

He sinks into me, groaning as he does. It's been weeks since we've been together, so I know this is going to be fast. I gasp when he continues to thrust into me and he reaches forward to put a hand over my mouth, muffling the sound I'm making. Like I'd thought, it doesn't take long for us both to lose our control, him spilling into me as I bite onto his hand to stop me making any noise as I climax.

"I missed you, Zo," he murmurs into my ear once he's caught his breath.

"You have no idea how much I missed you," I growl. He pulls out of me, pulling his trousers back up. I turn to him, kissing him, nothing but reckless abandon between us.

"I can't wait until tomorrow," he says, a longing in his tone.

"Me either. I need to get cleaned up. Give me a minute, then go downstairs," I suggest. I kiss him again, wishing we could go downstairs together, hand in hand, not a care in the world.

I leave him in my room as I go to the bathroom to clean myself up. I'm still in the bathroom when I hear Caterina's voice.

"Aiden, please, don't," she pleads. I frown to myself and step out of the bathroom, wondering what is going on. Jonah, Caterina, and Aiden are on the hallway.

"What's going on?" I ask.

"Aiden's just got a stick up his ass again, right bro?" Jonah rolls his eyes.

"They're both high," Aiden tells me, his tone disgusted, and he shows me what he has in his hand, a small bag, remains of white powder visible.

"What?" I exclaim, looking at Jonah and Caterina in turn. Jonah, I'm used to him getting high. After university, any time there was even the hint of a party, he'd do a line of coke, but Caterina…never. Now, as I look at her, I can see the haze in her eyes.

"He's lying, Zoey. I don't know why you stay friends with him. He's a bad guy." She has a pout on her face, but she takes a step towards him. I've seen this version of Caterina a few times, the woman who is determined to get what she wants, which, right now, despite all the time that has passed between them, appears to be Aiden. I wonder how much of her reaction is genuine emotion, and how much is an over-inflated ego from doing a line of coke.

"He's a good guy," I murmur. Aiden steps away from her and the expression on her face turns to a sneer.

"He's a bad guy who breaks hearts," she spits.

Aiden sighs. "Caterina, it has been years, get over it. I have. I've moved on, you should too."

"No, you haven't. If you'd moved on, you'd have told Zoey about it, and she'd have told me." Caterina frowns. There's a second of peace and then everything seems to slot into place for her. She looks disgusted. "You two?" she exclaims.

"What?" Jonah laughs. "I bet she's a freak in bed, right? Such a shame I never got my chance on the Zoey express, but I guess there's always time."

Aiden shoves Jonah and his reaction, his immediate defence of me, sets Caterina off.

196

"How long?" She turns to face me, her voice a high-pitched screech. I could deny it, wait until she's calmed down, until the alcohol and whatever else she is on has worked out of her system before telling her the truth, except I don't want to lie. I'm tired of lying, hiding the person I love.

"Five months," I admit.

"You fucking bitch," she spits. "He broke my heart, he left me without warning, and even though you knew how much it would hurt me, you fuck around with him?"

"You need to stop lying, Caterina. You know why we broke up. You know what happened," Aiden says, voice firm. His gaze is on me, though, checking how I am.

"Don't you dare," Caterina snaps at him.

I'm suddenly aware there is some vital information that I'm not privy to.

"Don't what? Finally tell Zoey the truth, about how I caught you in bed with Jonah?" Aiden snaps back.

The words he says are like a grenade going off and I scoff. There is no way Caterina and Jonah slept together. There is no way Caterina has spent three years lying to me about the reason of their breakup, telling me Aiden's decision had been out of the blue. I look at Caterina and then Jonah and the sick feeling in my stomach makes me realise that what Aiden says is true.

"We were high," Jonah protests, but I'm not sure if he's telling me or Aiden.

"Every time you were together?" Aiden mocks.

"It never meant anything," Caterina snaps. Jonah looks as if she's slapped him.

"You slept with Jonah? You were doing drugs with him? How did I not know?" I stutter.

"Don't act high and mighty to me, Zoey. What you've done is worse, you've broken my heart more than Aiden ever could," she cries.

"You've spent years telling me Aiden had no reason to break up with you. I can't believe you lied to me," I exclaim.

"How about you lying to me for months, about you screwing the man I was going to marry?" Caterina shoves me. I stumble backwards. By the time I've righted myself, Caterina has whirled on her heels, rushing downstairs. I hear the slam of the front door. I glance at Jonah and Aiden, then rush after Caterina.

I find her in the driveway, in her car, trying to get the key in the ignition.

"Caterina, get out of the car." I shout, stepping closer to her car.

"No, I can't stay here with you."

Her words are punctuated with the roar of the engine in her sporty car.

"Cat, you've been drinking, taking drugs. You're in no fit state to drive," I scold.

"Leave me alone, Zoey. You don't give a shit about me, so stop pretending."

I don't stop to think, I fling open the passenger door of her car and get in next to her. I twist in my seat to look at her.

"I love you, Cat. Come inside."

"You don't love me. You'd never have slept with Aiden if you did. You could sleep with anybody you wanted, and you chose Aiden," she whimpers.

"We didn't do it to hurt you. We…" I start and she lashes out, her hand cracking against my cheek.

"Do not tell me you're in love. Neither of you know the meaning of the word. He's probably only fucking you to get back at me for the times I was with Jonah," she cries. Her words sting as much as the slap, but I know how Aiden and I feel about each other. The fact I don't immediately cry and agree that Aiden has used me seems to anger her. "Get the fuck out of my car," she snarls.

My cheek stings, but I feel like I deserve it.

"I'm not letting you drive away." I stare at her, hoping she'll relent, but her face is a twist of pain and disgust.

"I said, get the fuck out of my car," she repeats, every word dripping with hatred.

"No. If you're driving off anywhere, you're driving me, too."

Aiden rushes out of the front door, then down the driveway. He climbs into the backseat of the car.

"Caterina, stop this," he barks.

Caterina gives a scream and then she throws the car into gear, speeding away from the house. I scramble for my seatbelt, watching as Aiden does the same in the backseat. I look at his expression and I can tell he feels like we have completely lost control of the situation.

"Cat, you're my best friend and I love you. Please pull over so we can talk. I didn't want to hurt you. I was scared about what you might say. I kept it to myself because I was afraid."

"Afraid I'd tell you what a fucking bitch you were? Or were you afraid I'd tell you to choose between us? Well, you are a fucking bitch, and you're going to have to choose between us. Who is it going to be, Zoey? Him, or me?" she snarls. She reaches the end of our road, a side street, and then she spins the wheel of the car furiously, catapulting us onto the main road.

"Pull over," Aiden snaps. I watch as Caterina shakes her head, forcing the car to go a little faster. I look at the speed on the display. She's doing at least thirty miles above the speed limit for the road and shows no signs that she's going to slow down.

"Please, Cat. I'm sorry," I cry.

"You being sorry doesn't erase the betrayal. I'm never going to forgive you for this," Caterina sobs.

"Stop the fucking car, Caterina." Aiden shouts from the backseat.

"Fuck you, Aiden," Caterina snipes and then she turns to look at him, taking her eyes from the road, and whatever she was going to say to Aiden vanishes as she loses control of the car.

The wheels clip against the kerb, the car going too fast for Caterina to get control again, and we're skidding onto the opposite side of the road.

"Zoey!" Aiden shouts.

"Aiden," I cry, and then the car smashes into the little wall surrounding a front garden of a house, and everything goes black.

I don't know how long the darkness engulfs me but when I next open my eyes, I want to scream. The pain is the worst pain I have ever felt in my life, my arm feeling like torture. I look down and want to vomit when I see the bone poking through my skin.

"Zoey." Aiden's voice is frantic as he pulls on the passenger door. I look at him through the window. There is blood running down his face, starting above his eye. The whites of one eye seems stained red, completely replaced by the colour of blood.

"Aiden," I cry. I blink a couple of times, the pain in my arm intensifying every second. "I smell smoke," I murmur, half to myself. A couple of more blinks helps me focus. The front of the car is on fire.

"Zoey," he gasps as he gets the door to yield to his strength. As soon as the door is open, he leans in and unclips the seatbelt. "Can you walk? I need to get you out of the car," he says. He reaches for his head, wincing.

I nod and get out of the car. I hold my injured arm with my other, howling in pain. The pain in my arm is like fire but the fear of the flames against the car is enough to make me move. I want to get as far away from the heat and the smoke as possible.

"Caterina," I exclaim. Aiden leads me away from the car, guiding me by my unbroken arm.

"Don't look, Zoey, keep your eyes on me," he begs. Everything about him, from his tone to the tension in his hands warns me to listen, except I turn. I look back at the car and the road, see what he is afraid of, then everything fades away, and I see nothing but darkness.

∞∞∞∞∞∞∞∞

When I was a young child, in a rare period that my father was in a loving mode, I'd fallen from a climbing frame and broken my arm. I'd been taken to hospital and given strong drugs to numb the pain. I remember coming around from the drugs after they'd set my arm, a numbness in me, haziness all around me. My father had been by my bedside, smiling at me when I'd looked at him, and he'd called me his little fighter, telling me it was a battle I'd won.

It's this that I think of when I open my eyes, the same numbness in me, haziness making everything look fuzzy, except I'm convinced this is a battle I've lost.

"Aiden," I murmur. He lifts his head from where he has been resting it.

"Zoey." It's the only word he manages. He sounds too choked up to talk. I squint at him through the haziness and raise my arm so I can touch him gently on his face. The blood from earlier has been cleared from his face but there is a neat line of stitches, starting above his eyebrow and running down towards his eye.

"What happened?" I ask.

"You broke your arm, an open fracture. You've been in surgery, they had to pin it," he explains, and I look down at my arm, see the cast.

"Where is Caterina?" I stare at him and his expression changes.

"Oh, Zo," he says, his voice breaking.

"Where is Caterina?" I repeat. There is a second of silence.

"I'm so sorry, Zoey," Aiden cries.

I squeeze my eyes shut and dig through my memory. I hear the echo of Aiden's words. *'Don't look, Zoey, keep your eyes on me',* and I remember how I'd looked behind me, expecting to see Caterina, ready for her to restart the argument. My stomach twists when I remember what I'd seen instead, the windscreen of the car missing, Caterina's body lying crumpled and bloody in the road, her neck at an odd angle, her eyes wide open and vacant.

"No," I whimper.

"I'm so sorry," he chokes out.

"No." This time, it's more than a whimper. It's a desperate wail, it is anguish pouring out of me, it's the end of my world.

∞∞∞∞∞∞∞∞

Aiden takes me home when I'm discharged. I don't think he'd left the hospital since I'd been admitted. Somebody must have visited as there are clean clothes for me to change into, and Aiden's bloodied shirt is replaced by a plain top.

Aiden holds me tightly in the back of the taxi he'd booked. I flinch every time the driver brakes, every time the car speeds up, even though he's only driving the speed limit of the road. The driver takes a convoluted route back to my house, but I realise it's because Aiden's instructed not to go down the road where the accident happened.

The house is clean and tidy, all evidence of the party gone. I don't know who cleaned up. I don't know how long it had taken for the people at the party to be aware that we were no longer there. How long had Jonah stayed after Caterina had driven off? Had he come after us, seen the devastation? Had people at the party heard the ambulance and police sirens?

Everything in the house reminds me of Caterina. Her things are everywhere, there are so many pictures of us dotted around the house, pictures she'd insisted taking of us and putting on display, telling me I was her family.

I go straight to my bedroom and climb into bed, fully clothed, shoes still on. I pull the covers over me and sob underneath them. I don't think I'll ever find the strength to get out again.

Aiden climbs onto the bed with me. He removes my shoes. He scoops me into his arms, spooning himself behind me and I let him hold me as I sob.

The only things that make me aware of time passing is whenever Aiden gives me my painkillers, always coupled with something to eat. Simple food like soups but still things he has to urge me to eat, telling me I'll get sick if I don't. He brings me glasses of water and only when he's satisfied that I've had enough will he let me collapse back onto the bed, drifting in and out of sleep, nightmares

201

meaning I never feel rested. All the while, he holds me tight, and he never complains that I haven't spoken since I'd realised Caterina had died.

One night, I wake and find Aiden asleep. Every time I've woken up, he's always been awake, alert, but it's been days since the accident, and he must be exhausted. He doesn't stir as I slip out of bed. I'm in my pyjamas but I go downstairs, put my shoes on and search for my car keys. I know it's stupid because I can't drive given my arm is in the cast, but I need to go where my nightmare just took me.

"Where are you going?" Aiden asks. I turn to look at him. He is standing on the staircase, dressed in his sweatpants and a tee-shirt, his hair ruffled from sleep. I open my mouth but can't find a way to make the words come. Instead, it's tears on my cheeks again. "Come on," Aiden says, putting his shoes on and then he digs through one of the coats hanging on the coat hooks, pulling my car keys out. I know he hid them. I know he did it because he knew at some point, I'd try to find a way to get myself to where I need to go.

I follow Aiden outside and we get in my car. He helps put my seatbelt on then straps himself in, starting the car and heading in the direction of the accident. He parks up on the road and helps me out of the car, but he doesn't follow me when I cross the road. I wonder if he knows this is something I need to do for myself.

The wall Caterina's car had slammed into has been cordoned off, warning tape around it where the wall had become unstable. The road has been cleared of debris, but to me, I can see what it was like after the accident, the glass on the ground, the smell of oil and engine fluids. I get a hazy memory of being in the back of the ambulance, the flashing blue lights making the glass on the ground shine blue. I remember how I'd howled when I'd seen a policewoman pulling a big blanket over Caterina's body, hiding her away from the prying eyes of the people who had come out of their homes during the commotion. Another memory jolts me, how I'd turned to Aiden and sobbed, 'this can't be real,' before the ambulance doors had closed and I'd given into the pain of everything. I wonder how many times that night Aiden had to confirm again that Caterina had died.

Just past the area where the accident happened, there is a sea of flowers. Bunches and bunches of colourful flowers, a couple of teddy bears, all laid in tribute to a beautiful, smart, wonderful woman who had been taken far too soon. I kneel to look at some of the flowers, reading the cards.

Caterina, rest in peace, you beautiful soul.

I'll miss you forever.

Gone too soon.

God called you to be his angel, fly high.

My baby girl, words will never be enough to describe how much we will miss you. You've taken a part of our hearts with you. How are we going to survive without the light of our life? Love forever, Mum and Dad.

I'm so sorry—Jonah x

I pick up the flowers that Jonah had put down. I grab hold of the petals with my hand, pulling them from the stalks. The thorns of the white roses dig into my skin. I want to burn these flowers and his card. He doesn't get to be sorry. None of us do.

"Hey, come on," Aiden soothes as he steps behind me. He crouches down and loosens the grip I have on Jonah's flowers. He puts the now damaged bunch back in the pile, covering with a couple other offerings so they're not visible. He guides me to stand and then walks me back to the car. All I know is the overwhelming grief has given way, a pinprick of fury has found its way into me, and I'm terrified about what will happen when the rest of it breaks through.

∞∞∞∞∞∞∞∞

I'm asleep on the sofa but the sound of the front door opening wakes me. I keep my eyes closed because I don't want to talk to anybody.

"How is she?" The voice is male, older.

"How do you think, Dad?" Aiden's response is sharp. They're in the hallway, but I can hear their conversation. Aiden probably thinks it's safe to talk, probably thinking I'm asleep after pacing most of the night after getting back from the accident site.

"It's a tragedy, for everybody concerned." Richard sighs. I imagine him standing in the hallway with Aiden. He's shorter than Aiden, blonde haired, stocky framed. I'd met him so many times but always as his son's friend, the best friend of the woman who was set to be his daughter-in-law. He always reminded me of Jonah, like when he adopted his second son, it was somebody who could pass as his biological child.

"I hope you're not here to talk about Jonah," Aiden snaps.

"He wants to see you. He's distraught, Aiden."

203

"I'm sure he has enough people around him. I'm not leaving Zoey by herself," Aiden says.

"Jonah told me that you and Zoey are apparently an item." There is a disapproving tone to Richard's voice.

"Yes. I love her. We'll get through this together."

"You and Jonah have let these two women come between you two for far too long," Richard mutters.

"Zoey is the innocent one in all of this," Aiden snaps back. The tears prick in my eyes because I know I'm far from innocent.

"I wish you'd never met either of them." Richard sighs.

"Every day, I wish I'd met Zoey first. I love her, I want to marry her. You need to accept that."

"What I need is for you to come talk to Jonah. He needs your forgiveness. He's punishing himself over what happened."

"What bit is he punishing himself over? Sleeping with his brother's fiancée? Giving her drugs? Telling me it was just blow and banging? He should get over it, I did. Or is he punishing himself for giving coke to Caterina when she was already wasted?"

"None of you are innocent. Yes, Jonah gave her the coke, but she drank the alcohol, all by herself. She was the one who got in the car. You and Zoey were the ones fooling around behind her back. Please, come talk to Jonah. He loved her."

"I'm sure he did, as much as Jonah is capable of loving anybody but himself," Aiden mutters.

"Please, Aiden."

"I can't forgive him, Dad. Did he tell you he held me back, stopped me going right after them? I should have been there sooner, if he'd let me go, I could have taken the keys from Caterina, I could have stopped her getting in the car, I could have stopped," his voice trails off and my heart breaks when I hear him sob. There's a shuffling sound and I imagine Richard holding Aiden, letting him spill his grief and guilt.

I squeeze my eyes shut and try to block out their conversation. I didn't know Jonah had stopped Aiden from rushing after us straight away, but Aiden shouldn't feel guilty for that.

We have far bigger things we should feel guilty about.

∞∞∞∞∞∞∞

"I'm not sure she is up to any visitors." Aiden sighs.

"Please, Aiden."

The sound of Caterina's father makes my stomach twist and I want to throw up. It's early morning. I've showered for the first time in forever and the only reason I have is because Caterina would have killed me if she knew I'd turn up at her funeral looking like a walking disaster. The black suit and white shirt are new, something she'd encouraged me to get weeks ago, telling me I could wear it at the next company conference. I was supposed to wear this as I stood next to her in front of all our employees and we celebrated in their hard work, gave out awards and told them all how proud we were. Instead, I'm going to wear it as we bury my best friend, and then I'm going to burn it, because I never want to see it again.

"She hasn't spoken since she got out of the hospital." Aiden's voice cracks a little.

"I understand," Ronan murmurs.

I walk out of the living room and look at Ronan. He is wearing his suit, dressed for his daughter's funeral, but somehow finding it important to come to my house first. Caterina's house, not mine, I remind myself.

"I'll leave you to it," Aiden says when he sees me, and he heads upstairs, leaving Ronan and me in the hallway.

Once we're alone, Ronan's face crumples. He crosses the distance between us, pulling me into a hug.

"Oh, my sweet girl, you look how I feel," he cries. I bite my lip. I can't cry anymore. I feel like I've used up a lifetime supply of tears. "Look, I'm only here for a quick minute. Jess and I won't be stopping after the funeral. We all agreed to get away and mourn in private, so I wanted to talk to you now, okay?"

I pull out of his embrace and nod at him. There are words in my head, but I can't bring myself to form any of them.

I'm sorry.

I'm devastated.

I'll never forgive myself.

I loved her.

I'd give anything to take it all back.

She told me to choose, and my first thought was I wouldn't give up Aiden, and now she's gone.

I'd trade my life for hers.

Ronan follows me into the living room, and I sit on the sofa. He doesn't take a seat and I get the sense he's being literal about his quick minute.

He clears his throat. "I don't know if you know, but Caterina had a will, and she left her half of the business to you. There will be some formalities we need to sign, but you'll be the full owner of the business. She always said you were the heart and brains of it, I couldn't think of anybody who would do a better job."

I want to tell him I can't do it. I remember the day we'd been setting up the company structure, when I'd told her I'd pass my share to her in the event of my death because I had nobody else to give it to. She had hundreds of people she could have left her share to, but she left it to me. I wonder if she'd still say the same, after what I'd done.

Ronan shakes his head, clearly impacted by Aiden sharing the knowledge that I still haven't uttered a word.

"No protests, Zoey. I can support you if you need help with the business, but I know you're capable of doing it by yourself. Now, the house, Caterina left that to me and Jessica. We're going to put it on the market, but you can stay here as long as you need. You can just let us know when you're back on your feet and ready to move, or if you want to buy it, okay? There is no pressure, no deadline, we just don't feel like we can keep this place."

I have no plans on buying this house. The house holds far too many memories, and I'll never get past the images of Caterina rushing away from me once she'd found out about me and Aiden. I'm only here because going to Aiden's feels like it would be more betrayal.

Ronan looks at me, sympathetically. "We'll get through today, okay? An appropriate send off for our beautiful girl. If you need anything, please get in touch. Look after yourself," he says. He doesn't say anything else. I wonder if it's because I'm a reminder of happy times in his daughter's life, or whether he knows about me and Aiden, how we caused her so much pain in her final hour.

I say nothing when he leaves.

I say nothing when Aiden tells me it is time to leave for the church.

I say nothing to any of the other mourners when they offer me sentences of sympathy.

I say nothing to Caterina's family when they hug me.

I say nothing when the reverend asks if anybody would like to say a few words about Caterina, inviting us to share memories.

I say nothing when I stand by her graveside and throw soil onto the top of her coffin.

I say nothing at the wake when I hear people commenting on her death, talking about her blood alcohol level, talking about their surprise that cocaine had been found in her toxicology report.

I say nothing when people ask me how I'm doing.

I say nothing when I run out of the hall where the wake is being held, out into the gardens, breathe in the fresh air, feeling like my lungs are on fire, hearing Aiden at my heels.

I'm gasping for breath when I see Jonah, sat on the bench.

He stares at me.

"I'm sorry," he whispers. On the bench next to him is a bunch of white roses, like the ones he'd put down at the accident site, and I think of his card of apology, stupid words that mean nothing because no amount of writing 'I'm sorry' is ever going to fix what happened. He stands, picking up the flowers, taking a step towards me. It's now that I see that the card attached to the flowers is written to me. *'Zoey, I'm sorry for your loss. Jonah.'*

Now, the fury breaks through. Like red-hot lava that I cannot contain, it pours out of me. I grab the flowers from him, grateful I didn't break my dominant arm because I need my full force. I smack the flowers against him, once, twice, three times. Petals fall off, landing at his feet. Like before, the thorns on the rose stems dig into my skin and when one of the petals falls to the floor, there is a smear of my blood on it.

My words find me, and the first words I've spoken since my world ended are bitter, full of venom.

"I hate you. These flowers…are you fucking kidding me? Sorry for my loss? My loss? She was my best friend! She was by my side for everything. She was my family! She was the first person who ever cared for me. She was the first person I could trust. She was perfect and wonderful, and you blew through her life and did what you always do, you fucked it up. No amount of shitty white roses and shitty condolence cards is ever going to make what you did okay," I scream.

I throw the damaged bunch of flowers onto the floor. They land next to his feet, on top of the petals already spilt. I turn to walk away because I don't trust myself to not hurt him further. I don't care if my arm is broken. Part of me wants to tackle him to the ground and hit him until I no longer feel like I'm going to explode.

"She wasn't a saint," Jonah cuts in. I whirl to face him.

"You do not get to smear her character. Anything bad about her was because of us, because of you. You played a hand in ruining her. The cards written for her, saying she'd been taken too soon, they make me sick. God, it should have been you. I wish it had been you," I spit.

"You know what, Zoey, I know exactly what it's like to lash out at somebody because you're angry with yourself. So, go ahead, you take that anger you feel about yourself and what you did, direct it at me, make yourself feel better by blaming somebody else," Jonah growls.

His words have so much truth behind them that I feel like they might break me. The fury recedes slightly, replaced by the despair, the grief, the guilt, the shame. I fall to my knees, the mud smearing across my trousers.

"She died hating me, and there is nothing I can do to fix that," I howl. "I'll never be able to tell her how sorry I am. I'll never be able to hear her say she understands; that she forgives me. I'll never be able to tell her how much I loved her and that I never wanted to hurt her."

"Zoey," Aiden says from behind me, sounding choked up. He takes a couple of steps towards me, reaching to help me from the floor. I wave his arm away.

"I wish she'd never met either of you," I sob. "No, I wish she'd never met me."

"Let me take you home," Aiden suggests.

"Please leave me alone," I gulp. I haul myself from the floor. Aiden follows me, but Jonah remains where he was.

"Zoey," Aiden calls. The tears are blinding me now as I stumble around the side of the building. I know there will be a row of taxis waiting and I want to get into one and tell the driver to drive until they run out of petrol, and I'll set up a new life wherever that may be.

"I can't do this right now, Aiden. I can't. I can't," I repeat the mantra. He looks tormented, like he thinks the best course of action is to scoop me into his arms, smother me with kisses, wipe away my tears and tell me everything will be okay, but sensible enough to hold back.

He watches as I get into the first taxi, blurt out the address for home. Before the taxi driver can drive away, Aiden opens the back door. For a second, I think he is going to get into the back with me. For a fleeting second, I hope he will.

"I'll give you the time you need, Zoey. I love you. I'll give you the space you want. I'll wait until you're ready to forgive me." His voice breaks on the last part of his sentence.

"I love you Aiden, but don't wait." I refuse to look at him. He shuts the taxi door for me and watches as the driver pulls away.

There's no point Aiden waiting for me to forgive him. It isn't him I'd need to forgive, it's me, and I know I won't ever be able to get over what I did, and what it cost me.

What I did, it cost me Caterina, and now, as penance, I'll let it cost me Aiden, too.

16

Zoey

I wake up, alone. I know there was no chance that Aiden would have stayed in bed with me last night, but there is a part of me that feels disappointed when I see I'm alone. There is also a part of me that worries about how it will be between us when I go downstairs.

Last night was spectacular, as it always has been with Aiden, and I don't regret a single second. I just don't know how Aiden might feel this morning, especially given the added complication that he's supposed to be providing security. I'm pretty sure that climbing into bed with a client is not something written into a contract. He might regret what happened, regret that he's gone against his morals.

Not that it's the only time we've crossed boundaries and gone against our morals.

I slip out of bed, my joints and muscles feeling like they've had a workout, even after sleeping all night. I feel like I've gone a million miles from Monday. Monday, I was panicking about seeing Aiden again, Friday, I'm waking up naked in bed after spending the night with him.

I walk into my ensuite, switching the shower on and stepping in when the water heats up. I wash my hair, noticing that my wrists feel slightly sore from where Aiden had held me last night. It's a nice soreness, a reminder of the passion, a reminder that he is always so willing to give me what I want, what I tell him I need.

I finish my shower, wrapping myself in a large towel before pottering to my wardrobe. It's Friday, casual clothes at work rather than anything formal. I pick out some clothes and dry my hair, feeling like the time taken to blow-dry my hair gives me enough time to calm my nerves, although I'm still a little nervous when I finish my make up and start getting dressed. I look at myself in the mirror when

I'm finished dressing. Red chiffon top, black leather skirt, sheer black tights, my hair up in a ponytail, and a little more makeup than I'd usually wear. It's all more than I'd usually look like on a casual Friday, but it's an outfit that makes me feel good, and outfit that I know turns heads. I try not to focus on the fact it's Aiden's head I want to turn. As far as I know, last night was a one off. Our history is too complicated to resolve by one passionate, exquisite night between us.

I take a deep breath before heading downstairs.

Aiden is in the kitchen, stood at the hob where he has a pan of water on the heat, waiting for it to boil. There are slices of bread already in the toaster, just waiting for the lever to be pushed down.

"Good morning," he says, flashing me a smile.

"Morning," I reply. I take a tentative step towards him. "About last night," I start, but the voice trails off as I lose my train of thought when he turns stares at me.

"Yes?"

"I know it's an awkward situation, and I don't want you to feel like I took advantage of you last night," I explain. There's a bemused smile on his face.

"Do you seriously think you took advantage of me? I was worried that I took advantage of you."

"You only did what I wanted," I remind him. Aiden reaches for me, catching me by my elbow like he had done last night.

"I didn't do anything that I didn't want to," he says. I find myself lost for words, too focused on his touch against my arm.

There's a second of silence between us. One. Two. Infinity. I don't know who moves first, but one second, we're staring at each other, the next, we're locked in a tight embrace, his lips on mine, my fingers in his hair. His kiss is tinged with a desperate hunger. The feel of his tongue on mine is like a shot of adrenaline. As my fingers twist into his hair, he growls against me and kisses me harder, his hands roaming to cup and grab my ass. The only reason I'm not jumping into his arms, wrapping my legs around him, is because my leather pencil skirt doesn't have enough give. I curse my decision for clothes.

My heart races like a greyhound around a track and I don't care about anything else in the world but this, this feeling in my heart, the way his body feels against mine. It's only when the saucepan boils over, water frothing onto the hob, causing it to hiss and fizzle, that I feel a little bit of clarity return. But when Aiden pulls away, his eyes are bright, his facial expression awed and shocked, and I'm fairly sure I'm wearing the same stunned expression on my face.

"I'm glad you don't feel taken advantage of," I murmur. If I didn't think he'd find it hilarious, I'd clutch my chest and fan myself as I try to return to a state of normal.

Aiden grins at me. "Stop distracting me. I was trying to make you breakfast, you know, to make up for my extended break last night."

I watch him take the pan from the hob, clean up the spill of water, then put the pan back on so he can poach some eggs.

"This is all very domesticated," I comment. I lean against the kitchen counter, mostly because I need a second to gather my thoughts and raging hormones.

"I heard you getting ready, I thought I'd start breakfast, that's all."

"I'm glad things aren't weird between us. Or, weirder than they were before. I know things have been weird this week, but I'm glad to see we didn't mess anything up last night."

"Not weirder. Are poached eggs okay?" he asks.

"Sounds great."

I watch him crack some eggs into the boiling water, put the toaster on, get the butter out of the fridge.

"I'll drive you to the coffee shop and office, we'll meet Isabelle there," Aiden says.

I nod. "I guess we'll see what fun today brings." I try to sound nonchalant, failing miserably.

"I'll keep you safe, Zoey," he promises.

"Do you think I need to show that letter to the police today? I'm sure they're sick of seeing me."

"I can take it, if you like," he offers.

"I was thinking about that photograph. It's weird that I'm the only one who is still alive," I say, and I feel the usual pain I feel when I think of Caterina's death. It's changed slightly over the years, less a fresh pain and more a dull ache. I'm sure I'll feel sad about Caterina's death until the day I die.

"Who were the others in the photograph?" Aiden asks. I can tell he's trying not to look worried, but he fails. Maybe it's because I know him so well, that I'm sure I can say what every expression on his face really means, but I can tell he's bothered.

"Dominic Ackerley-Jones and Laurel Hopewell."

"What happened to Laurel?" he asks. He doesn't need to ask about Dominic because he already knows. Aiden was the one I'd run to when I'd discovered what Dominic had been doing at work, and Aiden had been the one I'd gone to the day Dominic died.

"Laurel had an aggressive cancer. She died just a few months after being diagnosed," I explain.

Aiden frowns. "It's a little odd that the one photograph somebody decides to print out is of you and three people who have all died. Somebody either found a random, old photograph on your company website and happened to find one where you're the only living person, or somebody knows the details behind them."

I think for a moment. "Laurel's death was posted on the company website, a condolence to her family."

"What about Caterina?" he asks, tone gentle, like he always is when we speak about Caterina.

"There were a couple of posts, I think. Somebody else handled it. They asked me to write it but...I couldn't," I admit.

"You were grieving," he soothes.

"My first week back at work, I sat and tried to write the post people had encouraged me to make. Not so much as aiming it as condolences towards her family but acknowledging the loss we'd all suffered. I think I managed to write the opening sentence and couldn't write another word. Somebody else wrote some posts and gave them me to sign off on, and I just approved them as whenever I tried to read them, I...well, I just couldn't do it."

Aiden butters the toast and dishes up the poached eggs. He puts the plates at the breakfast bar, and we sit up together.

"Did you publish something about Dominic?" he asks.

"I would have to check, but I don't think so, not after what happened. We would have on the internal website, but I don't think we would have on the social media site. Maybe somebody else did. It's not like people don't remember Dominic, but nobody really mentions him. Laurel and Caterina, they're different, people speak about them with affection, talk about how missed they are."

"Perhaps it's just a big coincidence. It seems a bit random to single out these people. We should still take it to the police though. Maybe Officer West can be on his usual form, as I enjoy watching you put people in their place." Aiden grins at me.

"I'll be glad when this is all over, so I never have to deal with him again."

"I'm still waiting for some checks to come back on people, but maybe we'll need to cast a wider net and look at more people from work, especially given the photograph was taken from the company website."

"You still think this is aimed at me, rather than the company, don't you?" I ask.

He nods. "Yes, the wording and the threat is all about you. I know it's unnerving, but that's where we should put our attention. I don't believe this is anything to do with an upset employee. Besides, Isabelle tells me she'd consider applying for a job at your company, she says everybody looks positively thrilled to be at work every day, she's started to think you put something in the water." He ends his sentence with a tease in his tone and a grin on his face.

I laugh. "Don't get jealous, you could always apply."

"Would you have me, Zoey?" he asks, and I'm not sure we're joking about job adverts and positions. I poke my egg and watch the yolk ooze out onto the toast. Aiden does the same with his and, like he senses that he's overstepped the invisible line that exists between us, he clears his throat. "I assume you do casual Fridays based on your outfit. Did you tell Isabelle?"

"Yep, Isabelle knows its casual today. I'm kinda looking forward to seeing what she turns up in." I smile to myself.

"I'm not sure Isabelle knows how to relax," Aiden says with a laugh.

"I'm going to be grilling her about her date most of the morning." I take a forkful of my breakfast and watch Aiden's expression. He may have said that there hadn't been anything between them, but that doesn't mean there has never been any feelings.

Instead of looking jealous or upset, Aiden looks thoughtful.

"Did she say it was with a guy called Max?" he asks.

"She didn't say who, just that she had a date. Who is Max?"

"A guy she's been on and off with for a long time. I hope they make it work this time. They're a good couple, just…well, he struggled with a few things in his personal life. He pushes her away, thinking it is better for her than being with him," Aiden explains.

I know the feeling. I wonder if Aiden is thinking about our history, or relationship.

"You said Isabelle wouldn't be interested in you because you have emotional baggage. What makes Max different, that she's willing to take on his?"

Aiden shrugs. "Because she loves him. You know what it's like. Sometimes you love somebody so much that you want to carry all their baggage for them. You want to pick up all the pieces and make everything okay."

My stomach flips. When Caterina died, I'd shattered into a million pieces, sharp edged fragments that would have made it impossible for Aiden to hold me together without me hurting him. It was easier for me to let him go, than to watch how I'd hurt him.

"It sounds like he thinks it's easier to let her go than hurt her," I comment.

"Sometimes, when you think you're setting somebody free to avoid hurting them, you're hurting them more," he replies.

We fall silent and focus on our breakfast. When we're done, I clear the plates and put everything in the dishwasher. I grab my things, shove the letter from yesterday into my bag, and then get myself ready for work, adding my black boots to finish my outfit.

"I'm ready if you are," I tell him.

Aiden smiles with me. "You look really good, Zo."

"I know it's a different style to usual," I comment, looking at my skirt and top. He shakes his head.

"Not your outfit, though you do look amazing, as usual. I just meant that you just look relaxed and happy," he explains as he unlocks the front door. We step into the porch together.

"I had a really good night sleep, thank you. Much better than your warm milk suggestion." I grin at him. He laughs as he locks the front door, opening the porch for me so I can step out into the sunshine. It might be early, but it looks like it is going to be a beautiful day. The idea of going to the beach tomorrow and sitting on the sand in the sunshine feels amazing.

"I'm glad to hear it," Aiden replies as he locks the porch door. As we walk towards his car, he takes his mobile phone out to set the motion detectors. I try not to think about how somebody still did what they did to Simba, apparently not caring that the cameras are in place. It makes me wonder what could happen today.

Aiden doesn't push me to talk as he drives me to work, almost like he can sense I've things on my mind. He pulls into a space outside the coffee shop, and we walk in together. Friday traffic is always light, but this morning seemed non-existent and we're much earlier than we need to be for meeting Isabelle.

"Do you want a drink?" I ask. "We have time before meeting Isabelle, we could sit in here and have a drink," I suggest. For a second, I'm convinced he'll say no, that he'll tell me I shouldn't be staying here and should get to the office.

"A tea would be good," he concedes. We reach the counter and Mike smiles at me.

"What will it be today, Zoey?" he asks.

"Vanilla latte and a large tea, to drink in, please. I'll order takeaway drinks later," I tell him.

"Take a seat, I'll bring the drinks over. You can pay when you order the takeaway," Mike offers. I give him a big smile and then Aiden and I head to the table in the corner. I know it's the area where there are pictures of me and Caterina on the wall.

"You two look so young," Aiden comments, staring at the pictures on the wall behind me.

I look at the pictures of me with Caterina. We were so young when we started the company, the pictures make us look like we were still children.

"The one with the stack of paperwork, it was the year we were starting out. We'd come here to work because we were far more productive than trying to work at home. Mike used to bring us drinks throughout the day, though he'd always switch us to decaf for the afternoon, telling us that he couldn't deal with our buzzing energy in the afternoon if we had additional caffeine in us." I smile at the memory of those first months when we were trying to get everything started. We were so enthusiastic and excited, and Caterina never wavered in her faith that we'd be a success.

"I recognised the one when you'd signed for the building. Caterina had sent me a copy. She'd told me she was so proud of you."

"I sometimes wonder how she'd feel about things now. I don't even know if she would have stayed with the business, or if she'd have tried to force me to leave because I wouldn't have been able to buy her out. I've spent years wondering if she'd be happy with what I've done with the company, feeling like I don't deserve the success because the whole business was handed to me on a plate, based on a will she'd made before she knew what I was doing," I tell him.

"I know she would have been proud, Zoey. I'm sure, if she'd survived, she'd have eventually accepted you weren't doing anything to hurt her. Your friendship would have recovered, it was always stronger than a guy. I know she'd have come around in the end," Aiden soothes, and he sounds like he really believes that Caterina and I would have been okay.

"I still miss her." I bite my lip to stop myself from crying.

"I know, honey." His affectionate nickname makes me think of happier times, before everything had gone so off the rails. Aiden clears his throat. "Isabelle mentioned you'd told her the office next to yours is Caterina's. She commented that she'd never seen her in the building."

"Did you tell her Caterina had died?"

"Yes, but I asked Isabelle not to mention her to you, I know it upsets you."

"I still refer to it as Caterina's office, it's a habit, I guess. I cleared her things out of there last year, so the office is empty. I took everything to her parent's house, but I haven't felt like I can use that office for anybody else," I admit.

"Do you see much of her family?"

"Not really, just occasionally. They're all doing okay, but you know she was the vibrant one of her family and it's clear they miss her," I explain, and I feel a dull ache in my chest as I think of Caterina's family. They'd never blamed me for the accident, even once it was clear that Aiden and I had been together, that Caterina had found out just before she died. Her parents have told me specifically a few times that they have never blamed me, or Aiden. It doesn't make a difference, because I blamed me.

Before Aiden can reply, Mike arrives at the table, my coffee and Aiden's tea on a tray. He's added two pastries.

"The pastries are on the house," Mike says, smiling before he walks away.

"He seems like a nice guy," Aiden comments, as if he can sense that the conversation about Caterina is getting too much for me.

"He is. He's really looked after me over the years." I take my cup of coffee from the tray. I glance over at Aiden. "Please tell me you didn't do a background check on Mike and his family," I scold.

He laughs. "Not as such, just a quick glance into their social media. There was nothing to warrant anything further. Besides, from what I can gather, you're single handedly keeping this place in a healthy profit. From what Isabelle tells me, I'm surprised there is still coffee available for anybody else."

I drink some of my coffee and think about what he's just said. It's not the first time he's referenced something that Isabelle has told him about me and my day. It shouldn't surprise me. It seems logical that they'd exchange details about what is going on so that the other person is aware of the finer details and updates.

"You won't say anything to Isabelle about last night, will you?" I ask, and my fingers clutch a little tighter around my coffee cup.

"I will have to," Aiden replies. He drinks some of his tea, like he hasn't just told me he's going to tell Isabelle we had sex last night.

"I don't really want her to know," I shoot back, my cheeks feeling warm. All I've told Isabelle is that I knew Aiden from university. The curious tone she has whenever she asks me for more details makes me think Aiden hasn't ever told her that our relationship had been anything more than friendship.

"She needs to know about the latest letter you had, she needs to know everything about the threats," Aiden explains in a gentle tone.

"I wasn't referring to that, you idiot. Glad it made a lasting impression," I snort.

He smirks. "Oh, believe me, it's left a lasting impression. I don't think I'm going to think of much else when I try to get to sleep later."

"Me either," I murmur. I'm pretty sure I'm going to find it hard to focus on work today.

I think back to last night, the way his hands had felt on my body, the way his eyes had seemed to turn a shade darker when I'd climaxed against his hand, the skilful way his tongue had teased out the second orgasm. I put my coffee cup down because I don't feel like I can be trusted to keep my grip on it, not when my whole body seems to have suddenly been set alight with a demand to repeat the whole process, right now.

The expression on Aiden's face makes me think he's having the same thoughts as me. I lick my lip and his pupils dilate. I wish that I'd let things in the kitchen unfold differently. I wish I'd taken his hand and led him back upstairs to my bedroom. I wish I'd told him I didn't need to go into work today, that I could work from home instead, punctuating my meetings by climbing into bed with him.

More than ever, I wish I'd met him first, that he could have been mine without the strings that first connected him to Caterina.

"Zoey," Aiden starts, sucking in a breath and seemingly trying to make his facial expression look a little less hungry, "of course I wouldn't tell Isabelle that. Not just because she'd have some stern words to say to me about keeping my mind on the job, but because whatever happens between us is only ever between us. It is nobody else's business what we get up to."

I force myself to take a couple of steadying breaths, afraid I'm on the verge of asking Aiden to take me home. I know it wouldn't be sensible. I shouldn't pull him back into a tangled mess with me, not because there is a hanging threat in front of me, but because I've already hurt him more than anybody should ever hurt somebody they love, and I'd vowed never to hurt him again.

"Do you think we can still go to the beach tomorrow?" I ask once I'm sure I'm in control of my thoughts again.

"Providing there are no additional incidents today, I think it should be okay," Aiden agrees, shifting in his seat and taking a sip of his tea.

"I will be on my best behaviour," I promise.

"I mean from whatever psycho is playing the game," he points out, a wry smile on his face. He checks his watch. "Isabelle won't be long, you should probably order your takeaway drinks, give Mike time to make all the drinks you order for the masses."

I laugh. "It'll be four drinks, you idiot. One for Isabelle, one for Abigail, one for the security guards."

"How the hell do you keep track of what coffee they all prefer?"

"I make it my job to know everything. I took my eyes off the ball once before, I said I'd never do that again."

"What happened with Dominic wasn't you taking your eye off the ball, it was him manipulating a situation to his advantage. Besides, remembering his coffee preferences wouldn't have stopped him stealing from you," Aiden reasons. I know he's right, but it doesn't stop me from shuddering. Dominic's betrayal is a dark part of my history, a stain on my company.

Before I can answer, my mobile phone starts ringing in my bag. I reach for it, frowning a little when I see the caller display is for the local police station.

"Zoey Taylor," I say as I answer. I cross my fingers for it to be anybody other than Officer West.

"Ms Taylor, it is Officer West," the voice on the line replies, and I pull a face. "We have had a development in the case. Can you come to the station this morning?"

"What kind of development?" I ask.

"We have made an arrest. If you can come to the station, we will go through everything with you. Perhaps you can bring Mr Slater, so he knows to put a halt to his amateur investigations," Officer West adds.

"I'll come over now," I reply, and I disconnect the call because the guy irritates the hell out of me. "Dickhead," I mutter.

"What's going on?" Aiden asks, and his posture has changed. He looks rod-spined and ready for action.

"The police say they've made an arrest," I explain. Aiden pushes his unfinished tea into the centre of the table and rises out of his seat. One hand is on his mobile, looking like he's sending a text.

"I'm telling Isabelle to meet us at the station. She can wait for you there before taking you to the office when we're done," he suggests as I wrap up the two pastries in some napkins to take away with us.

"You should go home, Aiden. You need to sleep."

"I think we already established that I'm going to be too busy thinking to sleep," he teases, his expression looking less harsh and alert to before. "Besides, if this is all done and dusted, if they've arrested the right person, you don't have this hanging over you and you won't need any more security," he points out.

Despite everything, when I stand to join him, paying Mike before leaving the coffee shop, there's an uncomfortable feeling in my stomach. I knew it was coming, but it appears the day I will have to say goodbye to Aiden again is here much sooner than I'd ever imagined, and I'm no longer sure I have the strength to do it again.

17

Aiden

Zoey sits in my car, texting away on her work mobile as I drive us to the police station. I don't need to ask her what she's typing. I know she'll be asking Abigail to rearrange her morning appointments, even though she's the boss and going through something difficult. I know she'll be apologising for not turning up with coffee, even though she probably has dozens of different places her staff can get coffee in the day. I know she'll be sending a load of apologies that she doesn't need to send because she takes everything like a personal failure.

I'm nearly at the station when my phone beeps and the automated reading app I use kicks in, the system alerting that it is a message from Isabelle.

Yeah, no worries, I'll see you at the station. Hopefully this will be the end of it all.

End of it all. I hope it's the end of the threat hanging above Zoey, but I know it's the end of my time with her and that stings more than I'm willing to admit. I knew this day would come, and I wanted it to be quick so Zoey wasn't hurt, but I still wish things were different between us. Especially after last night, and this morning in her kitchen.

"I've cleared my schedule for today. If this is it, if they've arrested somebody so that this stops, I think I'll get a taxi home and just work from home," Zoey says.

"I can drive you back to yours. You'll need to decide what you want to do with all the CCTV and motion detectors," I remind her.

"Honestly, Aiden, if this is all done and dusted, you can remove everything. I don't like the idea that I'm constantly under surveillance. I'll be happy being back to normal, not having to worry that something is going to happen." There's a frown on her face as she talks. I know a lot of people who are not comfortable with being filmed and recorded, especially in their own home, a place where they'd want to chill out and relax.

"I can do that, if that's your preference, and if this is really over."

"You don't think it is?" Zoey wonders.

"It'll depend on what the police say, to be honest. I don't want to worry you, but I've seen cases before where somebody is arrested and it's a mistaken identity or an error. I don't want that for you, I don't want you to feel like everything is okay and then be blindsided when the police decide they're wrong," I say. I pull my car into the parking section outside the police station. I cut the engine to the car and, for the first time since Monday, she doesn't immediately look like she's going to jump out of the car. "Are you okay?" I ask.

"Yes, just suddenly overwhelmed."

She sounds weary and exhausted. I smile at her.

"And there was me, thinking you'd finally learnt to wait for security to get out of the car first," I tease. She rewards me with a small smile and then her hand is on the door handle to get out of the car.

"Come on, let's get this over with, I guess," she says.

I walk with her towards the entrance of the police station. Officer West appears to be waiting for us near the reception desk.

"Ah, come through, I'll update you with what we have discovered. You can wait here, Mr Slater." He looks at me with a smug expression.

"Aiden will come with me, per the terms of my contract," Zoey shoots back. There is no such clause in the contract, but I'm not going to admit that.

"Fine. We can talk in here." Officer West gestures towards an office door to his right. Zoey follows him into the office, and I follow her, the two of us getting settled next to one another on one side of the desk.

"Who have you arrested?" Zoey asks.

"Does the name Ross Smith mean anything to you?"

Zoey frowns. "No, nothing. Should it?"

"We picked him up near your home this morning. I was doing a routine patrol. He had an envelope containing letters addressed to you, and he was wearing the same balaclava that was visible on the footage at your house."

"I don't know who he is, though." Zoey is still frowning.

"What connection does he have to Zoey?" I ask.

"We haven't found a connection, yet, but Mr Smith is well known to the police as being somebody who actively participates on questionable websites, particularly vocal about his hatred towards women." Officer West explains.

"You're telling me that this was nothing to do with me, that I'm just some random woman he's directed his delusions on?" Zoey sounds sceptical. I don't blame her, either. This doesn't reconcile to what I expected, either. I don't believe the person making threats against Zoey is a stranger. There's too much coincidence in the photograph she'd received in the post yesterday.

"That is our working theory," he replies.

"But you could be wrong," I point out.

"He was wearing the same balaclava and had letters to post. I hardly think he's an innocent person in this," he huffs.

"I'm not suggesting he is innocent. I'm just suggesting that he could be working with somebody else."

"There is no evidence to suggest that." Officer West shrugs.

"He has absolutely no connection to Zoey," I argue.

"Aiden," Zoey chides, putting her hand onto my knee. Officer West rolls his eyes, like he's vindicated in his assumption about my relationship with Zoey. It pisses me off because he's right, I've crossed a line I shouldn't when working for Zoey, but it's still me and Zoey, there was always more to us than what threat was going on, and nothing like what he thinks.

"We will continue to question Mr Smith but, so far, we are convinced he was working alone. He insists he is the mastermind behind everything, that he wanted to make a point, take a stand." Officer West looks like he thinks the conversation is over.

"He knew specific things about Zoey. He knew where she lived, he sent a photograph printed from her company website where she is the only person who is still alive. That's either a massive coincidence, or he is getting information from somewhere." My words are fast because I don't feel calm with this situation. I'm not used to feeling uncomfortable when a case resolves. This doesn't feel finished to me.

"Mr Slater, I appreciate you're probably upset that you're not the one who played the hero, but please leave this job to us. We know what we are doing." There's a smirk on his face.

"Aiden, come on, let's go," Zoey says, standing up.

"Give him the letter you got yesterday," I urge her. She blinks, like she's forgotten about it, and then fishes around in her bag, pulling out the envelope. She slides it across the table.

"What do you expect me to do with this?" Officer West asks.

"Your fucking job," I snap. Before he can reply, I stand with Zoey, and she almost pulls me out of the room.

"Well, you weren't holding back, were you?" she mutters as we exit the police station.

"I'm sorry, he just pisses me off," I reply. As we walk towards my car, I see Isabelle. She's stood next to my car, a questioning expression on her face.

"Well, is it over or not?" she asks.

"According to the police, yes," Zoey replies.

"But not according to Aiden, I'm guessing?" Isabelle asks her question to Zoey, but she's looking at me, assessing my facial expression.

"It seems like irrefutable evidence," Zoey responds with a shrug. "They caught the guy red-handed, Aiden."

"Are you going into the office, Zoey?" Isabelle asks.

"No, I was going to work from home. I've already cleared my schedule."

"Well, how about I drive you home?" Isabelle starts, and before I can speak, she shakes her head and gives me a wry smile. "Zoey and I can talk in the car. She wanted to know all about my hot date. You can follow us, and we can decide the next steps when we're at Zoey's house."

"Okay," Zoey replies, and she takes a step closer to Isabelle.

"Fine, I'll see you at Zoey's," I mutter, zapping my car to unlock it. I watch Isabelle and Zoey head towards Isabelle's car, the two of them smiling. I'm sure Zoey's already asking questions about Isabelle's date.

I watch them drive off and I follow them out the car park and towards Zoey's house. The whole drive there, I'm wondering how quickly Zoey is going to decide she's comfortable with the police assessment, telling me and Isabelle the job is over. It should be a relief, that the situation is resolved, but it doesn't seem like everything is finished yet, not just the threat, but everything between me and Zoey, either.

∞∞∞∞∞∞∞∞

I park my car on Zoey's driveway, next to Isabelle's car. The three of us get out of the cars, Zoey and Isabelle carrying on the conversation that they seem to have had in the car. I fall back a little as we walk to Zoey's front door given it seems like Isabelle's giving intimate details about how she feels about Max. I know a lot about Isabelle and Max, but it's different when Isabelle tells me directly, rather than me overhearing something.

Zoey unlocks the porch door and then the front door. Isabelle turns to look at me.

"Don't freak out when she talks, okay?" she murmurs, and then she steps into the porch behind Zoey.

I know it means Zoey's made up her mind already, that we're here to get our stuff, clear out the house, end the contract.

Zoey locks the front door behind us, leaving the porch door unlocked. She walks towards the kitchen, Isabelle and I behind her.

"Okay, so, I'm putting my trust in the police and what they've found. I've had threats from the guys in those groups before, usually via work, but I shouldn't be surprised that it escalated to being something at home."

"Zoey," I start, but she ploughs on like I haven't spoken.

"I appreciate everything you two have done for me, for accommodating me when I know I'm not the easiest person when it comes to accepting help." Zoey gives us both a wry smile, then she flicks the kettle on.

"You've been a walk in the park compared to some, right Aiden?" Isabelle grins.

"Practically an angel," I say, voice low.

Zoey glances over at me. She takes three cups from the cupboard.

"I know you don't agree with me, but I'm ending the contract now. I'll obviously pay according to the contract, but I think it's the best way forward. I need to get on with things like normal." She sounds firm, and I know there is no way I will be able to change her mind.

"Why don't you keep some of the security things for a while, just to give you a bit of extra reassurance?" I suggest.

"No, that's not how I want to live." Zoey's chin juts out, her shoulders back.

"At least keep the security lights we have put up," Isabelle coaxes. Zoey nods and I curse inwardly that I was the one who suggested she keep everything else, she's more agreeable when it's Isabelle's suggestion.

"I'll make a start at taking everything down," I say.

"Don't you want a drink?" Zoey asks.

I shake my head. "No, it's okay."

I don't wait for a reply, I head down towards Zoey's study so I can start taking down the motion detectors. The little step ladder I'd used is still stashed next to the bookcase she has in here, so I drag it into place and reach for the motion detector in here, ready to take it out.

"You think I'm making a mistake, don't you?" Zoey's voice comes from the doorway. I turn to look at her.

"It's your decision, Zoey, but I'm not sure things are properly resolved. But if this is your choice, then this is your choice." I shrug and something flashes across her expression, almost like I've hurt her.

"Don't be like that," she says, and I'm surprised to see her eyes well with tears.

"I'm not being like anything, I swear. I'm just concerned, okay?"

"Okay," she replies with a nod, and then she wipes her eyes.

"Why are you upset?" I step down from the step ladders. I stand in front of her.

"My decision, my choice," she murmurs, and I realise what I've said to upset her.

"I wasn't talking about the past two years." I sigh.

"I just thought…"

"I was just talking about the decision to remove the security features, that's all," I promise.

She takes a deep breath. "I know we have things we'll need to talk about, like what happened last night, but I feel way too fragile to even think about things right now. I think I need a few days to decompress, and I'm sure you're not in the right frame of mind to talk about it yet, either. Do you think we can maybe talk next week?"

"Of course. Look, let me get everything sorted and then Isabelle and I can get out of your hair," I suggest.

"Okay. Isabelle declined my drink offer; she's gone upstairs to make a start on taking stuff down. I'm just going to get my laptop set up in here, is that okay?"

"It's your house, Zo," I say with a small smile. I step back up on the step ladder so I can finish what I started. Zoey picks up the laptop bag she'd left at the doorway then takes a seat behind her desk, pulling her laptop out of the bag. She doesn't glance my way again, and I rush to get out of her way.

I join Isabelle upstairs, taking the step ladders with me.

"Here, let me get that," I offer. Isabelle's gathered all the motion detectors that have been placed at lower levels, on the windowsills, and tiptoeing to reach one above Zoey's bedroom door.

"So, dare I ask, would any of these cameras have caught something inappropriate?" Isabelle asks.

"Why on earth would you ask that?" I ask, laughing. Despite Zoey jumping into my arms in the hallway, I know there is no recording because I'd made sure nothing was pointing directly at her bedroom door, wanting her to be comfortable with the cameras being in the house.

"I can tell the atmosphere between you two has changed."

"Nope, you're imagining things," I say, setting up the step ladder.

"Yeah, one of these days, you and I are going to sit down and talk all about your little history."

"Maybe the same time you tell me the details about your hot date," I tease. Her face lights up and I laugh. "It went well, I take it."

"I'm trying not to get too excited, but I feel like this is it, like we're finally going to get back on track."

"I'll be keeping my fingers crossed for you. You deserve a happy ending, Issy."

"You do too, Aiden," she replies quietly.

One day, I'll tell her about my history with Zoey. I'll tell her about the heartache, the pain, the year Zoey couldn't bring herself to speak to me, the year I wanted to go to her, every single day, but didn't, because I'd been too afraid I'd hurt her further if I ignored her request to stay away.

I know Isabelle will be sympathetic. Her relationship with Max is less complicated than the one I have with Zoey, but still complicated. They'd been together for almost a year when Max had fallen ill with encephalitis. Isabelle had been working away, Max's illness had progressed seemingly unchecked in her absence. He'd suffered from hallucinations and when Isabelle had come home, he'd lashed out, hurting her when he didn't recognise what was true and real around him. Although Isabelle understood, Max had struggled to forgive himself, regardless how many times Isabelle and the doctors reminded him that he wasn't in control of himself at the time. Max's recovery had been long and slow, and he's pushed Isabelle away several times as he struggles to get back to his full self. I know Isabelle loves him, and I know of Max well enough to know he loves Isabelle too.

Maybe there's hope for them, as well as for me and Zoey.

We work together in silence as we take all the units down, putting them into the box Isabelle appears to have found to store the items. We work down the hallway, back down the stairs, throughout the downstairs floor of the house. I disconnect the CCTV system, still a little wary that Zoey's made this decision. When we're done, I knock on Zoey's study door, then open it.

"Hey, are you all done?" she asks, looking at us from the desk.

"Yeah, everything has been cleared out. I've left the security lights, though," I tell her.

"Thanks. Thank you both, for everything," Zoey says.

"It was nice meeting you, Zoey." Isabelle smiles at her. Zoey gets up from her desk, walking towards us. She gives Isabelle a brief hug.

"It was nice meeting you. If you ever want a career change, you let me know," she offers.

"Don't you dare." I laugh when they break apart.

"As much as I think your company is awesome, I'd be so bored by the office life." Isabelle giggles.

"Damn, and there was me thinking I had a replacement for Abigail if she decided to find another job." Zoey chuckles.

"I hope everything goes well, Zoey." Isabelle hitches the box onto her hip. "I'm going to get off, I'll catch up with you later, Aiden."

"I'll walk out with you," I say. Zoey stands with her arms folded across her chest, watching me and Isabelle as we walk towards the front door.

"Aiden," she calls to me, just after Isabelle steps into the porch.

"Yeah?" I turn to look at her. She doesn't say anything immediately, and she looks conflicted about what she wants to say.

"Thank you," she says, eventually.

"Bye, Zoey," I reply. I step into the porch and then out into the front garden, nothing but the sound of the front door shutting behind me.

I walk with Isabelle towards the car, we load everything into the boot. Isabelle gives me a quick hug before she gets in her car and drives away.

I get into my own car and start the engine. I don't drive off immediately. Instead, I take a deep breath. I take my mobile out of my pocket and log into the work system, end-dating Zoey's contract with yesterday's date. I submit a quick update of the police assessment and then I close everything down.

I dig around for the contact card that Officer Kim had given me. Without thinking too much of the consequences, I key his number into my keypad and then connect the call.

"Officer Kim." He sounds calm and professional.

"Hi, this is Aiden Slater. I wanted to talk to you about the Zoey Taylor case. I understand you have made an arrest," I say. I hear him sigh.

"I'm not going to discuss an open case with you. I understand we contacted Ms Taylor to give her an update."

"You did, yes, but I'm not convinced the guy you have was working by himself. I appreciate you're still conducting your interviews, but I wanted to check you would still look into the threat Zoey got yesterday. We passed the details onto West, but I was hoping you'd look at it. Please."

I hate the idea of pleading for some action to be taken, but I'm not convinced the other police officer will take everything seriously.

"I will catch up with West and I'll make sure the latest item is investigated. I'll give Ms Taylor a call as soon as I have an update."

"Thank you," I reply. There's a small silence between us.

"Is there anything else I can help you with, Mr Slater?"

"No, it's fine. Thank you," I add, and I hang up.

I put my mobile into the centre console and then drive towards my place.

I try to tell myself that I wasn't waiting on Zoey's driveway in the hopes that she would come out and ask me to talk today. She'd said next week. I know what Zoey is like when she has made her mind up.

Zoey has trusted me with her life. Her heart, on the other hand, that's another matter, and I've only got myself to blame. Caterina's death had fractured us, and I've had years to regret my decisions. I should have pushed Zoey harder to tell Caterina sooner. We should have been in control of the situation before we were discovered, to ensure Caterina was able to process everything without the added impairment of alcohol and drugs. I should have been the one to tell Caterina that I'd fallen in love with Zoey. I should have given my blessing for her and Jonah to be together. Instead, my choices broke Zoey's heart, causing her to put up barriers to protect herself from getting hurt again.

The one thing I know about Zoey is that despite all the barriers she puts up, the prickly exterior when you try to get too close, she's kind enough to reach out when somebody is in pain, even when she's in pain herself. I know this because at the worst time of my life, even when she hated me, she turned up and held my hand.

18

Zoey

There is a sea of young, enthusiastic students in front of me as I stand at the podium, finishing my talk. I'm slightly proud of myself for managing to get through the talk without turning into a blubbering mess. It's much harder than I ever thought it could be, standing at the university I attended with Caterina.

A hand in the audience shoots up after the lecturer asks if anybody has any questions, and I smile at them, encouragingly.

"Thank you for talking to us today, I appreciate seeing somebody who did the same degree as me, standing there and being so successful. I wanted to ask; how did you manage to move forward after your personal tragedy? Did you ever consider giving up?" The student smiles at me like it's a friendly question but it feels anything but friendly. It's a fucking dagger in my heart.

I clear my throat and wish I could pause everybody, just to give me a moment to compose myself. More than a moment, because I don't know how to continue faking a smile now.

"Any other questions?" The host seems to sense that my brain does not feel engaged. I can't answer this question.

There is a flurry of questions which are easier for me to answer. Questions about the business, what our recruitment requirements are, what issues I foresee the business will need to adjust for, what trends I am seeing in the market.

I answer the questions and keep the smile on my face. I know I look like a woman who doesn't have a care in the world, a well pulled together adult. My suit is a designer label, and in an effort to look my best, I had my hair done this morning at the hairdressers, perfectly neat French plaits and I had my make up done, too. Hair, suit and makeup, a barrier for the world.

When the students file out, the host smiles warmly at me.

"I am so sorry for the first question," she gushes.

"It's fine. Kids nowadays, right?" I joke.

"Are you staying for the lunch?" she asks as I gather all my things. I'd originally said I would stay, but I'm now exhausted.

"I'm afraid another commitment came up."

"Of course, maybe next year," she suggests. I nod, but I know there is no way I will be here next year.

I walk out and find my car, sinking into the seat and locking myself in. If I was a smoker, right now I would be reaching for a packet of cigarettes. If I was an alcoholic, I would be reaching for a bottle. Instead, my addiction has me reaching for my phone, launching the social media app, finding Caterina's profile.

I scroll through her pictures, pictures I feel like I know by heart. I've looked through these so many times in the last year that when I scroll, I always know what picture is coming next. There are so many pictures of us together. Loads of us with Aiden and Jonah. Picture after picture of Caterina, beaming out to the world. She was flawless and vivacious in every photograph. It's been almost a year and every day I am dumbfounded by the knowledge she is gone.

I scroll through her photographs, stopping at the very first one of us together. We'd taken it when going out together for the first time, a few days after we'd moved in together. In the picture, she is holding me close, looking up at me, making a kissing gesture at me with her lips, and I am laughing. She'd captioned the photograph with the words 'when you go to university to find your future but find your soul mate instead'.

As I look at the picture, I remember vividly how I'd felt that day. I'd had friends at school, but my difficult home life had me hiding parts of myself. I could never invite a friend home, to see my sullen and angry father, my timid and agreeable mother, to sit in the oppressive air that hung in the house. It had driven a wedge between me and my friends. With Caterina, I didn't have those barriers. I could be open and honest and free with her, and I loved how she took me under her wing.

I trace my finger down the image of her face. As usual, a tear rolls down my cheek. Everything I have ever read about grief tells me the first year is the hardest. The help groups on the internet seem insistent that you have to get through every anniversary before you can pull yourself back together. I've been ticking off those anniversaries. I've got through what would have been her birthday, the anniversary of when we launched the business, the first Christmas. Tomorrow, I'm getting through the first of my birthdays without her. Four days after that, it'll be the anniversary of her death, then the only thing I have is the anniversary of her funeral.

The second year has got to be easier because I can't keep going the way I am. I'm better, but I'm nowhere close to being whole. Existing rather than living. Work keeps me focused, though in the beginning even that had been tough.

The first day back, before I could summon enough courage to go into the building, I'd wound up in the coffee shop that Caterina and I had spent so much time at before, early in the morning before any other customer was there. Mike, who had been serving us for years, told me he was sorry about Caterina. It was the first time since her funeral that anybody had said this to my face. Aside from the occasional conversation with Caterina's family, I'd been projecting an image of a woman without a care in the world. With strangers, I'd faked conversations about my plans and how great everything was. When Mike had been so kind, I'd broken down crying. He had come around the counter and given me a big hug. His wife, Sally had said some soothing words and then she'd helped me fix my makeup so I could go into work. I'd survived the day but cried all the way home.

Now, every day, I go to work, I keep my focus on things, and I still cry in my car on my drive home. The first couple of weeks after I went back to work, I'd go out at lunch and cry, the sympathy and grief of my employees too much for me to take.

Every day, somebody mentions Caterina, tells me how much they miss her. Everybody had loved her. Her sparkling and mischievous nature had provided balance to my more serious one. When we'd held company wide conferences, she was the one who seemed to get everybody to smile, got them on their feet, got them energised. There's a small cloud of gloom that seems ever present at the office now. I still haven't found the strength to clear out her office. Everything is as it was when she left it, even down to the post it notes she'd written and stuck on piles of paper. Once, I sat in her chair and traced my fingers over the notes she'd written. I know I'll have to get around to clearing the office but I'm not ready. I'd moved out of Caterina's house as soon as I could, and her office is the only place that I can go that feels like she's here.

I close my eyes for a moment to stop the tears, then I close her social media page. Over the year, I've become more disciplined in how much time I allow myself to look, the same way I've tried to discipline myself to spending less time in her office. I tell myself it is helping, but I'm not convinced it is, not when the loss I feel seems ever present, like a permanent haze blocking out the sun.

I look down my list of connections on my social media page, studiously ignoring Aiden's name. Aiden has stood by his decision to wait for me to reach out, and I've stood by mine when I'd told him not to. I haven't spoken to him since the day of the funeral. The guilt of losing Caterina is still too much to live with. It'll haunt me until the end of my days. I never allow myself to look at his page. I know one day, he'll move on and find some other woman, if he hasn't already, and it'll break me all over again.

Jonah's profile is not anything I shy away from opening. His posts are dark and often reference Caterina. In the early days after she died, his posts always seemed to be an echo of my thoughts and feelings. Once, he'd posted *'grief is the wound, anger is the scar that remains.'*

There's a part of me that feels sorry for him, I expect he loved Caterina more than I ever realised, but the fury I feel has always stopped me forgiving him. So, I know his grief, and I know his anger.

We all played our part in her death. I punish myself the most, but Jonah is second.

I open Jonah's page and for a moment, I am confused at what I am seeing. Since yesterday when I'd looked, his page seems to have gone crazy. There are so many messages on there, not from him, but about him.

Jonah, you were a great friend.

I'm so sorry you couldn't overcome your demons.

Rest in peace, buddy.

The gasp I give makes me jump, even if it's me making the noise. This cannot be true.

For the first time in nearly a year, I open Aiden's profile. His page is relatively quiet, no postings made from him in the year. Like mine, straight after Caterina's death, there was a load of condolences posted, friends we'd had who were so sorry for our losses, dumfounded by the news, reaching out in the only way they knew how. After those posts, there is a gap in the time until yesterday when the messages have started.

Aiden, so sorry for your loss

If you need anything, let me know.

I drop my phone into my bag and start my car. I have no idea if Aiden is still living at his flat, but that's where I drive. I park my car and walk down his path, the same path where I'd thrown myself into his arms when he'd come home, the same path he carried me down, asking if I was done pretending that what had happened between us didn't matter.

I knock on the door and prepare myself for somebody other than Aiden answering the door. I don't know what would be worse; having a stranger living here, Aiden having moved without me knowing, or Aiden's girlfriend answering the door, wondering who I am, reminding me that I am an unwelcomed visitor.

Instead, when the door opens, it is Aiden who stands in front of me. The sight of him takes my breath away. He looks like he has lost a little weight since I last saw him, or at least some of his muscle definition. His grey-blue eyes hold my gaze.

There's a pause between us. One. Two. Infinity. Then, without saying a word, he opens the door for me to come inside.

As soon as the door is shut behind us, I slip my arms around him, I pull him close to me. For a minute, he sobs against me, my shirt getting wet with his tears. I hold him closer, my heart breaking.

He pulls away from me, clears his throat and wipes his eyes.

"Do you want a drink?" he asks.

"What are you having?" I ask.

"Come through."

He walks through his flat, me behind him. Inside the main living area, on his dining table, there is a bottle of vodka and a glass next to it. The bottle looks half empty, and I don't know whether this was because he's already had half today, or if he's not yet started.

Aiden grabs another glass from the cupboard. He puts it onto the table and pours two generous measures of vodka. He hands me a glass and then he clinks his against mine before he drinks his serving, barely stopping for breath. I drink mine and put my glass on the table.

"How many have you had?" I ask, and I spot the second bottle of vodka, this one empty.

"Not enough," he replies, and his voice cracks. He looks like he hasn't slept in far too long.

"Do you have anything urgent to do today, are you seeing your parents?"

"No. They were on holiday and can't get a flight back until tomorrow night. I've done what I can do so far, I identified his…" Aiden's voice breaks and the enormity of what he has had to do hits me. He may have had a fractured relationship with Jonah, but Aiden always loved him, forgave his transgressions. Having to formally identify his brother's body must have been traumatic.

"Come with me," I coax, offering my hand. He takes it and lets me lead him through to his bedroom. I try not to think of all the times we've made this walk before, sometimes him carrying me, often with us stumbling if we were walking together because we'd be busy trying to undress each other as we walked, too impatient to wait until we reached the bedroom. More than once, we'd had sex against the cabinet in the hall, not able to wait a second longer.

When I open his bedroom door, he doesn't flinch. The room is slightly disorganised, the bed unmade but everything looks clean. I walk around the bed to draw the blackout curtains. There is still a little light in the room given the bedroom door is still open, so it is light enough for me to see things. I walk to stand in front of Aiden, unbuttoning his shirt and slipping it from his body. I unbutton the trousers he's put on and pull them down his body, slightly grateful that he's got boxer briefs on underneath. Once he's undressed, I slip out of my jacket, my shirt, kick off my shoes and take off my trousers. I push Aiden gently to get him to sit down on the bed and then I close the bedroom door, banishing all the light. I move to the bed as carefully as I can, given it's so dark, and get into the bed beside him.

I pull him to lie against me and I wrap my arm and leg over him. I let my hand rest against his chest, feeling his heartbeat under my palm.

"I'm so sorry, Aiden," I whisper into the darkness. His only response is the shudder of his body as he cries. I hold him tighter. He cries until he falls asleep, but I don't let go of him. Instead, I hold onto him, pretending that I can keep him safe from the demons, my own tears soaking onto his bedsheet.

∞∞∞∞∞∞∞∞

In the morning, Aiden gets up, disappears into the bathroom, and then comes back to bed. He smells of minty toothpaste. He gets back into the bed, occupying the space he'd taken before. He doesn't say a word, but I hold him close and let my fingers stroke across him so that he knows I'm awake.

Eventually I get up and go to the bathroom. I tell myself he won't mind too much if I use his toothbrush, so I brush my teeth and go to the loo before going back into his bedroom, still wearing only my underwear. I get back into bed and start to resume the same position we'd had before but this time he gestures for me to lie the other way, for him to hold me instead. I lie against one of his arms and he wraps the arm around me, his hand on the bare skin of my stomach.

"What day is it?" he asks.

"Tuesday. The fifteenth," I clarify.

"Can you do something for me, just for today?" His voice is tentative.

"Anything, Aiden," I whisper back.

"Can we pretend, just for today, that nothing has gone wrong? Pretend it's just you and me in the world, that it's a year ago, and nothing bad has ever touched us?"

It feels like a big ask, to forget Caterina, to forget Jonah, to forget all the pain we have in our bodies and hearts. There's something about it that feels freeing, to put everything to the back of my mind, to forget and pretend, if only for the day. The grief and the sadness will be waiting for us tomorrow, but I can give Aiden what he is asking, if that is what he needs.

"I can do that," I murmur.

He kisses my shoulder. "I love you, Zoey," he whispers.

"I love you too, Aiden." This is not a lie; this is not pretend. My feelings for Aiden have not changed. He's still the other love of my life.

The hand he has resting on my stomach slips a little further down, his hand ever so slightly underneath the elastic of my underwear.

"Is this okay?" he asks, voice gruff.

"Yes, Aiden," I start, and then his hand slips further down, his fingers skimming over my pubic hair, his index finger searching for my sweet spot. I can feel his erection pressing against my spine. For the first time in nearly a year, I feel a stirring inside of me, and it feels like I've woken from a deep sleep, desperate for a release, desperate for him.

He moves the arm I've been lying on so that it curls around my body, resting on my chest. His fingers make their way into the cup of my bra. When his fingers skim across the nipple, I gasp and groan, twitching slightly, my back rubbing up against his erection. His own moan is still the sexiest sound I've ever heard.

Aiden keeps moving his fingers, alternating between the one hand rubbing against my clitoris and the other hand circling around my nipple. When he leans over and kisses and nips the side of my neck, I'm sure I'm going to ignite into a ball of flames. I've never been with a man who can make my body respond the way it does to Aiden, and even though it's always so easy for me to climax with him, he has never been a lazy lover.

When his finger slips inside me, I can't stop my thighs from clamping tight around him, keeping him in that position and I move my hips, grinding against him.

"Zoey," he murmurs when it's clear I'm on the edge.

"Oh God, if you don't fuck me right now, I'm going to lose control. Don't make me get off by dry humping you," I gasp.

"Doesn't feel very dry to me," he teases, moving his finger inside me again and making me feel like my eyes are going to roll back in my head.

"It's been a year, Aiden. I haven't even gotten myself off in that time," I pant.

"Me either, so don't be surprised that this is over fast," he warns.

I grind against his hand again and he growls, rolling us over so I'm flat on the mattress and he's above me. He works quickly to unclasp my bra, flinging it to the floor, then he pulls down my knickers and his boxer briefs. He kisses his way down and up my body in a V shape, from one shoulder, diagonally down my body, paying special attention to my breast and nipple, sucking and teasing before heading further south, burying himself between my thighs for a moment before heading back up, across my stomach, my other breast, stopping at my shoulder. When he's finished exploring with his mouth, he grabs both of my wrists, pulling them above my head and then holding them onto the mattress with one of his hands. With his other hand, he grips himself, positioning himself against me.

"Jesus," I pant.

"Is this okay?" he asks.

"Yes. Now, Aiden, now, please, now," I groan and then he's inside me, his eyes seemingly turning a shade darker. I hook both of my legs over each of his, using my ankles to push against the back of his thighs so he pushes harder against me.

"You're going to make this really fast," he warns.

"Then just do it again later." I writhe underneath him, and he gives into the desire, flexing his hips and moving against me. One more touch and I know I'm going to come undone.

"Look at me, Zoey," he growls, and we lock gazes as he moves against me again. I can't stop myself from coming undone. My eyes are wide as I orgasm underneath him. Aiden leans down to kiss me, murmuring how much he loves me, still moving inside me. It's only when I climax for the second time that he loses his own control, spilling inside me before kissing me.

Aiden lets go of my wrists, I wrap my arms around his body, my legs still hooked over his. I couldn't possibly hold him any tighter, everything about my position suggests that I don't ever want to let him go. He collapses slightly against me.

"Are you okay?" I ask. One of my hands works a way up his body, across his broad shoulders, up his neck. I run my fingers through his hair, curling them slightly against the strands. I know my question is stupid because Aiden is far from okay. I know how much this hurts him.

Aiden looks at me. "Happy birthday, Zoey. I wanted to be the first to say it," he says. It breaks my heart, remembering how special I'd felt last year when he'd phoned me at midnight, so eager to be the first. It also breaks my heart a little that there isn't likely to be anybody else who will go out of their way this year to wish me happy birthday, beyond the usual routine messages people will send on social media.

"This is an amazing way to wake up on my birthday," I whisper back, still only half playing pretend. If things were different, if he'd been mine first, if Jonah had always been Caterina's, then this would be how I'd be waking up for every birthday.

"Shower?" he asks, and I smile and nod.

We walk together to his bathroom. He starts the water for the shower, turning the temperature up because he always joked that I liked mine one degree less than scalding.

Once we're showered, we dress in his room. He gives me a pair of his boxers to wear instead of my own underwear and one of his tee shirts given my own shirt is crumpled and has marks from where he'd cried last night. He pulls on a pair of trousers and a casual looking top.

"What do you want to do today?" I ask him as I follow him out of the bedroom. I don't know how long he wants to keep up this charade that nothing bad has happened, how long he can keep it up.

"How do you feel about a walk on the beach?" he suggests.

"I need to go home first, to pick up some different shoes. We could get breakfast on the way. Is that okay?"

"Sure," he says, grabbing his car keys and wallet.

I follow him as he steps out the front door. He locks it behind me and we walk towards his car, leaving mine where I'd parked it. There's a small, fond smile on his face when he sees I'm still driving the car he'd helped me pick out, long before we first slept together, and I remember how he'd laughed at how I'd haggled the dealer to a low price, telling me I could help him buy his next one if that was the kind of deal I could get.

When we get into his car and he starts the engine, I input my new address into his sat nav system. There is an option to save the address, so I do, calling it *Home*.

Aiden drives towards mine, doing a little diversion when he sees the signs for a drive through restaurant. We eat breakfast in the car before he resumes the drive to mine.

He comes into the house with me. He doesn't say a word about my new place. I assume it's because it would be too much of a break in the game of pretend to acknowledge I'm living somewhere different, that I bought my own home, a place he's never seen before. Instead, he waits for me as I pack a few things into a bag and he sits on my bed as I change my trousers into a pair of jeans, add a pair of socks, select a pair of comfortable shoes.

Aiden drives us to the beach. I'm not surprised to find it mostly empty. It's too early in the year for anybody to want to be on the beach, so we have the place almost to ourselves, aside from a few dog walkers who are enjoying it being off-season and able to have the dogs off lead.

We sit on the steps below the colourful beach houses, take off our shoes and socks so our feet can sink into the damp sand. He holds my hand as we watch the waves coming further up the sand as the tide comes in. We talk about everything, except what is really going on. When an energetic dog comes bounding towards us, dropping a ball at our feet, we laugh and throw the ball, repeating the process when the dog keeps coming back, until the owner whistles and the dog runs off.

We walk along the beach for miles, our trousers getting damp when we stray too close to the waves. We talk about the holidays we are going to take, the destinations we'll see together, how he wants to show me the world before we settle down properly. We talk about how we'll get married in a church, and he tells me he thinks I'll be the most beautiful bride. We talk about the children we'll have in the future. He tells me he hopes our children will have my eyes, but I tell him I couldn't imagine anything better than our children having his eyes instead.

We stop for a late lunch in a quiet café near the beachfront, chatting to an elderly couple who sit at the table next to us. When the older gentleman asks

Aiden about what our plans are for the day, Aiden smiles and says he's spending it with the woman he loves.

Aiden drives us back to his place. We go straight to the bathroom so we can wash the sand and sea-salt from us, showering together. I wash his body and sink to my knees, taking him in my mouth, giving him the release he needs.

We eat a dinner he orders in. We sit and talk about things we'd seen in the day, gushing over the energetic dog, commenting on how sweet the elderly couple were. When we get tired, we walk to his bed, hand in hand. I kiss the scar that runs through his eyebrow, the one he got after being injured in the car accident. He kisses the scar that remains on my wrist from where I'd had my own stitches, then he runs a line of kisses up my arm until he meets my lips, kissing me for what feels like hours, like we're cramming in a year's worth of missed kisses into one night. We make love, it's beautiful and tender, and afterwards we murmur how much we love one another.

As I fall asleep, I realise it's the first day in almost a year when I haven't cried.

∞∞∞∞∞∞∞∞

I wake to the sound of Aiden tossing and turning in the bed. I open my eyes and can see his phone screen is lit, so I know he's just been on his phone. I can tell from the atmosphere in the room that the spell has been broken.

"What's the matter?" I ask.

"That was my parents, calling before their flight. They're coming here straight from the airport so we can start arranging the funeral." His voice cracks at the word funeral. I reach for his hand.

"If you want me there, I'll be there with you for the funeral."

"I do, Zo, but it'll probably be best if you're not. My parents…" His voice trails off and he doesn't need to elaborate that his parents don't like me, that they wouldn't want me at their son's funeral.

"What happened? How did…how did Jonah die?"

Aiden sighs. He shifts on the bed to hold me, his body spooned behind mine.

"He spiralled a lot since Caterina died. He ended up getting further and further into drugs. Dad sent him to rehab but as soon as he was out, it didn't take long for him to be back in the same habits. Mum and Dad tried everything, but nothing got through. Jonah had two more stints in rehab, long sessions of therapy, but I don't think he could forget what happened. He got into harder drugs, started taking heroin."

"Were you two talking?"

"Yeah, but it always felt like a battle. He blamed us for Caterina because you and I were in a relationship. I blamed him for giving her the drugs, and the way things unfolded that night. When he called me the day he died, I didn't pick up, Zo. What if…what if I could have said or done something differently and stopped it? He could have been calling for me to help him, to convince him not to take something, and I ignored his call."

Aiden's voice breaks as he talks, and I feel his pain. We both know what it is like to grieve and battle through guilt, and now we're doing it for a second time.

"You were a good brother, Aiden. You forgave him for so much."

"I did love him, but I was so angry with him at times, and I let that stop me from helping him. I'm sure my parents will tell me how much I failed as a brother." Aiden sighs and I feel a rush of anger.

"You did not fail as a brother. You forgave him for sleeping with your fiancée. You were still trying to help him since Caterina died. If they say anything otherwise, they're lashing out in grief."

"When he went into rehab the second time, my dad told me how much he wished we'd never met you and Caterina," he admits. I'm not surprised. I never told Aiden that I'd overheard him and his dad talking after Caterina died.

"Let your dad hold me responsible. It wouldn't be anything less than I deserve; especially given the way I treated Jonah." I feel a ripple of shame about my last words to Jonah. Aiden tightens his arm around me and I'm sure he's holding back, not telling me just how much his dad is going to hold me responsible for what happened to his son. It wouldn't make a difference. I already hold myself responsible.

"Maybe in the future, he'll see Jonah for the way he really was, a flawed person who we all loved, but couldn't save from himself," Aiden says.

"Why didn't you ever tell me about Jonah and Caterina sleeping together, or that she was doing drugs? She said that night that you'd promised."

"You remember the weekend that Caterina and I broke up, when I'd come home and by the house to surprise her?" he starts.

"Yeah, I was in pain because of my tooth. You got me some medicine and stayed with me for a while."

"Once I was sure you were okay, I went to Jonah's. I thought I'd made a mistake about the weeks and that I'd forgot Caterina was with her family. I got to Jonah's and Caterina's car was outside. I think I knew as soon as I saw the car that it wasn't good because I didn't knock on the door. I let myself in, and I found the two of them, having sex. I could tell they were both high. They tried to justify it; told me it didn't mean anything. I told Caterina it was over. She begged me not to tell you what she'd been doing. I agreed, on the condition she got help and she stopped taking drugs, and never did drugs again with Jonah. I knew it wouldn't have been the first time she'd taken something, and I didn't want to see her lose the control she thought she had on it. I've seen what drugs can do to people, and no matter what she'd done with Jonah, I didn't want to see that happen to her."

"What happened between you and Jonah?"

"Caterina left after we'd made our deal. Jonah told me everything. They'd meet up some weekends, either when you were busy, or Caterina would lie and say she was with her family. They'd do a couple lines of coke, they'd go out and party and invariably, they'd go to his and 'do more blow and bang', as he eloquently put it. It had been going on for ages."

"You could have told me so many times," I murmur.

"I'd promised, and I'd seen nothing to tell me she wasn't holding up her side of the bargain. Jonah was doing twice-weekly drug tests to prove to my father he was drug free, and I assumed that if he was clean, so was she, so I just kept up with my side of it."

"She was so unfair to you, though."

"It didn't matter to me. If she was staying off the drugs, I didn't care what she said about me, and I know it'll sound stupid, but I didn't want to hurt you by telling you the truth. The minute I saw that she was high again, I was so angry with them, that I'd been keeping a secret from you but they'd carried on."

"Do you think they were still hooking up after you'd found out?"

"On and off, according to Jonah, yes. He told me after she died. After we'd split, Caterina had admitted Jonah's version of how long they'd been together before I found out, so I had no reason to doubt Jonah tell me after she died that they'd still been together. It's part of the reason Jonah spiralled."

"I had no idea about them," I murmur. Not once had I ever suspected Caterina and Jonah had been together. Jonah had always been friendly, flirty, often downright outrageous with women, but he'd always treated Caterina with respect, never crossing the line with her in front of me. Maybe that should have been my clue to know he did care for her, more than I realised but it never occurred to me. Caterina had spent ages encouraging me to give Jonah a chance, all while she was sleeping with him behind Aiden's back. Her deceit doesn't change anything though. The secret I'd kept from Caterina had led to her death, and I'll carry that with me for the rest of my life.

"I spent since the night of the accident wondering if me revealing the truth was something that pushed Caterina to run away. If I hadn't told the truth, maybe we'd have just all argued on the hallway and that would have been that." Aiden's voice cuts through my thinking.

"There's so much I wish I had done differently," I admit, throat tight, a tightness in my chest.

"I know," he soothes.

"It's all been such a mess, Aiden, and now they're both gone," I cry. I feel the weight of their deaths on me, every decision I made and everything I said to them, making me feel guilty.

"Zo?" Aiden whispers in the darkness.

"Yeah?"

"Nothing has really changed, has it? We're still broken, aren't we?"

Yesterday, we had played pretend. Pretended nothing bad has ever happened to us. Pretended that that glorious future we'd painted was our life, but that is all it is, just pretend.

I think of Caterina and Jonah, both still gone.

I think of Aiden's father who holds me responsible for Jonah spiralling.

I think of my relationship with Aiden, too tied up with our emotions about Caterina and Jonah to exist independently of the events of their deaths.

I think of how much shame I feel about betraying Caterina, now laced with the shame of how I'd treated Jonah, compounding everything, weighing me down more than ever.

"I'm so sorry, Aiden," I cry.

This time, he holds me as I cry. I'm sure, as we both fall asleep, we both know that by the time morning rolls around, I'll have left, and I know when I leave, the tears will come with me.

19
Zoey

I watch Aiden's car from the upstairs window as he remains on the driveway much longer than necessary. He never glances up towards the house, and the whole time he is there, I'm not sure if I should go out to him.

It would be so easy to go outside, sit in his car with him, hold his hand, tell him how much he means to me, ask him to come inside so we can talk. Except, what is easy isn't always what is right. I've hurt Aiden too much in the past.

Over the last two years, I've wanted to go back to him so many times. Lizzie, ever honest, reminds me whenever I talk about Aiden that he would never be able to forgive me for what happened to Jonah.

When Aiden's car finally reverses off the drive, I head back to my study, checking the front door is locked as I pass it. I sit back behind my desk, checking all my emails and replying to everything as quickly as I can, picking up all the questions that have been sent to me. Abigail clearly has everything in hand, she's managed to rearrange my diary and give me the upcoming Monday free of meetings so I can have the day off, like I'd asked her this morning as Aiden had driven me to the police station.

Monday would have been Jonah's birthday. He would have been thirty-three. I've no idea if Aiden would want to see me, but aside from the last two years where we had no contact, on days like this, we'd meet up. Still broken, but temporarily reunited to get ourselves through our worst days, always finding that nobody else could get us through those days.

Shaking my head to focus, I email Abigail to tell her I'm available by phone for anything urgent. I grab my personal mobile and text Lizzie to tell her that I'm okay, that the police have arrested somebody. She texts back to tell me she'll call me over the weekend.

I work through the rest of the day, eating the pastry Mike gave me at breakfast for my lunch. At six-thirty, my work mobile pings, a message from Abigail, telling me to log off work and enjoy the weekend. I'm surprised how late it is and that I've spent most of the day hunched over my laptop.

I stand and stretch. I can't decide if I'm hungry or exhausted. I settle on exhausted, like the events of the week have caught up with me. I switch off my laptop and put it away, walk through the downstairs section of the house, checking the windows, even though I know they're still going to be locked. I lock the porch and then relock the front door, heading upstairs to my bedroom. I strip off, shower and get myself ready for bed. It might only be early evening, the sun might still be shining in the sky, but I'm ready for bed. I close the curtains and clamber into bed, catching the scent of me and Aiden on the bedsheets.

I wrap myself into the quilt, squeeze my eyes shut, letting the scent of us wash over me as I drift off to sleep.

∞∞∞∞∞∞∞∞

The sound of the doorbell ringing wakes me up. I'm startled as I look at my watch, trying to work out what day it is. My watch says it's eight and for a moment I'm not sure if it is the same day and I've only been asleep for an hour, or whether it's the next day and I've slept until morning. It takes me a moment to realise I've slept through the night.

The dream I was having lingers on me like a cloak that's been slipped around my shoulders. I blame the scent of Aiden on the bedsheets, it's like smelling him in my sleep conjured him into my dreams.

The doorbell rings again. I roll over, still disoriented. I grab a cardigan from the wardrobe, pulling it on as I head downstairs. I open the front door and start laughing when I see Lizzie is stood outside my porch door. She's wearing a big sunhat, sunglasses with large frames, and a sundress. She looks dressed for the beach.

"What are you doing here?" I laugh as I open the porch door. I rub the sleep from my eyes, stretch a little so I'm more alert.

"Surprise!" Lizzie exclaims.

"I am totally surprised! I thought you were away until next week."

"Yeah, but I got the weekend free, and I didn't see the point in hanging around by myself in a hotel, so I thought, stuff it, I'm going to go see my bestie. I can drive back on Sunday night so I'm ready for the Monday training."

"You're a very dedicated friend." I grin. She follows me into the house.

"I am indeed. So, I'm guessing you don't have plans for today? I'd hate to have driven all this way to be given up for a better offer."

"Nope, free all weekend. What were you thinking?"

"I thought we could go to the beach." Lizzie gives me a big smile.

"Well, clearly, I'm going to need a minute," I say, gesturing at my pyjamas.

"Chop, chop. I've packed up a lunch in the cool box in my car, I've got the suncream and the beach towels. The only thing I need is you, so move your butt."

"Make yourself comfortable, I'll be as fast as I can," I tell her, and I head towards the stairs.

"We'll grab breakfast on the way," Lizzie calls to me.

I rush up the stairs, going back to my bedroom. I grab my tankini from the drawer, and a sundress from the wardrobe to wear over it. I get freshened up in the bathroom, get changed. I grab my mobile, bag and sunglasses and then head downstairs to where Lizzie is waiting for me, pacing in the hallway.

"That is the fastest I've ever got dressed." I laugh.

"I am very impressed. Come on! Let's go grab some breakfast and then find a good spot on the beach," she says, a grin on her face. I follow her out of the house, locking the doors behind me, looking forward to getting to the beach.

∞∞∞∞∞∞∞

The sunshine feels glorious, as does having my feet sunk in the warm sand. My sandals are discarded on the sand, next to Lizzie's flipflops. We've spread the beach mats that she'd packed out on the sand, both of us stripped off to our swimwear, our clothes discarded in a little pile next to the cool box.

"This is amazing," I announce, feeling utterly content. I never used to think much about the beach, not until the day Aiden and I had spent our first day of playing pretend together. Since then, it's felt like a calming place for me, though, as usual when I'm at the beach, my mind is thinking about Aiden.

"It's not even the height of summer yet, but if this weather keeps up, we're going to have an amazing one," Lizzie comments.

"I think I'm going to come to the beach more. I look for it every day out my office window, I don't know why I don't come more often," I muse. I bury my feet further into the sand. I look down the beach, out towards the waves. It's still early in the morning but the beach is busy, there are lots of families with young children who are jumping over the little waves, screeching as they try to run away from the water.

I know the water will be cold, regardless of how much the sun is shining, but I'm tempted to take a swim later, to feel the salt water on my skin, to lie back in the water and look up to the vast blue sky, to feel like I'm insignificant.

"I can't work out if you're just happy that the police arrested somebody, or if something else is going on to make you look so happy." Lizzie comments. Her face is half buried under the sunhat, she's refusing to take it off, claiming she has no interest in premature aging.

"I'm clearly thrilled that somebody has been arrested. It was nice to go to sleep last night without thinking about somebody in the house," I say, though there was a part of me that had missed knowing Aiden was around.

"I don't know how you slept a wink, knowing a stranger was wandering around your house when you were vulnerable." Lizzie shudders.

"It wasn't that bad. They kept me safe when I thought I needed it and I barely noticed they were there," I protest, but I'm suddenly thinking about the night I'd asked Aiden into my bed. I noticed everything that night. Even now, my skin heats up as I think of his hands on my body.

"Have you kept any of the security measures up?"

"No, I asked them to take everything down. I don't want to live my life thinking there is somebody out to get me all the time. It's my house, I want to feel comfortable and relaxed there."

"Well, I am glad everything is resolved. I hope they lock this person up and throw away the key." Lizzie wrinkles her nose at me.

"Me too."

"So, what else have you got to tell me? What else has been going on since I saw you last, crazy people aside?" Lizzie prompts.

"I have been thinking a lot about Aiden," I admit.

Lizzie rolls over on the beach towel so she's facing me. She tips the brim of her sunhat up and inches her sunglasses down her nose, staring at me with a quizzical expression on her face.

"Aiden as in your ex?"

"Yes." I nod. I should tell her that Aiden was the person who provided security, but something holds me back. I know she won't see it as anything but a mistake, she's been quite firm about her opinion of my relationship with Aiden.

"Have you spoken to him?" she asks. I shake my head and stare out to the water. It's easier to lie when you're not looking somebody in the eye. I should know, I had plenty of experience doing it.

"No, I've just been thinking about things a lot this week."

"Please tell me you're not thinking of getting in touch with him?" she groans.

I laugh at her reaction. "Well, that kinda tells me what you think about it."

"I just think you'd be setting yourself up for a fall. There's so much baggage between you. Your best friend, his brother…that's a lot of blood to run between you."

"You make it sound like we murdered them," I scoff, though she's hit a nerve. For years, I blamed myself for Caterina's death, and for years I was sure Aiden knew I'd contributed to Jonah going off the rails, resulting in his death. If thinking about Caterina's death hurts my heart, and thinking of Jonah's makes my throat tight, how does it affect Aiden?

"Even if that was something you could get past, do you think he'd ever really trust you? I mean, I don't want to sound bitchy, but you did cheat on Caleb," she points out. "Aiden doesn't sound like the type of person to willingly date somebody who cheats given what Caterina did to him."

"I know that," I reply, tersely.

"I know you think you two had this big love affair that was more than what you've ever had with anybody else, but I worry that you'll try to get back with him and it'll explode again. How do you think his parents would react? Don't they blame you for Jonah?" she prods.

"Yes," I murmur, but I don't know for sure. I have no idea how their opinion of me has changed over the years. They might still wish I'd never met Aiden or Jonah, that along with Caterina, we could be erased from their sons past, rewriting the history.

"Whatever you were thinking about with Aiden, forget it. I've told you before, you need to move on. I can help you find a lovely guy. Somebody who doesn't have so much darkness around them."

"Aiden doesn't have darkness around him," I scoff.

"He sounds like he does, from the history you've told me. Besides, you don't know what he's like now, you haven't seen him in two years. He could be married. He could have a kid. His whole life might be perfect, and you want to waltz in there and change everything?"

I know Aiden isn't married. I know he doesn't have any children. I know he isn't even dating anybody. I know I wouldn't be messing up a relationship, but I don't know if I'd be doing anything good in his life. If I ask Aiden for another chance, there's every possibility I could hurt him.

"You're right. I'm probably just in a weird mood with everything that has been going on."

"That's probably completely normal, Zoey. You've had a horrible week. I just hate the idea of you getting hurt or being disappointed. Whatever happened in the past, it should stay in the past."

"I guess you're right. Forget I mentioned anything. I should be chilling out and relaxing with you, not getting myself all confused." I give her a big smile. She gives me a little nod and then settles back on the beach towel.

Despite what I've told Lizzie, my mind is still on Aiden. She seems satisfied with my response to her opinion, but I know I'll need to talk to Aiden, to see what he wants, to see where things could lead us, to take that gamble. The thought of talking to him makes me feel a little terrified, something I'm not used to.

I'm a strong woman. I make difficult decisions every day of my life. I have lived my life with the mantra that I will not yield under pressure, I taught myself to thrive on it, to take all the pressure and pain and turn it to something productive. I've taken my worst hurts and poured it into my business, pretended that everything was okay. The only person who has ever known that I'm not okay has been Aiden. He's the only person who I'm ever able to be vulnerable with. He's the only person with who I allow myself to lose control with, the only person I've ever yielded to.

Nothing has really changed since that first night I succumbed to him. He's still the man I want to dance in the storm with. Despite the two years between us, the night we had spent together had been like fire, like he lit my soul alight again. It's never been like that with anybody else. Only ever him.

Except, fire gets you burnt, and I'm scared that this time I won't survive it.

∞∞∞∞∞∞∞∞

"I feel so lazy," Lizzie complains late in the afternoon. The sun is still warm, though the crowds at the beach has thinned out, families getting home for tea, young adults likely leaving to go out for parties and drinks. We've spent most of our day prone on the beach towels, turning occasionally in the sun.

"I feel very sandy," I say with a laugh as another family trudge past me, kicking sand in my direction as they walk too close, laden down by their deckchairs and windbreakers. Once they've got further up the beach, I sit up and brush the scattered sand from my legs.

"I'm in danger of falling asleep right now," Lizzie warns.

"Do you want to head off? I know you had a long drive last night to get home. I still can't believe you came home for the weekend."

"We probably should head off. I've got to set off tomorrow to get back for Monday training." She pulls a face.

"Are you going to tell me more about this training?" I ask. She shakes her head.

"Trust me, you'd be totally bored. Bored as fuck," she declares. Another family walks past at the same time, the mother tutting at Lizzie's language, covering her child's ears.

"Come on, let's pack up, before you can upset other sensitive ears," I joke.

"What are you planning tonight?" she asks.

"Nothing. I'll just watch a film, I think," I say, trying to ignore that thoughts of Aiden pop into my head.

"I'm going to take a long hot shower, get the sand from me," she declares, getting up from the beach towel. She waits for me to get up before picking the towel up, the sand blowing in my direction. I feel it on my face and in my mouth.

"Gross," I complain. "Maybe this is why I don't come to the beach as often as I should. It's all fun and games until you've sand in your mouth."

"Grab the cool box, I'll deal with the towels," she offers. I focus on making sure everything is packed back into the cool box, throwing in the cans of pop we've just finished. She stuffs her things into the beach bag, I pick up both sets of footwear and we walk up the beach towards the car park.

"Seriously, Lizzie, thank you so much for today," I say once we reach her car. She opens the boot for me to put the cool box in.

"No problem. Get in the car, I'll drive you home. I'll even let you pick the songs we listen to on the way home."

251

"Oh, now you're being way too nice." I laugh because Lizzie never lets me have control of the music when she drives.

I get into the car and she closes the boot then gets in beside me. She starts the car and drives in the direction of my house, never once complaining about the music I've put on to play.

∞∞∞∞∞∞∞∞∞

I wave Lizzie off as she drives away from my house. I watch as her car disappears down my street, then I let myself into the house. I rub my feet against the mat in the porch, trying to dislodge as much lingering sand as possible. I lock the porch door then let myself into the house.

I rummage around in the beach bag for my purse and then I drop the bag onto the floor near the front door, pulling my car key from the drawer in the side table. Talking with Lizzie about Aiden has stirred a flurry of emotions in me, and I know I'm not going to settle for a peaceful evening if I don't do what has been on my mind. I leave the house, locking up again, head to my car. I drive to the local florist to buy two bunches of flowers, and then I drive to the cemetery where Caterina is buried.

I know the steps to her grave like it is muscle memory. In the first year after she died, I'd come here a couple of times a week. Sometimes I'd run into her mother, and we'd sit and talk about how wonderful Caterina had been, talk about how much we missed her. As the years passed, my visits became less frequent, and I'd run into Jessica less. I think we both adapted to time our visits to avoid the other, a self-preservation process for me because Jessica reminded me so much of Caterina.

I can tell somebody has been to the grave recently as there is an almost dying set of flowers placed below the headstone that announces Caterina's name to the world, telling the world how much she was loved, how much she will be missed.

I kneel so I can put my flowers with the others.

I've always felt silly talking at a grave. It makes me feel self-conscious. So, instead of speaking the words out loud, I think the conversation in my head, hoping that, in whatever form that exists after this lifetime, she's able to hear me.

I still miss you, Cat. I've never had a friend like you, and I know I never will. I'd still give anything to re-wind to that night and do things differently. I just

252

can't let that price be Aiden anymore. It's breaking me in half. I hope you understand. I hope you can forgive me. I love you, Cat.

I run my hand over the top of her headstone and then head back to my car so I can drive to another cemetery, this one closer to the house Aiden grew up in. I'm less familiar with this cemetery, I have to read the headstones for the dates to get a sense of where I need to be. I find the year Jonah died, walk down the line of headstones until I find his. There's a bunch of white roses at his. I wonder if they are from his mum and dad.

I put my flowers into the second insert at the bottom of his headstone. Like at Caterina's grave, I don't talk out loud.

I'm sorry, Jonah. I'm sorry I wasn't a better friend. I'm sorry I didn't help you when you were hurting. I'm sorry for everything.

I take a deep breath, and then I head back to my car, my heart still tight in my chest.

∞∞∞∞∞∞∞∞∞

I make sure I've locked the doors when I get home. I grab my beach bag from where I left it and walk towards the utility room, stripping out of my clothes so I can put everything into the washing machine, trying to avoid traipsing sand through the house upstairs.

I take my mobile phone out of my bag. I fire off a text to Aiden, asking if we can get together on Monday. I put my mobile phone onto the counter as I rummage around in the ironing pile to find something to wear so I can avoid having to duck under the windows given I've stripped off and all my curtains will still be open in the daylight.

I pull on the oversized tee-shirt and then head upstairs for a shower. I try not to think about how Aiden might reply to my message, but the thoughts are in my head as I wash my hair, they're in my head when I dry myself after the shower, and still buzzing around in my head as I dress in a pair of jeggings and a comfortable top. The thoughts are still in my head as I tidy the bathroom, they're still there when I go downstairs to make myself some toast. They're still there when I have a cup of tea. I'm pretty sure they'll be in my head until Aiden replies and puts me out of my misery.

20

Aiden

"I'm sorry I haven't been in a while," I say, kneeling at my brother's headstone. I used to feel self-conscious when talking out loud in the cemetery but now it feels like second nature. I've seen enough people talking to themselves in the cemetery over the years, though my visits to Jonah's grave are not as frequent as my parent's would like.

Mum comes every week. She likes the idea that Jonah has fresh flowers every week. I don't think Jonah would give a shit about flowers, but if it gives my mother some comfort, I'm not going to point that out to her.

There are two bunches of flowers that Mum put down before jetting off to France with Dad. The purple flowers still look fresh, despite them being a few days old, but the roses look a little worse for wear. She's filled in both metal inserts for flowers which is not like her, usually she leaves one free because she knows I always come to Jonah's grave around his birthday. Mum and Dad are never in the country when it's this time of year, like the anniversary of his death, they like to get away. Like being in a different country would ever be enough to help them forget the pain that their second son is dead.

I put my flowers into the spare metal insert. They're not roses, like Mum prefers. Roses always make me think of Zoey, finally talking at Caterina's funeral as she destroyed a bunch of white roses Jonah had tried to give her. Instead, it's a bunch of sunflowers, bright and loud, like Jonah had been in life. He may have been an asshole sometimes, but he always stood out in a crowd.

"So, Zoey's doing okay, I think. She's not with Caleb anymore, if you can believe it. Still breaking my heart, though," I say, running my hand over the top of the headstone.

It's weird, sometimes, talking to Jonah like he's still here. It's weirder given our relationship was never easy. Even as kids, it was difficult. Like me, he took time to adjust to the new house, the new parents. Both of us knew what it was like to have had an unreliable home before, though mine was never with the fear of being beaten. I'd had three years living with Mum and Dad before they adopted Jonah but still, we distrusted each other for months, like we both thought the other was a threat. It took us an age to trust each other, but through our adolescence there were always setbacks, and we'd fight often, sometimes just verbally, sometimes ending in a scuffle. We'd always forgive, though, get through whatever our argument was, right until I'd found out about Caterina.

I'd told him that night that he was dead to me.

For my last year in the army, I only heard about Jonah through my parents. They'd ask me to forgive him, and I'd tell them no.

After I got out of the army, I'd see him from time to time at our parents' house. He'd turn up, unexpectedly, on days I was visiting. I always assumed it was my mother who had told him I would be there, but I found out that it was my father. We'd have stilted conversations in front of our parents, but eventually it was easier to talk to him, nothing of any depths, but at some point, I stopped wanting to hate him. It was never lost on me that this was around the time that I started noticing Zoey as more than my friend, knowing that I was truly over Caterina, that I was falling in love with Zoey, seeing the possibility of a future with her, wondering if she could ever feel the same about me.

When Caterina died, my relationship with Jonah changed again. For ages, I couldn't stand the sight of him, nor could he stand the sight of me. It was only once I'd accepted that we were both grieving that I started to talk to him again. He was grieving for Caterina, a woman who had been taken too soon, and I was sad that Caterina was gone, but I grieved for Zoey and the future we should have had.

Despite accepting we were both grieving and talking, my relationship with Jonah was strained. He blamed everybody for Caterina's death, including himself, and I couldn't find it in me to be gracious enough to tell him he shouldn't feel guilty, and I couldn't cope with every time he called me, raging or upset, not when I had my own battles to get through, not when I was frustrated with him, for what he was putting my parents through. And then he died, and I never got the chance to tell him I loved him, that I forgave him, that I hoped he loved and forgave me too.

"I bet you and Caterina are up there, together, laughing at what a pair of idiots we are, right?"

I sigh to myself, looking up to the skies, like there's a chance I'd see Jonah and Caterina, up in the mythical heaven. I'm sure if he had the opportunity to speak to me, he'd tell me I'm a dickhead and I should run to Zoey, hold her close and beg for a second chance. Despite everything, I'm sure Caterina would tell me to keep 'our girl' safe, to look after her and make sure she's happy.

My mobile buzzes in my pocket. I'm grateful that I seem to be the only person in the cemetery given I'd forgotten to turn the volume down. The last thing somebody who is grieving at a grave side wants is a mobile phone ringing in the background.

I walk away from Jonah's grave, heading towards the gates that lead to the car park, answering the phone as I go.

"Hey, Dad, how are you and Mum?" I ask.

"I saw you closed Zoey's case. Sounds like everything was wrapped up," he says. I sigh, hoping he doesn't hear my frustration.

"I thought Mum had you under strict instructions to be relaxing?"

"I always keep an eye on the business, but I'd asked for updates on this one, once I knew who the client was."

"Yes, right, we're no longer providing security."

"I'm glad everything was resolved successfully," he says after a moment of pause. I reach my car, zapping the lock so I can get in.

"I bet you are," I mutter.

"I assume you're not going to see Zoey again?"

"I don't know." I sit back in my seat, feeling frustrated. "I know you wouldn't want that, but whatever happens, it's my choice."

"I know it's your choice. I just wish..." Dad's voice trails off.

"I know, you wish that me and Jonah had never met either Caterina or Zoey," I mutter. I've heard this many times over the years.

"No, I just wish that you didn't always end up so utterly heartbroken whenever the two of you interact. It's hard to watch, Aiden. It was bad enough watching Jonah falling to pieces because he couldn't be with Caterina. I hate seeing the same with you."

He's never said this to me before. He's always talked about Zoey and Caterina being destructive forces in our lives, and since Jonah died, his opinion of Zoey has not been complimentary. The first year, he'd walk out of the room if her name ever came up in passing.

Mum was more understanding. She never blamed any of the four of us for anything, not even the cheating between Caterina and Jonah, or the secrets Zoey and I had kept from everybody. Mum had just told me love makes you do funny things, like it justified everything, but God knows we had used that justification ourselves. If Zoey and I spoke about the secrets we were keeping when we were together, one of us would say something along the lines of *'we love each other so much, it couldn't possibly be wrong'*, and I'm sure Caterina and Jonah would have had similar justifications.

"I promise to keep any heartbreak to myself, okay?" I feel bad for being an ass, but I'm frustrated. I feel like a teenager, being told by a parent to stay away from the love of their life in case they're a bad influence.

My phone beeps. I glance at the screen and see there is a text message from Zoey. I ignore it, trying to focus on the conversation with my dad.

"Aiden, you're my son, I love you, it isn't wrong for me to want to protect you, no matter how old you are. If you settle down and have children, you'll see what I mean." Dad sighs, as if he can sense my frustration.

His comment doesn't do much to dampen my frustration. I'd imagined that future with Zoey, we'd planned for it. We'd talked about our future when we were together and we'd reiterated the same promises when she'd come to me after Jonah had died. We may have said we were pretending nothing had hurt us, that life was normal, but the things I'd pledged to her on the beach that day, they were my hopes for the future, the life I wanted to have with her. I'd told her again, when she was with Caleb, what kind of life I wanted with her. I'd told her I knew we belonged together. I told her I wanted to live my life with her. I knew I was ready, ready to be stronger than all the things that seemed to lay as blockages between us, but she wasn't. I'm not sure if she ever will be. I'm still holding off on the future I want because the woman I want it with doesn't seem to want it with me.

"How is Mum?" I ask, changing the topic. I can't talk freely with my dad about Zoey. Talking about Mum is an easy topic. I know how hard she finds Jonah's birthday, or any anniversary to do with him.

"She's doing okay," Dad replies, voice gruff. I'm sure what he means is that Mum is trying to be stoic, something she does in the runup to the anniversaries, until she breaks down and looks like her heart is breaking all over again.

"Give her a hug from me. I've just been to Jonah's grave. The purple flowers are nice," I comment.

"We only put down white roses," Dad replies.

"Oh, right," I say, thinking about the flowers that had been left. If the purple flowers aren't from my mum and dad, I wonder if it is possible Zoey has been here today.

"Are you still okay to pick us up from the airport when we get back?"

"Of course," I reply, still thinking about the flowers.

"I thought you might still be angry with me about my reaction at the airport when you told me it was Zoey's case. I'm just worried about you, Aiden. I'm glad the case is wrapped up, though."

"Me too."

"Okay, well, I'm going to find your mother, before she tells me off for not relaxing."

I laugh. I know my mum will be fighting a losing battle with my dad for years about him relaxing. Maybe I get my own stubbornness from being his son.

"I'll see you soon, Dad."

Dad says his goodbyes and ends the call. I flip to my message apps, opening the message that arrived earlier from Zoey.

Aiden, I'm so sorry about the way we left things. I have been thinking about you all day. I was at the beach with Lizzie and all I could think about was you. I know I suggested we wait to talk, but I'm off work on Monday. I know it would have been Jonah's birthday, and you probably need a distraction rather than me complicating things. I know I could offer to 'pretend' for a day with you, but I know you don't want that, and I don't want it either. If you are up for an honest conversation, can we meet on Monday to talk, to see where that leads us? Zoey x.

I'm glad she's acknowledged that I don't want to play pretend days with her. We'd done that, on and off, since Jonah died. Days where we'd pretend that we were together, that nothing had ever hurt us, living the lives we should have had. Days that I'd told her I couldn't do any more.

I type back a message.

Zo, this week has been a wild one, but all it has done is remind me how much I love you. Let me know when you want to meet. Love, Aiden.

I watch the screen, looking for any indication that she's seen the message, that she's typing back. I watch for a few minutes, the text remaining delivered but unread. I drop my phone into the centre console of the car and start the engine, driving home.

∞∞∞∞∞∞∞∞

I walk around the flat, feeling oddly off kilter. I make myself busy, doing the jobs that I've neglected when at Zoey's, changing the bedding, emptying the dishwasher.

When my phone buzzes, it jolts me as I wasn't expecting it. My heart seems to kick up a level, hoping it's Zoey, but instead it's a message on my work mobile, from one of the team who runs background information.

Hi, Aiden. I know the case is closed, but this stood out as being unusual and I thought I'd highlight it to you. I've updated it in your latest case files.

I grab my laptop and log into the system. I open Zoey's case. There's a new alert under the background section. I open the attachment, it's an update on Zoey's best friend. The information is generic, usually there would be nothing interesting in this information, except for the section on previous names. Despite Zoey being insistent that Lizzie had never changed her name, the document confirms that Lizzie is known as Elizabeth Ackerley-Jones, not Chapman.

As soon as I see the name on the phone, it hits me like a lightning bolt. It's an unusual surname, and I have a moment of dread, realising Lizzie must be related to Dominic, a man who worked for Zoey before he died. I'm certain that if Zoey knew that Lizzie was related to Dominic, she would have told me, she'd have explained how they had become friends. I recall the conversation with Zoey about how she'd met Lizzie, how she'd apparently just kept bumping into her.

The world isn't so strange that this is a coincidence. The chance that they would randomly form a friendship and then discover they were connected by Dominic seems astronomically slim.

It strikes me how calculated it would be, if Lizzie did know about Zoey's connection to her brother. Like Caterina's death, like Jonah's death, Zoey isn't responsible, but it doesn't mean Lizzie believes that, and isn't looking to find a way to hold Zoey accountable.

The idea I've overlooked something so simple sends a chill through me. I promised to protect Zoey, and I've left her defenceless against somebody who she'd never suspect, a woman she's spent the day with, even though she was supposed to be away until next week.

I call Zoey's number, getting no answer. Without thinking, I rush out of the flat.

I get in my car, racing to Zoey, my mind filled with the events of Dominic's death, wondering what Lizzie believes happened to her brother, and what she could be planning next.

21

Zoey

Four Years Ago

"Zoey, I have Caleb for you, shall I put him through?" Freya pops her head around the office door. I smile at her.

"Yes, please."

She disappears back to her desk and then my phone rings, her transferring the call.

"Zoey?" Caleb says once I answer.

"To what do I owe this pleasure?" I sit back in my chair and check my watch. I've a little time until my next meeting.

"I know you're not into all the mushy stuff, but I wanted to give my girlfriend a call on our anniversary," he says.

"Oh, it's our anniversary, is it?" I tease. He laughs and I grin to myself. He has an infectious laugh.

I met Caleb two weeks after my birthday last year, the birthday I'd spent with Aiden. When I'd got home from his, broken hearted and laden down with guilt, I'd caught my reflection in the mirror and couldn't believe what I looked like. My reflection reminded me of what I'd seen in Aiden, somebody shrunken, a shell of themselves. I'd decided that I'd make a conscious effort to pull myself together, to fake it to the world until I'd made it. Two weeks later, Caleb was at one of the meetings I was having with prospective audit companies, tendering for a bid. I'd chosen a different company and the day after I'd rejected the bid of the firm that he worked for, Caleb phoned me to ask me out.

Nine months after we started dating, he moved in with me. He travels a lot for work, up and down the country, working on client audits, though he tells me he wants to move out of practice into industry. I tease him occasionally, asking if he only asked me out to lay down the groundwork for working for me.

Caleb tells me he likes how strong I am, how I'm not like any of the women he knows. It should be a compliment, I'm sure, but there's part of me that knows Caleb doesn't know the real me. He only knows what I choose to let him see, and that's not a lot. He knows nothing about my parents. I think he assumes my mum and dad are both dead. He knows nothing about Caterina. He knows nothing about Jonah. He knows nothing about Aiden. I've spent a year with Caleb, being with his friends, meeting his family, keeping my own history to myself.

It's better that way.

"Even you aren't so busy you haven't realised it's our anniversary, though I do love that you're so laid back about this kind of crap. Most women would be upset when their partner goes away for ten days without them," Caleb points out.

"Well, I am very understanding." I twirl the cord of the telephone around my fingers, my eye falling to the scar on my arm. The only time Caleb had mentioned this scar was when we went on holiday together as the pins in my bone had set off the body scanner. He'd never pushed further than my explanation that I had pins in there, never asked how it had happened.

"Much more than the other guy's girlfriends. Marie is calling Harry every five minutes. I'm glad you're not needy like that," Caleb comments. Harry is one of his best friends. They're both away with mutual friends Zack and Alexander, on a 'boy's holiday' in Las Vegas. I hadn't minded when he told me, I'm used to Caleb travelling, plus it's coming up to our annual audit and I'm going to be snowed for a couple of weeks.

"So, aside from calling me to remind me there are such things as anniversaries, and to mention how other girlfriends are complaining, what else are you calling for?" I tease.

"Just to tell you I love you," he says, and I get the sense of the smile from his tone.

"I love you too," I reply, and I tuck the phone between my ear and neck so I can scratch my arm. I do love Caleb; I just know it's a different type of love to what I had with Aiden. I often think the type of love we'd had was the type you only experience once in a lifetime, the type of love that never really leaves you.

"I know you're not likely to be sitting around and pining for me, but I'll be home on Sunday, okay?" he reminds me.

"Although I am far too busy to be sitting around pining for you, I am looking forward to you being home." I laugh.

"I'm going to book a table for us for dinner when I get back. Actually, we should make it the day after, I'm sure I'm going to be jetlagged. We can celebrate our anniversary then."

"Sounds great," I reply, and I shake the mouse on my laptop to wake the screen again. I can see I've had a load of emails come through in the short window I've been on the phone. Freya does an excellent job of managing my inbox for me, sorting out all the things she thinks are unimportant, but the volume that is still left for my attention is often staggering. I'm sure there are days where I do nothing but answer emails, or rather, I have evenings at home, holed up in my study, catching up on emails.

"Zoey?" Caleb's voice is a little raised and I realise I've zoned out of the conversation.

"Oh, I'm sorry, I was trying to multi-task," I admit.

"I'll let you get back to it. Go conquer the world, my boss babe," he teases. We say our goodbyes before we hang up, but I'm still focused on the emails in my inbox.

I put the phone down and roll my neck after sitting in an awkward position. I open the email from Dominic, my chief accountant. The attachment is an in-depth breakdown of the annual accounts. I move my chair closer to the desk so I can read through. I have a hazy memory of last year, my brain seeming to drift into trances when I tried to focus on the attachment. The year before, just after Caterina died, I don't remember what I did. The first few weeks back at work was a blur.

I open every attachment that Dominic has sent me. There is a complete breakdown of everything, the debtors, creditors, the asset listing, the bank data, the profit and loss summary. He's completed with commentary and year on year trends, highlighting certain areas he'd think I would be more interested in.

I dig out the same version of the file that we'd had last year and the year before. Everything looks sensible but when I pull up the file from three years ago, I can see our spend is higher than it used to be. I compare the files for the four years. Year on year, spend is increased in our cost of sales line but it is much higher than I'd expect it to be, it doesn't seem to fit with the growth of the business or market factors. Where most other lines are increasing at steady percentages, cost of sales looks like an outlier.

I frown a little as I look over the numbers again. I look through the attachments from Dominic again. He's very thorough but he hasn't included a transactional download of the accounts, he's always joked I'm too busy to be 'in the weeds.'. I have always hated the sentence because it makes me think he assumes I'm sitting in my office all day, filing my nails, disconnected to my business.

I know Dominic will be busy, preparing other files and preparing for all the audit requests that will come through shortly. Instead, I email Omar, one of the finance analysts. He's on a rotation scheme I'd set up last year, he's spent time in various departments and prides himself on knowing his way around the system. I ask him to run me a transactional listing of the account that has caught my eye, for the last five years.

I sit back in my seat, check my watch again. I've ten minutes until my next meeting and I know it will take a while for Omar to run me the data I need. I'm not used to having a gap in my time, so I am relieved when my mobile phone buzzes. I pick it up, half expecting it to be Caleb but Aiden's name pops onto the screen, and my heart seems to hitch, as it always does.

After I'd left Aiden's flat last year, we had no contact with one another, not until I'd messaged him on the anniversary of Jonah's death. My message had been simple, just a note that I was thinking about him and that I hoped he was okay. He hadn't replied and I thought maybe he'd changed his number, moved on, but then my phone beeped at midnight as the day ticked over into my birthday. He'd wished me a happy birthday, telling me he hoped he was the first. I'd spent an hour in bed, thinking about the birthday before, the day we'd played pretend for as long as we could before the bubble burst.

Since then, for the past couple of weeks, we have exchanged messages. They're all focused on the present, inconsequential details about our day. I haven't told Caleb that I message Aiden, mostly because he has no idea who Aiden is, but it doesn't feel like I'm doing anything wrong as the messages are so innocent.

The way my heart beats a little faster when each message arrives is probably not as innocent as the topics.

Aiden, on the other hand, knows about Caleb. I told him about Caleb the day after my birthday, when I'd replied to his birthday message, and we'd started asking the serious questions like how we were really doing.

His message today reads: *'Finally home and washing the city from me. How's the audit going, you made any of the newbies cry yet?'*

I chuckle to myself. Aiden's been away in London for a week with some mysterious rich client. I know Aiden enjoys travelling for work, but I also know he loves when he gets home.

I send a message back: *'Not yet, but it's only Monday, can't start the week too hard.'*

I put my phone back on my desk. I'm sure he won't reply, when we do message, they're usually infrequent. Sometimes we message in the morning and then nothing until late at night.

I look back at my laptop and can see I've a message from Omar. He's clearly keen to make an impression as I didn't expect anything so quickly. He's even pivoted the data by supplier and by financial year, removed all the noise from accruals to leave purely spend with suppliers. I appreciate he's gone to the extra effort as it saves me a bit of time.

I read through what he has sent me and then I pop out of the office.

"Freya, could you please rearrange the meeting with HR? Until tomorrow, please. Send my apologies. I'm also going to ask Omar to come see me, so can you send him through when he gets here?" I ask.

Freya, ever professional, nods and smiles. Her fingers are already on her keyboard, no doubt cancelling the meeting with HR and apologising profusely on my behalf. I'm sure they'll understand, it's only a quarterly meeting to go through the uptake of employees into various benefits we offer.

I leave Freya and go back to my desk, emailing Omar, asking him to come and see me.

It doesn't take long for him to arrive, the slightly timid knock on my door making me smile. I've seen Omar around the office with other people and he is always confident, professional, and I remember being very impressed with him when I'd sat in on one of the assessment centres we ran when recruiting for his cohort of colleagues. However confident somebody is, there is something unnerving about being called to the boss's office, especially unexpectedly.

"Hello, Zoey," Omar says as he comes into the office. His smile is confident but there is something about his expression that shows me he's nervous. I don't think he even looked this nervous when being interviewed and asked why he wanted to work for my company.

"Take a seat, Omar, and relax. You're not in any trouble." I smile. He looks grateful as he slips into the seat opposite me.

"What can I do for you?"

"Are you busy this afternoon?" I ask. I can see he's not sure the best way to answer. "It's not a trick question, Omar, I'm not trying to suggest your twiddling your thumbs at your desk." I laugh.

"I have things to do, but nothing that can't wait until tomorrow. What do you need me to do?" he asks.

"You sent me through the spend analysis. I have a couple of suppliers that I wasn't expecting, or the spend looks unusual. I was hoping you could dig me the copy invoices out. There are a few, unfortunately. I was hoping you would keep this to yourself, is that okay?"

"Sure, Zoey. I can get you the copies. Just send me the ones you are looking for. I'll send them through as soon as I can."

"Thank you." I nod. He gets up and walks towards the door before turning back to look at me.

"Is there a problem with the suppliers?" he asks.

"I hope not," I murmur. Omar doesn't ask any further questions, and he heads out of the office, shutting the door behind him.

My phone beeps, a reply from Aiden. *'Ha, are you trying to lull people into a false sense of security?'*

I smile to myself but don't answer. I go back to the laptop screen, sending Omar the suppliers I'm interested in after looking through the other emails I'd had, hoping that when Omar sends through the copy invoices, I'll be able to put the nagging feeling to bed.

It doesn't take long for Omar to send me the copy invoices. He's created one email, telling me it's all the invoices for this financial year. There is a note that he'll send the previous financial years as soon as he can.

As soon as I open the invoice attachments and scan through them, I can tell my nagging feeling isn't going to get put to bed.

I reach for my mobile and reply to Aiden. *'I know it's been forever, but are you free for dinner tonight? Can I come around to yours?'*

His response is a short confirmation, telling me he's home all day. I put my phone back, looking back at the invoices, the frown still on my face.

∞∞∞∞∞∞∞∞∞

I arrive at Aiden's at seven. I'd stopped at the shop on my way to his and stand awkwardly on his pathway, holding the bottle of wine I'd picked up.

He answers the door a couple of seconds after I'd knocked. He looks so much better than the last time I'd seen him, in all senses of the word. He's got his muscle definition back, his hair is cut neatly, his skin is back to a healthy colour. It's the first time I've seen him since just after Jonah died and I hadn't braced myself for how the sight of him would make my heart race.

It's been a year and God, it still hurts.

"You look so good," I blurt out.

He grins at me. "You do too, Zo."

I know I look healthier than the last time I'd seen him. At the time, I hadn't appreciated how much the emotions I was feeling was affecting me physically. The day I'd arrived to see him last year, once the professional makeup and hairstyle I'd had done for the talk at university was removed, he'd have seen how dark the circles were under my eyes, how gaunt I looked, how flaky my skin was. Even my nails were brittle and bitten down. I know I look so much better now than I did then. It's mostly down to me trying to sleep properly, to look after my skin, keeping my outer presenting self in good condition. Underneath, I still feel like a jumble of broken parts some days. I wonder if the same is true for Aiden.

"How are you?" I ask as he opens the door wider for me to come inside.

"I'm fine, but what's with the frown?" he asks. He leads me through to the living area. There's no judgement from him that I haven't been here in over a year and now I'm here, it doesn't feel like five minutes have passed.

I hand him the bottle of wine and then I take a seat on the sofa. He sits next to me.

"I was looking through the accounts at work and found some anomalies. I did some digging and it's not good Aiden," I blurt out.

"What do you mean, what kind of anomalies?"

"There are a couple of fake suppliers that have been set up, where we have made payments to them," I admit.

Aiden gets up from the sofa and a minute later he is back, two wine glasses in his hands. He puts them on the floor so he can open the bottle of wine and he pours us both a glass.

"Tell me everything," he says as he hands me my glass.

I drink my glass without pausing for breath and he pours me another as I tell him about the accounts that I'd found. The first one that had caught my attention was a supplier Caterina and I had used ages ago, one that had gone bust shortly before she'd died. I remembered the supplier as the name rhymed and Caterina had joked it was her favourite name. Since Caterina died, the supplier account had been reactivated, and my company had made a payment a couple of weeks after I'd gone back to work, for fifty-thousand pounds. The payment was made to an account that, upon further scrutiny, doesn't belong to the supplier. I tell him about the other accounts, new accounts for business I don't recognise, regular spend being put through their accounts. I tell him how each individual value is small, in the grand scheme of things, but that when added up, the total is significant. I tell him how each invoice is registered with the same banking details, listed as if they're subsidiaries of a parent company, sharing the same bank account. I tell him how the investigations I've done online show that all the companies look to be hastily set up to look genuine but aren't. I tell him the amount I've calculated so far, money stolen from the business, and he winces because it's an obscene amount of money.

"It's fraud, Aiden. It's been going on since Caterina died, and I missed it," I explain, and my voice cracks on the last part of my sentence.

"Do you know who it was committed by?" he asks.

"The invoices are approved by Dominic, my chief accountant. I asked somebody to dig out the reactivation request from the first supplier and the setup paperwork for the other suppliers, they were signed by him, too."

"Have you confronted him?"

"I have scheduled a meeting tomorrow, with him and I've asked HR to be involved. I don't want to think it is him, but I can't think of another explanation."

"How do you think he's going to react tomorrow? Do you need any support? I know it would be unconventional, but I could be there," he offers. His unwavering support makes me feel buoyant, but I know it won't last long. The enormity of what Dominic has done is going to hit me again later.

"I'm worried he already suspects something. When I asked our setup team about one of the setups, they'd replied and copied in Dominic. He knows I'm looking at things. Maybe I should have said something today. I just don't know what I'm going to do about it. I'm going to have to admit this to the auditors, I'm going to have to disclose the fraud. I'm going to have to get the police involved. This is all so much." Again, my voice cracks.

Aiden takes my glass of wine from me, putting it on the floor with his, and then he pulls me close for a hug. There's a small part of my brain that seems to sigh in contentment as I remember how safe I always feel when I'm with Aiden.

"It'll be okay, Zo. What has Caleb said?" he asks. I've told him a few bits about Caleb, including what his job is. Caleb rejoices at finding shit like this in the accounts of companies he looks at.

"Caleb is away, but I haven't told him. I know all the things he'll say, what he'll ask. He'll want to know how I let this happen, why I didn't see it, how I let one person have so much control of a process," I explain. I don't move out of his embrace.

"Zoey," he says, gently. I don't move. I can't look at him. "If the fraud started after Caterina died, it's clear to me that Dominic took advantage of the situation. If Caleb doesn't understand…"

"He doesn't know."

"Know what?"

"About Caterina," I admit. "You're the only person I can talk to about her."

Aiden pulls away from our embrace. I brace myself for him judging me, telling me how terrible it is that I haven't told the person I'm living with about the person who I still grieve for. I brace for him asking how it is possible I've hidden the truth for so long and prepare to be judged if I have to tell him how I've hidden away every trace of Caterina at my house. There are no photographs of us together on display in my house. All the photo albums have been put away, to stop me looking at them, especially as Caterina's parents had deleted her social media page just after the anniversary of her death and I knew I couldn't keep staring at photographs and punishing myself.

I can punish myself without the photographs.

Instead of the questions, there is sympathy in his eyes. He cups my cheek with the palm of his hand and his thumb strokes across the skin.

"Every day, I wish things were different," he murmurs.

"It still kills me to talk about it all," I whisper.

There's a beat between us and I feel so exhausted. I feel like no matter how hard I work to get my life together, how hard I make myself stand tall and behave like I'm in control of everything, I'm always falling to pieces. There is always something, waiting to trip me up.

"What do you want to do, Zoey?" he asks.

"Honestly?"

"You can always be honest with me," he reminds me.

"I want to lie down. I want to sleep."

"Okay."

Aiden gets up and he reaches for my hand. He leads me to his bedroom. I slip out of my shoes and jacket. He pulls back the covers on his bed and we get in together. He spoons himself behind me, holding me close.

"I'm so tired, Aiden. Holding myself together all the time, knowing the next disaster is always on the horizon. It is exhausting. You know what I mean, don't you?"

"I know, honey, I know," he soothes, and he holds me closer until my mind stops racing and I fall asleep.

∞∞∞∞∞∞∞∞

My mobile phone is what wakes me. For a second, I'm afraid it's Caleb, wondering where I am. I haven't done anything with Aiden, but I know it'll be seen as poor form to have spent my one-year anniversary with Caleb asleep in Aiden's bed.

I reach for the phone from inside my jacket on the floor. Aiden stirs and gives me a small smile.

"Zoey Taylor," I say as I answer the phone, sitting up in the bed. A quick glance at my phone shows me it is six in the morning. It's later than I'd usually get up, but I know I've had some solid sleep.

"Hi Zoey, I'm so sorry to call you so early. It's Liam, I'm on security today. There's been an incident. I wasn't sure who to call."

I know Liam. He's worked security for the last six months. He's built like a brick house but right now he sounds like a lost kid.

"What's the matter?"

"I need to call the police, but I wanted you to know. How quickly can you get to the office?" Liam asks.

"I'll come now. What's going on?" I ask, getting myself out of bed. Aiden follows my lead.

"Just get here when you can, please." Liam replies, and then the call disconnects.

"What's going on?" Aiden asks.

"I don't know. Something at the office. Maybe a break-in? The guard from this morning sounds freaked out." I frown as I look down at my crumpled shirt. I should go home and change but Liam sounded anxious.

"Go freshen up. I'll come with you," he offers.

"Yeah, that'll look good, me turning up at the office in the clothes from yesterday, with a strange guy in tow." I manage a laugh.

"I have one of your shirts here, so at least you can have a clean shirt." Aiden smiles.

I don't need him to tell me it's the shirt I was wearing the day I'd turned up at his over a year ago, left behind as I'd disappeared from his life again.

I head to the bathroom to freshen up, wash my face and tidy up my hairstyle. When I get back to the bedroom, he has the shirt out for me.

"So, some random woman's shirt in your wardrobe never raised red flags for the women you dated?" I joke.

"That would suggest I bring women back here." He shrugs. There's a little jolt in me when I realise this place, his flat, it's always been our place.

"I'll message in a bit and let you know what's going off," I say as I pull the clean shirt on. I gather the rest of my things and Aiden sees me to the door, waving me off.

As I drive to the office, I find myself panicking about what seemed to have Liam so off kilter. He's never usually somebody who appears rattled. My mind seems to go in a million directions, imagining the building up in flames, or razed to the ground so I'm relieved to find the building still standing, looking as it always does when I pull my car into the carpark. There are only a couple of cars in the carpark when I park up. There's a sporty car parked in the far corner of the carpark, the neon orange paint making it impossible not to see. It's Dominic's car, and I wonder if he's in the building now, causing a fuss. Maybe he's aware I'm investigating some transactions and he's trying to shred files or something before I can find everything. Maybe that's what has Liam so freaked out.

I find the lobby of the building deserted. It still too early for any of the staff to be in, so I am not surprised there doesn't seem to be anybody around. As I walk across the lobby, the glass of the windows illuminates with a flashing blue light and I realise it's the arrival of a police car, stopping near the barrier to the carpark. Liam appears out of nowhere, crossing the lobby so he can deal with the arrival of the police, and then I see there is an ambulance that arrives behind the police car.

It takes a second for my brain to engage. Liam looks at me, a warning look on his face.

"Don't, Zoey," he says, but I'm already sprinting through the lobby, ignoring the lifts because I don't want to wait, instead heading to the staircase. I take the

271

stairs two at a time, heading to Dominic's office. I don't need to go into the office. Liam has left the door to Dominic's office open, and I can see the thing that has Liam so spooked.

Dominic's body lies on the floor, the noose of the rope still tied around his neck.

"Oh my God," I gasp, and I want to throw up.

I hear Liam's footsteps, followed by the police officers who have arrived.

"I had to get him down, to…check…I didn't know what to do," Liam explains, sounding shellshocked.

"Oh my God," I repeat.

"Ms Taylor? Can we have a word?" One of the officers asks, and it sounds like I'm underwater. When I sway, Liam reaches to catch me and all I can think is how much I wish I'd accepted Aiden's offer to come with me, because he's the only person in the world who has ever managed to keep me steady.

∞∞∞∞∞∞∞∞

I have enough sense about me to activate the work disaster plan, instructing everybody bar key members of staff to stay at home. I follow up with a message on the alert system, reminding the team they'll be on full pay, and further communications will be sent soon, that I'll let them know when work will be back to normal.

I text Aiden to tell him what is going on. He offers to come to the office but instead I tell him I'll come back to his later.

I spend the first part of the morning with the police. I explain the situation I'd found yesterday; tell them I was concerned Dominic was aware that I was investigating transactions. I hand them copies of the evidence I'd found so far. I find out from Liam that Dominic had left a note on his desk. I half expected it would be an apology for what he had done but instead it was a rambling on the pressure he'd felt working for me, pressure he couldn't take another day. I'm not sure how any pressure would justify him stealing so much money from the business.

The police and ambulance service that arrived are quick in removing Dominic's body from the building. It's still not fast enough to prevent some people seeing it, early starters like Freya who faints and has to be taken home by Liam, somebody who still looks shaky himself.

Key staff members arrive, heads of departments. I explain what has happened to Dominic, and I explain the situation about the payments. We talk about what will happen next. I know the next few days will be brutal. There will be team members who will mourn for Dominic, and there will be team members who will wonder what they'd missed, how somebody could have acted with such deviousness under their noses. I reassure the managers of the setup team, the finance team, and the payments team that nobody will be punished for not spotting Dominic's actions. I should have been the one to see the irregularities. I shouldn't have let this go on for as long as it has.

Before the staff members leave, I warn them that there will be a thorough investigation and processes will have to be strengthened. I cannot let anything like this happen again. I tell them that once we're through the shock of everything, we will assess every hole in the processes that left it open for Dominic to deceive us, we will find every flaw in the system and we will fix them, together.

Once the last team member has gone home and the second security officer has promised me that they'll lock up shortly, I head back to my car. It's still early in the workday but I feel exhausted. I should go home. I should crawl into bed and get the sleep I will need to get me through the next few weeks, the police investigation, the forensic review of the business accounts to see what else I have missed, the scrutiny by the auditors, but I find myself driving to Aiden's place. Not just because I'd said I would go, but because there isn't anywhere else where I feel I can possibly relax after what has just happened.

Aiden is at the doorway as I walk up the drive. As soon as the door shuts behind me, he pulls me into his arms.

"I'm so sorry," he murmurs, then his lips press against my forehead. I drop my things onto the floor and cry against his chest.

"I have so much blood on my hands, Aiden."

"These hands?" he asks, pulling away, taking mine in his, bringing them to his lips so he can kiss across my skin. "Nothing there," he soothes.

"I feel guilty."

"What Dominic chose to do was his own choice. It had nothing to do with anything you did. What other choice did you have? Ignore that he was stealing from you, carry on letting him steal from you, just so he didn't have to face any consequences?"

"I feel like I make a choice, and somebody dies. Dominic. Jonah. Caterina."
I hiccup.

"No, honey, that's not true."

"Yet they're all dead."

"You did not put a noose around Dominic's neck. You did not inject heroin into Jonah's arm. You did not put a drunken and drugged Caterina into a car. I know what it's like to wish with all your heart that things were different, but it doesn't mean you can blame yourself," he soothes, and he wraps his arms around me again, holding me close. Minutes pass and I feel so tired.

"Aiden?" I ask. I look up at him. I know why I've come here instead of going home, calling Caleb and telling him what has happened. "I closed the business for tomorrow. I know it's a lot and I know I have no right to ask, but can we pretend?"

"When is Caleb home?"

"Sunday afternoon."

"I can be free until Sunday," he offers. I know it's a lot I'm asking from him, and I am so grateful for how he's graciously going to let me pretend that everything is okay.

We spend the rest of the day in his living room, curled on the sofa, watching television. When Aiden makes us some food, I text Caleb and tell him I'm busy but add that I hope his holiday is going well. I switch my phone off so that I'm not disturbed.

Aiden and I eat and then we watch some more television. He runs me a bath. I ask him to join me, and I watch as his grey-blue eyes darken before he steps into the bathroom with me. We undress and I lie against his body in the bathtub, his arms around me. I feel safe and secure, hidden away from everything. When we get out of the bath and dry one another, it feels like the most natural thing in the world to hold hands as we walk together towards his bedroom.

When I kiss down his body, sink to my knees in front of him, he asks if I'm sure. I nod and take him in my mouth, listening to the initial hiss of desire and carrying on until I hear him moan and then he pulls away, lifting me from the floor, whispering as he puts me on the bed, telling me all the things he wants us to do together. The only thing I can think about is Aiden, he occupies every brain cell. When he clasps my hands with his, I writhe underneath him. When he enters me, there's a string of curse words from my mouth, followed by me telling him just how good he feels, how much I've missed this, how much I want him. When we climax, I'm wide-eyed and wondering if I've ever felt so good before, knowing the answer is the last time I was with Aiden.

We both know it's an illusion, a fantasy world we're creating together because it is so much better than our reality. We both know the scars are still there, literally and figuratively, the losses still make us ache. We both know that when Sunday arrives, I'll leave him behind and go back to my normal life. We both know this can't last, but when he tells me he loves me, I tell him I love him too, and I know that's one thing I'll never have to pretend.

22
Zoey

The sound of the doorbell ringing makes me jump. I wonder how long it will take me to adjust to being in the house by myself. It seems strange that Aiden was only here for a few days, yet it feels like a lifetime. I try not to focus on the acknowledgement that I miss him. Dealing with my emotions about Aiden seems too exhausting to do right now, so much so that my mobile is still in the laundry room, to stop me refreshing the screen every five seconds.

I walk towards the front door, unlocking it. Outside the porch stands Lizzie, a bottle of wine in her hand, a huge grin on her face. She's changed from the beach, no longer wearing her sundress. She's wearing jeans and a top, her hair looking freshly washed.

I unlock the porch door, laughing.

"What are you doing back here?" I ask.

"Well, I had my hot shower, got rid of all the sand and wondered what to do with the rest of my night. I know you said you were going to watch a film, but I thought we should round up the night by having a good drink." She holds up the wine bottle, like I haven't already seen it.

"Where is your car?" I look out on the driveway.

"I assumed after we finish this bottle of wine, we can hit the good stuff you keep in the study. I decided to leave the wheels, I can taxi home like a drunken degenerate."

Lizzie steps into the house and I lock the porch behind her, following her into the house, relocking the front door.

"You could always stop over," I offer. I think of Aiden sleeping over the other day, idly wondering if the sheets in the spare room still smell like him. I wonder if my own bedsheets will still smell of him. There's a small part of me that is looking forward to getting into bed, pulling the covers around me and inhaling the smell like some lovestruck idiot.

"Sounds like a plan. We can get hammered and I'll help you forget this horrible week."

We walk through to the kitchen. I lean against the breakfast bar, watching as she makes herself at home, dropping the overstuffed tote bag she has onto the floor, putting the bottle of wine on the side.

"Looks like you'd already decided you were staying over," I muse, looking at the tote bag.

"I assumed it would be something you offered." She gives me a little shrug.

"Of course. It's a nice surprise. I thought you'd have been sick of me after today." I smile at her.

"Never," she vows.

"You're a very good friend."

Lizzie glances over at me, a small smile on her face. Down the hall, in the laundry room, I hear my mobile phone ringing.

"Do you need to get that?" she asks.

"It'll wait," I reply. I hear the phone stop as it transfers to my answerphone, then the ringing starts again.

"Are you sure you don't need to get that?"

"I'm sure. It might be the police, trying to give an update after the arrest, but I don't want to talk about that tonight. A drink sounds perfect."

The phone stops ringing and doesn't start again. I go to the cupboard where I keep my snack food items, pulling out a large bag of tortilla chips. I find a jar of salsa and jalapeños. I know I have grated cheese in the fridge, some cheesy nachos sound like a great idea to go with the wine.

"I still can't believe somebody killed Simba, that's just awful," Lizzie says as I'm halfway to the fridge. I stop walking, resting my hand on the worktop to steady me. Talking about Simba makes me feel sick. I look over at Lizzie. She pulls two wine glasses out of the cupboard.

"I know, poor Simba. He was so innocent in all of this. It takes a disturbed person to do something like that to an animal." I force myself to sound normal, I wouldn't want her to think she's upset me by bringing up the topic.

"Hanging him on your door is sick," she agrees. She places the wine glasses on the side and then reaches for the bottle of wine.

I don't know why her words catch me off guard. I tap my finger on the worktop as I think about her words.

"Sick," I murmur back, still trying to put my finger on what about her sentence is bothering me.

"Well, at least it's all over. No more monitoring in the house, worrying that your every move is caught on camera." Lizzie opens the wine as she talks.

"Yeah, that's all gone," I reply. I shake my head to clear my thoughts, but the nagging feeling is still there, like my brain is trying to remind me of something. I watch her pour the wine.

"What's the matter? You look really freaked out." Lizzie laughs as she walks to stand next to me and hands me my wine glass.

"I didn't tell you that," I blurt out.

"Tell me what?" she asks, looking surprised by my tone.

"I didn't tell you that Simba had been hung on my door. I'd said he'd been left on my doorstep."

"No, you told me he'd been hung."

"I don't think I did." I frown, trying to remember the full conversation we'd had that night.

"You did, because I remember it upset me. That's how my brother died, you know." Lizzie stares at me.

"You never mentioned a brother," I whisper, and the icy feeling of dread seems to tingle the whole way down my spine. I know I didn't tell her that Simba had been hung from the door. I know I didn't, not in any of our phone calls, messages, or today. I also know that Lizzie has never, ever, mentioned that she'd had a brother.

"Yes. He was struggling, working for a demanding boss. She was a bitch, never satisfied by the work he was doing, she pushed him to the edge," she starts. She sips a bit of her wine and then leans for the bottle, like she's dissatisfied by the amount she has in her glass and already wants to top up.

"That's awful," I murmur, trying to keep my expression neutral when my brain seems to be screaming for me to run. Lizzie's fingers are still wrapped around the wine bottle.

"I was sick in hospital when he was under that pressure, he tried to shield me from it so I could get better without worrying about his whore of a boss he had, but I saw his suicide note, about how his boss had driven him to the brink." There's a pause in her talking and then she laughs, humourlessly. "Do you know what I thought when I read his suicide letter? My first thought was his boss was a cunt, a sinner who would have to pay for my dear brother's life."

Bitch. Whore. Cunt. Sinner

My brain registers all the words.

"Lizzie," I start, but she glares at me.

"Do you know what his boss then tried to do? After she'd worked him to the point that he put a fucking rope around his neck and hung himself in his office? She tried to tell the police that he'd been stealing from her company. Can you believe that? Talk about deflection of guilt, right, Zoey?" she scoffs.

"Lizzie…"

"Not your turn to talk yet, Zoey." Lizzie laughs and wags a finger at me, her other hand still gripping the wine bottle.

"But…" I start again, but before I can say another word, Lizzie lifts the wine bottle, cracking it against my cheek. The force of it stuns me more than anything, the wine bottle and the force not heavy enough to do any real damage, but it's enough to make my eyes water, make me stumble backwards, enough for Lizzie to advance on me, pushing me to the floor. She kneels in front of me, still holding the wine bottle.

"I swear to God, Zoey, if you move one more time, your death is going to be far more painful and far less poetic than I have planned. The death I have planned for you is quick, do not piss me off, otherwise I'll make you suffer," she snarls.

"You and I have been friends for eighteen months; how could you possibly want to kill me?" I ask, astounded and frightened. It's possible I'm not engaging all my brain cells, because it's clear her friendship has been nothing but an act on her side.

"I spent months planning this, and eighteen months biding my time," Lizzie snarls.

"Please, don't do…"

"Do you think hanging Simba from your door was maybe a bit on the nose? I did wonder if it was too obvious, but even a hanging cat wasn't enough to make you think of what you pushed my brother to do," she snaps. "Too busy lamenting about what you could possibly have done, never thinking about the people you've really hurt."

"I don't know what you think happened, but you're wrong. Dominic was stealing. His suicide note was a bunch of lies. The police investigated. Everything pointed to Dominic." I know pushing these facts on her is a risky strategy. She could lose her temper and lash out, but I am desperate for her to see reason.

"You expect me to trust a corrupt police officer, somebody who probably didn't want to investigate properly. They just went along with evidence you'd fabricated and tried to smear my brother's name."

"Lizzie, there was so much evidence. Documents he'd signed. Fake accounts he'd set up. There was a money trail, leading right to him. I tried my best to keep it quiet, because I didn't see the point in smearing his character after he'd died, but it was out there, it was true what was reported. Please believe me, Lizzie, I never did what Dominic had put in his letter, he had been a valued employee who I cared about. His death devastated me, no matter the circumstances leading up to it."

"Stop saying his name," she shouts.

"I'm so sorry for your loss," I start but she shakes her head.

"You're not sorry, and you're *responsible* for his death. Do you have any idea what that did to my family? My mother never recovered. She had one child in hospital, battling a terrible illness, and another child in the morgue, the centre of a false police investigation. I vowed that I would get better, and I would get revenge. It took me ages to get over my illness, and then I sought you out, biding my time, plotting my revenge," Lizzie snarls.

"Dominic was," I say, but she looks furious with me. She smacks the bottom of the wine bottle against my mouth. I taste the blood in my mouth as my teeth bash against my lips.

"I told you! Do not say his name," she screams.

I stay in my position on the floor, raising my hand to my lips, touching them gingerly. Lizzie reaches over across the floor, grabbing her tote bag.

"Please, Lizzie, listen to me," I whisper.

"Sorry, I've planned this for so long, I don't want to get distracted. Admittedly, you did a few things I didn't expect after I sent you the package, like hiring personal security, but it made the game a bit more fun. I had to get a little more creative as you'd involved the police. Surprisingly easy enough to find a fall guy though, some innocent incel sap who wanted notoriety, even if I was pulling all the strings. You should have seen him, he almost wet his pants when I gave him Simba's body to hang on your door."

"You killed Simba," I whimper. "But you've been away." I struggle to comprehend everything that is happening.

"I've been right here the whole time, watching, adapting when I needed to. Simba was a whim, but all wars have innocent casualties, especially a dumb cat like Simba who'll walk down the street to anybody with a treat," Lizzie cackles as she pulls things out of her bag. She pulls out a long, thick looking rope. The sight of it makes me whimper. "Poetic, right? I have spent months imagining you hanging from the beams in your kitchen. Every time I had to put up with you, I visualised it." Lizzie seems to vibrate in anticipation.

"I don't understand," I whisper. "You've pretended to be my friend for months."

"I had to find a way to get close to you. I didn't want to just murder you, where is the fun in that? I wanted to mess around with you, so that when we got to this point, you'd know who I was, you'd feel the betrayal. So, once I was better, I watched you for ages. I followed you to places, worked out who you are as a person. Then it was easy to insert myself in your life. Every time you confided in me; you just make me more certain I was doing the right thing. You're an awful person, Zoey. Not only are you to blame for my brother's death, but wow, your best friend, too. It's like a sign from the universe for me to do the world a favour. I'll play the sad friend for a while, but I know I'll be smiling inside." Again, she has a sickening smile on her face.

"They'll know it was you," I whisper, but it feels like an idle threat. The whole week has seemed beyond reason, police suggesting that I was concocting the story, or that Aiden was manipulating things, the likelihood of anybody suspecting Lizzie seems remote. If Officer West is the one who investigates whatever she has planned tonight, nothing will be investigated properly.

"Nobody would ever suspect me. Nobody is ever going to connect the real me to you, and everybody will think you killed yourself for your guilty past, like they did with Dominic."

"Aiden will know," I murmur. "He'll have background checked you, even if I had told him that you wouldn't hurt me."

Lizzie stops pulling the rope out of her bag. She looks like she is thinking and then she snorts.

"Why am I not surprised that a sinner like you lied to me about your security person? No wonder you had all those questions about Aiden today. Hiring a former lover who you have big history with, not a smart move, Zoey," she tuts.

"He'll know," I warn, my voice a little loud and a whole lot stronger.

"Nobody will know," Lizzie smirks. She pulls the rest of the rope out of her bag, and then she puts her hand back into the bag and pulls out a surgical scalpel. "Perfect, don't you think?" she asks, waving the scalpel in front of me.

I try to keep my expression neutral, but I can't help but think about what Lizzie's plan is. She has a rope and a sharp blade. I don't know which scares me the most.

"Please can we talk?" I plead.

Before she can answer, the doorbell rings. Lizzie leans forwards, holding the scalpel against my throat.

"Who are you expecting?" she snaps.

"Nobody. I don't know who it is." I gulp, the scalpel scratching against my throat as I talk.

"They'll go away, don't you dare make any loud noises," she snaps at me.

"Lizzie, please listen to me. What happened to Dominic was awful, it was a tragedy, and there isn't a single day that I don't wish I had done things differently." I know exactly what I sound like as I talk, I sound like a woman who is pleading for her life, trying to reason with somebody who is not willing to listen to reason and truth.

The doorbell rings again.

"For God's sake, they better go away, otherwise I'll make them," Lizzie growls.

"Whoever is outside, they have nothing to do with this. This is between me and you. Please, Lizzie," I beg.

There's a part of me that knows it will be Aiden on the doorstep. I don't know why he's here, whether it's to talk through the text I sent, or maybe he's feeling sad and just to talk about Jonah, given it's nearly what would have been his birthday. No matter what happened between them, Aiden still loved his brother, and the upcoming week will be difficult for him. I'm confident that it is Aiden who keeps ringing my doorbell, but I'm also confident that him being that side of the porch door, two locked doors away from Lizzie and her delusions, he's safe. It's far better for him to be outside than here with me.

Lizzie assesses my expression as the doorbell rings again.

"Oh, you think it's Aiden, don't you. Some knight in shining armour. You know, it's kind of sad how you seem to pine for him," she mocks.

"Leave him alone."

"It's like you've given me a gift. I was just going to fuck around with your head and then go for the finale, but this is perfect. I'm going to let him in. One last fucking around with you before I watch you hang in the kitchen." Lizzie sounds like she's planning something trivial and fun, not calmly discussing how she plans to kill me.

"It won't work. Nobody would believe I killed myself, especially now you've injured me, and Aiden wouldn't keep quiet." I sound a lot braver than I feel, and then it dawns on me what Lizzie means by her comment about one last thing to fuck around with me. She'll hurt Aiden in front of me.

"It's perfect, Zoey! You say Aiden is the only one who would suspect I had something to do with this, and that clears him out of the way. A lover's tiff. Murder suicide. So easy for me to tell this story, how my poor best friend turned to a former lover in her hour of need, dredging up all the terrible memories and all the betrayals. It'll be so easy to suggest it turned into a fight, that you lashed out, and the guilt pushed you over the edge. They always suspect the ex. They never suspect the best friend, but you know that more than anybody, right. I bet your precious Caterina never suspected your betrayal, did she?" Lizzie taunts.

Over eighteen months, I've opened up to Lizzie and told some of my secrets, and now she's using it all to destroy me.

The doorbell rings again, a frustrated triple ring. I wish to God that Aiden would just go away. Give up on me. Save himself.

"Let him go, please. You can do anything you like to me, but please leave him. I beg you," I choke out.

Lizzie pauses for a moment.

"I'll get rid of him, but I swear, if you make a sound, I'll slit his throat," she hisses.

"I won't," I promise with a sob.

She grabs the rope and roughly grabs my ankles, tying them together with the rope. She seems to know as well as I do that I will be able to get out of these, but it'll take me longer than the time it'll take her to open the door to Aiden. I know by the time I'm free, she'll be within striking distance of Aiden. Even if I get there quickly, his strength will mean nothing given she's got him unprepared.

Lizzie gets up, scalpel still in hand. She strolls out of the kitchen with such calm confidence it shocks me. As soon as she's gone, I start trying to get out of the rope. It chafes at my ankles and my heart pounds in my chest. I can hear the doors opening, the sound of their voices travelling down the hallway.

"Hi, it's Aiden, right?" Lizzie sounds full of the joys of spring.

"Where's Zoey?" he asks. The tone of his voice is not particularly friendly, and I'm sure he somehow knows. He knows something about Lizzie. I curse inwardly. He's never going to leave it alone now, no matter how much I'm silently willing him to, how much I'm praying to God that he'll keep Aiden safe.

"I'm so sorry but she doesn't want to talk to you. She's very upset. She asked me to tell you to leave her alone."

"I need to speak to her, urgently." Aiden sounds firm, and closer than before. It sounds like he's pushed his way through the door and into the house.

"I didn't say you could come in. Please leave, Zoey doesn't want you here," Lizzie protests. She's half right. Right now, I do not want him here. Right now, I wish he was anywhere else in the world.

"Zoey?" Aiden calls, sounding closer again.

"If you don't leave, I'll call the police," she warns.

"Go ahead." Aiden again sounds closer. Then the only sound is a crack, a big thud, followed by a crash.

"Well, I'll give you one thing, you're fucking persistent." Lizzie's cackling laugh sounds like it's right next to the kitchen.

Now I'm free of the ropes around my ankles, I scramble to my feet, rushing out of the kitchen. Lizzie is closest to my position, partly blocking my view, but I can see Aiden's body is flat on the floor, somehow looking so much smaller than normal. His eyes are closed. My large brass table lamp lies on the floor next to him. There's an angry looking welt at the front of his head.

"You promised," I scream at her. She barrels towards me, pushing me backwards. My body slams into the doorframe of the kitchen, the force of it taking my breath away.

"Jesus, Zoey, I'm telling you I'm going to kill you, and you're pissed off because I broke a promise to let him go?"

Lizzie pushes me again, this time into the kitchen. I can tell she's trying to herd me back towards her original goal. She shoves me harder. I fall backwards onto the ground. She clambers on top of me, pinning me down. She grabs the rope and holds it against my throat, forcing it against me, wrapping it around her hands to give her a better grip across my throat. There's a satisfied glint in her eyes as I gasp for breath, my eyes watering.

For a second, my brain seems to go haywire with fear but then all I can think about is Aiden, telling me it only takes a couple pounds of pressure or a couple of seconds to render somebody unconscious. It's like he's whispering it in my ear, and it unlocks another memory, how he taught me to get away from an attacker, how to survive if my life depended on me fighting back.

Now it's more than my life on the line. It's his life, too.

I grab Lizzie the way he'd taught me all those years ago, catching her off guard, twisting us so she's no longer on me but pinned on the floor instead. I pin her down for a second, too busy taking a deep breath to do anything useful.

With shaking hands, I grab the rope, yanking it out of her hands.

Think, Zoey, think.

I drag Lizzie towards the metal leg that holds up my breakfast bar, the one I know is screwed into both the floor and countertop, an immovable object in the kitchen. She's kicking and snarling at me, but I force her into a sitting position, ignoring as she lashes out and kicks. I force the rope around her arms and chest, looping behind the metal leg, knotting, looping around again, knotting, repeating the process until I'm sure she's secure and I've run out of rope.

There's so much I want to scream at her, to call her names, to tell her exactly what her brother took from me, but this all pales into insignificance to how much I want to get to Aiden.

I rush out the kitchen, ignoring as Lizzie snarls behind me, sounding like a rabid wild animal.

Find your phone. Call for help. I tell myself. The second I see Aiden; I know I can't go past him to find my phone.

Mercifully, Aiden's phone appears to have fallen from his pocket as he fell and I grab it blindly, calling the emergency services. I blurt out my address and beg for an ambulance and for the police.

"We had a call from this address shortly before your call, can you confirm you're safe?" The woman on the other side sounds calm and measured but I can't answer her. Instead, I shove the phone in my pocket. I am not calm.

I sink next to where Aiden is lying prone on the floor. I clamber onto him, checking his neck for his pulse.

"Oh God, Aiden, you cannot die on me. Wake up," I plead. I can feel his pulse under my fingers, but it does nothing to stop the pounding of my heart. I can't work out if a pulse is supposed to feel like that, all I know is that he has one.

"Zo," he murmurs.

"Aiden," I exclaim. I lean forwards, my chest on his. "I thought I'd lost you. I thought she'd killed you," I cry.

"I have a thick skull," he says, his mouth twitching into a small smile.

"Maybe that's something I should feel very grateful for, given I told you I was fine by myself."

"Where is Lizzie?"

"She'll be secure until the police arrive. I tied her up, very tightly."

"Kinky."

"Don't make jokes right now," I scold but I'm laughing through my tears. I stay lying on his chest, feeling it rise and fall with every breath he takes. A movement that reassures me. I match my breathing to his.

"Zoey," he murmurs again.

"Yes?"

"Your knee…It's on my dick," he says.

I sit up and laugh. My knee is in an awkward position, but I hadn't thought of being graceful when I was so desperate to check on him. I wipe my eyes.

"It's so small, I barely noticed. The ladies must be disappointed."

"You and I both know you're never disappointed," he growls, and he pulls me back onto him.

"Are you sure you are okay. It sounded like you took a real whack to the head."

"I better be okay. I'd hate the idea that my last words were about my dick."

"Oh yeah, what do you think more appropriate words would be?"

"I love you."

"Strong statement," I let out the breath I appear to be holding.

"Absolute truth," he replies, and he lifts his head as if he is trying to get up.

"Don't move, Aiden. You could have a concussion. The ambulance is on its way."

"I need you to know, Zoey, I love you. I always have. I always will."

"I love you too, Aiden."

The words burst out of me in a similar way to how the emotions seem to burst out of my chest. I'm so tired of denying my feelings for him. I've kept him at a distance since I lost Caterina, believing losing him is my penance for hurting Caterina, but I know I can't live my life like that, not even for another day.

I get up from my position on him, staring down at him, taking in every inch of his beautiful face.

Aiden's eyes seem to focus on me for the first time. He smiles and reaches for me but then his expression changes, and he looks almost fearful.

"You're bleeding," he stutters.

I look down and, on my shirt there is a stain, a bloom of bright red blood. I frown and lift my shirt so I can feel my skin. Under the fabric there is a smear of blood, but nothing else. It takes me a second to realise, and the dread trickles through my body, from my head to my toe. I put my hand to Aiden's stomach, the dark fabric of his shirt seems saturated in his blood. I pull his shirt up. Under his shirt, across his abdomen, are two small but deep gashes.

"No…No…" My words are a gasp, a desperate wail. I put my hand over the wounds, my hand quickly sticky with his blood. For the first time, I notice how pale his skin looks.

"I love you," he murmurs. I press tighter onto him.

"Don't you dare. Don't you dare leave me," I cry.

His eyes close.

The tears sting my eyes.

My heart pounds in my chest.

Two years ago, Aiden gave me an ultimation. Two years ago, I chose to sever our link, believing it would be the best way for us to survive, to live happy lives. I've spent every day for two years regretting my decision, knowing I was wrong, wondering if I could ever find my way back to him.

Despite what I'd decided then, I know I can't live my life without Aiden. I've always known.

Now, my tears spill down onto Aiden's body, mixing into the blood. I gasp for breath and feel like my lungs are going to explode, and I know, without a shadow of a doubt, I won't survive this.

23
Zoey

Hey, how are you?

The text that arrives is innocent enough, but it still makes my stomach flip over in a series of summersaults.

I text back. *Good thanks, Are you free tonight?*

After the gym, why?

Dinner? I ask.

Sure, I'll be home about six.

I don't reply because he knows I'll be there. I flip my phone over, face down onto the desk, turning my body back towards my laptop screen, focussing on my emails.

∞∞∞∞∞∞∞

I arrive at Aiden's house at five forty-five. I sit on the little wall that encloses his front garden as I wait for him. Like all the other times I've sat here, I think about the first time I'd told him things were over, and he'd asked me to come over to talk.

After everything that happened after Dominic, when I'd run to Aiden for comfort, I didn't walk away and ghost him like I had done before, but we acted like it hadn't happened. We just fell into a friendship where we'd message and occasionally meet up, neither of us ever mentioning how we'd spent that week together.

For the most part, over the last two years, friendship has been all we have had. Aiden met Caleb. I've met women that Aiden has dated. Aiden doesn't think much of Caleb. A few weeks after I introduced them, Aiden told me he thought

Caleb was like the warm wet lettuce that ruins the burger it's been put on top of. I wasn't offended. I don't particularly like the women Aiden has dated, and I've made comments about them, too. But we carry on, neither of us wanting to talk about how complicated things are between us. Mostly, we keep things on the straight and normal between us, except for the times we fail and cross the line.

We crossed the line when I lost a big client I was trying to land. The shame of not being the best, being their preferred choice, it had left me feeling like I needed to lick my wounds, and I knew there was nobody else in the world I wanted to do that with aside from Aiden. So, I'd turned up, telling Caleb I was out with people from work, and Aiden and I drank our way through far too much alcohol, toasting our failures. When he'd told me that his biggest failure in life had been not grabbing me and holding me close after Caterina's funeral, it had snapped the restraint in me. We'd tumbled onto the sofa together, mouths locked together in a desperate kiss. We'd kissed until I was dizzy with need, he'd asked me if I was sure, and I'd nodded, telling him to take me to bed. I'd left in the middle of the night and Caleb never once asked me where I'd been, never seemed to notice that I was freshly showered, lips still swollen from my desperate kisses.

We'd slipped again when I had booked the anniversary of Caterina's death off work. I'd spent the day with Aiden, we'd walked hand in hand down the beach and got caught in an unexpected downpour of rain, soaking us through to the bone. He'd driven me to his to dry off, and it had seemed so natural to let him help me out of my clothes in his bedroom, for me to help him out of his, for us to kiss and touch, for him to lie me on the bed, asking if I was sure, for us to make love, hands clasped together, whispering how much we loved each other, marvelling how right this felt.

I'd fallen again when Caleb was out of town, the first time he was working in the New York office after changing jobs, moving out of practice to industry, a job that had global offices and required his travel. I'd felt peaceful all week. Rather than missing the man I lived with, I recognised that I felt relieved to be by myself. I'd asked Aiden to dinner at my house. When he got up to leave late in the evening, I had pulled him close and asked him not to leave as everything had felt so perfect between us. I'd taken him upstairs to my bedroom, the first time we had sex in my bed.

I can count on one hand the times we've slipped, the times I've cheated on Caleb. I can recall every time with Aiden with such vividness that it's like watching a movie. I remember how my skin tingles, how my heart races. Mostly,

I remember how right it feels, that it's almost felt like I was cheating on Aiden when I went home to Caleb, rather than feeling like I've betrayed the man I lived with, the man I'm supposed to love.

The sound of the approaching car cuts me out of my daydreaming. It's still before six, but it's Aiden's car arriving, parking up behind mine. When he gets out of the car, I'm taken back by how he looks. He's clearly just finished a workout or class; he's dressed in jogging bottoms and a tee-shirt, his hair damp.

"I'm sorry, I thought I'd be home before you," he apologises as he walks towards me. Home before me, not home before I turned up, like this place is as much mine as it is his.

I stand to join him, following him down the pathway towards his front door.

"Kickboxing, jiu-jitsu, or the standard gym?" I ask.

"Jiu-jitsu," he says, grinning at me as he unlocks the door.

"Rolling around on the floor with a bunch of sweaty men, I can see the appeal," I tease. He smirks at me as I walk through the front door with him.

"Speaking of sweat, I think I need a shower. Do you mind?" he asks. He drops his bag to the floor, yanking his tee-shirt off. My eyes roam down his stomach, looking at his muscle definition, the terrain that I know by heart. When I force my eyes upwards, to look at his face, he's looking at me, a bemused expression on his face.

"Sorry," I murmur.

"What are you sorry for?" he asks, his voice suddenly gruff.

It's been months since we've been together, the last time had been at my house, what started as one night in my bed but ended up with him staying the whole time Caleb was away, when I'd asked him to make believe that this was our life. It had been glorious, cooking dinner together, cuddling up and watching television together, making love whenever the mood took us. It had almost reminded me of the days we'd spent at his, before Caterina had found out about us.

Since the night at mine, nothing.

Except, now, I'm sure where the evening will take us.

I step forwards, closer towards him, rest one of my hands on his chest. I can feel the way his breathing changes, slightly hitched.

"I was staring," I say, teasing him with a small smile on my face.

"See anything you like?" he asks, his voice low.

"Always," I whisper.

"What's spurred this on?" he asks, his head bowed so he can murmur into my ear, nuzzle my neck.

His lips on my neck sends a shockwave through me.

I sigh. "Nothing. And I can't stay too late. Caleb is at home."

He groans slightly but then I pull his face to mine, my lips meeting his, and any hesitation is gone. We're wrapped around one another, we're fire and ice, nothing but heat and steam between us.

∞∞∞∞∞∞∞∞

"Do you ever wonder if this is how Jonah and Caterina felt, when they were together?" I murmur, my fingers tracing across Aiden's arm as we lie in his bed. One of his legs is over mine, one arm under my neck. We've made love twice this evening, once in the hallway then in his bed after he'd finally got into the shower.

"How do you feel?"

"Not guilty," I admit.

"I know I should, but it isn't guilt I feel, either," he says, kissing the top of my head. There's a beat of silence between us. "Don't you think it's time we face up to the truth?" he asks.

I pull away from his embrace so I can look at him properly.

"What truth?"

"That we belong together." He says this with a soft voice, his gaze holding mine.

I sigh. "Aiden."

"I love you, Zoey, desperately. I know why all my relationships fail. It's because you are the woman I love. Nobody is ever going to make me feel the way I feel when I'm with you. I know we belong together, Zoey, and I've been waiting patiently for you to realise it too, for you to forgive me and come back to me."

I sit up. Aiden seems to sense the change in the atmosphere, and he sits up too.

"I love you, Aiden, but…"

"No buts, Zoey. There aren't any. You and I, you know we work. You know I'm the man who has your back, I'm the man who makes you feel safe and secure. I know you don't love Caleb, not like the way you love me."

"It's too complicated." I frown. He's not wrong about my feelings for Caleb. It's a fraction of what I feel for Aiden.

"It's only complicated if you keep letting it be complicated," he replies.

I get out of the bed and go to the hallway, grabbing my clothes, taking them back to his bedroom so I can get dressed. Aiden reaches for some clothes to pull on as well.

"So, this is all my fault?" I ask.

"No, I'm not saying that. I'm just as culpable as you. I just want to stop all the bullshit."

"I don't want to have this argument with you." I pull on the underwear he'd seemed to have so much fun removing earlier.

"Because you don't want to face up to the truth, Zo. I don't want to keep doing this. I don't want to only get a piece of you. I mean it when I say I love you. Every little piece of you, honey, and I know you feel it too. I don't want to carry on being that shitty guy who sleeps with you behind Caleb's back."

"You don't even like Caleb, don't try to say this is some bro-code thing," I scoff.

"No, I don't like him, he's not right for you, but I still don't want to be that guy, having sex with you and you running back to him. I might not feel guilty, but it doesn't make me feel good when I spend time with you and watch you slink off home to another man."

"What do you want from me, Aiden?" I glance at him as I pull my shirt back on. He stares back at me, his grey-blue eyes clear, like he's just had an epiphany.

"I want you to admit that Caleb isn't who you love. I want you to admit to yourself that you love me, that you know we belong together. I want us to be a real couple, not just some hook up. This…" he starts, and he waves an arm, gesturing between his body and mine, "this is everything, Zo. You're my heart, you're my soul mate, you're the love of my life. I want us to have that life we planned, honey. I want the holidays, the wedding, the kids, the laughter and the long, loving marriage. I want to hold you when you're sick, if you're sad, I want to wipe away your tears. I want to be there with you for your highs and your lows. I want to laugh with you, and I want to hold you when you cry. I want you to turn to me when you need somebody to hold you, without there being somebody else you need to get back for. I want to come home from work and listen to every single detail of your day, and I want to bore you with the details of mine. I want to walk into the front door of our house, for us to kiss and hug and be so grateful to be home together. I want to sit and drink in our back garden, play hide and seek with our kids, I want to live that life we planned."

I'm stunned. All I can do is stand in front of him, half dressed.

"I…" I start, but my voice trails off because I don't know what to say.

"Mostly, I want you to accept that it's okay for you to love me more than you loved Caterina," he cuts in like I haven't spoken, and the words take my breath away. "I love you, Zoey, but I can't watch you walk away from me again. So, you've got to make a choice. You've got to decide if you want a life with Caleb, or if you'll finally admit that you want a life with me, that it would be *okay* for us to be in love with one another."

The force of his words still has me in a stunned silence. I pull on the rest of my underwear and my trousers. I step into the hall, gather my bag from the floor. I hear him follow me into the hallway.

"You're asking too much from me," I tell him.

"Yeah, I know. I'm asking you to forgive what happened with Caterina. I'm not saying it's going to be easy, but we can get through it together."

I hesitate at the door.

"I don't think I'm strong enough to do it," I whisper.

"You're the only one who can choose to be strong enough for it, but I wish you would. I know exactly where our life should go together, Zoey, but you're the only one who can make the decision. You don't need to hide your pain from me, hide the scars on your heart, because I know them, I have them, but it always hurts less when I'm with you," he says, sighing and when I look back at him, he looks defeated.

"I have to go." I reach for the door handle.

"Zoey?" he calls.

"What?"

He still looks defeated, but he squares his shoulders and stares back at me.

"Don't come back until you've changed your mind."

I step outside. I close the door behind me I manage to keep the tears from coming until I'm in my car.

Halfway home, I pull my car to the side of the road. I call him, he answers on the first ring.

"This can't be it," I whisper.

"Then come back. All you have to do is come back and tell me you're going to live your life with me. Tell me you'll be with me. Tell me you give yourself to me, like I give myself to you. Tell me we can rise above all the sadness. But, I mean it, Zoey, don't come back and tell me this until you mean it," he warns.

I can't find the ability for the words in my head to come out. Through my tears, I end the call. I know what he wants from me, but I can't give him that. Not yet. Not right now. Not when I still feel so broken inside. But...one day. One day, I'll be strong enough.

I can only hope that by the time I'm strong enough to give Aiden what he wants, he'll still love me.

24

Aiden

Throughout my life, I have had the luxury of travelling the world, where waking in a different bed, in a different location was the norm. Sometimes, when travel was back-to-back, in the minutes between sleep and fully alert, I'd wonder where the bed I was waking up in was located.

Somehow, waking up in a hospital bed never gives that moment of uncertainty. I don't know if it's the feel of the bed, the smell of the place or the unbearable stuffiness that seems ever present in hospital, but as I return to consciousness, I know I'm waking up in a hospital bed.

I don't know what day it is. I don't know what time it is. I don't know how long I have been in hospital. All I know, based on the stiffness in my bones, I have been out of it for a while.

I open my eyes and look around. Yes, I'm definitely in a hospital bed. I'm in a private room. It's larger than one of the wards that are often used in hospitals, where only a generic curtain provides privacy from the poor soul in the next bed. There is a vase of flowers on the dresser next to my bed. The blinds are slightly slanted open, giving a little natural light in the room. On the table tray that is at the side of the bed there is a jug of water and a glass.

And in the corner of the room, curled up in the big armchair, is Zoey.

I stare at her, assessing how she looks. She has a bruise on her cheek, purple and angry looking. There is a welt around her neck. Her lip looks swollen.

I failed her. She might be breathing, but she's been hurt because I underestimated who was trying to hurt her. I missed it, and when I turned up at Zoey's house to tell her about Lizzie, I barged in, forgetting everything my experience has taught me. I turned my back on the threat and let her take me down, I put Zoey in danger.

I don't know how long Zoey has been asleep, so I fight my instinct to call her name. I lie still for a minute and assess what I can. There's an IV drip in my right hand. My temple is tender and a quick skim of my hand across my abdomen suggests I've had stitches. Based on the minor discomfort, I'm pretty sure I've got a catheter inserted in me too. My throat is dry and sore, so I try to reach for the jug of water.

It's only the slightest noise as I reach for it, but it wakes Zoey.

"I'll do that," she says, getting out of the chair.

She stretches slightly when she walks. She stops at the edge of the bed, pouring me a glass of water. I'm already propped up slightly in the bed so when she passes me the cup I drink half. She puts the glass back on the table. All her movements seem stiff and formal. I wonder if I dreamt what she'd said to me as I was on the floor in her hallway, or if she regrets it now that we are out of the tense moment. It wouldn't be the first time we'd declared our love and she'd backed away from me.

"What happened?" I ask. My voice is slightly croaky. It confirms to me that I've been out of it for some time. Maybe over a day.

Zoey looks at me. She doesn't answer. Instead, she crumples into silent tears, her body shaking but no noise coming out. For a second, she looks undecided on her course of action but then she lowers the guard at the side of my bed, climbing on the bed with me, tucking herself into the space at my left side, cautious of the wires connected to me.

"You nearly died," she sobs.

"Hey, I'm clearly made of tougher stuff than that," I soothe.

"You lost so much blood. They said you were in hypovolemic shock." She's still crying. I understand why she is scared. Hypovolemic shock is dangerous. If the doctors mentioned hypovolemic shock, it means I lost a significant amount of my blood volume. It means that I could have died. Except I didn't. Instead, I'm lying in bed, the woman I love in my arms.

"Zoey, I'm alive. Feel me breathing. Feel my pulse. I'm here, with you."

"I didn't know she'd stabbed you. I should have been faster to get to you, but I didn't know. I didn't even know it had happened when we were talking, you were so calm. The doctor said it was probably shock, but I should have known. I could have been too late." She gulps and her body shudders against mine.

"I'm the one who didn't know until it was too late that Lizzie was the threat. Look at you. You're bruised and bloody and it's my fault."

"Not your fault," she murmurs. "I've a couple scrapes, you're the one who was seriously hurt." She makes a sound somewhere between a hiccup and a sob. I stroke her hair.

"How did you get away from her?"

"If you believe it, I did a jiu-jitsu move."

"You remembered." I smile and kiss the top of her head.

She looks up at me.

"I remember everything between us, Aiden. Every conversation. Every touch. Every time."

Her eyes seem to search mine. I don't know whether she is looking for my reaction to her words or if the shock of what happened with Lizzie has made her doubt the words that I'd said to her when I was lying on the floor in her house.

"Zoey?" I ask with a sigh.

"Yes?"

"Are you done trying to pretend that we don't belong together?"

I feel like I'm holding my breath, waiting for her to decide my fate. I know if she says no, there will be a part of me that does die, a part of me I'll never get back. The part that I gave to her so long ago that I only really feel fully myself when we're together.

"Aiden...I'm done fighting it. I'm exhausted. I'm so tired of punishing myself. I can't change the past. I can't change what happened. I'll always love Caterina and regret what happened, but me pushing you away because I don't feel like I deserved to be happy, that doesn't bring her back. Nothing can. No amount of penance I pay will change anything. So, instead, I'm choosing to be happy, and hoping that she would want that for me, too. For us."

"Are you sure about this?" I whisper, still holding her close, scarcely able to let myself believe that she means it.

"I'm sure about you. I'm sure about us. I don't want to lose us again." She pauses for a moment and then clears her throat. "I don't want to push you away again. It'll kill me."

Before I can respond, to tell her it would kill me too, the door to the hospital room opens. I look over and see a very disgruntled nurse.

"The beds are for the patients." The nurse scowls as he talks but when Zoey attempts to move, I hold her closer.

"I'm fairly sure this is my best medicine," I joke.

"Not when I need to check your vitals."

"I'll go get myself a coffee. Maybe something to eat. Do you want anything?" Zoey asks and then she looks at the nurse. "I mean, is he allowed to eat yet?"

"Clear fluids only until the doctor has done their rounds."

Zoey gives me a kiss on the cheek and then gets off the bed, leaving me with the nurse. I miss the warmth of her body against mine and I hope the nurse won't take too much time, as I'd happily lie in bed with Zoey for the rest of my days.

∞∞∞∞∞∞∞∞

The disgruntled nurse tells me his name is Neil, that he's been on a long shift, that it's Sunday evening, and it is hospital policy for the beds only to be used by patients. I can't work out if he's tired or just always disgruntled but I make a half-hearted promise that I'll keep the bed for myself.

Neil seems happy enough with my vitals and decides it is okay for the catheter to be removed. When he takes it out, I'm glad I was unconscious when it was inserted, it's not a pleasant experience but I've heard it's worse going in. I'm also partly glad that Zoey is out of the room. Neil also takes my IV drip out given the latest bag hung has finished and now I'm awake I can take care of my own fluids.

By the time Zoey is back in my hospital room, I'm back in bed after the first tentative steps Neil made me do around the room before he left me alone, and the doctor is halfway through telling me what procedures they'd done. When Zoey steps into the room, the doctor smiles at her.

"Hello, Zoey," he says.

"Hello, Doctor Worth, how are you?" she asks as she settles herself in the seat she'd been in earlier. They clearly met when I was unconscious.

"I was just updating Aiden on everything."

"When do you think he can come home?" Zoey asks. The word 'home' on her lips sounds like a promise. The doctor smiles and turns his attention back to me.

"So, I'm going to recommend you stay in the hospital for another night, just as a precaution. We can release you in the morning. When you go home, we'll recommend a period of rest, that you stay hydrated, and that you avoid strenuous activity. Your stitches can come out in a couple of days, we'll make an appointment for you to come back to the clinic." The doctor stands.

"Thank you," Zoey says.

"Overall, you're a lucky man, Aiden." The doctor smiles at me.

"I know I'm lucky," I reply, looking at Zoey. She flushes slightly.

"I'll come by and check on you in the morning." The doctor puts my chart back at the bottom of my bed and then leaves, shutting the door behind him.

"Come here," I call out to Zoey. She crosses the room and clambers back onto the bed with me, tucking herself on my left side again.

"Being discharged tomorrow seems positive," she comments, her hand stroking across my chest.

"Maybe, but I think it would be best if I'm with somebody who is willing to keep an eye on me, what do you think?" I tease.

"If you think I ever want to let you out of my sight again, you're sorely mistaken. You might have to report me for stalking you." There is the smallest chuckle from her.

"Ah, but you must have let me out of your sight for a bit, given you've changed clothes since the night at your house," I point out and she stares up at me.

"Actually, these are courtesy of Abigail. What happened, it was on the news. She knew it was my house and she got worried when she couldn't get through to my mobile, given it's at the house. She went through the documents she had on her laptop and found your number. I recognised her number when your phone rang. Then she turned up with clothes for me and something for you. Apparently, I have a friend who doesn't want to murder me."

"I'd bet you have a load," I soothe. "I'm sure when you get home, there will be a flock of visitors for you."

"I think you're forgetting my house is currently a crime scene. I don't even know how I'll get back in. I abandoned the house to come to the hospital with you. I don't even have my keys. I just ran out and left the police to it. At some point, I'm going to have to go back and clean up. Or at least pay somebody to clean it up. I guess there are companies that do that." She shudders like she's considering what kind of messes companies like that have seen.

"We'll go to mine," I suggest.

"That sounds nice," she murmurs. I can tell her focus is still on what a disaster her house might look like. I want to lighten the dark thoughts that seem to be in her head.

"No strenuous activity feels like a punishment." I kiss her head as I talk.

She giggles. "Do you seriously have a one-track mind?"

"I think we'd better check there was no impact due to blood loss and the catheter they stuck up there," I joke.

"I think it's all impacted your brain," she says, still chuckling. I reach for her hand and curl my fingers around hers.

"Joking aside, it's not a one-track mind, unless we can call that track Zoey, because all I see is a beautiful future for us. I know we have things to work through, but I know we'll get through them together," I vow.

The knock at the door makes her move.

"I don't want to get thrown out by the nurse," she says as she goes to answer the door. Instead of a nurse or doctor, Officer Kim is in the doorway.

"It's good to see you awake, Mr Slater," he comments.

"I'll feel better when we're home," I reply. He's wearing his uniform and I feel significantly underdressed in my hospital gown.

"We're finished with your residence, Zoey. We have secured the property. You'll need to collect your house keys from the local station." Officer Kim steps into the room and stands, leaning against the wall opposite from the bed I'm in.

"Okay, I'll come and collect them once Aiden is released. I don't really want to leave him here alone," Zoey says.

"I can put you in touch with some companies that clean crime scenes. I'm afraid the hallway is in a bad condition," he apologises, and I can't help thinking of the state the house must be in. I wonder if I can sort it without Zoey having to deal with it herself.

"I appreciate it, but I'm sure you've not come out of your way to offer advice on cleaning services." Zoey frowns.

Officer Kim nods. "You're right. I want to give an update. Elizabeth Ackerley-Jones, or Elizabeth Chapman as you know her, has been charged with several crimes but the biggest charge is two counts of attempted murder. She will be in court next week to face charges and will be held in prison until the court case. We will assign you both a liaison support worker who will be in touch and go through what the next couple of months will look like. We'll also assign victim support," he explains.

"We appreciate the update," I say once it's clear Zoey is not going to respond.

"We're confident that she was acting alone, so you shouldn't have any further threat. I know that isn't a big comfort because of what you have gone through but…" he starts but Zoey shakes her head.

"It is a big comfort, actually."

He smiles at her. It's the practiced smile of somebody who has had to deal with people during the worst time in their lives.

"When you come to the station to pick up your keys, please ask for me and I'll update you on any developments. Have you any questions you want to ask before I leave you in peace?" he asks. Zoey shakes her head.

"No, but if we think of anything, we can ask when we pick up Zoey's keys," I add.

Officer Kim gives us both a smile and then he leaves us in peace.

I look at Zoey and she looks a little shellshocked. I hold my hand out for her. She moves her chair to the side of my bed, taking my hand.

"Attempted murder," she murmurs. "I mean, I know…but…it feels weird to hear it described like that."

"I know, honey. I'm sure it'll be a rollercoaster of emotions for a while. We'll get through it," I assure her.

"Together," she whispers.

"Together," I agree. I squeeze her hand. "Zo, you said earlier that what happened made the local news. Was my name released? I should phone my parents, in case they're checking the local papers," I say, thinking of how terrible it would be for my parents to find out through the media. It's a small possibility given they're in France, but I'd hate to put them through it.

"They're on their way here. I called them."

"You called my parents?" I ask.

"Yes, I've spoken to them a couple of times. I've been keeping them updated. They were struggling to get a flight, but they managed to get one, they should have landed by now."

"When did you call them?" I wonder, still surprised she took that step.

"I called them when the doctors started asking about your next of kin. I got your dad's number from your phone. He gave me permission to act on your behalf until they could get here," she explains.

I'm stunned. Stunned that she contacted a man who unfairly held her responsible for his other son going off the rails. Stunned that my dad trusted her enough to act as a proxy, to make decisions about my life. There isn't anybody else I would trust after Zoey, but it must've been hard for him to come to the same decision.

"How are they?"

301

"Your dad put the call on loudspeaker so your mum could hear as well. Aiden, she made a sound that I never, ever want to hear again." Zoey shudders as she talks, and I imagine how my mother would have sounded. I've heard her make a noise like that before, the day we buried Jonah.

I squeeze Zoey's hand again.

"Thank you for contacting them."

"I should have told you earlier. I just lost my focus when you woke up, then it's just felt like non-stop."

"You're going to still be here when they arrive?" I ask. She looks suddenly upset.

"If you think it's best, I'll go."

"That is not what I meant, at all. If you're comfortable, I want you here. I'm being serious when I say my future is with you. My parents will need to adjust to that."

"I'm not expecting them to roll out the red carpet for me, but they seemed appreciative of the updates I've given them. Maybe there's hope for us, after all." She gives a shrug and then a little yawn.

"Did you sleep much?" I ask.

"No, I don't think so. I kept fighting it, I was scared if I took my eyes off you, something bad might happen."

"Get some sleep, Zo," I suggest.

"I'm just going to rest my eyes for a minute."

She rests her head on my bed. I stroke her hair and it doesn't take long until she's asleep.

∞∞∞∞∞∞∞∞

Zoey is still in a deep sleep when my parents arrive.

"Aiden," Mum exclaims as she rushes towards me. "My beautiful boy," she cries.

"I'm fine, Mum. Superficial wounds. I'll be out tomorrow. You didn't have to rush home, but it is good to see you both." I laugh softly.

"It is good to see you, son. I was worried." Dad pulls a seat out for Mum to sit in, but she sits on the edge of my bed instead, her hand on my ankle, looking like she needed to touch me to make sure I'm not a hallucination, to give herself physical proof that I'm still alive and breathing.

"It was a very stressful journey home," Mum says.

"Wouldn't she be better at home?" Dad looks at Zoey. Immediately it raises my hackles. I wasn't expecting it to be sunshine and rainbows between us all straight away, but I'd hope for something more than instant dismissal for her.

"Where do you think she should go, Dad? Her house is a crime scene. My blood is staining her carpets, and I'm here. Where else would she be?" I ask, trying to keep my tone even. Partly because getting annoyed with my dad is pointless, but mostly because I don't want to disturb Zoey.

"I just meant that she doesn't look very comfortable," Dad apologises, and his words stop any response I might have had.

"Perhaps she could come home with us tonight." Mum sounds tentative.

"Okay, now I'm starting to think I really did die, and this is an elaborate construct of heaven," I mutter.

Dad frowns. "Please don't make jokes."

"Almost losing another son provides a lot of perspective on what is important, Aiden," Mum chides.

"We will find a way to make things up with Zoey," Dad adds.

"The only thing you need to do is accept her because I love her. One day, I'm going to marry her, if she'll have me," I say.

"I remember you saying something very similar a few years ago." Dad smiles wryly.

"We're just glad you're okay." Mum still looks teary.

"I hope this will be the last time you take an active job, Aiden."

I knew he'd seize the opportunity to remind me how much he wants me to take over the business from him.

"Dad," I groan. I'm too tired for this conversation. My groan disturbs Zoey. She shoots upright, looking out of sorts when she sees my parents.

"Oh, I'm sorry, I didn't mean to fall asleep," she apologises.

"Thank you for taking care of Aiden," Mum gushes.

"I'm thirty-two, Mum, I'm not sure I need any taking care of," I grumble.

"You don't feel emasculated having a woman take care of you, do you?" Zoey teases. "If so, I'll remind you that technically, I saved the day. Maybe I should change jobs and go work as a bodyguard."

"One jiu-jitsu move and she thinks she's Rambo," I joke, looking at my parents who seem relaxed in her presence. I'm sure it's just the relief of a good outcome after what happened, that there will still be bumps in the road between my parents and Zoey, but I feel almost hopeful that this will all be okay.

"Rambo, I get it now," Dad snorts.

"What have I missed?" Mum asks.

"We use codenames on the work system when we're doing a job. Zoey's file had her listed as Rambo," he explains.

"You are a menace." Zoey laughs. She looks at my parents. "He's called me Rambo since the day we met."

"I always knew you were a tough cookie." I shrug. She reaches for my hand and curls her fingers around mine. I'm sure if my parents weren't in the room, she'd risk saying something cheesy like how we give each other the strength to be tough, but instead, she squeezes my hand and smiles, and I feel my heart swell.

∞∞∞∞∞∞∞∞

Zoey declines the offer to go home with my mum and dad. She thanks them but tells them she wants to stay with me again. She sleeps in the chair, pulled close to my bed, falling asleep with her hand in mine.

After I'm discharged from the hospital, Zoey and I catch a taxi to the police station so we can get her keys. I wear the clothes that her assistant had dropped off, surprised at how well they fit, but Zoey laughs and tells me that Abigail is exceptionally detail oriented and good at sizing people up.

"Are you sure about this?" I ask when the second taxi drops us outside her house. My car is still on her driveway, looking half abandoned given how fast I'd left it that night to get to her.

"Are you?" She looks at me with a concerned expression. I'm not sure if I'm ready to step foot into the house where we were both attacked, where I saw Lizzie and thought I would have to fight for Zoey's life and ended up fighting for my own. A house where just one little change to the events could have left either of us without our life, the other broken hearted.

"Yes," I reply. I'll be the strength she needs, and she'll be mine.

She puts her key into the porch door to unlock it and then does the same to the front door. I take her hand as she pushes the front door open. We step inside together and even though I'm prepared, it still takes me by surprise. The same fear I'd felt the night she was attacked rushes through my body.

Zoey shudders. "I don't think I can live here. All I can see is you, bleeding out in the hallway," she admits. I don't know if it's just a gut reaction, she might change her mind, but for now, I'm happy to take her away from here.

"Then let's pack you a bag and you can come to mine, once we've met the cleaner," I suggest. She nods and we turn in the direction of the stairs, both of us trying not to focus on the pool of dried blood on the floor in the hallway.

"Oh God," she mutters.

"It'll be gone soon. Come on, Rambo, upstairs," I coax.

I pull her past the dried blood. My dad had messaged Zoey this morning, telling her he was sending somebody around at one to clean up. The fact he'd messaged Zoey and not me had taken me by surprise, but it's another little bolster that things might be okay between them in the future.

We walk up the stairs together. She leads me towards her bedroom and when we're inside, she guides me to sit down on the bed. It's still a little sore to move comfortably but I try not to grimace so that she doesn't worry.

"So, how much am I packing?" she asks as she pulls a holdall bag from her wardrobe.

I grin at her. "Pack everything."

"I'm not sure everything I have will fit into this little bag," she teases. She opens one of her drawers and I can see it's her underwear.

"Oh, please tell me you're packing all of that."

"What, these ones?" she asks, and she picks out something that looks incredibly skimpy in a blue fabric. There is a definite rhythm change in the beat of my heart. "Or are you looking at this one?" She holds up what appears to be a matching bra. It takes me a second to realise I've seen this underwear set before. I've inched these down her body before and then buried my head between her thighs.

"Pack them all," I growl.

"I thought you were supposed to be avoiding strenuous activities," she teases.

"I'm pretty sure the doctor just meant you should go on top for a while," I joke. She takes a step closer towards me.

"Aiden, my love, I'm going to enjoy going on top, and I'm going to enjoy giving my jaw a workout when I blow you. I missed you so much, and I love you," she tells me.

As always when I'm with Zoey, it's like she has a direct line to my dick.

"Zoey," I growl.

"Yes, Aiden?" she asks with a smile.

"Say it again."

"I'm going to enjoy going on top," she starts. I reach for her hand.

"Try again."

"I'm going to blow you?"

"Try again," I pull her closer.

"I missed you…"

"I missed you too, but try again," I say, and she lands on the bed next to me.

"I love you," she concludes. From the grin on her face, I know she knows exactly what I was aiming for.

"There's the magic words." I pull her closer and her lips meet mine. I kiss her softly as her lip still looks a little puffy. When she pulls away, she is smiling. "I love you too. Not pretend," I add.

"Aiden," she says, her tone soft. "It was never pretend. Even those beautiful days we had, the ones we said it was pretend, it was never a lie when I said I loved you. I've always loved you."

"I've always known that, honey. I was just waiting for you to realise."

She grins at me. "Perhaps I'm a slow learner."

"You're a slow packer, that's for sure." I tease.

Zoey gets off the bed and I watch as she throws some of her underwear into the bag and then some of her clothes. Everything she packs looks like casual clothes, jeans and tops, denim skirts and nightclothes. There doesn't seem to be any work clothes going into the bag.

"What is that look for?" she asks, a smile on her face.

"They're not your usual work clothes," I comment.

"I'm going to take some time off work."

"I think you earnt it," I muse, my gaze falling to her neck, where an angry looking bruise is forming. The sight of it makes me shudder. We haven't talked yet about how Lizzie attacked her, what she did to Zoey. When I tried to ask her last night, before she'd fallen asleep, she'd shaken her head and told me she didn't want to talk about it yet.

"Maybe, but aside from that, I meant what I said in the hospital, that I wasn't going to let you out of my sight. So, we're going to spend some time together, we'll lock ourselves away in your place at night, in the day we'll go out. We'll reconnect," she says as she sits down on the bed next to me.

"You mean this last week wasn't enough reconnection for you?" I joke. She swats my arm.

"Well, this week has been *delightful*, but I think maybe next week we can aim for a little less interaction with the police, fewer stitches, and a whole lot less blood."

"I think we can do that." I smile. She shifts on the bed.

"Do you think, maybe, we can go to the beach in the week? I'll drive."

"Anything you want. Pack bikinis, honey," I reply. She leans towards me and kisses me. I pull her closer, still counting my lucky stars for how everything has ended up like this.

∞∞∞∞∞∞∞∞

"Welcome home, honey," I say to Zoey as I open the front door. She stands on the path outside my flat and doesn't follow me through the front door. I turn to look at her and I wonder if she is going to change her mind.

"I've always loved this spot," she comments.

"Why?" I laugh, feeling more relaxed.

"This is the spot where I was standing when I realised that I'd love you for the rest of my life," she replies.

I want nothing more than to recreate that day, to have her jump in my arms, wrap her body around mine, for me to carry her through the hallway. Coming home to find her on my doorstep, so happy to see me, it had felt amazing. She looks like she's thinking the same.

"Zo," I start with a growl.

She grins at me. "Relax, you'd bust your stitches. I really don't want to take you back to hospital."

"Come on, let's get you unpacked."

Zoey steps through the front door and shuts it behind her. She follows me towards my bedroom. She puts her bag on the bed, unzips her bag and I help her hang the clothes in my wardrobe. She stifles a yawn when she puts the last of her things away.

"Sorry," she apologises, a wry look on her face.

"It's been a long day already, and I'm sure it's been a few nights since you had a proper sleep," I remind her. We'd stayed at her house longer than I had expected; the cleaning up team insisting they were going to do a thorough job. I suspect it was an instruction given by my dad, part of him trying to make amends with Zoey.

"Maybe we should have an early dinner and then get some sleep," she suggests.

"Why don't you have a lie down now? We can have dinner later."

"Will you lie down with me?" she asks.

"Of course." I smile. She turns and stands in front of me, unbuttoning the shirt I have on, followed by the trousers. She winces when she sees the dressing over my wounds. "I'm okay, Zo," I murmur. She strips out of her own clothes, down to her underwear. I reach for her, caressing her face. She pushes her cheek against my palm.

"I know things recently have been a rollercoaster, and I'm never going to forgive myself for your new scars, but I'm so happy right now," she says.

"There's nothing for you to forgive yourself for, you know that, right? Please don't let this be another thing you punish yourself for. There was never anything you needed to feel guilty about." I pull her towards the bed.

When she lies down next to me, I pull her close. She fits against my body like she always has, like we're designed to fit against one another.

"I missed this," she whispers against me. We're both quiet for a moment.

"Zo, do you forgive me for what happened? For what happened to Caterina?" I whisper. I want, desperately, for us to have our happy ever after, to be together forever, but if there is the smallest piece of her that holds me responsible, it'll eat away at us.

Zoey looks up at me, her eyes wide.

"I never needed to forgive you. I needed to forgive myself. I always blamed me most of all. For a while, I blamed Jonah, but it was only me deflecting my guilt, like he said, and another thing I felt guilty about after he died." She's quiet for a moment, her hand on my chest. "After you gave me that ultimation, I got some therapy," she adds.

"I should never have given you that ultimation."

"No, you were right. We needed to change the status quo. It was wrong for me to keep coming to you for those pretend days, I was wrong to be cheating on Caleb. I was wrong to put you in that position. So, after that night, I went home and really thought about everything. A couple of weeks later, I started therapy."

"How did you find it?"

"My first therapist was awful. He seemed convinced that I had repressed my sexuality and I had been in love with Caterina. When we spoke about my childhood, he told me I must be suppressing memories of sexual abuse. My dad was an asshole, but he never abused me. I loved Caterina, but not the way he thought. I hated that therapist," she admits.

"He sounds like he needs his licence revoking."

"I complained, then I found a different therapist and tried again. I felt raw after the sessions. Turns out I had layer upon layer of shitty supressed emotions, not what the first therapist thought but just emotions I'd not dealt with. I spoke to the second therapist about everything, including how I felt that by being apart from you, I was somehow making it up to Caterina. I told the therapist about how Caterina had shouted in the car that I had to choose between you and her," Zoey says, her voice faltering. She takes a deep breath. "I told the therapist how when Caterina had issued that ultimation, my first thought was *'I'm not giving up Aiden'*."

She's never told me this before. I can feel the tension in her body where I hold her.

"Oh, Zoey," I murmur.

"There was so much I felt guilty about, not just that she was gone, that she'd died hating me, but that was one of the last thoughts I'd had when she was with me. I told the therapist everything and I eventually started to feel like I was getting better. When I felt stronger, I wanted to come to you, to beg for a second chance, but then my dad died, and it threw me through a loop. I wanted to get myself through that. I didn't want to turn up again being some broken husk of a person, so I had more therapy. Then Caleb left, and I felt better, I wanted to come to you, I wanted to ask you if you still had feelings for me given so much time had gone by. Lizzie told me I was being crazy and that I would just be messing up your life. She said you'd never be able to trust me, because of how awful I'd been to you, so I convinced myself you were better off if I stayed away."

There's a burst of frustration in me, knowing that Zoey confided into somebody who had been manipulating her from the start, through their entire so-called friendship.

"She was an evil piece of work," I murmur, and I kiss her temple. I run my finger against the side of her neck, where the welt is, and I shudder slightly. As far as I'm concerned, Lizzie can rot in prison.

"On Saturday, at the beach, she told me you'd never trust me because I cheated on Caleb to be with you, and you'd never trust a cheater after what Caterina and Jonah did to you," she tells me.

I kiss her temple again. I can feel the tension in her body. Being cheated on by Caterina ripped my heart out at the time, but I know Zoey.

"You and I, I know we're the real deal. I trust you, and you can trust me. Our love was what always pulled us back together, and I know nothing will pull us away."

"I trust you too, Aiden," she says, her body relaxing.

"Lizzie was wrong, and based on her motives, I think you can ignore anything she ever said to you, okay?"

"I'll tell you one day all about that night, but I don't want to focus on what happened right now. There'll be a lot to unpack about what happened, maybe I'll go for a few more therapy sessions, but for now, that's not where my mind wants to be. I want us to just enjoy being together, is that okay?"

"Whenever you're ready, Zo," I promise.

"I'm too tired right now," she says with a yawn. "I'm going to enjoy blowing you later though," she says, stifling a second yawn.

"Go to sleep, honey." I chuckle and hold her tighter. It doesn't take long until she's asleep against me, holding onto me, even as she falls into a deeper sleep. I keep holding her, feeling like I've got everything I'll ever need from life, knowing I'll never want to let go again.

25
Zoey

Epilogue

"Did you get the quote back for the celebrations?" I ask.

"Yes, it's within the budget you set, and that includes an additional glass of mimosas or juice upon arrival," Abigail replies.

"Okay, if it is within the budget, go ahead and book it. I know you sent a placeholder appointment, but can you please update with the location when it's booked?"

"Zoey, everything is fine here, I promise." Abigail smiles at me through the video screen.

"I know you'll have everything in hand, but could you check how much it would be to hire a few buses to get people there, we used one company before, their details should be on file in…" I start but the expression on her face stops me talking.

"Look, you know I'm a very reliable, competent person, right?"

I grin. "Yes, I know that, Abigail."

"Then leave this place to me. Please. Go enjoy your time off, and by off, I mean switch off your laptop," she chides.

"Okay, I promise." I smile at the screen.

"Goodbye, Zoey. Say happy birthday to Aiden for me," Abigail replies. She gives me a little wave and then disconnect the video call.

I skim through the last emails that has come into my inbox but there is nothing that requires an immediate response, so I shut down my inbox and then power down my laptop, putting it away in the drawer of the coffee table. I stretch and chide myself for working hunched over on my laptop on the sofa, even if I haven't been on long.

I potter across the floor of the living room, shrugging out of my top as I walk towards the back of the villa, through the open bi-folding doors and onto the paved patio of the back garden.

"There's my girl," Aiden calls. He's on one of the sun-loungers by the poolside. He pushes his sunglasses up from his face, resting then on top of his head, his grey-blue eyes holding my gaze as I walk towards him, kicking off my flipflops.

"You're a fine sight to look at, Mr Slater," I say as I unbutton the shorts I'm wearing, shimmying out of them, leaving me standing in front of him in just my bikini.

"I think you are the finest sight, Mrs Slater," he growls.

When I get to his sun-lounger, he reaches for my hand and pulls me closer towards him. I sit on his lap, a leg straddled on each side of his hips. I run my hand down his chest, my thumb skimming over the scars he has on his abdomen. They've faded in the last two and a half years since Lizzie stabbed him but they're more pronounced now given we've spent the last ten days in the sunshine and the scars are the only area not tanned.

"I was a little longer than I thought. I'm a terrible wife, abandoning you on your birthday," I say, kissing against his neck as I talk. Aiden runs his hands up my back, his fingers tickling against my spine.

"You've already given me a great start to my birthday, and I think you're the most amazing wife, even if you're a workaholic," he says, and I can feel the curve of his lips against my shoulder as he smiles.

"I think you should perhaps look in the mirror before you call anybody a workaholic," I tease.

"Well, for a couple of workaholics, I think we're doing well, spending ten full days in paradise, so far," he replies.

The last ten days have been pure bliss, even if we have been working occasionally, me trying to keep on top of everything with my business, Aiden trying to juggle running his father's business as Richard spends less time at work, as well as juggling studying for his post-graduate degree.

This getaway is our celebration for our one-year wedding anniversary. People say the first year of marriage is the hardest, adapting to new roles, but if that's true, the rest of our lives are going to be easy as this first year of marriage has been perfect. I couldn't think of anything better than getting away to celebrate with the man I love. Our time away has been blissful, we have spent time exploring the island, hand in hand, or just relaxed in the villa or by the poolside, snuggled up with one another. Evenings have either been long dinners at intimate restaurants, or food we've cooked together, eating in the garden. We've ten more days before we're due home, the longest time we've had off work together since our honeymoon.

"I'm loving our anniversary holiday, Aiden, I'm going to do better at not being a workaholic. I managed it on our honeymoon," I remind him, and I can't stop my mind wandering back to our honeymoon. Three weeks where we'd been away together, neither of us mentioning the word 'work', just talking about our dreams for the future and reminiscing over our beautiful wedding day.

We'd married in front of his family and our friends, Isabelle standing as Aiden's best man. Richard had offered to walk me down the aisle in absence of my own father and although I don't believe a woman needs to be given away, I'd said yes, strengthening my relationship with Aiden's parents. Despite everything, we have grown close, and I enjoy spending time with them. Aiden had looked emotional when he'd seen us walking down the aisle together.

We'd both welled up when exchanging our vows, promising each other the same things we'd promised years ago on the beach, knowing that neither of us would let anything break those promises ever again.

After the wedding and the ceremony, Aiden and I had spent the night at the flat, him carrying me over the threshold and us making it only halfway down the hallway before we were both half-undressed.

"We're both busy people, Zo, don't apologise. We both know we put each other first." He kisses my shoulder. I know he's right. We both might get swept up in our work, but Aiden always knows how to bring me back to the present, to what is important, and he tells me I do the same for him. There are still days I find hard, still days he finds hard too, but we get through them together.

"So, were you doing anything productive, or have you just been topping up your tan?" I ask, pulling back a little from Aiden so I can look at him properly.

"I was house-hunting, actually," he replies, and he pulls his tablet from the floor.

"Oh, anything worthy?" I ask. I change my position on the seat, turning to lie back against him. Aiden slips his arm around me, his left hand on mine, touching over my wedding ring, his tablet in his right hand, swiping for the page he'd been looking at.

"I wondered if this one would take your fancy," he says, and I take the tablet from him to look at it properly.

I'm not expecting much because we have seen so many houses and been disappointed. I loved my house, right until the moment Lizzie had tried to kill me and Aiden in it. Not long after Lizzie was arrested, I put the house on the market. Despite the incident in the house, it had sold quickly. I'd moved some of my things into Aiden's flat and put the rest in storage, the two of us planning on finding a new home together but it's taking much longer than we'd anticipated.

There's part of me that loves living in Aiden's flat. It's comfortable and it holds so many memories, but I know Aiden is right when he reminds me that it is not a long-term solution. His flat was only ever a base for him, though I suspect he'd kept the flat longer than he'd thought he would do, for sentimental reasons, to know I'd always have a place to find him, the same way he'd never changed his personal mobile number.

"This is in a great location," I muse, looking over the details for the house listing on the tablet.

"Close enough to the beach for you to see it, for us to walk to if you wanted, close enough to the office so you don't get stuck in the traffic, close enough to my office," he says.

"The rooms are all a good proportion," I comment. Usually, we find houses where the living room will look perfect, but the kitchen is too small, or where one bedroom is lovely, but the others are tiny.

"Four bedrooms, the kitchen is amazing, almost as good as the one in your old place."

"I like that it has two rooms downstairs so we could each have a study. You know how badly it goes when we share a study," I joke. The second bedroom at his flat operates as a home office, but usually we get distracted. More than once, I've abandoned any idea of working and ended up having sex with him over the desk instead. It's certainly helping in a better work-life balance.

"The garden looks good, too," he replies. "Off-street parking, and it wouldn't take much to secure the place, you know, from any potential threats."

"Are you anticipating any threats?" I laugh.

"You can never be sure, and you know your safety is my number one priority," he says, voice husky against my ear. He nips the lobe, and it makes me shiver with anticipation.

"Nobody would dream of trying to hurt me, not when I have a strong, protective husband, and my own badass skills to protect me. Plus, I can protect you, I do remember saying I'd be able to take your ass in a fight," I tease.

"Well, you know how much I love to wrestle with you," he murmurs against my ear and his tone is so suggestive, I know he's not talking about actual wrestling. My mind wanders to how we'd spent the morning, how I know we'll spend the evening. As soon as my mind wanders and thinks about Aiden kissing his way down my body, I feel a thrill rush through my body.

"It's my favourite way to relax," I murmur.

"Mine too, honey," he replies, and his fingers skim across my wedding band again.

I don't wear an engagement ring, even though he wanted to get me one. I had been the one to propose to Aiden. We'd got past the anniversaries of some of our worst days, remembering and honouring both Jonah and Caterina. Even after therapy, even after forgiving myself for what happened, there are times I find myself sad, when I miss both Caterina and Jonah. The strength Aiden and I had given one another to get us through those days had reminded me that we're stronger together. I'd left work early one afternoon and sat outside the flat, waiting for him to get home from work. When he'd walked down the path, a smile on his face, I'd run to him, throwing myself into his arms. Between kisses, I asked him if he would like to marry me. Between kisses, he'd carried me towards the door, telling me yes, then carried me towards the bedroom.

"How do you feel about keeping the flat?" I ask.

"We can, but the memories are here, Zo," he reminds me, and he lifts his hand to skim a finger over my forehead.

"I know that. I just feel connected to the place, and I've never felt it this strongly before. It's not like I have a childhood home that I feel nostalgic about," I explain.

"Then we'll keep it. We're in a position where we can hold onto it, if you want to."

"I know deep down that it's not the place that I feel connected to, but you, just like how the coffee shop makes me feel close to Caterina. I'm sure I'll eventually feel okay letting go of the flat, but for now, I'm not ready."

"I understand, honey. It's where our love story started," he soothes. The bonds of our friendship have been there since the beginning, but he's right, our love story started there.

"Just so we're clear, our love story ends with the two of us hand in hand in some retirement home, when we're old and creaking." I joke.

He laughs. "Maybe we'll even have settled on a house by then. Stop stalling, Zoey."

I flick through the photographs on the property site.

"It does look perfect," I agree.

"Do you want to make an appointment to see it?"

"Why don't you offer the asking price, and we'll view it when we get home? I can't imagine there being anything about it that we don't like, it looks perfect."

"I'll phone the estate agent in a bit. Do you really like it? You're not just fed up looking?" he asks.

"I love it. I think you've found what we thought was elusive."

"Oh, I know I've found the elusive," he says, pulling me closer to his body, leaving me with no doubt that he's talking about me, about us and our love.

I settle in his arms and sigh contentedly before looking back at the tablet.

"This bedroom would make an excellent nursery," I say.

"I think the garage could be converted into a…" he starts, but then he stops talking. I grin to myself. "Sorry, what did you just say?" Aiden asks.

"I said…" I start, looking up at him.

"A hypothetical nursery?"

"Well, hypothetical for the next couple of months. I think for the next eight months or so, I'll keep them in this nursery," I say, running my hand across my stomach.

"Seriously?" He sounds awed, like a man who has just seen the stars for the first time, trying to describe what they look like.

"That's usually what happens with babies, Aiden," I tease.

"You're pregnant?"

"I know we said we'd just see how it went, forgo the contraception, but it happened a little faster than I thought. What are you thinking?" I ask. He gives me the widest smile ever, his eyes shining bright.

"I think you're right, that would be an excellent nursery."

"I was going to tell you over dinner tonight, as another birthday gift, but you gave me the perfect opening, too good to miss." I smile at him. He rubs his hand across my stomach.

"Honey, you have no idea how happy you've made me."

"Well, I think you're forgetting just how happy you make me every single day. I love you, Aiden," I murmur.

"I love you too, Zo. Always have. Always will," he vows.

He holds me close, one hand still resting on my stomach, thumb and one finger circling across the skin. As always, when I'm in his arms, I feel safe, secure, utterly loved and cherished.

"I know you don't expect me to be a stay-at-home mum, but I was thinking I would take a year off work, and then go back part-time," I tell him.

"Whatever you're comfortable with, honey."

"I want our children to have a better start in life to what we did when we were young," I say, and my voice is shaky. I think about seven-year-old Aiden, alone after his birth parents died, in the care system until Richard and Grace adopted him. I think of my own childhood. I don't want either of those starts for our child.

"I'm not your father, you're not your mother, and neither of us are my biological parents. You're going to be an amazing mother, Zoey, whether you work full-time, part-time, or are a stay-at-home mother," Aiden soothes.

"I have absolutely no doubt that you are going to be an amazing father, Aiden. I'm pretty sure you'll insist on background checks for playdates, but you're going to be amazing." I twist so I can kiss him, and he grins at me.

"Background checks are not a bad idea at all."

I chuckle and settle back in his arms. He kisses my forehead. The warm sun beams down on us and I don't think there is anybody in the world who feels more content than I do.

"Aiden?"

"Yes, Zo."

"It's really warm out here, do you fancy coming back to bed with me for a bit?"

"You want a nap?" His laugh makes me grin.

"Oh, Aiden, I wasn't thinking about a nap," I tease, and I get up from the sun-lounger. I hold my hand out for him and a second later, he's on his feet, sweeping me off my feet and into his arms.

"Well, if my wonderful wife wants to go back to bed for some afternoon fun, on my birthday no less, who am I to argue?" he murmurs. I hold onto him as he carries me towards the house, our laughter echoing around us, nothing between us but love and hope for a beautiful future ahead of us for our family.